I0768675

leaf it to me

KIRBY FALLS
BOOK 2

LANEY HATCHER

CANDACE

They said you can't go home again.

Well, Thomas Wolfe said it.

Which was kind of funny because the early-twentieth-century novelist was born about twenty miles up the road from Kirby Falls.

But I completely understood the sentiment.

Perhaps better phrasing would be . . . you can't go home again and expect everything to be the same. Or maybe, you can't go home again and expect everyone to welcome you with open arms. And then there was the lesser known proverb: You can't go home again because you'll fuck everything up, and why couldn't you just stay in New York, Candace?

But the fact remained. I did go home again.

I flew into Asheville the second week of August when the humidity was thick enough to slather on my momma's award-winning buttermilk biscuits. I watched as hazy blue mountains grew bigger and sharper in my rounded airplane window until they parted on either side for the lone runway that would drop me within fifteen miles of my hometown.

Kirby Falls had been in my rearview for just over seven years.

I'd lit out of town on graduation day, my maroon cap and gown balled up in the backseat of my best friend's 1996 Toyota Camry, and hadn't looked back. We'd had a plan—Lo and I—and a little bit of money, and we'd decided to leave our hometown behind while we could.

I'd never had to explain it to Lo. She'd always just gotten it. The overwhelming desire to break free, to do something completely different than the rest of your family. Lo knew what it was like to have an itch beneath your skin and a fire in your belly driving you to grow up faster and prove yourself. She knew because she felt it too.

We'd bonded over being the youngest children among overachieving siblings. My brother, Brady, had three years on me, but his personality beat mine by miles. He was warm and funny and everyone's favorite Judd. And that wasn't just my warped perception. You could ask anyone in our hometown.

Then, there was my big sister, Joan, who was nine years my senior and basically my parents' dream child. She was responsible and dedicated and had known from a young age that she wanted to help run our family's apple orchard.

Lo had three older sisters, and they'd each been valedictorian on their respective graduation days. My friend figured, why bother? She'd never loved school the way her sisters had, and her solid C average throughout her high school career reflected that.

Community college the next town over had been Lo's destination at the end of that magical post-graduation summer, but before that, we'd been determined to spend three whole months getting as far away from Kirby Falls and our responsibilities as possible.

I wondered what Lauren "Lo" Walker, my former best friend, would say when she heard I was back in town. Swallowing around the sudden golf ball that had formed in my throat, I lowered the shade on my window as the plane taxied briefly before depositing me—and the forty-eight other passengers—at our gate.

I watched as everyone hurried to grab their bags from the overhead compartments while a whole lot of nothing happened. The flight attendants hadn't even opened the cabin doors yet. Rolling my eyes at my overeager fellow passengers, I pulled out my cell phone and turned off airplane mode. My finger hovered over the text thread with my brother before tapping.

Brady: Text me when you land.

Me: Will do. Thanks for volunteering to pick me up.

Brady: Oh, I didn't volunteer. Mom's paying me.

Me: Shut up.

Brady: You shut up.

Brady: Have a safe flight. Can't wait to see your stupid face.

I rolled my eyes again—this time at my doofus brother as I reread our exchange from before I'd boarded at LaGuardia.

Now, I peeked toward the front of the plane to see the progress of the line. Still not moving.

I typed, *Just landed. I'll let you know when I'm at baggage claim.*

Staring at the screen, I waited a few moments but no dots appeared to indicate my brother was typing. I slid the phone back into my pocket and started gathering my laptop bag and purse from beneath the seat in front of me.

The flight had been a short one, just a couple of hours. Long enough to get in the air, request my standard in-flight ginger ale, and then land between the rolling hills of the Blue Ridge Mountains.

We deplaned directly outside into the humid August heat and onto a gray ramp that zigzagged a few times before setting us on solid ground.

I breathed in the late afternoon air. It felt like inhaling through a sweaty gym sock, but I couldn't help but smile.

My eyes landed on the tree-covered hills in the distance and the bright sunshine. My everyday landscape of glass-and-metal skyscrapers had been replaced by mountains and so much blue sky that I could hardly take it all in.

The pace was slower here. I could feel it in the way the breeze picked up and my heartbeat evened out. The wind cut through the oppressive moisture for just a moment and then helpfully whipped some brown hair out of my ponytail. I grinned, tucking the strands behind my ear and scanning my surroundings once more. Some strange emotion was working its way up my tight throat, causing my nose to sting and pressure to build behind my eyes.

The gentle breeze rustled out another welcome, the mountains a faint whisper in the distance that said, *Why were you gone so long?* and *Welcome back, honey.*

I was home.

Well, about twenty minutes from home, but I'd done the hard part. I'd gotten here. Even if I was dragging more heartache and baggage than the two checked bags I'd been allowed. That luggage was well over capacity as it held nearly all the clothes I owned plus a good helping of failure and regret.

I was subletting my tiny apartment in New York City for the next five months. The idea of selling all my furniture and putting all my belongings into storage had felt like admitting I was never coming back.

This trip down south was just temporary. It had to be or what was the point? Coming home for good would make everything I'd done in the last seven years —everything I'd worked for and achieved and sacrificed—utterly pointless. I couldn't give it all up. Retreating to Kirby Falls was the best short-term solution to my problems, but if I stayed . . . I'd be doing more harm than good and undoing every bit of progress I'd made. I didn't want to let my parents down. They'd sacrificed so much for my education. And they'd be disappointed if they knew the truth. That was why they could never find out about the mess I'd left behind in Manhattan.

When I passed the security exit, I pulled out my phone, but there was still no reply from Brady.

Rounding the corner to baggage claim, I stopped dead in my tracks. There, waiting beside the unmoving carousel, was my brother, my mother, and my father. Brady held a sign on lined notebook paper that read *Welcome Home Candy Cane.* And my momma had a handful of colorful balloons while my dad clutched a bouquet of white roses—my favorite.

I squealed and hurried over. My parents stepped forward and hugged me tight, balloon ribbon bouncing off my face and making me laugh in the process.

"We're so happy you're home, Candy Girl." Mom sniffed and I could tell she was one more squeeze away from crying in the middle of Asheville Regional Airport.

I pulled back to look at them, feeling my own emotions clog my throat. Dislodging a white ribbon from around my ear, I grinned. "Thanks, Momma."

Amy Judd was a petite version of me. I had her hazel eyes and brown hair—minus her beauty shop–added caramel highlights. But I'd gotten my height from my dad.

His smile was wide beneath his dark mustache. "Hey, Candy."

"Hi, Daddy." I was so happy to see my family that I barely registered the use of my old nickname—the one I'd shed when I went to New York and didn't want to sound like a small-town cocktail waitress or an exotic dancer. "I didn't know y'all would be here. Brady said you couldn't make it."

Brady squeezed between our parents and pulled me in for a tight hug. "Yeah, well, I lied, dummy. I can't believe you thought they'd be too busy to welcome their little girl home."

I was five eight, but Brady had a good six inches on me. His arms wrapped around my head and nearly suffocated me before he stepped away. "Good to see you, baby sister."

"You too, loser." I felt the skin of my cheeks stretch to accommodate my smile.

Peering casually beyond the balloons and the flowers and the three people crowding me, I noticed that not all of the Judds were present and accounted for. "Where's Joanie?"

Brady and Dad shared a look over my mother's head. But it was Mom who replied easily enough, "She had some work to do at the farm."

I frowned. "You're open on Mondays now?"

"No," my father replied. "She's just keeping an eye on things. You know your sister."

Not really, I wanted to say but didn't.

Joan had always been this gruff, nebulous presence in my life. She was nine years older than me and had never really had time for a tagalong little sister. And as far as I could tell, she did everything perfectly, always. I mostly spent my childhood and adolescence watching her in awe from afar, like the lions at the zoo.

"You'll see her later," Mom assured me. "We're all having dinner at the house together to celebrate you being back."

The house being the two-story Craftsman farmhouse on my family's property. We'd moved in when I was about five. It had been my grandfather's home—as had Judd's Orchard—before he passed away. My father, Nick, had inherited the land, the farm, and the house, and he'd been running things ever since.

"Oh," I said, covering my hurt with a bright smile. "That's good." I wondered what my mother had offered Joan to get her at the dinner table celebrating my return. Probably a new tractor. My sister only cared about one thing and that was the farm.

Thankfully, the baggage carousel turned on with a jolt, drawing our attention to where luggage was coming down the ramp.

I spotted my large black rolling cases, and my brother and dad snagged them off the belt.

"Jesus, Candy," Brady wheezed beneath the weight of my bag. "What did you pack? All the makeup and beauty products required to make you presentable?"

"You jerk." I whacked my brother on the chest as he laughed.

"Alright, children," Mom said, aiming for stern but landing somewhere in the neighborhood of unbearably fond. "Let's all go home."

The ride from the airport didn't take long, but I enjoyed every moment. It was interesting to see the way the area had grown and changed. And the scenery was always a stunner.

Brady and I rode in the backseat like we were eight and five again, my nose disturbingly close to the window on my side. Mom kept up a constant stream of chatter, updating me on neighbors and happenings around town.

I took in the changes as we passed through the tiny community of Miller Creek on the way to Kirby Falls. They had a Pizza Hut and two grocery stores now amid all the lush green farmland. Our route also took us by Legacy Hills Assisted Living, and I thought back to visiting my grandfather there as a small child.

"And we have the Orchard Festival coming up in a few weeks. You've always loved that, Candy."

I nearly winced at being referred to as Candy once again by my father. All my work colleagues—former work colleagues, I corrected inwardly—and friends in the city called me Candace. I risked a glance at my brother. He'd give me endless shit if I asked them to use my full name now instead. He'd probably announce the name change in the Kirby Falls Facebook group to really drive the humiliation home.

I'd just talk to my parents about it later.

"I do love the Orchard Fest," I replied with a smile for my dad in the rearview mirror. "I can't wait to help work it."

Unofficially, I was back in Kirby Falls to visit before I started a new position in January. I'd told my parents I was excited to help out at the farm and implement some new marketing strategies that I thought might help their bottom line.

Judd's Orchard had been in my father's family for three generations, and it had always been profitable. But there were lean years when disease or weather had affected the crops. My family's farm was making ends meet, but the income between seasons often resembled living paycheck to paycheck.

While I definitely had some ideas to help the farm turn a bigger profit, I wasn't being entirely truthful regarding my return to Kirby Falls. My plans did include going back to New York, but I didn't have a position waiting on me in January or anytime soon. I didn't even have a houseplant waiting on me.

"And we are so excited to have you, sweetie." My mother's voice pulled me out the guilty thoughts swirling inside my head. "We're just so grateful to have you home and that you're willing to invest your time and energy into the farm."

"Mom," I said, desperate to stop her. I did not need any of her praise. If she knew the truth of my unceremonious departure from Blakely Hammond Marketing, she'd be much less impressed by my return.

"Especially when you could be in the big city, putting your degrees to good use," she added.

I swallowed around the hard lump in my throat. That golf ball just kept making an appearance. I only had those degrees because of my parents—their generosity and their sacrifice in sending me to an amazing college.

"Don't be silly." I worked hard to make my smile anything but brittle, but I could feel the cracks along the edges. "I'm happy to be back. And thankful that you're letting me stay."

A hand hit me on the arm, but there wasn't any force behind it. Brady was just getting my attention.

Turning, I met his gaze across the backseat.

My older brother was watching me strangely, a confused vee taking shape between his dark eyebrows. "Don't be stupid. This isn't some friend's couch you're crashing on, Candy Cane. This is your home."

"That's right," my mother added from the front of the car.

I nodded and returned my gaze to the passing landscape, but I no longer saw the hills in the distance or the trees filled to bursting with green leaves. I only saw my failures flashing before my eyes—on repeat and in great detail—until we turned onto the private road that would take me home.

The farmhouse came into view and a sigh escaped me, fogging the back passenger window just a little.

It was just how I remembered it. Ten-year-old Candy had thought the two narrow windows flanked by slate-gray shutters on the second floor looked like eyes while the wraparound porch resembled a wide, smiling mouth. I'd always loved this house. It was where I felt safe and secure and loved.

My mother's pink crepe myrtles were still wild and overgrown, no matter how much my father trimmed them back every winter. The farm truck sat parked in the same place it had been throughout my entire childhood—between two trees to the right of the driveway.

My eyes eagerly scanned the property for any changes, but all I found was relief in faded memories.

From the way the worn staircase creaked on the third stair from the bottom to the way the kitchen pantry always smelled like tea, this place held so many memories of comfort and stability. The family meals around a scarred claw-foot dining table. Fighting with Brady over the television remote. Waking up early and finding my dad in the kitchen, already dressed and ready for work on the farm with a thermos of black coffee and a white powdered doughnut wrapped in a paper towel.

My nose stung as the car pulled to a stop.

I was home.

Joan sat on my parents' front porch. She took a sip from a giant water bottle and eyed the car warily, like it held a troop of killer clowns instead of exactly one hundred percent of her immediate family.

But I was determined to make this go well, so I took a deep breath and opened the back passenger door, ensuring my smile was wide and genuine. "Hey, Joanie."

My sister—the person I'd admired my whole life—stood and walked down the six porch stairs in her old work boots. "Hi, Candy. Welcome back." Joan sounded like she always did, straightforward and a little gruff, but there was a chill in her demeanor that had my shoulders tensing.

It all devolved into painful awkwardness from there. I went in for a hug and Joan froze.

"I'm sweaty and gross," she said, putting her hands up to ward me off. "Been out here all afternoon." With a quick glance down my body, she added, "Wouldn't want to get you all dirty."

"Oh. Okay. Sure." My black trousers and silk button-up felt suddenly tight and uncomfortable.

Joan had been twenty-seven when I'd left home. We were in a family group chat together—one she rarely participated in. And I'd seen her on three separate Christmases, when I'd met my family in Virginia to celebrate the holiday with my mother's family. There hadn't really been video calls or even phone calls in the intervening years.

Joan had mostly always been an adult. The adultiest adult in any room. Our dad liked to joke that she was born forty-five and just got progressively more middle-aged every year. The last time Joan and I had any meaningful sort of relation-ship, I'd been a dumb teenager, hell-bent on escaping from her favorite place in the whole world.

I knew she didn't understand me, and I wasn't even sure I wanted her to. The prospect of being found lacking was highly likely, and her criticism didn't feel like the sort of thing I could handle right now.

My parents joined us and shifted our awkwardness face-off into a rectangle of unease.

With two hands full of luggage, Brady called helpfully from the trunk of the car, "I'll take these up to the apartment."

Frowning, I glanced between my parents. "I'm not staying in my old room?"

Mom smiled and squeezed my arm. "We thought you'd like your own space. I set you up in the apartment over the garage."

"Yeah, the one they remodeled for Mamaw," Joan added, something in her voice sounding like a challenge. I couldn't imagine why she felt the need for that. There was never any competition between us, not one I could win, anyway.

Of course, I knew about the apartment. Mamaw Murray—my maternal grandmother—had suffered a stroke several years ago. My parents had made accommodations for her here so that she had family nearby that could help with her care. It was why we stopped meeting for Christmas in Virginia. Mamaw had relocated to Kirby Falls out of necessity.

Joan snapped her fingers like she'd just remembered something. "That's right. You were too busy to come to your grandmother's funeral."

I could feel the blood leave my face. Guilt and shame fought for control as I shifted on my feet.

I hadn't attended Mamaw Murray's funeral. I'd been on deadline for my internship when she'd passed away last year. The bridge troll I'd worked for wouldn't give me the time off, despite my red eyes and visible grief over the loss of my last remaining grandparent. He'd told me that if I left, he'd fire me and never provide a decent reference as long as I lived. I'd called home crying and so damn ashamed.

But I'd survived that internship and gotten the recommendation I needed to land a better position with Blakely Hammond Marketing this spring. Though that hadn't worked out like I'd wanted either.

"Joan," my mother hissed in admonishment.

"I wanted to be there," I managed to say through my embarrassment, gaze straying toward the grass beneath my feet.

Before my mother could rush in to make things better—as was her way—Joan sighed. "I need to get back to it."

"But—" Mom started.

"I'll be back in time for dinner," Joan assured her, and then stalked off into the rows of apple trees lining the property, her long, lean form eating up the space.

I watched her back disappear behind thick green leaves, and then I watched some more. Vaguely, I could hear my parents juggling the flowers and the balloons and beckoning me to come into the house when I was ready. But my mind snagged on all the things I'd missed.

Not just the big things, like holidays and birthdays and the funeral for my grandmother. But the small things too. Being back in Kirby Falls made me suddenly very aware of the years I'd been away. I'd never seen my brother's apartment in town. I didn't know where Joan lived. I couldn't even imagine the spaces they occupied or who they spent their free time with. Did my sister have a dog? Did Brady still hang out with Floyd Ellerby and Jase Wilcox and Cole Abernathy, like he did in high school? Did my family still get together for pizza nights down at Apollo's on Main Street?

I didn't have answers to any of those very basic questions, and for what, because of the dream I'd been chasing? Doing whatever I could to live up to my parents' expectations and trying to figure out a way to take a country girl with good grades and a bright future and make her special. My goals had always been lofty. I had wanted to make something of myself. Be someone that Nick and Amy Judd could truly be proud of . . . in a different way than my siblings.

In the process, I'd done my level best to distance myself from my hometown and my Southern accent and my nickname and the way people saw me.

I sighed as seven years of regret and self-doubt worked to tighten every muscle in my body with unease.

In the distance, I could hear the rumble of a truck. It was coming from the direction of the farm. The Apple House, the main building that both acted as the storefront and housed the machinery for sorting, washing, and pressing apples for Judd's Orchard, was deeper on the property, a short quarter of a mile behind my parents' house. There was a separate entrance farther down the highway for farm visitors, but there'd always been a dirt path between our home and the public-facing structures for easy access.

Now, there was a white truck coming up the drive with its windows down and a man in a hat behind the wheel.

My mom stepped out onto the porch as the vehicle slowed beside the farmhouse. "Mercer!" she called. "Stop for a minute. Come on over!"

Ah. So this was the other farm employee I'd heard so much about. And the only full-time non-family member on staff.

The man I didn't know stopped the truck and climbed out. He was a big guy, solid and strong looking. His chest was wide and his arms were muscled, thighs thick in his light-wash denim. The skin exposed beyond his tee shirt was white but deeply tanned, likely from working outside so much. I couldn't see a whole lot with that hat in the way, but his hair looked like it was light brown, or perhaps it matched his dirty-blond facial hair. His eyes were shadowed beneath the bill of his cap, so I couldn't make those out either. Figuring I'd probably stared long enough, I forced myself to glance away.

My parents had talked about Mercer being a wonderful employee over the last several years. I knew they thought highly of him—a surrogate son for Amy and Nick Judd to dote on. He apparently helped Joan in the fields but also provided coverage at the Apple House when needed, grading and selling apples and handing out buckets for the u-pick side of the operation.

My brother strolled around the side of the farmhouse. I guessed he'd gotten my luggage sorted.

I stood a little taller as I watched Brady approach the handsome man, who looked to be around my age. They did a familiar hand-slap thing that male friends seemed to be born knowing how to coordinate.

Suddenly my mother and father were by my side without me realizing how they'd gotten there.

"Come say hi," Mom called across the twenty or so feet separating us from Brady and Mercer.

I smiled as they approached. As Mercer came closer, I was able to see the blue gray of his eyes that I'd been unable to make out before. He smiled too, and I couldn't help but notice the fullness and shape of his lips beneath his scruffy beard.

Before my parents had a chance to introduce me as Candy, I stuck out my hand and said brightly, "Hi, I'm Candace. You must be the famous Mercer I've heard so much about."

The hand that had been partially extended toward my own halted briefly as Mercer's expression morphed into one of frowny confusion. But then his big fingers managed to curl around mine, and he gave a warm squeeze.

I kept smiling and shaking as Mercer's eyes—that cool blend of blue and gray—searched my face. His lips flattened and joined the frowning party his face was currently throwing.

"Did she hit her head while I was gone?" my brother asked from Mercer's side.

I glanced at Brady. "What?"

He raised expectant eyebrows. "That's Mercer. Mark Mercer."

My eyes quickly shot to the man in question. I was still shaking his hand.

"You know Mercer. He was in your grade," Brady continued. "He went to our high school, doofus. Graduated with you and everything."

Um, what?

I let my mind drift back to the halls of Kirby Falls High as I took in the handsome face of the not-so-stranger before me. I didn't remember the name Mercer. And surely I would have remembered seeing this guy. But when I compared his to the faces of the teenagers I'd gone to school with, I came up empty.

"Oh," I said, like an idiot. My thoughts spun, trying to place the present-tense version . . . whose hand I was still holding.

I was only twenty-five. High school hadn't been *that* long ago. I should really be able to figure this out. Why couldn't I come up with a single memory of this man —this good-looking, solid, capable presence staring at me very thoughtfully? What was wrong with me?

Quickly, I gave a final squeeze to end the longest handshake in the history of greetings and lied, "Of course! I'm so sorry, Mercer. I must be all muddled from travel."

I fought a wince as my brother's eyes went wide in my periphery.

Muddled from travel.

Why had I said that? I wasn't a Regency romance heroine.

Muddled. Oh, Jesus.

"It's really good to see you," I added quickly. My hand felt sweaty with panic. Thank God I'd finally let go of him. "And of course, I've heard all about you from Mom and Dad. They just think so highly of you and love having you here at the orchard."

And then I shut my trap and prayed for a head injury, so I would, at least, have something to blame the memory loss and my sudden nineteenth-century vocabulary on.

Alas. Nothing fell from the sky to put me out of my misery.

We all just waited in awkward silence for Mercer to call me a liar and a fraud.

It wasn't anything I didn't already know anyway.

MARK

Wow.

She *really* didn't remember me.

I forced my face to do something that could hopefully pass for a smile and said, "Welcome home, Candace."

She'd been Candy back in high school. Maybe she'd forgotten her own name right along with mine.

She was trying to play it off and be polite, but she was a shit liar. Her smile looked like a photograph of a smile, copied and pasted onto her face, instead of the real deal.

There was a part of me who acknowledged that, yes, I did look different now, and we'd never really run in the same circles. But our graduating class had less than one hundred people.

Plus there had been that thing that one time.

Anyway.

Of course, I remembered *her*. Candace Judd had been the valedictorian of our class and the president of a handful of clubs. She'd organized events and led volunteer work. And if that hadn't been enough, she'd been popular and well-liked among her peers. Candy hadn't been head cheerleader, but she had run track and cross-country and been both homecoming and prom queen.

The part of me that had been a scrawny seventeen-year-old nerd took Candace's convenient memory loss as my due, but it still stung a little. Like a thorn I hadn't expected while pulling weeds.

Amy raised her voice over her daughter's well-meaning rambling. "Mercer, why don't you stay and have dinner with us? I have chicken and dumplings in the slow cooker."

"Thank you, but I should get back to work. I'm finishing up a few things and then heading home."

Plus, I'd seen Joan stalking along the path between the orchard and the house with *quite* the facial expression. Someone needed to protect the farm equipment from her obvious wrath.

"I'll see y'all tomorrow," I said with a wave and backed away.

Candace took a tiny step forward, like she might stop me. "Bye, Mark. It was good to meet—to see you!" She fought her wince, but I caught it.

Lord, she was trying hard. Bless her heart.

I smiled—authentically this time—and nodded.

I watched long enough to see Brady roll his eyes and wrap his arm around Candace, directing her toward the front porch. He sighed out, "God, you're hopeless," and then threw me a wave over his shoulder.

Climbing back inside my truck, I felt a little twist of guilt when I shifted into drive. I didn't actually have any work left. It was ten after five, and I had been on my way out when Amy flagged me down.

I kind of wished I'd kept on driving.

Despite her unintentional dig, it was good to see Candace back in Kirby Falls. Her parents never passed up an opportunity to talk about her—her life in New York City, her job, how amazing she was, or how proud they were of her. I was happy for them to have her back.

Nick and Amy Judd were good people. In the three years I'd been working for them, they'd always treated me like one of the family. I got invited to dinners and cookouts and birthday celebrations and holidays regularly. I had a good friend in Brady Judd and a good co-worker in Joan. She was quieter and less intentional in her friendship, but it was there. I knew I could count on her for damn near anything. And the Judds had never once made me feel like the home-town tragedy I was. They ignored the gossip and nosy neighbors. They were the closest thing I had to a family.

I moved to Kirby Falls in middle school, during my seventh-grade year. I'd already been a bit of an outcast because I was new. Most of my classmates had known each other since kindergarten. A brand-new student, much less a midyear transplant, was pretty rare around these parts. Add in the fact that my homelife looked a lot different than most of my peers', and you had a recipe for a loner in the making.

My neighbors had been the first folks to welcome me to North Carolina. The Prices were a charitable bunch. Reverend Price was the preacher at Kirby Falls Baptist Church, and his wife, Peggy, was generous and involved. Their only daughter, Hannah, had been in my grade at school and was the first person to offer me friendship. I'd held on tight and given her my undying devotion as a result. Even now, after all that had happened, I wasn't sure if I regretted it or not.

I rolled the window up on the truck and let the air-conditioning cool me down. The summer months were a killer down south, and this week made it feel like autumn was a ways off and not right around the corner.

The orchard would be opening this weekend for the season. Judd's Orchard was only open to tourists and visitors from mid-August through November 1. Thursday through Sunday, we'd welcome tourists onto the farm. They'd be eager to pick early-ripening apples and sample the items from the refreshment stand. Amy worked behind the counter, handling the apple slushies and the apple cider doughnuts and the apple slices with caramel. Brady and his dad, Nick, rotated between stations in the Apple House—either selling tickets, passing out buckets for the u-pick customers, and manning the merchandise counter in the front, or grading and washing the apples used for pressing in the back. I was mostly in the fields with Joan, but I pitched in where needed. I helped pick and prepare the produce we sold locally, and we all did our part to cover the weekly seasonal farmers' market and scheduled Kirby Falls events.

It was tight with just the five of us full-timers, but we managed.

I worked during the off-season too. A farmer's work was never really done. Joan and I had pruning to do in the winter when the apple trees were dormant. And in the spring, we kept an eye on the fields for any sign of blight or disease. We brought in bees to pollinate, hand-thinned the trees to guarantee longevity and production, and administered pest control.

The whole county was big in agriculture. Across the highway, Grandpappy's Farm did good business too. Their public-facing operation was a year-round affair. With more acreage and a wider variety of produce, they catered to tourists on a much larger scale. They went all out with hayrides and corn mazes and even an apple cannon.

I'd interviewed with William Clark before accepting my position here with the Judds. Between the two apple farms, I'd been more comfortable with the smaller setup. I couldn't imagine working in the Clarks' large General Store, which stayed open year-round, or being part of a whole team of farmers who worked the fields planting everything from cucumbers to potatoes to pumpkins to apples.

I liked where I'd ended up, and I liked the people I worked for.

And it appeared we'd have one more Judd on the property this fall. I wasn't sure how Candace's presence would affect the consistency and balance we'd established. However, it wasn't my place to question it. Kirby Falls was more Candace's home than it had ever been mine.

Nick and Amy had warned me just over a week ago that their youngest daughter would be returning to North Carolina. They'd said she'd be using her marketing know-how to work her magic behind the scenes. So if all went according to plan, I shouldn't have to deal with Candace Judd at all.

Maybe today would be the only awkward amnesia-riddled encounter I'd have to endure.

I thought of her fancy black slacks and her silky-looking blouse, not even *muddled* from travel. Her brown ponytail, sleek and sophisticated, just made her seem that much more put together and untouchable. Her gorgeous hazel eyes were the perfect swirling combination of green and gold and warm brown. Unlike me, Candace had a face you couldn't forget.

But something about that copy-and-paste smile made me wonder about her—

probably more than I had any right to, even now, twenty minutes later, as I turned toward my house.

Candace had always been tall and beautiful, even when she'd been Candy, captain of the debate team and cross-country star. Now, though, she was elegant in a way that teenagers couldn't really manage. She looked like she knew the best restaurants to recommend and always ordered the priciest thing on the menu. Like she drank wine instead of beer and had a ten-step skincare routine. The years of city life had turned her into someone unknown and unpredictable in a town filled with the same old, same old.

I wasn't sure how the polished young woman would fit back into farm life here in Kirby Falls. But I guessed that she'd be welcomed with open arms and widespread curiosity. That was what happened when a successful hometown favorite returned.

Reaching toward the visor over my head, I hit the button to open my garage. The house was quiet, as usual, when I entered. I lived at the end of a quiet one-lane road between the orchard and town.

When I reached the kitchen, I hit preheat on the oven and dropped a frozen pizza inside. No sense in cooking something real when it was just a party of one.

Setting the timer, I figured I'd have enough time to do some watering.

After grabbing a beer from the fridge, I slid open the back door to the deck and stepped outside. The garden in my backyard was full to bursting this time of year. I'd left the center of the yard open and lined the perimeter with raised beds. Colorful spots stood out from the plantings on the left, where yellow and orange bell peppers were ripening. The tomatoes were on the opposite side of the yard but were no less vibrant. They'd be producing well into September. I grew heirloom varieties in bold reds and striped yellows and pinks. The zucchini and summer squashes had their own space in the back near the fence line with plenty of room to spread out alongside the vine-like cucumbers. And the blackberries twining through the lattice below the porch were nearly done producing for the year.

First, I went around checking to see what could be picked. With my arms full of zucchinis and cucumbers, I briefly considered dropping some off with my next-door neighbor but then decided to just bring them inside for the time being. After depositing the vegetables on my kitchen counter to wash later, I went back outside by way of the back porch and started watering all the plants that needed it, sipping my beer as I went.

I could have set up an automated irrigation system to ensure regular soil hydration, but I was always home in the evenings. Besides, I liked to monitor the rainwater the plants received and supplement as needed. I'd spent several hours this past weekend weeding the beds, so my work tonight was nearly done.

My phone vibrated in my pocket just as I turned off the sprayer. I pulled my cell out and saw a text.

Brady: Here's your weekly invitation to trivia night at Trailview, even though I know you won't come.

I sighed, staring down at my phone.

Brady Judd asked me to join him at Trailview Brewing nearly every week. And every week I said no.

The familiar weight of guilt made my feet feel heavy as I climbed the porch steps.

I liked Brady. I really did. He was a good guy and a good friend. Brady had been a senior when I'd been a sophomore. But in a lot of ways, I felt like the older one between the two of us. He just wore his youth so blatantly. Brady had this carefree quality that made him seem like a perpetual frat boy. He lived to joke around and play pranks and tease. He had freedom, though, that other people didn't. And he hadn't lived the life I had—growing up fast out of necessity—so he couldn't really understand my inclination to keep to myself.

None of that was Brady's fault, but it did make things, like invitations to trivia nights at a local brewery, a little more complicated. There was a reason I chose to avoid Kirby Falls. I didn't go out. I spent my free time at home, for the most part.

And tonight—like most nights—I didn't have it in me to deal with an evening in town and the folks I might encounter there. So I texted back a quick, *No, thanks, man. See you tomorrow*, and put my phone away.

I snagged the small food and water dishes from the back porch and brought them inside to refill. The cat would probably be by soon for his supper.

Eyeing the placement of the sun in the sky, I briefly considered heading up to Juniper Point for some shots of the sunset. With the cloud cover moving in tonight, it had the potential to be a dramatic one with a sky full of pinks, purples, oranges, and everything in between.

But I figured the popular spot would be packed with tourists this close to the start of the season.

So I went inside, checked on my pizza, and finished my beer.

Twenty minutes later, I'd eaten and cleaned up. I peeked out the window to see that the cat hadn't shown up yet.

My phone buzzed from its place on the kitchen table, and I frowned. It wasn't like Brady to keep trying—not again on the same night, at least.

Wenn: Want to hit Craggy Peak tonight?

As I stared down at my phone, the only sounds I could hear were the clock ticking on the wall and the distant call of a bird somewhere outside. A quick scan of my kitchen and the living room beyond showed absolutely nothing going on.

I thought about it for all of ten seconds before replying.

Me: Sure. Meet you at 9. I'll get the beer.

Wenn: Bring that cider, if you've got it.

I peered out the back door one last time to see the bowl of cat food still untouched. Then I went to grab my gear and put a couple of ciders in the cooler.

The drive up to Craggy Peak took about thirty-five minutes. I got to catch an amazing view of the sunset after all, it just happened to be outside my side passenger window as I maneuvered the twists and turns on the Blue Ridge Parkway.

I parked next to Wenn's massive Jeep and transferred my camera, equipment, and belongings to his backseat. He was just walking back from the direction of the visitor center when I finished up.

"What'd you barter tonight?"

"Peach strudel bars," Wenn replied and then hopped in the driver's side.

My friend had an arrangement with the visitor center employee on duty. For over a year now, Wenn provided baked goods, and the worker looked the other way while we used the access road off the main trail at Craggy Peak. There was the area that tourists and locals were allowed to hike and visit, and then there was the narrow, bumpy path that was roped off and intended only for park employees and law enforcement.

As was our routine, Wenn pulled right up to the dirt drive, and I hopped out and unlocked the chain as he drove past. Then I climbed back in and we continued our rough journey out of the trees and on toward the lookout, where the landscape flattened beneath our tires and the hills spread out below us.

At just over five thousand feet in elevation, Craggy Peak provided a nice view of the surrounding area. You could see nearly to Tennessee from our vantage point. Wenn and I came out here, usually once a month when the weather was good, to shoot long-exposure photos of the night sky and mountains.

I'd taken a random photography class in college, and half a decade later, I found myself with an expensive hobby and intermittent income from selling prints online.

Wenn and I had met a couple of years ago at a photography group meetup in Asheville. He was quiet, like me. Maybe that was why we'd gravitated toward one another. Our friendship had pretty stable boundaries. We didn't grab dinner or go out for a beer at a brewery. Wenn had never been to my house, and hell, I didn't even know where the guy was from. But every now and then, he texted me to come out to Craggy Peak. He'd pass me some sort of baked good that tasted like heaven on earth while I provided the beer. Then for a few hours, we'd sit in peace and mostly quiet, in between taking photographs of the night landscape.

Wenn's tall, broad form moved around his Jeep, getting out a tripod and setting up camp chairs for us. I brought out my own gear and dropped the cooler in between our seats. The moon was bright enough for us to see what we were doing without the aid of headlamps or lights. And turning on an electric lantern would have messed up our exposures anyway. We performed all our usual tasks in silence, but it was a different sort of quiet when you shared it with someone else.

Twenty minutes later, when we were sitting comfortably and the night air was still in the low eighties, Wenn popped the top on some ancient Tupperware and passed me the contents.

Peach wasn't my favorite stone fruit by a lot, so I had low expectations. But when I took a bite, the cinnamon from the strudel topping blended perfectly with the sweet, ripe peaches. The base of the bar was some sort of vanilla shortbread. Combined with the texture of the cream cheese layer, it was all just ridiculously delicious.

"Man, that is good," I said after I swallowed.

Wenn's dark eyes stayed fixed on the barely visible horizon, but I could tell he was pleased by the compliment. "Thanks. I had a basket of peaches I picked up in South Carolina that I needed to do something with."

I took another bite and finished chewing before I mentioned, "I brought you a bag of zucchini from my garden. Left it in the backseat. In case you want to make any more of that chocolate chip zucchini bread."

Wenn nodded. "I might just do that. Thank you for the produce."

"Where do you learn to make all this stuff?"

I was tempted to take a third bar.

My friend gave me a scrutinizing look, so I backpedaled. "Hey, I wouldn't have asked if I thought it was a secret. I'm sorry."

A sound left Wenn's lips. It would have barely been amusement on anyone else, but it was practically a guffaw from the quiet man.

I didn't know Wenn's story, not really. He liked his peace and quiet. He was generous with his baking, but a stingy bastard with his words.

While we were friends, I'd never really felt like it was my place to ask why he had a picture of a woman and a kid as his lock screen when he'd never mentioned having any sort of family. I didn't initiate deep discussions. I didn't know why he went months without texting sometimes, or why he had trouble sleeping. I kept our interactions simple. I thought my friend got the only sort of socializing he could handle. So I called it good and didn't push.

Wenn seemed like the kind of guy who'd be easy to scare off. And the sad truth of it was, I liked having a friend who didn't know about my recent past either.

When you lived in a town as small as Kirby Falls, everyone knew your business and your history—or, at least, they sure as hell thought they did. It was inescapable.

But my friendship with Wenn was easy, and I wanted to keep it that way.

"It's not a secret," he clarified, amusement still lingering. "It's just embarrassing. I follow this home baker on social media. She shares recipes and makes step-by-step baking videos that are entertaining."

I waited for the embarrassing part. "So . . . you, like, have a crush on her?"

Wenn snorted. "No. She doesn't—you can't even see her face in the videos. I just know it's weird for men to enjoy baking as a hobby."

It sounded like my friend had some toxic masculinity in his background, which was also none of my business.

"Plenty of male top chefs in restaurants, all across the world," I challenged lightly and then took a sip of my cider.

Wenn nodded thoughtfully, like maybe he knew that already.

"What's it called? Maybe I'll look the videos up."

"It's called *Not Your Aunt Linda's Kitchen*," Wenn replied. "Her name is Melinda, and she takes traditional recipes and puts a unique spin on them. Makes a lot of substitutions for people with dietary restrictions."

"That sounds really cool. Don't worry. I'll keep your dirty little secret."

Wenn laughed—a real one this time. "Thanks, Mercer. I knew I could count on you."

I let loose a big sigh. "That's me. Dependable Mercer."

Wenn's gaze cut my way. "What's that self-deprecating sigh about?"

I was so surprised by my friend's genuine interest and rare personal question that I actually answered. "It's just, that's who I've always been. The reliable friend. The one who gets walked on and looked over. The dependable sucker."

It was dark now but not so dim that I couldn't make out Wenn's deep frown as his eyebrows drew together. "That's not what I meant. I——"

"No, I know," I interrupted. "Ignore me. They're my own hang-ups."

And they were. Wenn couldn't know that calling me dependable triggered the part of me that felt used and manipulated. There was no way he could have anticipated my reaction. I was Mercer: the loyal, trustworthy employee. The responsible friend. Need someone to call when your car won't start? I'm your guy. How about when you need coverage at the farmers' market on Saturday? Just ask Mercer. He's got you. Or if you happen to find yourself knocked up in college, risking public scrutiny and being disowned by your religious, conservative family? Yeah, get Mercer for that, too.

Wenn didn't know all the complicated emotions tied to being the dependable one or what it had cost me. So I distracted him with a different truth instead. "Hey, you wanna hear something funny? The girl I had a huge crush on in high school just came back to town today, and, get this, she didn't even recognize me."

The man occupying the camp chair beside me stayed quiet, so I laughed to cover up the awkwardness of the last thirty seconds and explained who Candace Judd was and that she was back on her family's farm for the first time since high school.

"She held out her hand and introduced herself like we didn't have honors chemistry together junior year," I admitted.

Wenn groaned. "Jesus, that is rough. Is she clueless or just mean?"

I was already shaking my head. "No. Neither. I looked different back then. I can't really blame her for not recognizing me right off."

"Different how?"

I thought of puberty and how it hadn't been kind. Somehow I'd had acne from fourteen to nineteen but hadn't grown past five one until after high school graduation. "My face was a mess. I wore glasses—cheap, basic frames because that was all my aunt could afford. I was scrawny and small. The summer after graduation—the summer Candace left—I shot up so fast that my bones ached."

With a commiserating glance, Wenn said, "I was a late bloomer too."

Taking in his imposing form in the tiny camp chair, it was hard to imagine Wenn as anything but the large-framed, muscular man before me. He looked like an action star or a professional athlete, maybe a soldier or an MMA fighter.

But it was nice to imagine that we had something like teenage awkwardness in common. I was six feet tall now and had taken up strength training and weight lifting in college. I wasn't the skinny nerd who enjoyed art class and dreaded PE, like I used to be. And I wasn't the eighteen-year-old guy growing too fast for his body to keep pace with. There had been a time when I couldn't eat enough to keep my belly full. Mrs. Price—Hannah's mom—had loved inviting me to have dinner at her house next door. I'd been the only one at the table who wasn't a picky eater. I ate everything she put in front of me, and the leftovers she'd send home with me too.

The Prices had been more than my neighbors. Hannah had been my best friend. Mrs. Price had treated me like a son, and the reverend had taught me how to grow a garden, drive a car, and shave my face. They'd done their best when they realized my homelife wasn't ideal. But it had never been their job to fix what was broken in me.

Having your deficiencies exposed made you vulnerable. And in the long run, having the illusion of a family was worse than growing up without one.

I'd been raised by my aunt after my mom took off when I was a baby. Having a kid hadn't worked out for my young mother, and I'd never known my father in any capacity. My aunt Autumn was pretty sure my mother hadn't even been sure of my paternity.

I barely had memories of my mom. A few old photographs in a shoebox in my closet and a hazy image of a blond woman humming "Blackbird" as she held me. There wasn't much to go on and even less to miss.

Aunt Autumn had been bitter and resentful, having to raise a kid she'd never asked for. I'd been clothed and fed, so I couldn't complain too much. I had it better than a lot of kids out there. The best thing Autumn had ever done for me was move us to Kirby Falls when I was twelve. I'd had people who cared about me and a place to call home.

For a little while, at least.

"So, what are you going to do?" Wenn's deep voice yanked my thoughts out of the past, and not a moment too soon.

"About what?"

"About the girl—Candace. Are you going to tell her who you are? That you have history together?"

Taking in the darkness beyond and the sweet scent of honeysuckle growing on the hillside, I let myself picture her friendly but mortified expression from this afternoon. And then I smiled.

"Nah. I'm going to let her figure that out on her own."

CANDACE

I stacked another box in the corner of the room and then batted away the plume of dust that erupted as the cardboard joined its brethren.

The small office located behind the counter in the Judd's Orchard Apple House hadn't been used with any sort of regularity since my grandfather was alive. My mom and dad were usually too busy to have a use for it, and anything requiring a computer was done up at the farmhouse.

When I'd broached the subject of cleaning out the space and using it for myself, my parents had been all for it. Just like with everything else I'd ever attempted, Nick and Amy Judd supported me wholeheartedly.

I'd done a cursory glance through the farm's social media accounts and was surprised to see the orchard was pretty active on Twitter. Less so on the other channels, but the content was solid. The photographs that were posted of the farm were irregularly spaced and infrequent, but they were beautiful. The shots of apples on the trees and all the merchandise and refreshments available had blown me away. I couldn't wait to implement a consistent marketing and advertising plan around the already stellar content.

In fact, I'd already been snapping photos around the farm to supplement. I liked getting shots of people in action. I'd caught my mom's smiling face at the refreshment stand and my dad sorting and washing apples for the press. I'd even taken several pictures of Joan and Mercer at work, but I made sure to crop them or at least keep their faces hidden. Joan because I didn't want to incur her wrath, and Mercer, well, I got the impression he was a pretty private guy.

So here I was, my first week in Kirby Falls, organizing old files, discontinued signage, and neglected storage items, getting this old office ready to be mine.

There was a battered wooden desk and a rolling chair, the back support adjustable, and the seat a dull avocado color with the texture of worn burlap. The chair squeaked whenever it rolled or when I sat on it or just generally breathed in its direction.

The wood-paneled, windowless room had three filing cabinets along the front wall and no artwork to speak of. But there was a largemouth bass mounted on a plaque behind the desk alongside the oldest analog wall clock I'd ever seen, permanently frozen in time at four thirty-two.

I used the bottom of my tee shirt to wipe sweat off my forehead. Even with the door propped open, there was little air circulation to speak of. I'd need to allocate some funds to purchase a portable air conditioner, or I'd never be able to work in here as summer slowly wound down to fall.

Inexplicably, the next box I searched through held six bowling trophies from down at Lucky Strike Lanes and some old Kirby Falls postcards from over the years. I thumbed through the stack, noting how much the town had changed. At one point, there'd only been a single stoplight on Main Street. I took in the blue-and-white sign over Apollo's. When I'd ridden with Mom last night to pick up pizza, I'd noticed a new-and-improved logo directing restaurant-goers to one of our family's favorite dining options in Kirby Falls.

I'd already emptied the desk drawers and wiped everything down. My laptop was perched on the scarred oak surface, just waiting for me to brainstorm ideas for the farm. I had quite a few things I wanted to run by Joan and my parents, just to see what would be feasible. But so far, Joan had been keeping her distance.

She had shown back up at my mother's dining table two nights ago for chicken and dumplings. But my sister had been quiet while my parents kept up a running commentary and I fielded their questions about New York. I'd felt uneasy and barely able to drink my sweet tea as I avoided talking about my unceremonious exit from the city.

As far as my family knew, I had a better opportunity lined up later in the year. The Christmas holiday had seemed like a good arbitrary timeline, but even though we were over four months away from December 25, I could feel the deadline looming, and my lies holding me hostage.

I hefted the final box off the filing cabinet and rolled my eyes when I opened it and saw it was packed full of stuff from my brother's bedroom which had been converted into a craft room for my mother. There was a stack of car magazines, a collection of greeting cards held together by rubber bands, a soccer medal from his senior year, and his high school diploma, still in the protective holder embossed in gold with *Kirby Falls High School Class of 2012.*

I'd have to ask him if he still wanted any of this crap. I also unearthed ticket stubs in an old Altoids tin that, somehow, still smelled strongly of peppermint, and a smudged and faded handwritten note on folded notebook paper. Before I could read it and happily invade my brother's teenage privacy, I caught sight of his yearbook at the very bottom of the box.

Smiling to myself, I sat down in the green chair as it squeaked in protest.

"Would you look at this, Lance Bass," I mumbled to the mounted fish, who I'd recently named. Unsurprisingly, he had no comment.

Excitedly, I flipped through the pages until I found my brother's goofy, grinning face in his senior portrait. The guys all wore those faux tuxedo shirts while the girls sported off-the-shoulder, V-neck maroon velvet tops.

Then I kept on flipping until I got to the sophomore class photos. My finger scanned the list of alphabetical names until I found mine: *Candy Judd.* I sighed. They hadn't even used my full name in the high school yearbook.

The black-and-white image smiled back at me. That was the year I'd tried swoopy bangs and long layers. My over-plucked eyebrows were regrettable, but I still looked bright-eyed. Youthful in a way you couldn't manufacture, no matter how many retinol-based serums you had on your nightstand.

My gaze scrutinized the sea of familiar faces. I saw Laramie Burke, who'd always been a firecracker. I wondered absently if she was still helping her family across the highway at Grandpappy's. Then my eyes drifted and found Lauren Walker as the very last photo in the bottom row. *Lo.* My former best friend.

Nostalgia and sadness fought for the top spot as my finger traced the features of her sassy, smiling face. I remembered she'd specifically worn a crop top on school picture day to show off her new belly-button piercing, risking an in-school suspension if the assistant principal caught her violating the dress code. She'd made it until the last period of the day, when Mr. Pritchard had finally spotted her and written her up. And then the pictures came back a month later, and they'd been cropped too high to even see her midriff.

I could feel the faint smile on my lips as I recalled the memory. Apparently, nostalgia won out.

I continued scanning the youthful faces, most I'd known all my life. Then I sat up straight, my attention snagging on the name *Mark Mercer*. My gaze flew past his likeness three times before I made myself double-check the listing to the right, indicating his position on the correct row and column.

My heart was beating hard when it finally settled on the face of fifteen-year-old Mark. Mercer was his last name, not his first.

I sighed and covered my face with both hands.

That was Mercer.

I peeked out from between my fingers at the waiting image. He was small even in the frame of the photo. Thick-rimmed glasses framed long-lashed eyes. Acne spread liberally across his forehead and chin as the sullen boy stared straight at the camera. Mark wasn't smiling, but he wasn't frowning either.

I couldn't believe I'd forgotten.

I guessed he went by Mercer now. But I'd known him as Mark, the quiet kid who hardly ever spoke up and never drew attention to himself. He'd been close to Hannah Price, the reverend's daughter. I found her photo on the row below, two columns over. She'd been prim and reserved. Short brown hair that came to just below her chin and the ghost of a smile as she posed in her collared shirt beneath a sweater vest.

Hannah and Mark had kept to themselves throughout middle and high school. They partnered on projects and ate together in the cafeteria. Hannah had rarely been included in social events or invited to parties. It was well-known that Reverend Price was a strict man. No one wanted to subject themselves to being tattled on by his daughter or risk his wrath when they were sitting in one of his pews on Sunday morning at Kirby Falls Baptist Church.

I tried to remember if we'd had any classes together—Mark and I—but the memory wouldn't come. I thought there might have been a technology course where he'd sat at the computer desk behind me, but I couldn't really remember.

He'd been a nebulous presence in my middle and high school career. Not in my circle of friends and not on any sports teams or in any groups or clubs. He wasn't a member of the school newspaper with me or on any of the various committees I'd served on. We'd coexisted in the same universe, our orbits coming close on occasion but, typically, with light-years in between.

However, there had been one instance involving Mark that I definitely should have recalled when I was shaking his hand and introducing myself like an idiot two days ago.

Groaning, I covered my face again and remembered every awkward moment of the past.

It had been the week of graduation. I'd been rushing through the hallway, nearly late for class. I couldn't recall which one or even where I'd come from, but I'd heard a voice trailing after me, calling my name.

I remembered feeling shocked to turn around and find Mark Mercer standing there, four inches shorter than me and looking like he might throw up at any moment.

Mark had asked to speak to me privately. I'd probably frowned, confused and slightly annoyed to be sidetracked like this. The bratty part of teenage Candy that lived pretty close to the surface had likely cringed, thinking Mark might have been working up the nerve to ask her out.

But then he'd informed me quietly that I had a stain on my pants. With cheeks burning, he'd all but shoved the hoodie he always wore into my arms and told me I could wrap it around my waist.

Teenage Mark had bolted before I could even so much as mumble a startled thank-you. I'd looked up and down the busy hallway full of my peers before positioning the black sweatshirt around my waist and tying the arms in front.

Then I'd raced to class and explained the situation to my teacher, who'd excused me to the PE locker rooms to change into my workout clothes and grab an emergency tampon I had stored there.

I'd carried Mark's oversized hoodie in my backpack for the next two days, hoping to run into him and return it. But I didn't see him again before graduation. The black sweatshirt, with a logo of a band I'd never even heard of, got packed with my things and accompanied me across the country in the back of Lo's Toyota Camry. I'd forgotten its origin over the years as I'd pulled it out and worn it around my cold apartment in the wintertime.

I stared at the photo of young Mark Mercer and thought about how kind and brave he'd been to approach me that day. He'd crawled out of his little introverted shell and saved me from embarrassment.

Squinting down at the page, I tried to see the man this boy would become. My eyes attempted to find Mercer's square jaw, the strong, compact lines of his body, and the faint smile lines that lingered at his temple. But clearly, the kid I'd been vaguely aware of—the one who'd done me such a kindness—had years of growing to do still.

I couldn't believe I hadn't recognized Mercer as my former classmate when I'd been reintroduced to him two days ago. Well, I mean, I *could* believe it because Mark had changed so much over the years. He no longer resembled the boy I remembered.

I still felt like a jackass for not realizing it though. And I wasn't sure if bringing it up the next time I saw Mercer would be the right thing to do. I didn't want to draw attention to my blunder, but I still kind of wanted to thank him for what he'd done that day. I'd never gotten the chance. I decided I'd play it by ear when I ran into him again. To hear my parents tell it, Mercer was on the farm all the time and often joined them for dinner.

"What's going on in here?"

My sister's sharp voice had me jolting in the squeaky chair. I slammed the yearbook closed like I'd been caught with porn, and a poof of dust erupted in front of my face.

Hacking and waving away the particles, I finally managed to make eye contact with Joan and reply. "Oh, hi! I was just cleaning out the office."

Joan's blue eyes narrowed from beneath the bill of her ball cap. "For what?"

I nearly lost my nerve under her scrutiny but then straightened. "Mom and Dad said I could use it while I'm in town. That it's just been sitting here empty."

"Well, yeah. We're all too busy working to sit behind a desk all day."

Nodding, I tried not to take her comment personally. Joan was a hard worker, and her job had physical requirements that mine didn't. But just because I wasn't outside all day or doing manual labor didn't mean my work lacked value.

"I know," I said evenly. "I actually have some ideas for the farm I wanted to run by you. You're the expert, and I'd really love your input before I bring any of these concepts to Mom and Dad."

My sister regarded me coolly, like I was a salesman trying to talk her into a time-share and swindle her life savings. "I don't have time for that. Talk to Mom and Dad all you want, but there isn't disposable income for trendy marketing schemes. Not beyond the advertising we've always done. Don't take advantage of them, Candy. They've never been able to tell you no."

Hurt and defensiveness had me frowning. I would never take advantage of our parents. And I knew that the farm hardly did more than break even most years. My whole childhood had been centered around budgets, frugal spending, and making ends meet. Sports fees and uniforms had been a luxury. Soccer for Brady and track and cross-country for me. My prom dress had been from the clearance rack at Belk. There hadn't been a family vacation for the Judds until I'd been nearly fourteen. We'd prayed over the orchard's yearly harvest at every dinner and sold to reliable vendors who gave us a fair price for our apples. There'd been kitchen table bills and constant saving for the rainy day fund. We'd never been a family who splurged or spent excessively.

Did my sister think I'd been away so long I'd forgotten that?

"I'm just looking for ways to help, Joan," I admitted quietly, unable to hold her accusatory gaze.

I registered a sigh from the doorway and then the scrape of boots over cement flooring as she walked away.

Maybe it was history or the years between us, but Joan always had the ability to make me feel like a child. I'd forever be seven years old, trying to impress all the grown-ups in the room with a dance routine.

I didn't think she did it on purpose, but my sister consistently flattened my self-confidence. It was why I worked hard in my relationships with my peers and co-workers to never quash someone's enthusiasm. No one liked to feel bad about the things that made them happy.

And I was energized and eager to take my ideas for the farm and turn them into quantifiable profit for my parents.

Or, at least, I had been until Joan made me seem like an opportunist and an idiot to boot.

I wanted to be respected. I wanted to be a valued co-worker and a member of this orchard team. I wanted to be a good daughter and sister.

But I didn't think I was any of those things currently. Mostly, I just seemed to be in the way.

Joan already thought the worst of me, I winced considering what she'd think if she knew the truth about my return to Kirby Falls. While I was excited to be with my family and put my marketing education and experience to good use here on the farm, I was also home to lick my wounds.

Back in May, I'd been hired by Blakely Hammond, a really prestigious marketing firm. Things had been going great. Well, they'd been . . . pretty good. I'd learned a lot about the inner workings of a large office, but then I'd made the mistake of mixing business with pleasure. In retrospect, starting up a romantic relationship with my boss hadn't been the best idea. There had just been so many things I hadn't realized at the time. Like the fact that Emerson—my former boss —was stealing my ideas and passing them off as his own. I'd thought I was helping, being a team player and an even better girlfriend, but in the three months I'd worked there, Emerson continually took credit for my work, lying to me all the while.

We'd kept our relationship secret, like he'd insisted. I definitely didn't want to appear unprofessional, but Emerson wasn't like anyone I'd ever dated before. He was older, for starters. Ten years my senior and more sophisticated by a long shot. He'd encouraged me to take leisurely, romantic lunch breaks with him and to meet him at hotels late at night. I'd never questioned why he didn't invite me over, and I'd been too embarrassed to have him come to my tiny third-floor studio apartment.

Looking back, I could see what an idiot I'd been, but it didn't make that particular pill any easier to swallow.

One day, a frazzled-looking woman with a baby on her hip had burst into Emerson's office while I'd been in the hallway. I'd watched in horror through the clear glass windows as he'd taken the baby from her and smiled and reassured her through whatever crisis had been going on.

"The little wife has a meltdown at least once a month," his administrative assistant had whispered to me conspiratorially. I'd been frozen in front of her desk, watching the drama unfold with dawning horror and sinking dread. "Comes barging in with the baby. Probably locked herself out again."

Emerson had glanced over and spotted me by then, but the rest of the story was just a tragic tale best left in the annals of human resource training videos.

A knock sounded that had my head snapping up and out of the pathetic Lifetime movie spinning on repeat in my head.

"Hey," Brady said with a strained smile. Add that to the fact he hadn't called me butthead or buttmunch or some variety of butt-focused name indicated he'd seen Joan stalk away from me.

"Hi."

My brother took in the meager offerings of the room. His eyes touched on the stack of boxes in the corner, the filing cabinets, the yearbook I held in my lap, and the wall-mounted Lance Bass—my new best friend.

Eventually his blue eyes—the same shade as Joan's—settled on me where I hunched behind the desk. "She'll come around," he said sympathetically. "Just give her some time."

I nodded.

"You've been gone a while, Candy Cane. And Joanie, well, she's never been good with change."

"I know."

"What you got there?" Brady asked, taking a step closer to the desk.

"Just a yearbook." Then I stood and indicated the open box full of his stuff. "I found some of your crap while I was cleaning up. You want it?"

He was already poking at the contents.

While Brady was occupied, I slid his yearbook into my bag beneath the desk so I could thumb through it again later.

"Mom was pretty eager to get her craft room situated," my brother said. "She packed everything up for me. I guess I must have missed this box."

Brady had gone to college at the University of Tennessee in Knoxville. He spent four years there and then came back home with a degree in public relations. He'd been content to live with our parents for a while. I had the vague sense he'd moved out when he'd been twenty-four or twenty-five, but since I hadn't been back to Kirby Falls, I'd never been to his home.

"Can I see your place sometime?" I blurted.

"Yeah, sure," he replied without even glancing up from the box he was digging through.

Maybe I was quiet for too long, thinking about what a terrible sister I was, because his eyes cut my way.

"You really want to see my apartment downtown?"

I nodded quickly. "I want to see where you live." He looked mildly alarmed, so I added, "So I can judge it and you accordingly. And offer my expert decorating advice for your bro pad."

Brady snorted, then returned his attention to his old things. "You can come over whenever you want, buttface."

I rolled my eyes, but I was grateful I had at least one sibling who wanted me around.

I blamed nostalgia, weather, and my sweet tooth for making me pull into the parking lot of the long-closed Sears department store.

The tiny hut that housed Bev's Sno-Kones still sat at the back of the faded asphalt lot. The building was worn with faded cream paint on the outside and a dark V-shaped roof over the top. There was a large cooler behind the building as well as two trash cans. A window on the left side served as a drive-through for Kirby Falls' residents while the window on the opposite side of the small building was for walk-up customers.

The lines weren't too long today, just a handful of people standing single file on the right and three cars waiting in the drive-through lane.

I parked my mother's Volkswagen Passat and hopped out, squinting to see the signage on the outside of the building as I approached.

Judging by the hours listed, Bev's Sno-Kones still opened and closed whenever they felt like it. On hot summer days, you could usually count on lines wrapping around the building, but if it rained, they typically closed up shop. But most afternoons in May through September, you could swing by and get a snow cone or lemonade or soda poured over delicately shaved ice.

I had memories of Mom and Dad bringing me and my siblings by for a treat, usually early on in the summer, before the farm opened up for apple picking. We'd spend a Saturday swimming in Lake Archer and then drive back to Kirby Falls and wait, still wrapped in beach towels, at the order window with sunburned cheeks. I always got the bubble gum flavor.

Something new I noticed was a converted van parked off to the side and out of the way. It looked like Bev's now offered shaved ice on the go. Catering and party rentals were available, or so the side of the van proclaimed. I made a mental note to add it to my notebook when I returned to the car as something to check into.

There were no welcoming picnic tables for you to stay and enjoy your purchase. No umbrellas to shield you from the punishing heat. Nope. Bev wanted you to take your shaved ice and be on your way. Loitering typically got you some side-eye from behind the order window.

Now though, I didn't recognize any of the workers who were slinging sugar syrup. It just looked like two teenagers in there.

I was standing in line on the hot pavement, scanning the board listing all the flavors when I heard an obscenely Southern voice from behind me. "Candy Judd, as I live and breathe! How are you doing, honey?"

Turning, I found Vera Sterling, Kirby Falls' biggest gossip and busybody, approaching from the parking lot. She skipped right over the two people in line behind me and came to stand at my side. I gave the preteen boy and pretty blond woman apologetic smiles before Ms. Sterling threw her arms around me for a hug.

"Hello, Ms. Sterling," I mumbled against her shoulder, resisting the urge to tell her it was *Candace* now.

She pulled back and beamed. "Well, it is just so good to see you!"

I nearly winced as her clutching hands gripped my shoulders so she could get a good look at me. I could only imagine what she was seeing.

I hadn't thought too much about my appearance when I'd run out of spray cleaner and needed to make a quick trip to the store. Despite the fans my dad had dropped by the office, it was still pretty hot in there.

I was thinking about it now as Vera Sterling took me in with a slightly shocked expression. My brown hair was piled up on top of my head in a messy bun. I could feel the shorter strands at my nape and temples damp with sweat. I wasn't wearing a lick of makeup, and my oversized-tee-shirt-and-jean-shorts combo left a little to be desired. Especially for a fifty-something church lady who rarely went out without her face on.

"What has that New York City done to you, Candy honey?"

I tried for a smile. "Oh, I was just in the middle of cleaning when I needed to run to the store. Then I decided to stop by Bev's here and see if the shaved ice was as good as I remembered."

She still looked a little disappointed in me.

Vera Sterling owned a bed-and-breakfast downtown that catered to tourists. She'd gone to church with my family for as long as I could remember. But she was a nosy woman who made everyone's business her own. I could only imagine how fast the news of raggedy Candy Judd would make the rounds on the Kirby Falls hotline. A report of my appearance would probably end up in the town's Facebook group.

Small towns and entitled opinions. Some things never changed.

"Well, Bev's sure is a welcome treat on such a hot day," Ms. Sterling offered with a sweet smile as we shuffled forward in line.

I nodded.

"I am just so glad to see you back home, young lady. And I know your parents must be thrilled. All Amy ever talks about is how darn proud she and your daddy are of you."

I swallowed hard and made myself maintain eye contact. Ms. Sterling didn't know she was pushing on a tender spot. She was just telling the truth. My parents *were* very proud of me and so supportive.

But I didn't deserve their constant praise. The fact that I was back home right now proved that.

Ms. Sterling went on, "And such a big-city professional! Well, it's hard to envision right this minute. But this town has always known that little Candy Judd would accomplish great things."

Clearing my throat, I managed, "Thank—thank you, Ms. Sterling. That's very kind."

I was saved from further conversation when the window slid open and a bored-looking teenage boy awaited the next order.

"You go ahead," I said to Ms. Sterling. "I still need a minute to decide."

And then I slipped to the back of the line behind a woman with short blond hair who looked really familiar.

I was so distracted by Ms. Sterling's words and the reminder of what a phony and a failure I was—crawling home with my tail between my legs after my "big-city" disaster—that I barely noticed when the woman in front of me turned around with a big, pretty smile.

"Hi, Candy. You might not remember me, but I'm Bonnie Jensen—used to be Bonnie Clark. I was a few years ahead of you in school."

"Oh, hi!" I replied as her face clicked into place with the aid of her introduction. She was one of the Clarks from Grandpappy's Farm. Her family worked the attraction across the road. "Yes, of course. Laramie was in my grade."

"That's right," she agreed. "How are you liking being back?"

"It's great," I said automatically.

Her smile widened knowingly. "You'll get settled. I imagine it takes some getting used to after living somewhere bigger and brighter for so long."

"Yeah." I nodded, grateful that she hadn't called me on my fib outright.

While it had been nice to be back in Kirby Falls, it had been a challenge too. I loved seeing my parents, but things with Joan had been rocky. The mountains that gave me peace, but after seven years in the city, it was too quiet at night, and I had trouble sleeping.

"So what are you up to now?" I asked, hoping to take the focus off of me.

She tucked a strand of short blond hair behind one ear. "Oh, I married Danny Jensen, and I teach art at Kirby Falls Elementary School."

"Wow!" I wanted kids of my own, but I couldn't imagine trying to wrangle twenty of them every day while they wielded tiny paintbrushes and glue sticks.

Bonnie laughed. "I know. It's not for everyone, but I like it. I love the school and my students."

"Do you have any kids of your own?" I figured someone who willingly inter-acted with other people's children and enjoyed it probably had plans to create their own offspring.

Her light brown eyes dimmed just a little, and I felt like an asshole for asking. "No, not yet."

"Me neither," I said quickly. "But someday I hope to meet the right guy and it'll all come together, you know?"

Bonnie grinned and nodded. "So are you helping out at the orchard this season?"

"Yeah, I am. Are you at Grandpappy's while school is out for the summer?"

She laughed. "Oh, no. I'm the worst farmer in the bunch. Do more harm than good, I'm afraid. Plus school starts back up next week. I'm busy getting my classroom ready."

"That's me over at that orchard. Joanie is the one with all the know-how. I'm just using my marketing background to hopefully help boost sales. And I'll be working at the farmers' market and festivals and such."

We scootched forward as Vera Sterling left with her snow cone in hand. I kept my gaze firmly on Bonnie, lest I accidentally invite more conversation from my nosy neighbor.

With a sly glance over my shoulder, Bonnie said quietly, "She's gone. You're safe."

I breathed out a huge sigh of relief and we both laughed.

"She is just the same," I said.

"She sure is," Bonnie agreed. "But don't let Vera Sterling discourage you. She's eager for some hot gossip to spread around about why you're *really* in town. But most everyone else is just happy to have you home."

I considered that and felt a pang in my midsection.

Bonnie was a near-stranger. I knew *of* her and had seen her around Kirby Falls in my youth. The fact that she—or anyone else who wasn't my family—even noticed or cared that I was back was heartwarming.

But there was indeed hot gossip surrounding my departure from New York. If Ms. Sterling ever got her ears on my accidental affair and subsequent firing, all of Kirby Falls would know within the hour. And my parents would be unbelievably disappointed in me.

"You go on ahead," Bonnie offered as the kid in front of us finished up. "I'm picking up a bunch of snow cones for my husband and the guys at Begley Auto, where he works. You'll be in line forever if you're behind me."

I thanked Bonnie and stepped forward to order my medium bubble gum shaved ice from the bored teenager. Then I chatted with Bonnie some more while I waited.

After a few minutes, my pink-topped white Styrofoam cup was placed on the ledge and the worker requested $3.50. I grabbed my debit card out of the front pocket of my jean shorts and handed it over.

The teen looked at the plastic rectangle in my outstretched hand and sighed audibly before pointing to the very obvious sign on the outside of the building that read *Cash Only* in big bold red letters, underlined twice.

"Crap," I muttered, digging in my back pockets like some bills or change might magically appear there. I didn't carry cash. Who carried cash? "I'm so sorry. Do you take Apple Pay? Or Venmo? I can PayPal you directly."

The teenager sighed again.

Before I could offer him my favorite kidney or my firstborn child, Bonnie stepped up next to me and held out a five-dollar bill. "Here you go."

"No, I couldn't," I insisted as mortification burned a path up my throat.

She gave me a look that said, *Girl, it's five bucks*, before thrusting the money into the hand of the waiting employee.

"Thank you," I rushed out. "I can Venmo you."

Bonnie grinned and shook her head. "Let's call it a 'welcome home' present."

I thought for a moment. "How about you let me help you carry all your snow cones to your car, and I take you out for a drink sometime to say thank you?"

Bonnie hurried to catch the change the worker thrust in her direction. "You don't need to do all that."

"I want to. Plus you'd be doing me a favor. I left Kirby Falls before I was old enough to drink . . . legally. I'd love to have a new friend to show me the ropes."

The smile Bonnie gave me was warm. She had a tiny gap between her two front teeth that made her even more endearing and adorable. "You got it." She unlocked and handed me her phone. "Here, put your number in while I order all these snow cones."

I gratefully accepted her cell. No matter how old you got, asking someone to be your friend, whether on the playground at recess or beside the shaved ice shack, never got any easier. I felt relieved that I might have found someone new in a place where I was surrounded by so much history.

While Bonnie rattled off her long order from a piece of scrap paper, I added my number to her contacts. *Candace, not Candy. Thank you very much.*

A text message came through just before I finished up. I didn't intentionally invade her privacy, but the notification practically highlighted the message at the top of the screen, directly over where I needed to finish typing my details. Plus, it didn't help that the text from Danny was in all caps.

Danny: WHY THE HELL AREN'T YOU BACK YET?

I glanced up to see Bonnie's attention still focused on ordering. I waited for the notification to disappear and then I finished up what I was doing and turned the screen off.

Bonnie's rude husband was none of my business. I didn't know her very well yet, but I still felt annoyed on her behalf. Maybe Danny was just in a bad mood. Maybe he wasn't always a douchebag. Hopefully, he didn't make a habit out of treating his wife that way.

I swallowed down my uneasy feeling and met Bonnie's gaze when she turned back to me. Smiling, I told her, "I texted myself from your phone so that I'll have your number too. I'll message you this week about grabbing a drink."

"Sounds good!"

While we waited for her eight snow cones, we chatted some more about her job at our former elementary school. I asked about the teachers who were still around, and we laughed about the old PE teacher, who'd apparently scarred us both as children with his short shorts.

Eventually, she got her to-go trays and I helped her get settled in her SUV, thanking her again for bailing me out at Bev's.

We said our goodbyes, and I made my way back to my borrowed car feeling lighter than I had when I left the orchard.

That first bite of bubble gum snow cone flooded my body with sugar and memories. The sweetness of both had me smiling out the windshield of Mom's Passat. My sister's dismissal from earlier in the day was buried beneath pink shaved ice and potential.

four

MARK

I hadn't bothered checking the schedule this weekend to see who I'd be working alongside in the farmers' market booth. I figured it would be either Joan or Brady, so it didn't really matter.

Nick and Amy usually picked two weekends a month and worked together while Joan, Brady, and I rotated in and out.

I hadn't expected Candace to put herself on the schedule or participate in that side of things when it came to orchard responsibilities. And I definitely hadn't expected it her first weekend in town. In truth, I thought she'd be pretty hands-off with the crops and produce.

So, I was doubly surprised to see her boxing up apples alongside her brother when I got to Judd's early Saturday morning.

"Good morning," she said when she noticed my slow approach up the steps of the Apple House. She wasn't quite as put together as she had been earlier in the week, right off the plane. But she looked relaxed and comfortable in a white orchard tee shirt, flowy skirt, and her brown hair long and wavy. There was a softness to her now. Still beautiful, just in a way that was approachable rather than intimidating. Despite the years away, Candace looked like she belonged here, and it was a shock to the system.

I'd never seen her in the context of Judd's employee, only its long-lost daughter.

But I supposed she had grown up on this farm, and she'd probably worked her share of Saturdays, as a teen and adolescent who was part of a family business.

"Good morning," I finally replied once I stopped gawking at her like a preteen with a crush.

Brady sat nearby on the surface of the worn worktable, booted feet swinging, while he scrolled on his phone. "Hey, Mercer."

"You're up early," I told Candace once I'd returned her brother's greeting.

She grinned and tossed a thumb over her shoulder. "You thought I'd be hiding out in the office."

My gaze followed the direction she indicated, and I saw the door behind the counter open for the first time in my three years of employment. "I didn't even know there was an office back there."

"I cleaned it out this week. And while I do plan on using it while I'm here, I also intend to help where I can." Her eyes slid away from me as she closed the sides of the box before scooting it aside. "Earn my keep."

Speaking of earning one's keep, I should probably be helping prep the produce to load up and bring downtown for the farmers' market this morning. I reached for the flattened cardboard and folded it back into a box shape before joining Candace behind the worktable.

"I don't think you need to worry about that. You're from here. Your parents are thrilled to have you home."

Her hands stilled for a moment. "I know. I still want to help though. And taking a shift at the farmers' market lightens the load, right? You okay being stuck with me today?"

Oh, so she was working the farmers' market. Not just loading produce or helping out at the orchard today.

"Yeah, of course," I hurried to say after a moment of hesitation.

"Good," Candace said with a grateful smile. "Plus, I'm sure Joan still hates being away from the fields, and I'm sure Brady here is thrilled to have another warm body to man the booth."

It was true. Joan hated dealing with the public and answering questions about the farm. And while Brady was personable and a natural salesman, he did get bored easily and often looked for ways to keep himself entertained. Usually, by messing with a certain dark-haired employee at the Grandpappy's tent.

Candace's presence on the farm would be a help. I just hadn't anticipated it, was all.

"You're right about that," her brother agreed without looking up from his phone.

"It'll be nice to have another pair of hands around." Then I offered her a small grin that she readily returned.

"Have you seen some of these comments, Candy?" Brady asked abruptly, blue eyes wide.

"What comments?"

Then Brady started laughing, which was never a good sign. "Holy hell. These women are thirsty."

His sister straightened and moved quickly to his side so she could see his screen. "Oh, no," she muttered a moment later.

Frowning, I wondered what the hell was going on. "What's wrong?"

But then both Judds raised their heads and met my gaze. Candace looked pained while Brady appeared ridiculously pleased.

"Candy asked if she could help out with social media and post some photos she's been snapping around the farm this week, and, let's just say, some posts are more popular than others."

"I'm really sorry, Mark," Candace said. "I was just trying to help."

I looked between them, not getting it. "What are you talking about?"

"She posted a thirst trap of you, and now the ladies—well, mostly ladies—of Instagram are taking notice," Brady explained, then laughed again. "God, these comments. They are ridiculous. *Is that an apple in your pocket or are you just excited for apple picking? He puts the spice in pumpkin spice.* Oh, listen to this one by CeCeSlater. Man, that's a great username. Anyway, CeCeSlater commented, *Lumbersnack material?* and then tagged some friends to weigh in. And someone else said you could handle her apples any day."

"Geez," Candace said, reading over her brother's shoulder, expression mortified.

There was a picture of me on one of the farm's social media accounts? Attention was literally the last thing I wanted. I moved forward and snatched the phone out of Brady's hand.

"Hey!" he protested, but I didn't care.

As I scrolled up to find the image in question, I heard Candace say, "I didn't post your face, Mark. I wouldn't do that. I respect your privacy. But I was sharing photos from around the farm. I had some of Joan and Brady and Mom and Dad. I just wanted you to be included too. You're an important part of Judd's Orchard. I didn't want to leave you out."

My fingers swiped through the photos, distantly aware that she was telling the truth. There was a shot of Nick and Amy in the Apple House, smiling with their Judd's Orchard tee shirts on. Another image showed Brady from behind while he picked apples and balanced on a ladder. Then there was Joan driving the tractor, gaze forward and focused as she hauled the giant apple cart out of the fields. With the light behind her, Joan was basically a dark silhouette.

The last picture in the carousel was of me holding an apple. Candace must have taken it when I wasn't paying attention, right here in the Apple House. I was sorting and washing the fruit we'd harvested earlier in the week.

The image was cropped in such a way that you couldn't see my face, but my torso was clearly visible. My shoulders bunched, my biceps flexed, and the hard planes of my chest were on full display beneath my white tee shirt. I must have splashed water on myself at some point, because my stomach was wet, abs shadowed beneath the fabric of my cotton tee.

I got through reading three of the top comments before I felt a fierce blush climbing up my neck. When I raised my head, I saw Candace looking remorseful and wringing her hands while Brady held his stomach and laughed some more.

"I'm really sorry," she repeated. "I didn't realize it would, um, go that direction."

Her brother rolled his eyes. "You can practically see his happy trail, Candy. Jesus. You knew it would get good engagement. Don't lie."

Before she could object or apologize again, I cut in, "It's okay, Candace. I know you didn't mean any harm. And you're right. You can't see my face. No one will know who I am."

"Yeah, maybe they'll think it's me," Brady offered with a grin. He hopped off the table and took the phone from my waiting hand.

Candace snorted. "Yeah, right. No one would mix up the two of you in a wet tee shirt contest."

Surprise had my lips parting, and I turned to see her face go aggressively pink.

As if realizing what she'd said, Candace backpedaled. "I just meant that obviously you two are very differently shaped." She made motions with her hands as she spoke, separating them and going from large to small, before stopping abruptly and hiding them behind her back.

I fought the urge to laugh.

"Hey, now," Brady argued. "I go to the gym. No need to be rude."

Candace rolled her eyes but then moved back to the table to resume her work, unwilling or unable to meet my gaze.

Part of me liked seeing her flustered. I knew that what she'd implied didn't really mean anything. Brady was a fit guy, but he was lean from years of running and playing soccer. I was shorter and thicker, more muscular from weight lifting. I didn't hate the fact that Candace seemed to notice. She may not have remembered me from high school, though judging by the heat in her cheeks, I had her attention now.

But like I said, it didn't mean anything, and it didn't matter.

With her attention focused on packing apples, Candace said, "I'll be more careful in the future. I'm sorry for making you the target of unwanted internet attention, Mark."

"It's okay," I replied. "Besides, I just work here."

Candace paused at my words before meeting my gaze. Her hazel eyes were warm and earnest. "Yeah, and so do Joan and Brady. Mom and Dad may own Judd's Orchard, but you help keep it running, just like everyone else."

I appreciated what she was trying to do. Including me was kind of her. But this was a family business, and I wasn't family. The Judds were good people. The *best* people. They'd never once treated me like the town pariah I was. They welcomed me and accepted me for who I was, regardless of rumors and perception. But this was *their* farm. They didn't need my picture to represent their livelihood. The last thing I wanted was to reflect poorly on them or the orchard.

"She's right," Brady agreed. "You're part of this place, too, Marky Mark."

"Please don't ever call me that again."

He winced. "You're right. I regretted it immediately."

Candace was still watching me, so I said, "I appreciate that. Maybe just focus on highlighting other parts of the farm on social media."

She nodded. "Sure, I can do that."

"Thanks."

"Yeah," Brady chimed in, "we don't need him getting accosted on the street for being a juicy lumbersnack, now do we?"

I sighed, but Candace was ready. She pelted him square in the stomach with a shiny red apple.

"Oof," Brady wheezed. "You know the rule, buttface. You throw an apple, you have to eat it. No crop wasting."

"Worth it," she called, eyes narrowed, as she bent and retrieved the projectile from the floor. "Now, get out of here. We have actual work to do."

He shot me a grin, no doubt happy he'd irritated his baby sister. "See you later, Mercer."

I shook my head at their antics, but I felt the tug of a smile. The Judd siblings weren't perfect by any means, but they were entertaining.

Candace and I spent the next half hour packing up some Gala and McIntosh varieties and loading them in the farm truck. Then I drove downtown while she rode shotgun.

Candace was surprisingly quiet. Maybe she was still feeling embarrassed about the whole Instagram thing.

Eventually, with a flick of her wrist, she turned on the radio and navigated to an oldies station that broadcast out of Charlotte. Candace stuck her arm out the window in the early-morning air and let her loose hair blow in the wind. When I sneaked a peek at her, she had her eyes closed as the sunlight shone brightly over her features.

Despite my constant awareness of her, and some leftover awkward crush-adjacent feelings from high school, Candace was easy to be around. She had a soothing presence and was surprisingly laid-back. Not what I expected from a former gifted child and perpetual overachiever. Maybe she'd grown out of her people-pleasing tendencies and was comfortable in her own skin. It sure seemed that way.

I parked the truck, and with the two-wheel dolly, we unloaded the apples and made our way to the booth designated for Judd's Orchard. Candace also carried a bag full of merchandise, like hats and tee shirts.

We worked side by side and got set up well before the 9:00 a.m. start time. There were a few early birds and the usual suspects moseying around the farmers' market, but the out-of-towners wouldn't be by until later.

Candace offered to walk the block and a half down to Cubhouse Coffee Shop and pick up some caffeine for us before the crowds descended. I made the mistake of telling her my order first because she took off down the street, refusing to take any cash from me and ignoring my protests.

I wasn't sure how things would go today with us as co-workers. Part of me wondered if she'd want to talk about high school or if she'd even placed me in her adolescent memories yet. It was okay if she hadn't. There wasn't a whole lot worth mentioning from back then. She knew better than I did about what the friends from her circle were up to. Probably kept up with them on social media and whatnot.

"They had homemade strawberry Pop-Tarts," Candace said as she returned to our table beneath the white canopy. "I'm afraid I'm not strong enough to resist such temptation, so I got us some."

"You didn't need to do that." I accepted the bag she thrust in my direction. "Will you please take some cash?"

"Nope," she replied, popping the *p* and grinning at me. "My treat. Plus, I'm trying to buy your vote for favorite Judd co-worker. I fully expect to be ahead of Brady before we finish here today."

I laughed. "You pulled ahead of Brady just by breathing."

She cackled delightedly then took a sip of her iced latte.

"Thank you for breakfast," I said.

"You're welcome. Just be glad I wasn't the one doing the cooking."

I wondered at that. Candace's mom, Amy, was a great cook. Joan and Brady both knew their way around a kitchen too. Maybe being in New York and surrounded by some of the best restaurants in the world made Candace a little less self-suffi-cient with meal prep.

"Not a fan of cooking?" I asked.

She finished chewing a bite of Pop-Tart and then admitted, "I've just never been very good at it. Not like Mom, at least. Do you like to cook, Mark?"

I opened my mouth to answer, but Candace spoke again before I got the chance. "Can I call you Mark? I'm sorry, I should have asked before. Do you prefer to go by Mercer now?"

Now.

Maybe parts of high school were coming back to her after all. I *had* gone by Mark back then. Most people just called me Mercer now. I couldn't pinpoint a reason or particular moment when things shifted, but the Judds all called me Mercer, so that was what I answered to.

I cleared my throat. "You can call me Mark. That's fine." Then I glanced in her direction to find her watching me. "And you prefer Candace now?"

Her smile was small but appreciative. "Yeah."

We finished our coffees and pastries in comfortable quiet. Then Candace pulled out what appeared to be a stack of flyers and placed them neatly on the table, using an apple on top as a paperweight.

"I thought it would be good to advertise that it's the orchard's opening week-end," she offered, almost shyly, as I scanned the bright green paper.

It featured a coupon at the bottom for a free turn on the farm's giant bounce pillow. We typically sold wristbands for kids to enjoy it, and usually whoever was working behind the counter at the Apple House kept an eye on who was going in and out of the gate. It was a pretty low-maintenance attraction.

Offering the coupon here at the farmers' market would advertise as well as entice families with kids to visit the orchard. "This is great," I said, holding up the sheet of paper I'd snagged from the stack. "It'll let people know we're open for the season and get tourists to the orchard to hopefully buy some apples."

"That's the plan," Candace replied with a grin, tucking a strand of dark hair behind her ear.

Main Street was blocked off until 2:00 p.m., and the market crowd picked up as folks visited the booths lining the road. Candace let me take the lead with customers while she diligently bagged up their apples and I accepted their money.

"We should really set up PayPal or Venmo for the farm and offer those forms of payment," she said when there was a break in customers. "Some people don't always carry cash."

I nodded. "I'm sure your parents would go for that if you walked them through it."

We'd just settled into our chairs for a brief lull in foot traffic when I noticed Hilda Branson and Rose Brentwood strolling a few feet from our booth. Unease made its way along the muscles of my back, making everything tight with awareness.

There was a chance they'd pass right by. I took a breath and attempted to ignore the tension coiling within, but I was hyper-aware of the women's shuffling steps.

They were close friends of the reverend and Mrs. Price and regular parishioners down at Kirby Falls Baptist Church. I remembered them from my days as a member and all the various church events and picnics the Prices hosted.

Now, the two older women eyed me with a fair bit of contempt. This wasn't unheard of behavior. In fact, it was pretty typical. I was used to it by now and could usually ignore the glares and glances.

But something told me things would be a little more complicated today with Candace at my side. I rolled my shoulders back and tried to force away the anxiety that was slowly taking hold.

The women strolled a bit closer. Mrs. Brentwood, with her cane in hand, said, "Hilda, didn't you need some apples to make your pies for the bake sale?"

"Oh, yes. I do," Mrs. Branson replied, loud enough to be heard. "But I prefer to buy from the Clarks. They're all good Christian farmers." With a pointed look in my direction, she added, "Especially considering those present here today."

Mrs. Brentwood's gaze found her way back to our table and to me, sitting there quietly. "Oh, of course!"

I could feel Candace's attention on the side of my face, but I was careful to keep my eyes lowered. I didn't want to draw attention or cause any trouble with the locals, especially friends of the Prices. I focused on keeping my breathing even.

"What was that all—" Candace started to ask.

"Candy Judd, is that you?" Mrs. Brentwood's exclamation drew our attention as the elderly woman approached with her friend trailing behind. Her wrinkled face creased into a smile of genuine delight.

I didn't know what compelled me, but I corrected, "She actually goes by Candace now."

Both women on the other side of the booth shot disapproving stares my way, but I glimpsed Candace's smile and focused on that.

"Good morning, ladies," she replied easily enough, but Candace's hazel eyes were watchful and cautious.

"Well, it has been a good long while," Mrs. Brentwood continued. "I'm sure your momma and daddy are just delighted to have you back."

"It's nice to be home," Candace replied with a short nod. "How are you both?"

The older women chatted about their grandchildren and their volunteer work while Candace listened politely. The ladies angled toward my tablemate and completely ignored me. I could tell Candace was struggling with how rude they were being. She kept shooting me glances and frowning.

After a few minutes of catching up, Hilda Branson said seriously, "Well, despite the company you're keeping, we sure are glad to see you back in Kirby Falls."

My cheeks went hot with shame. I may have been used to the gossip and the knowing looks by now, but it was something else entirely to know Candace had a front-row seat to the display.

She straightened in her folding chair. "I don't know what you mean by that, Mrs. Branson."

But Rose Brentwood rushed to fill the awkward silence. "We look forward to seeing you at church. You'll be at the early service with your folks in the morning, I'm sure. You always were such a good girl."

Candace's gaze was still fixed on Mrs. Branson, and she didn't say one way or the other if she'd attend Kirby Falls Baptist Church tomorrow.

"I do hope you haven't let the big-city life influence you too much," Mrs. Branson said out of nowhere.

But Candace just laughed and crossed her legs. "No, ma'am. Not too much. I'm only stripping down at the Leather and Lace Lounge a few nights a week."

The women gasped and I choked on air. The Leather and Lace Lounge was the strip club just over the South Carolina line.

Candace was grinning as the two busybodies backed away.

"I'll be praying for you, young lady," Mrs. Branson called through pinched lips.

Unbothered, Candace waved cheerfully. "Thank you! I'll take all the help I can get!"

My teeth dug into my lower lip, but when I turned and met my new co-worker's expectant gaze, I couldn't hold back. We both cracked up.

When our laughter faded, our smiles lingered, and I noticed Candace was still watching me—likely waiting for an explanation.

She'd seen the way those ladies had looked at me and spoken about me and, finally, pretended I wasn't there. I might be used to the treatment I received from certain members of the community, but it was different watching Candace experience it firsthand. She hadn't even recognized me, so I doubted she kept up with small-town gossip. Her confusion was warranted.

But how did you tell someone your whole sordid life story? How did you explain your mistakes and your perceived misdeeds?

I didn't want Candace to look at me the way those women did. And I didn't want to lie to her face, which was what I'd have to do.

I didn't know how to confess that I'd married my best friend when she'd needed me the most, and I'd been used along the way. It wasn't my story to tell . . . at least, not all of it.

Hannah and I had been close since middle school, when I'd moved to Kirby Falls with my aunt. When we decided to go to college together at NC State University in Raleigh, I'd been relieved. Making friends had never been easy for me. So having Hannah there with me while we transitioned into adulthood felt safe and right.

But Hannah's life took a different turn in college. After a childhood and adolescence lived under the thumb of her Southern Baptist minister father, freedom took on a whole new meaning for her. She partied a lot and met new people. By the time junior year rolled around, I hadn't seen much of Hannah. We didn't have classes together anymore, as we'd both finished with general education requirements and settled into our respective majors—agriculture science for me and elementary education for Hannah. Our friendship was slowly dissolving, turning into something we were growing out of.

And that was fine. I didn't take it personally, and I didn't begrudge Hannah the life she wanted to lead. I had my own life to keep me busy, and I was tired of being blown off and ignored. But when Hannah turned up at my dorm room one night in a panic, I had no idea everything between us would shift yet again.

Hannah was pregnant and needed help. The father of her baby wasn't ready to be a dad, but Hannah didn't want to give the baby up. She begged me to marry her and claim the baby as my own to keep her family from disowning her.

At the time, I knew Hannah's fears were legitimate. Her parents would have never accepted a grandchild born out of wedlock. And seeing my friend terrified at the possibility of losing the only family she'd ever known was a stark reminder.

The Prices had always shown me kindness. They'd eased my path in a new town, and they'd given me a place to be that wasn't filled with the neglect and indifference of my aunt's house. Hannah had been my first real friend in Kirby Falls, and when she was scared and alone, she'd sought me out. I couldn't turn her away and watch her life fall apart.

So I married her. We announced her pregnancy shortly thereafter, and eight months later, nobody batted an eye when Lyndsey was born. She was perfect—the sweetest, most beautiful baby. At the time, I was too focused on Lyndsey to worry about my marriage to Hannah. We were friends again and navigating parenthood. There wasn't room for anything else.

As strange as it sounded, I was happy. I loved Lyndsey and our approximation of a family. My own experiences growing up had been so limited. I never wanted Lyndsey to feel unwanted or unloved. The late-night bottles and the colic never bothered me because I had this perfect little person to take care of.

We got an apartment off campus, and Hannah finished up her degree while I stayed home with the baby. When our lives brought us back to Kirby Falls the following year, Hannah got a job teaching at the elementary school while I came on board at Judd's Orchard. I put all the money I'd saved toward a little house for the three of us—the house I lived in now. And things were good . . . for a time.

When Lyndsey was just over a year old, Hannah asked for a divorce, seemingly out of the blue. She said she'd met someone else, and she was moving to Tennessee to be with him. That he was a good person and he loved her. He was ready to be a dad. They'd been in an online relationship for a while, and Hannah wanted a clean break from me. She'd said Lyndsey wasn't really mine anyhow, and if they left now, she'd never even remember me. Hannah seemed to think that was for the best. But the knowledge battered my already bruised heart. How something that felt so vital and beloved to me could only exist in my memories alone.

But I wanted Lyndsey to grow up safe and loved. I'd been saddled with a messy family life as a child and adolescent. I never wanted that for her. The confusion, the upheaval. Constantly wondering what I'd done wrong. I wanted Lyndsey to have stability and security.

So I didn't fight it. I let them both go. It nearly killed me to lose Lyndsey, but I wanted Hannah to be happy, and, by that point, it was clear that wasn't going to happen with me. If I had to break my own heart so that Lyndsey would have a bright and prosperous future, I would do it—over and over again.

But small-town gossip and perception painted me the bad guy—the deadbeat dad who let his family go without a backward glance or child support.

Hannah's parents didn't approve of our divorce, but they supported their daughter, especially when they had someone to blame for the drama and disruption in their lives. I didn't correct them. I kept my head down and my mouth shut. Hannah never wanted them to know the truth about Lyndsey's paternity, and it wasn't my place to reveal her secret. So I ignored the disproving stares and the gossip, and I kept to myself. And four weeks after Hannah had asked for a divorce, my family was gone.

My life was quieter after that. No more babbling in the high chair or singing songs at bedtime. Gradually, in the two and a half years since, I'd gotten used to the silence.

A few times a month I had to deal with locals who thought they knew my life or church ladies who felt like they owed it to the Prices to hate me on principle.

It didn't matter. Shit like that had never bothered me anyway.

Hannah was happy, and she was a good mom to Lyndsey—always had been. And Hannah's new husband loved them both. Based on news around town, things were going well for them in Tennessee.

There wasn't a place for me in their lives anymore.

But I still had to deal with the fallout.

At least when people thought they knew my story, I didn't have to answer questions or explain things.

Having Candace stare at me in confusion, awaiting an answer I didn't know how to formulate, was a situation that didn't come up too often.

So instead of addressing her unspoken questions, I replied simply with a shake of my head, "You can always count on small-town judgment no matter how long you've been away."

And then I ignored the way she kept looking at me, and I changed the subject. "The whole town will hear you're an exotic dancer before lunchtime."

Hazel eyes searched my face for another long moment before she shrugged casually and glanced away. "That'll spice things up around here."

It wasn't rational, but I wanted her attention back. I'd managed to divert her curiosity, and now I felt disappointed over it. That didn't make any sense.

Then I considered her words. I supposed Candace was used to bigger and better everything.

"I guess Kirby Falls can't really compare to New York," I mused, straightening the flyers on the tabletop when they were plenty straight already.

"It has its charms," Candace replied easily. "Besides, I've missed home. I'm glad to be back."

The rest of the morning at the farmers' market sped by as business picked up. Eventually, Candace got comfortable enough to chat with the customers. She seemed at ease with tourists, but every now and then a Kirby Falls resident would recognize her and she'd stiffen up. Neighbors and former classmates and coaches approached, and I'd see her smile go strained and her shoulders brace for impact.

I couldn't understand it. Candace Judd seemed universally beloved. Everyone who remembered her did so with a kind word and a fond recollection. She never once corrected them when they called her Candy, and I didn't step in again.

I witnessed her tension rise through every encounter until early afternoon when I couldn't stand to see another strained smile. I asked if she was hungry and told her I was starving. After passing her some cash, I asked if she'd care to pick us up some lunch at the Hogs Wild food truck set up down the street.

As I watched Candace walk stiffly away, I considered that maybe everyone had complicated histories with their hometowns. Even when their pasts seemed perfect and unblemished by scandal. Maybe coming home wasn't always what you thought it would be.

We ate our lunches quietly as the farmers' market mostly wound down. Candace had relaxed a bit since her return with our beef brisket sandwiches, but she still seemed cautious with me.

I missed the easiness Candace and I had shared this morning before those old women had stirred up trouble and the locals had dimmed her smile.

So, I did what usually helped people grow more comfortable—I gave Candace an opportunity to talk about something she was passionate about.

"So you got the office ready at the farm. Do you have some ideas for the orchard?"

Candace looked surprised by my question. "Yeah, I have some things I'm tossing around."

When she didn't offer anything more and silence settled over us, I smiled encouragingly. "Let's hear it."

"Oh." She fidgeted with the edge of the tablecloth. "You really want to talk about my ideas?"

"Sure. Haven't you gone over this stuff with Joan and your parents?"

Her eyes slid away briefly. "Well, I wanted to get Joan's opinion before I presented things to my parents, but she wasn't, uh, too receptive."

I fought a wince and nodded. I could see that. Joan was about as flexible as an eighty-year-old. She did things her way, and if you wanted to keep the peace, you did them her way too. I suspected she was feeling proprietary over the orchard and probably a little resentful to have Candace swooping back in to make improvements.

"Well, how about you test out your pitch on me? I'll answer any logistical questions you may have, tell you what's feasible from my standpoint. And then maybe you can give everyone a rundown at the next staff meeting."

Dark eyebrows lifted in surprise. "Y'all have staff meetings?"

"Yep," I lied. I could wrangle everyone together when Judd's was closed to the public. That wouldn't be too hard. "So, let's hear what you got."

"Okay," she replied, excitement bubbling through as she grinned.

Candace reached beneath the table for her bag. She dug around until she produced a notebook. It was spiral-bound and small enough to fit in her purse, but it was clearly well-used. I couldn't see the cover as Candace quickly started flipping through pages filled with colorful ink and her neat script.

"So, some of my ideas are pretty basic upgrades, like using PayPal and Venmo for payment, like I mentioned. And other simple things, such as local advertising and using incentives—like the bounce pillow coupon. But I think the farm could utilize some of the unused acreage on the farm for other popular u-pick operations. The tourist season has really expanded in Kirby Falls over the years. I requested numbers from the Agricultural and Festival Planning Committees, and I think now is a great time to further develop what Judd's Orchard offers."

I listened to Candace read off items from her notebook checklist and expound upon them in detail. By the time she hit her third bullet point, I realized she'd done her research and had some really good ideas. What started as an effort to get her talking again, and to get us back on even footing, suddenly morphed into me being a sounding board for Candace's grand plans.

She was radiant and energetic. Enthusiasm poured from her in big, sweeping hand movements and the velocity of her speech. Candace smiled a lot as she spoke, and I grew distracted by the sight. It was *something* to have all of her focus and attention. She was vibrant and animated, and I couldn't have looked away if I tried.

This might as well have been a company presentation, but with me as her lone audience member. I was glad for it. I'd never seen her in action as captain of the debate team, but I could easily envision it now.

Her excitement was palpable, as was her love for her family and the farm. This temporary gig at the orchard wasn't just her killing time until another opportunity came along in New York. She'd clearly researched and put effort into this.

God, Joan would hate it. All of it. But Nick and Amy would support anything Candace wanted to do. Brady would see the benefits and go with the flow, whatever was decided.

A lot of these things, if implemented, would make the orchard more profitable, but some of the long-term goals would require a lot of work and probably a few more hands to accomplish them.

"So what do you think?" Candace was bright-eyed and nearly breathless. And so damn hopeful. Her sincerity made me eager to give her whatever she wanted. She'd won me over and gained my support without even breaking a sweat. Respect and admiration had me smiling. It was, admittedly, a little intoxicating to see this side of her—one that fought to replace my teenage memories with its authenticity.

If Brady was a natural salesman, then Candace was an inspirational speaker. Maybe enthusiasm and charisma were genetic. Maybe it had somehow bypassed Joan Judd, who did not give a single shit about impressing anyone.

"I was not expecting that."

Her face fell like a dimmer switch.

So I hastened to amend, "I wasn't expecting to agree with nearly everything you said."

Candace's hazel eyes searched my face, like she was looking for the lie or waiting for me to say I was messing with her.

She must have been satisfied with whatever she saw because after a moment she smiled shyly and asked, "Really?"

"Really." I nodded. "But we're going to need a plan to get Joan on board."

She sighed as if she knew the battle awaiting her. One that was uphill . . . both ways . . . in the snow.

"I'll help," I offered.

"You will?"

Nodding again, I clasped my hands together and hoped that Joan wouldn't kill me for being disloyal.

"Why would you do that, Mark?"

I could have answered her a lot of ways. I could have said that I wanted her to succeed in Kirby Falls. I hoped she'd be accepted and find her footing at the orchard and with her family. And a little bit of the nerdy teenager still deep inside wanted a chance to show the most popular girl in school that things *had* changed since graduation. I didn't want to be invisible anymore.

But my reply wasn't any less truthful when I answered, "Change isn't easy, but sometimes it's necessary. I want Judd's Orchard to be successful. It's home to me too."

CANDACE

On Monday, I decided to take a break from the heat of my office, and the chilly attitude of my sister, and drink my lunch at the Lonely Mountain Winery.

I'd texted Bonnie a bit following our shaved ice encounter, and then just went for it today and invited her out for a drink. She'd recommended the vineyard less than three miles from the farm, citing a top-notch charcuterie board and notable chardonnay.

As an experienced cheese lover, I'd texted back an enthusiastic affirmative and told her I'd meet her there at noon.

"Hey," I said as I caught Bonnie up in a hug without even realizing it. I quickly pulled back and blurted out awkwardly, "I'm sorry. I'm a hugger. I didn't even think."

She laughed and yanked me back in, making me laugh. "You're fine. And I've never been one to turn down a free hug."

Grateful for her understanding, I cleared my throat and followed her to the outdoor seating area on the winery's wide patio.

"I can't believe I've never heard of this place," I murmured, settling into a chair beneath a wrought iron café table.

My attention was focused on the gorgeous long-range views of the Blue Ridge Mountains and the beautiful scene before us. Sure, I'd grown up here and I had plenty of memories of the landscape, but this setting never got old. Years in the city made me appreciate the clear blue of a perfect summer day and the hilly mountain range that meant I was home.

The longer I looked, the more I recalled, my senses lighting up with remembered summers gone by. The taste of a banana popsicle, cool and sweet on my tongue. The feel of the fine mist from the sprinkler when I used to chase Brady around the front yard. The sound of my mom's laughter when she and my dad danced in the backyard while my brother and sister and I caught lightning bugs.

"It's pretty new," Bonnie said, drawing me out of my tender memories.

She had on a calf-length pink floral dress with spaghetti straps, and her short blond hair was styled with loose waves that framed her pretty face. She wore round sunglasses and a ready smile.

I felt grateful, once again, that we'd bumped into each other at Bev's and that she had been free today for lunch, before school started later in the week.

Bonnie picked up her menu and said thoughtfully, "I think Reggie and Aurora opened up about a year ago. They're big *Lord of the Rings* fans."

"Ah." I nodded. That explained the name.

I reached for my copy of the food and wine list and scanned several items.

Prancing Pony Rosé: bright and refreshing, juicy pink fruit, subtle complexity, perfect for all manner of bar patrons, from elves to hobbits.

Miruvor Reisling: well-balanced, honeyed pear and white flowers, clean and refreshing finish, invigorating for the weary traveler.

Strider Cabernet: full-bodied and layered, vanilla and dark stone fruit, long-lingering finish, like busting open the doors of Helm's Deep.

Shirecuterie Board: crusty breads, herbed butter, wild blueberry jam, Fangorn Forest ham, seasoned potato skewers, and a variety of seasonal fruits and accompaniments. Enjoy from elevenses through supper.

I smiled. Apparently, everything on the menu featured a reference to the popular fantasy series. Neat. I loved a theme. Maybe the orchard could do a themed event.

I slipped my notebook out of my purse and jotted down a few quick notes to myself.

"Sorry," I apologized. "I just thought of something and had to get it down before I forgot."

Bonnie grinned, unbothered. "Farm stuff?"

"Yeah. The vineyard made me think about doing an apple-and-wine-pairing event. Maybe a way to collaborate and bring in business. I'd need to research a liquor license for the orchard."

"So how is everything going at Judd's?"

I sighed. "Oh, you know. I'm getting settled, but things are weird. My parents would give me the go-ahead on anything I wanted to try, but I'm not about to take advantage or step on toes. Brady doesn't care. He just does whatever someone tells him. And Joan . . ." I sighed again. "You'd think I was trying to lead a coup and oust her from the fields. Mark is the only one who's taking me seriously."

Bonnie gave me a sly look. "Mark, huh?"

"Mercer. Mark. He goes by both." My neck felt warm suddenly. Probably the lack of air-conditioning.

This wasn't the first time I'd thought about Mark since Saturday. Working the farmers' market together had been fun. At first, I thought he'd just been humoring me about my ideas for the orchard, but then he'd started asking questions and giving his own input. He'd given me his full, undivided attention, and I had to admit, I'd liked it.

When you'd messed up and let your boss steal your work for months, it was a damn revelation to have someone look at you like you were capable and knowledgeable about your field instead of giving the credit elsewhere or trying to gobble it up for themself.

Then there had been the unexpected side effects of having Mark's thoughtful attention. His blue-gray eyes and solemn face had flustered me in an entirely different way.

I may not have remembered Mark at first, but I was plenty aware of him now. He was, honestly, hard to ignore. Mark was a big, strong, good-looking guy. He obviously had some strength training in his workout routine because his biceps strained the confines of his Judd's Orchard tee shirt, and his thighs made me a newfound believer in the patron saint of leg day. The firm jaw, masculine features, and good genes didn't hurt either. His short, dark blond hair looked soft. And the matching scruff of his beard seemed to highlight the fullness of his mouth and the brightness of his smile when he managed to let one slip.

In the confines of the truck, I'd noticed his bright verdant scent. It must have had something to do with farming and all the time he spent in the fields. But his skin smelled like gardens and rain and the first blooms of spring. It was the relief you longed for in the middle of winter *and* in the heat of summer.

But it was more than his body and his face and whatever attraction was making me hyper-aware of his pillow-soft lips. I enjoyed talking to him and working beside him. He made me feel comfortable. And, as a woman, that wasn't something that happened every day.

Maybe it all came back to what he'd done for me in high school. It wasn't often that a teenager of the male variety had the situational awareness and the maturity to handle visible evidence of menstruation and then problem-solve it. Hell, there were grown-ass men who couldn't manage to pick up tampons at the store for their wives or girlfriends.

On a physical and instinctual level, I felt safe with Mark. In this day and age, that meant something.

He was quiet. Not so much stingy with his words, but intentional. It made me eager to hear what he had to say because his deep voice was a rare occurrence.

Yet I couldn't shake the sense that something was going on behind the scenes—something I wasn't aware of. Listening to those old biddies make their snide remarks and watching them cast their judgy stares Mark's way made me feel sure I was missing something—something big. Like I'd jumped in on book four of a fantasy series after all the world-building had been established.

What had gone on in Mark Mercer's life that made him the target of little church ladies?

Before I thought better of it, I asked Bonnie, "What *is* the deal with Mark? What's his story? Because there were some customers this weekend who shocked the daylights out of me with how rude they were to him. It was a weird vibe."

Bonnie bit her lip. "There *is* some gossip about him."

I wasn't typically a nosy Nancy. I felt like people had a right to their privacy, and, unfortunately, sometimes small towns did equate to small minds. Guilt nipped at me for asking, but despite my best intentions, I knew I was leaning forward in my chair, eager for the truth about Mark, more curious than I wanted to admit.

"Well, let's see," Bonnie continued. "He and Hannah Price got divorced a couple years ago. That's a big part of it."

I could feel my eyes bulge. "They were *married*." I didn't know why I'd lowered my voice on the last word—like *married* meant something dirty and I was in the middle of Bible study.

Bonnie nodded. "Yeah. Back in college. It didn't last long. Just over a year, if I'm remembering correctly. She used to teach kindergarten at the elementary school with me. We weren't close or anything though. She kept to herself mostly. Then right after her marriage ended, she took the baby and left. Moved to Tennessee and got remarried shortly thereafter."

"The *baby*," I all but hissed, feeling certain my jaw must be on the table. "Mark has a baby?"

She chuckled at my undoubtedly over-the-top reaction. I couldn't help it though. I was shocked. Beyond shocked. I was practically electrified by this revelation. Rationally, I knew that people got married and had kids all the time. It was actually one of my goals. In my five-year plan and everything.

I'd known that Mark and Hannah were close. They'd been best friends since middle school, but I couldn't say why I was so dumbstruck by the news. Of course, there were times when friendship blossomed into something more. That was what made the friends-to-lovers trope so popular in romance novels. But, I guess, I found it odd that Mark hadn't mentioned having a child two days ago, when we'd worked together for many hours. No funny stories. No anecdotes. No cute baby pictures on his lock screen.

"Yeah," Bonnie replied, fanning herself with her menu to circulate the humid air. "But he never sees her. That's the gossipy bit. Hannah rarely comes back to Kirby Falls and has full custody of the little girl. People say he didn't even fight for her or ask for partial custody rights or holidays or summer visitation or anything. They also say he doesn't pay child support."

"Oh." My shoulders slumped, and I sat back in my chair to absorb this news.

Bonnie nodded and then she made a face. Likely the same one I was making right now, the scrunched nose and lip curl of disappointment.

Of course, I knew that families came in all shapes and sizes. I was also aware that kids were running around without fathers in every corner of the globe. Some men carried on with their lives while their sons or daughters were raised solely by their mothers. There were dads and there were biological fathers and then there were sperm donors. And there was a difference between all three.

I knew all this. But I still had a hard time accepting that Mark Mercer was one of the latter.

Admittedly, I didn't know him. We'd gone to high school together, and we were co-workers now during this weird temporary limbo of my current life. But I hadn't known him when we'd graduated together, and I didn't know him now, not really. *Not yet*, whispered a knowing voice in my head.

My brain was just having a hard time reconciling the sweet, quiet, thoughtful guy from Saturday and the sweet, quiet, thoughtful teenager from seven years ago with the stereotypical version of a deadbeat dad.

If those were the rumors floating around about Mark, I could see now why the unofficial Kirby Falls Baptist Welcoming Committee had looked at him like he was something stuck to the bottom of their orthopedic shoes. Those women would always take the side of Reverend Price and his family, no questions asked. And despite the good Lord's directive to love your neighbor, Hilda Branson and Rose Brentwood had clearly taken it upon themselves to cast the first stone.

"Wow," I breathed.

Amid the shock and disquiet, remorse and shame made my belly tighten anxiously. I felt bad for asking about Mark now. But I never imagined the possibility that a divorce from the reverend's daughter fueled the gossip surrounding my co-worker. I'd assumed Mark had switched churches or stopped going altogether. Or it was some other minor offense that made those women so salty with him.

As a person with secrets of my own, I felt guilty for invading Mark's private life without his knowledge.

"Yeah," Bonnie agreed. "Want to order some wine and eat your very obvious feelings about this Mercer-related development?"

"Yes. Yes, I do."

We made our way through the open patio doors, and back inside to the bar.

An attractive Black man in his forties was already smiling at our approach. "Good afternoon, ladies."

"Hi, Reggie," Bonnie said. "This is Candace Judd. She's Nick and Amy's daughter."

Reggie's brown eyes widened, and he held out a hand. "It's nice to meet you, Candace. I've heard so much about you. I play poker with your father, and he and your mom were very kind to us when Aurora and I opened the vineyard."

I smiled and shook his hand. "It's nice to meet you. I love your place here."

"Thank you," Reggie replied. "We like it." Then he threw his hands up like he just remembered something. "And our daughter, Lucy, received the Candy Judd Award at Honor's Night when she graduated three years ago."

I stared, waiting for those words to make sense. When that didn't happen, and Reggie offered no explanation, I asked slowly, "The Candy Judd what now?"

"The orchard sponsors an award in your honor."

"But I'm not dead," I argued.

From my side, Bonnie laughed and covered her mouth. "It's not a memorial award, Candace."

"It's a cash award to help with books for college," Reggie finally explained. "The administrators select a deserving senior who exemplifies your dedication to education and community service. Lucy did a ton of volunteer work to beef up her college résumé. She's at Vassar now. We're very proud."

I was dumbfounded. I had no idea my parents sponsored an award like that in my name. That was . . . a lot. I didn't know that I deserved such an honor or recognition. I knew my parents were proud of me, but . . .

Feelings of guilt and shame twisted in my stomach. The thought of inhaling cheese and wine and hobbit food didn't sit right when faced with the knowledge of my parents' unwavering support—how it had taken shape into something like this. If they knew the truth about all my "success" in New York, they'd be devastated. I needed to get my life back on track. I needed to make better decisions and earn the faith they'd misplaced in me.

When Reggie asked what he could get me, I ordered a glass of rosé absentmindedly, and Bonnie told him we'd share the Shirecuterie Board.

Eventually, I managed to pull myself together, and Bonnie and I enjoyed a nice lunch over the next forty minutes. It was fun to have someone new to get to know. She was sweet and funny and I loved hearing stories about her students and her family.

Despite the sunshine and the good company, I couldn't shake the feeling that I needed to get going on my plans for Judd's Orchard. It was this itchy sensation under my skin, a tightness in my belly that required immediate action and results.

I was eager to prove myself and show my family that my return to Kirby Falls was a good thing. If I could just make some headway with Joan, I might feel better about things. But part of me knew that until I could prove my worth to my parents, I'd never feel like I was worth the investment or the sacrifice of sending me to an expensive college.

I intended to talk to Mark as soon as I got back to the farm and try to arrange that staff meeting to go over my plans.

For as much as I enjoyed lunch with Bonnie, I was just as eager to get back to work.

"Thank you all for letting me take the lead during this staff meeting," I said brightly from my position at the head of the worn dining table.

"Staff meeting?" Brady murmured with a confused look on his face, but I ignored him.

It was Wednesday. A day when the orchard was closed to the public. Mark had set up the meeting with my parents and siblings. And in the two days since my lunch with Bonnie, I'd had plenty of time to prepare my semi-casual presentation.

We were all gathered at the farmhouse on the screened porch beneath a swirling ceiling fan while my dad passed out lemonade for everyone. There had been countless family dinners out here during my childhood and adolescence. A wave of nostalgia had practically bowled me over when I'd taken my seat. My mom used to drink her tea out here every morning. I wondered if she still did. Maybe I'd ask if I could join her.

Mark caught my eye and gave me an encouraging nod. I managed to get a handle on my nervousness and unclench my jaw enough to smile in return.

"As I was saying, I have a few ideas I'd love to go over."

I'd found a black-and-white printer in the Apple House office and sweet-talked it into spitting out a tidy list of the topics I wanted to discuss today. And by "sweet-talked" I meant I cussed a blue streak while I waited for the ancient printer to warm up and accept my print job. Lance Bass had looked on disapprovingly.

After passing a copy of my bullet-pointed agenda to each person at the table, I took a deep breath and began. "Having reviewed tourist data from the Agricultural and Festival Planning Committees, I think this is a great time for Judd's to expand what it offers. Some relatively low-risk ways to do that include utilizing some of the acreage behind the Apple House for other u-pick operations. Raspberries or blackberries would be good options. Opening in July for a u-pick berry season would require relatively little maintenance and put Judd's Orchard on the map for summertime tourists. U-pick lavender fields offer another possibility for harvesting in the spring months. This would be great for brides and wedding planners, not to mention local craftspeople who extract essential oils for things like soapmaking. It could be another draw for the farm outside of apple season."

I swallowed and glanced around the table. My parents were smiling encouragingly my way. Brady was slouched in his seat and may or may not have been playing *Candy Crush* on his phone. Joan was frowning down at her handout, her face shadowed by her ball cap. But it was Mark's steady gaze that helped ground me. His attention gave me confidence and helped clear the nervous wobble threatening in my voice.

"There are a few big-ticket items we could outsource in the fourth quarter to really bring in the tourists. I think setting up a pumpkin patch for Halloween would be amazing. And instead of closing up for the season on November 1, we could sell pre-cut Christmas trees for the holidays. These options would require more upfront costs, since we don't have space on the farm to grow pumpkins or trees ourselves without a good deal of clearing and leveling. But I think it's totally doable. And I have some fun ideas to collaborate with other local businesses, like doing a pumpkin carving and hard cider event or an evening with Santa or even an apple-and-wine pairing with Lonely Mountain down the road. We could coordinate with local food trucks and bring them in every Friday to encourage their client base and get our customers to bring the family out, stay for the evening, and have dinner here."

There. I'd gotten through the big things. The ones that would require time and energy as well as monetary investment.

Joan shifted in her seat, and I could feel her disapproval rising like a kettle set to boil.

So I hurried to add, "There are some other avenues we haven't explored yet as far as advertising and social media. There are travel influencers I can reach out to in order to bring attention to Kirby Falls and our family operation. And I know social media is incredibly time-consuming, but I think we just need to be more intentional. Stick to a schedule and let the algorithm work for us. For the most part, the orchard has really amazing content. The photographs I saw on Facebook and Instagram were seriously beautiful."

"That's all Mercer," my brother said absently, eyes still glued to the phone in his hand.

My attention shifted to Mark, who looked decidedly uncomfortable. Then I asked, "What do you mean? Mark handles Facebook and Instagram?"

"No," Brady explained, "I do the posting. On Twitter too. But Mark takes all the photographs we use for content."

I looked to the man in question. His cheeks were a little pink beneath his scruffy beard. It probably didn't help that the white tee shirt he wore made his blush more pronounced. I found myself equal parts curious and amused.

Mark cleared his throat. "I, uh, dabble."

I forced myself not to show the surprise I felt. The photos I'd seen were fantastic. Beautiful compositions that perfectly highlighted the orchard's offerings. Mark could have sold his photography. That was how amazing it was.

A tiny voice in the back of my mind warned that I was a little too curious about my quiet, thoughtful, artistic co-worker. I was still trying to rectify the idea of the man who'd potentially abandoned his child with the Mark I was getting to know now.

He was obviously uncomfortable with this line of questioning regarding his photographs, so I decided not to push it. But I got the sense he more than dabbled.

"Well, I'm happy to help with our online responsibilities or make up a schedule for you, Brady, to ensure we're getting good visibility."

Brady shrugged. "I don't mind if you help out. I just want to keep the Twitter account."

I frowned. I hadn't done more than a cursory glance on that platform to see what our presence was like there. "Why?"

"No reason," he replied, but he gave me a sweet smile that made me suspicious and itching to reach for my phone so I could pull up the app.

Before I could give in to the urge, Joan pinned me with her narrowed blue gaze. "So all of your big plans basically boil down to opening early and staying open later? Extending our season and doing more with the same amount of staff and resources?"

My sister's direct stare and sudden questions were intimidating. I licked my lips and managed a few words. "Well, not exactly. I—"

"I thought," she interrupted, "this was supposed to be you providing all your expensive marketing know-how to help us sell apples."

The mention of my background and the value attached to my college education had me looking away.

Joan scoffed, removing her hat and dropping it on the table. "Your answer to breaking even is to work harder and longer. Am I getting this right?"

"Joan, honey," Mom admonished while my father said at the same time, "I don't think that's what Candy means, Joanie."

I wanted to defend myself, but my big sister always had this way of making me feel inadequate. Clarifying my statements seemed like a distant goal at the moment. First I needed to lift my head and make eye contact. It seemed simple, but I wasn't sure I could manage it. *Expensive marketing know-how* just kept repeating itself on a loop in my sister's rough, disbelieving tone.

Brady had joined in the discussion by now, and all the voices were swirling together.

It was like going back in time to when I was fifteen and I'd overheard my parents explain to Joan that they couldn't afford the new farm equipment she had her eye on because I had a trip coming up for the debate team.

I straightened my printout needlessly so I had something to do with my hands while everyone talked around me and over one another. I was the baby of the family again, unable to find my place within the business and completely useless in the grown-up discussions.

Suddenly, a deep voice emerged from the cacophony, snapping my attention to the seat at the far end of the table.

"I think what Candace is saying," Mark stated calmly as everyone stopped to listen, "is that for the orchard to continue being successful, it needs to adapt. Kirby Falls is changing. Tourist season is changing too. Candace researched the market and made her suggestions for things we could do to meet the rising tide. She's not saying we have to do all of it right here, right now, Joan. She's giving us options. That's why we're meeting. To discuss them."

Joan's features narrowed on Mark—suspicious and something else, surprised, maybe, at the way the typically quiet man had inserted himself in the discussion and essentially defended me.

"Maybe we can take a few days to think about what Candace has proposed," Mark said to everyone before shifting his gaze to me. "I'm sure she has some cost analysis to go over with us and income projections for the various projects."

I did. On a twenty-two-deck slide presentation. But I knew they weren't ready for that, so I just nodded. Mark returned the gesture. It was only a brief dip of his chin, but it felt like a show of support, a flag raised in my honor. It was enough to make me release a shaky exhale.

Gratitude filled me up, nearly to the top, for the way Mark had stepped in. But, somehow, there was still plenty of room left to feel embarrassed that I'd needed his help in the first place.

"I agree," Mom said with a pointed look toward my sister. "Let's take some time to think, and we'll meet again soon to figure out what we'd like to do."

Dad nodded. "Then I'm sure Candy can answer our questions, and we can figure out where to go from there."

Joan swiped her ball cap off the table and pulled it on roughly before standing and exiting the porch. The screen door had made the same loud snapping sound my whole life, but it seemed inexplicably louder and harsher when my sister was the one pushing through it.

Brady stood from his place to my right and ruffled my hair on his way out. "Make that social media calendar. I'll stick to it."

"Okay," I replied and tried for a smile.

My parents started in then, complimenting me on a job well done, despite the truth of how the meeting had actually gone. They moved to sit closer and ask me questions, wanting to know more about having pumpkins for sale in the fall and if I'd sourced any vendors.

As I spoke to them about local farmers who sold pumpkins wholesale, I noticed Mark standing at the opposite end of the dining table. He picked up the handout I'd provided, folding it carefully into fourths before heading toward the door.

I wanted to talk to him. I wanted to thank him for what he'd done. If he hadn't spoken up, I probably would have just sat there in paralyzed weakness while my family went round and round without ever deciding anything.

But before I got the chance to interrupt my mother's well-meaning praise regarding the u-pick blackberry idea, Mark shot me a small grin and then exited the porch.

My eyes stayed fastened on his movements—so purposeful and efficient. There was something quietly arresting about the way he wielded his careful strength. My attention strayed lower. And the way he slid the folded piece of paper into the back pocket of his well-worn jeans sure didn't hurt either.

One strong arm pushed open the swinging screen door, but just before it snapped back into the wooden frame, he caught the handle and closed it gently. It barely even made a sound.

MARK

Lift. Twist. Pull.

You wouldn't really think there'd be a preferred method to pick an apple, but there was.

We tried to teach the leafers—the seasonal tourists who frequented Kirby Falls to witness the changing leaves—the best way to fill their baskets and buckets, but it didn't always take. Most of them just grabbed the apple and yanked. However, the best way to pick cleanly and keep the tree healthy was to lift, twist, and pull.

That's what I was doing now, over and over, on the row of Honeycrisp apples near the rear of the property.

Judd's had about fifty acres, but only a portion of those were open to the public for self-picking. None of the produce was sold commercially to factories or grocery stores, but we did press our own apples for the cider we sold at the refreshment stand.

We planted extra crops for the most popular varieties of apples, and these particular trees were on the edge of the undeveloped land. Just beyond the dark green leaves currently occupying my field of vision was the uncleared acreage that spread out in the distance until it hit the tree line.

Back in the 1970s, when Judd's Orchard sold commercially to grocery stores and baby food companies and juice manufacturers, it had only been Nick and his dad and a few part-timers and seasonal employees running the farm. So they hadn't spread out as much, and the last fifteen to twenty acres had just never gotten any attention.

It was smart of Candace to mention using it. It was pretty far from the Apple House, but it would make a nice pumpkin patch or lavender field one day. I'd even visited other operations that took tourists on hayrides out to their pumpkin patches, so the distance might not be an issue if Nick and Amy decided to move forward with one of Candace's long-term recommendations.

One big obstacle, though, was the woman working efficiently and quietly at my side, picking bag slung over her shoulders.

It had been a week since the "staff meeting" where Candace had presented her big ideas, and Joan was still barely doing more than grunting in my direction. I knew she hadn't joined her family for dinner at all this week because Candace had mentioned it this morning when I'd stopped by the office in the Apple House to say hi.

She'd been typing away on her laptop, sunglasses perched on top of her head, and wearing a pale yellow tank top that had me noticing her sun-bronzed skin before I'd forced myself to look away. We'd chatted for a bit. Candace had wanted to know if Joan was speaking to me yet. I'd tried to reassure her that it wasn't out of the ordinary for her sister to keep to herself. But I could tell Candace was still worried over Joan's reaction to her recommendations for the farm.

I hadn't lied. Joan isolated herself at times. She could be personable and friendly, but those moments were few and far between. It was usually around kids at the orchard that Joan let herself be free with her smiles. She was good with children, despite how unpracticed she was with adults. But now she was shutting everyone out deliberately. And it was probably time to broach the subject, or I'd be lifting, twisting, and pulling for the next four hours beside a silent apple-picking sentry.

"You ever gonna talk to me again?" My gaze was still fixed on my task, but I heard the rustle of leaves to my left pause momentarily.

When Joan didn't answer and the leaves resumed their movement, I rolled my eyes as I gently tugged another mottled-red apple.

"I don't like to get involved in this stuff, but your family wants to talk to you, Joan. They asked for your opinion because you know best where this farm is concerned. Even if your opinion is to keep things the way they've always been."

Joan abandoned her crouch and stood to face me, hands on slim hips, eyes narrowed beneath the bill of her Judd's Orchard ball cap. "Oh, you don't like to get involved in this stuff. Is that right? You didn't seem to mind when you were helping Candy with her *staff meeting* and all her brilliant plans."

I resisted the urge to sigh and instead scrounged around for some courage under that icy blue glare. "They're good ideas. And you'd see that if you weren't so busy being angry that your sister was the one who thought of them."

She scoffed as she busied herself carefully dumping the apples out of the picking bag and into the basket.

"Candace wants to help," I said gently. "She loves this farm too."

And maybe she hadn't been here for the last seven years, but it was obvious to anyone who wasn't too angry and bitter to notice that Candace really did love this place. She was a hard worker—the first to volunteer for any task required and equally determined to help out so the shared load was lessened.

She'd helped her brother load up the produce for the farmers' market when she hadn't even been on the schedule. Then she'd worked concessions over the weekend with her mother in the refreshment stand. Candace made that social media calendar she'd mentioned, and she was dividing up the work with Brady. She was there, in the office, every day when the orchard was closed to the public. And then, Thursday through Sunday, she greeted out-of-towners and handed out buckets and sold merchandise and generally chipped in wherever she could. And she did it all with a smile on her face. She seemed to genuinely enjoy the tourists and spending time with her family. Nick and Amy were so happy to have their daughter back. There was no denying that.

And I couldn't ignore Candace's sincere desire to see this place succeed—to do more than break even.

"She left." Joan's words were clipped—jagged and bitten off, like they nearly didn't make it past her teeth on their way out. "She couldn't get out of this town fast enough. She shouldn't get to waltz back in here whenever *she* feels like it and make demands and changes."

I nodded because I could see where she was coming from, why someone like Joan—proprietary and possessive and fiercely loyal—would see Candace's well-meaning attempts as affronts.

I made sure my tone was soft and lacking all judgment when I said, "When does someone get to come home? What's the timeline that would have made it okay for Candace to return and be involved? When would you have welcomed your sister back?"

Joan sighed, equal parts resigned and bitter, and then closed her eyes and tilted her head up to the sky, sunshine highlighting the planes of her narrow face. "I don't fucking know, Mercer."

"Candace means well," I offered.

"I know that," she said before opening her eyes and frowning at me. "Why do you keep calling her Candace?"

I blinked. "That's her name."

Joan made a face.

"That's what she likes to be called," I argued, then swallowed uneasily as Joan kept right on watching me. I wasn't sure what she saw written across my features, but I sure as hell hoped it wasn't the ever-expanding crush I had on her sister.

The more time I spent with Candace, the more unsteady I felt. She was pushing me outside my comfort zone, making me want more—making me wish I was braver and bolder. She was endearing in a thousand ways.

The crush I'd had in adolescence didn't really compare to knowing the very real version of her now. There was so much more beyond popularity and objective beauty. Grown-up Candace had layers and depth that a teenage boy couldn't understand or appreciate. I'd seen past the friendly extrovert to the woman who got nervous talking to her own family. She carried secrets behind fake smiles, and the mystery of her made me curious beyond the boundaries of being co-workers.

Finally, Joan's scrutinizing gaze relented, and she said, "Well, what do you think we should do since you're captaining Team Candace?"

I ignored the snark and pretended we were having this conversation like adults—like we should have done a week ago with everyone present. "Her 'Friday night food truck' idea is extremely low-risk, and she's happy to handle the scheduling. It's a no-brainer. And I think we should try the pumpkin patch. And the u-pick blackberries behind the Apple House for next summer. I'll get those situated. You won't have to do anything. Let's see how a few of the special events go. Candace said she'd run those in the evenings. Again, you won't be expected to help."

"I don't mind working—"

"I know," I cut her off before she got defensive again. Joan was finally listening. I didn't want her to shut everyone out again.

"It doesn't have to be everything all at once. Candace didn't march in there and make demands," I reminded her evenly. "She gave us options and short-term and long-term goals. We can implement those as we see fit. We could hire seasonal workers after a time—"

"I am not having strangers in my fields, Mercer," Joan interrupted.

I barely resisted the urge to roll my eyes. Apparently, I—a non-Judd—was lucky I got to work in these fields at all.

"Okay. But maybe someone up at the Apple House or the refreshment stand. Surely you could trust other folks to sort and wash and run the press. Then your parents could cut back on their hours a little. Or we could stay open five days a week instead of four."

Joan appeared thoughtful. She was a hard-ass but she loved Nick and Amy something fierce. She was always worried they were working too much and overdoing it.

"I'll think about it," she finally said.

"And talk to your family?"

Joan gave another put-upon sigh. "Fine. I'll talk to them. But I'm not working the farmers' market with Candy. Brady is bad enough. You can stay on the schedule with her."

I never imagined I could get these sisters to reconnect. I wasn't a miracle worker, after all. I was just a man who was tired of an awkward situation at a job I loved most of the time.

Maybe a part of me was more invested in helping Candace than I should have been. And maybe another little part of me didn't really mind her being my booth partner at the farmers' market.

"I can do that." Before I thought better of it, I added, "But you know, it wouldn't kill you to get to know your sister, Joan. She's not—"

"Jesus Christ," she groaned loudly in frustration before striding off down the row.

Sighing, I realized I probably shouldn't have pushed. My gaze caught on the twenty or so apple trees that still needed to be harvested, the giant apple cart half full and the tractor waiting to deliver it back to the Apple House for grading and sorting.

My day just got a whole lot longer. Shit.

Fifteen minutes later, Brady came tromping across the grass wearing a bright red picking bag.

"What are you doing here?" I asked. *Lift, twist, pull.*

"I felt a disturbance in the force," he replied, grinning.

I stared.

Brady shook his head, obviously disappointed that I didn't find him amusing right now. I was tired and I was hot, and Joan had bailed on our afternoon task, leaving me to handle it alone.

"Okay, fine," he said. "Joanie told me you might need some help."

My gaze strayed absently in the direction she'd stomped off, and then I huffed out an incredulous laugh. She'd been pissed enough to stalk away from me but still made sure I wasn't busting my ass alone.

"You know, Brady, your family could really stand to work on their communication skills."

He stepped over to the ladder and basket his sister had abandoned and started reaching for apples. *Lift, twist, pull.* "Tell me about it."

"I couldn't help but notice that you are back on the farmers' market schedule with me," Candace said, cutting me an amused glance before she'd even said hello. "What happened? Did you draw the short straw?"

She was, once again, already boxing up the produce we'd be hauling downtown to the farmers' market this morning. I'd even woken up twenty minutes early to make sure I beat her here.

I smiled and joined her behind the worktable in the Apple House. "Just lucky, I guess."

She laughed, her even white teeth flashing briefly before she focused back on her task.

I wasn't about to tell her that her sister was still being a pain in the ass and refused to take a shift with her. So that left Candace paired with me every three weeks. September 1 was just around the corner, so we only had a couple more of these Saturday mornings scheduled together before the downtown market closed up for the season.

After a few minutes, Candace said, "Thanks for being willing to babysit the new hire."

I closed up a box of Honeycrisp before replying, "It's not exactly a hardship. You grew up here. You know what you're doing."

"It's been a while."

"Seems like it's all coming back to you."

"Thanks, Mark," she said, sounding grateful. "And I didn't get a chance to thank you for stepping in during the meeting the other day and bailing me out. I appreciate it."

Truthfully, I'd been relieved that Nick and Amy had vied for Candace's attention following the meeting. I'd seen Candace's expectant gaze and the gratitude waiting on the tip of her tongue.

But for some reason, I hadn't wanted her thanks.

Working with family was tough. Watching Candace slowly slip out of her professional role that day had been difficult. She'd sat there, tense and unmoving, through Joan's remarks like it was her due. I was in the unique position as an outsider, and while I wouldn't have normally inserted myself into their family business, I could see that they needed a new perspective to balance things out. And the very fact that I didn't usually speak up had the added effect of ensuring I was heard.

"I wouldn't call it a bailout," I said, not looking her way. "More of calling a time-out. Have y'all talked more about your plans yet?"

Candace shook her head. "Not really. Mom and Dad are adamant that I do whatever I want, but I don't want to step on any toes. So far, we've settled on the things I can manage myself, like scheduling events. I have another handout for today's market, this one advertising birthday parties and a hard-cider-and-apple-pairing event with Firefly on the Friday before the Orchard Festival. But that's all I'm really willing to move forward on right now. Still haven't heard from Joan."

I made sure my sigh was internal. I'd had that conversation in the fields with Joan three days ago. Maybe she was still thinking. More likely, she was trying to figure out how to swallow her pride.

"I think that pairing event will do well," I said. "Let me know if you need any help with it."

She smiled. "Thanks. I think I'll be alright. We're having it over at Firefly since I'm still working on the liquor license for the orchard. I'll just need to bring over the apples we'll be using and some extra to sell."

I was already mentally adding the event to my calendar. Not that it was all that busy, but I wanted to make myself available. Be a good co-worker. I didn't want Candace to have to tackle this first one on her own.

And if there was some other reason I was risking interacting publicly with Kirby Falls residents or looking forward to spending time with Candace, then that was something I'd worry about later. Like when this was all over and Candace was back in New York, where she belonged.

The rest of loading up and setting up went by easy enough. Candace wanted to act like she was the new kid on the block, but she was knowledgeable about the orchard and knew what she was doing. She didn't need to look to me for instructions, most of it was second nature for her.

An hour later, when we were sipping our Cubhouse coffees at our booth on Main Street, waiting on customers, I decided to ask Candace about her life in New York. I knew bits and pieces from what Nick and Amy mentioned, but I was curious about her.

"So, what made you settle in New York?"

If she was surprised by my question, she didn't show it. "Well, I went to Columbia for undergrad and grad school, so I was already in the city. Then I got an internship, so it just made sense to stay. There were more job opportunities there, and I'd finally gotten used to living in a big city."

"That makes sense. You liked it though?"

Candace took another sip of her apple crisp latte and licked a tiny dot of foam off her upper lip.

I swallowed and glanced away.

"I did like it—do like it there. It's fast-paced and exciting. There's always a takeout place open no matter the time of day. I used to take my lunch break and go for a walk in Central Park or visit a museum. I was never bored, that's for sure. It's different than home though. I like having space here. Quiet. Room to breathe, you know?"

I nodded because I did know. College in Raleigh, North Carolina, had been fine. It was bigger than Kirby Falls, but not unmanageable. But I liked the pace of where I lived now. I loved the mountains and the land and growing things. I couldn't imagine living somewhere like New York, with all its steel and concrete and noise and people.

It was interesting to me that Candace still thought of Kirby Falls as home. Seven years somewhere else might start to sway your allegiance. But maybe that was just the transplant in me talking. I wasn't born in Kirby Falls, but I considered it home all the same.

"What do you miss most?" I wondered.

She hummed a little and took another sip from her paper cup. Then, face bright, she turned to me and lightly nudged my knee with hers. "I've got it. There was this little pie shop three blocks from my apartment. It was never very busy, and they stayed open late. I liked working there on Saturdays and grabbing a slice of pie on my way home. The owners were an older couple from this small town in northeast Georgia. We used to talk about sweet tea and the mountains and everything we missed about home." Her hazel eyes drifted over my shoulder as she considered. "They were sweet to me. And they made the best pie. Don't tell Mom I said that."

I grinned. "What was your favorite kind?"

"Key lime. No, actually, this Oreo mousse pie they made once a month. And you had to get there early or it would sell out." She seemed wistful, attention distant, until her gaze snapped back to mine. She gave me another knee nudge that was casual for her, but had me hyper-aware. "What's your favorite kind of pie?"

Candace waited for my answer like it was a big deal. Like she was unearthing something mysterious and monumental about my personality. I was a little worried about letting her down when I admitted, "Apple pie is my favorite."

But she nodded agreeably, and her knee touched mine once more. "Classic choice. I approve."

As silly as it was, I liked having her approval. We were just talking about pie. It didn't really mean anything. But with the feel of her leg against mine, and the weight of her attention and focus, I was having trouble shepherding my thoughts.

It had been so long since I'd met someone new—someone who didn't think they knew everything about me. Wenn had been the last friend I'd made, and we didn't share our histories or personal lives. Hell, he didn't ask what sort of pie I liked. He just brought me whatever he was baking that week and hoped I wasn't allergic.

No, it had been quite some time since I had a person ask me something—innocuous or otherwise—about myself.

Briefly, I considered telling her about the pie shop in a strip mall over in Miller Creek, about fifteen minutes away. Pied Piper's was a family-owned place, and they made really good pie. I usually picked one up for holidays to bring to the Judds'. Amy always invited me for Easter and Thanksgiving and Christmas, and I never wanted to show up empty-handed, no matter how many times she told me to just bring myself.

I could just let Candace know about Pied Piper's. She was back in town. The place had only been open for a couple of years. It was unlikely that Candace knew about it. But some part of me—maybe the part that had her warm leg against mine and her lavender scent in my lungs—wanted to invite her to go . . . with me.

I knew Candace wasn't here to stay. And I knew we didn't know each other very well—we never had—but we were learning. We worked together. We had the orchard and this town in common. I probably (definitely) had a crush lingering somewhere in the background, but I could recognize that this new feeling was different. I hadn't known her back in high school, not really. I'd only been attracted to the idea of her—friendly, kind, popular, beautiful.

Now, she was real. And she was still all of those things, but she was also more. I knew that she was a hard worker, not a complainer, and laughed surprisingly loud. She was affectionate and casual about it. She loved her family and was a genuinely good person, every bit the daughter the Judds had bragged about over the years. She didn't take herself too seriously, and she had a surprisingly mischievous streak. She was upbeat and playful. Hell, she'd named the mounted fish in her office Lance Bass.

And I knew that her favorite pie was Oreo mousse.

I was a little surprised that a pie shop was what she missed most about the city. Not work or friends or her apartment. No mention of a significant other either.

Before I could mull that over or come to a decision about inviting her out for pie, someone approached our table.

Candace's knee returned to her side of the booth as she straightened to greet them. "Hello, Mr. Ammons. How are you?"

Nelson Ammons was our former biology teacher from Kirby Falls High School and a frequent farmers' market visitor. "Hello, Miss Judd. Welcome home." And then with a nod in my direction, he said, "Mr. Mercer."

"Good morning, Mr. Ammons," I replied easily. He was always polite but not much of a talker.

Our first customer of the day went about selecting a half bushel of our Gala apples from those arranged on the table.

Surreptitiously, I glanced at Candace. I recalled the way she'd stiffened up a few weeks ago, in that very same seat, after encounters with well-meaning locals—the ones who remembered her as Candy Judd, valedictorian and most likely to succeed.

She was watching Mr. Ammons cautiously, like he might bite. But after a moment, he simply pulled out his leather wallet and passed over exact change for his apples before nodding politely in our direction and then moseying off.

Candace stared after him, her lips parted and an expression caught somewhere between confusion and relief. Mr. Ammons hadn't brought up her accomplishments or her performance in his class. He hadn't even called her Candy.

"I always liked biology," she murmured softly.

"Me too," I said.

Still staring off in our former teacher's general direction, Candace mused, "Lo used to complain that he was so monotone that she couldn't stay awake. But I liked how calm and collected he seemed to be. I had an easier time understanding when someone spoke gently."

Lo was undoubtedly Lauren Walker. Well, Lauren McClain now. She and Candace used to be inseparable. They were as different as night and day, but they'd been close growing up. I wondered if they were back in touch since Candace was home.

"He was a good teacher," I agreed.

I'd been in that class with both Candace and Lauren freshman year, but I didn't expect her to remember that.

Candace bit her lip and surprised the hell out of me by asking, "What are the odds you had Mr. Ammons's class with me?"

"Pretty good," I admitted, but I softened the truth with a smile.

She covered her face with both hands, and I laughed.

"I'm sorry," she mumbled loudly behind her fingers.

Amusement lingered but I made sure my tone and my touch were soft and reassuring as I gently pried her hands from her cheeks. "It's okay."

Candace grasped my hands in hers, and I fought a jolt of awareness. She was an affectionate person, effusive and open with others. It didn't really mean anything that she was holding me tight and keeping me close. She couldn't know how rare this was for me. How good it felt to have her hands on me, even with the awkwardness of teenage memories hovering between us.

Candace's grip was firm and purposeful now. Her gaze met mine unflinchingly. I could see the bravery in it—the intention behind it too.

"I'm so sorry I didn't recognize you right off," she apologized earnestly.

Apparently, we were doing this. I hadn't planned to ever bring up how she'd awkwardly reintroduced herself to me weeks ago in her parents' front yard. I thought it would be easier for both of us to ignore it.

My embarrassment seemed to take a backseat to hers. Candace's cheeks were fiery, and she looked truly mortified.

"So very sorry," she insisted before untangling our fingers after one more deliberate squeeze.

I ignored the loss of her touch and moved my hands back to my side of the booth.

"It's really okay," I repeated, and bravely tapped her knee with mine. "I looked a lot different back then."

Candace smiled, clearly grateful. "And the Mercer thing threw me off. That's what everyone calls you now."

Not her though. I liked hearing my first name on her lips, especially knowing she was the only one who said it.

"I still feel terrible," she groaned.

"Don't. It's fine, I promise."

But she still looked miserable. We needed something to put us back on equal footing once more.

I wondered if she remembered that time in the hallway, right before graduation. Our one and only interaction back then. Probably best not to bring it up.

After a glance toward the Grandpappy's table, I leaned in close to Candace. I ignored that hit of lavender that lived on her skin, and how it felt for our shoulders to press together, and whispered, "Laramie Burke is at the booth right next door. I don't know if you know this, but she went to high school with us."

Candace pulled back, a surprised look on her face as she took in my mischievous grin. "Are you giving me shit right now?"

"Yep."

Then she started laughing. Her pleased amusement was so loud that it turned heads from across the street.

I loved it. I loved that I could make her sound like that—free and happy, and totally unselfconscious in her joy.

I wasn't a particularly funny guy. My humor was pretty dry, and mostly I was quiet and kept to myself. Candace was such an open, friendly person—such a charmer—that it was a little bit intoxicating to know I had the ability to put such a big smile on her face.

As the day went on, I pointed out two more classmates, a former lunch lady, and our assistant principal, all enjoying the farmers' market. Candace cackled and whacked me on the shoulder each time I whispered conspiratorially that she might not remember them, but they'd been acquaintances of hers once upon a time.

The teasing worked to smooth things over. I didn't want her to feel bad about what had happened her first day back in Kirby Falls.

People needed a chance to move on from the mistakes they made, especially when they were genuine in their remorse. It was hard to hold this one against her.

There were folks out there who didn't believe in *sorry*. They'd rather hold a grudge and give unnecessary weight to minor transgressions than ever move on. But I'd never been one of those people. I'd rather move forward than be stuck in the past out of nothing more than spite.

"Are you going to do that every time we see someone from school?"

With the echo of her laughter making my grin linger, I looked over from where I was condensing our remaining stock. "Nah, I'll cut it out eventually."

She grabbed a box from the pavement behind our seats and passed it to me, so we could start packing up for the day. "You said it yourself, you were different back then. I should be off the hook. Plus, I'm not totally sure the woman you said was Dolores from the lunchroom was actually her."

I chuckled. "I guess I'm not the only one you forgot."

We'd had fun today. I liked that I could tease her about this now. It soothed the twinge of hurt from that first day. Now we had this inside joke between us. It didn't really matter that I was the butt of it.

We hadn't rewritten history, but we'd put it in new packaging. One that wasn't quite so sharp around the edges.

Grabbing a carton for herself, Candace stood beside me and started carefully loading our unsold produce to return to the orchard and sell in the pre-picked bins at the Apple House. "But you've obviously changed. Not just in appearance," she added quickly.

When I turned my head, I caught her eyes tracing down the length of my arms, lingering on my biceps, before watching my forearms flex from the grip I had on the box in my hand.

Her attention snapped back to the apples she was loading up, but not before I caught her blush and the way she'd checked me out.

I fought my pleased grin and busied myself with my own task. I liked having Candace's eyes on me. I liked her flushed cheeks and whatever direction her thoughts had taken.

But before I could really enjoy the possibility that Candace might be attracted to me, she sort of stammered, "And—and you're a dad now, right?"

Surprise had me pausing with the box of apples in my hands. I quickly turned away to stack it with the others and to catch my breath. Of course, she'd found out. Of course, she'd asked. My life wasn't a secret. It was fodder for small-town gossip. Naturally, it would have found its way to her in the weeks since she'd returned.

"Uh, right," I finally managed, but it sounded more like a question than a confirmation. I still couldn't look at her.

My business was common knowledge, but I couldn't remember the last time someone had asked me about Lyndsey outright. The Judds never brought up her or Hannah after the divorce. They gave me space.

Brady had asked early on—right after Hannah had taken Lyndsey and moved to Tennessee—if I wanted to grab a beer and talk about it. I'd said no, and he hadn't mentioned it again. I'd been grateful that Brady and his family hadn't persisted, hadn't asked after the little girl who wasn't really mine, because I didn't want to lie to them.

The Judds were good people, and they supported me through a shitty situation and gave me privacy all the while.

So it had been quite some time since anyone had inquired about my former life. And it was the first time the lie had occasion to stick in my throat.

Hannah's truth was not mine to tell. She had her own family and her own life, and I never wanted to make things hard for Lyndsey. I loved that little girl. Losing her was hard enough. Reliving it now felt like some funhouse version of events, where the reality was distorted and impossible to decipher from the lies.

But I didn't *want* to lie to Candace. I didn't want her to have this impression of me—that I had a daughter I didn't talk about or acknowledge. That there was a baby out there whose picture wasn't in my wallet and whose presence I simply ignored.

I endured the gossip and the bad opinions of me because they came from people who didn't matter.

However, I couldn't be honest with myself and say I didn't care about what Candace thought. Somehow I didn't imagine she'd be able to ignore whatever it was she'd heard about me.

We stayed quiet and busy while we loaded up and headed back to the truck. My response obviously hadn't encouraged any more conversation on the topic. I could see Candace watching me from the corner of my eye as I drove back to Judd's.

I'd let a single choice define me for the rest of my life. And for the first time in a long time, I was reminded that trying to do the right thing didn't always work out.

seven

CANDACE

"Candy, honey, you alright?"

My mother's words pulled my attention away from the meandering path it had taken.

I smiled. "Yeah, Mom. I'm good. How's your book?"

We were on her screened porch this morning, the fan off since it was in the low sixties. I wore a pale blue sweatshirt, and Mom was wrapped up in a plaid robe she'd had since I was in middle school.

It turned out that my mother did still drink her tea out here most mornings. And when I'd asked if I could join her, she'd been extremely pleased. So, now I moseyed over from the garage apartment around 7:00 a.m. and brought my e-reader.

Some mornings we sipped our tea and read in companionable silence for half an hour, and others we chatted. I loved having this time with her. I'd missed out on so much over the years. Subtleties and nuance you couldn't really capture over the phone or on a video call.

Out here on the porch, with the birds chirping and the fog settled like a cozy blanket in the valley, it was the most relaxed my mother ever got. She was a hard worker and always busy with the orchard and the business and church and the community. Amy Judd was a go-getter. Seeing her at ease was something special and rare, and I loved these moments, just the two of us.

While Mom filled me in on the thriller she had spread across her lap, I couldn't help but wonder how many of these mornings I had left.

I should definitely be job hunting—at least seeing what was out there. If I kept to my timeline, I had less than four months to track something down and go through the lengthy interview process. But part of me—likely the one currently enjoying tea with my momma—didn't want to limit my options moving forward. There were opportunities a little closer to home. I could always job hunt in Atlanta or Nashville, or heck, even in Charlotte.

My parents loved visiting New York and seeing the sights. They were always interested in checking out the places I frequented and eager to spend time in the city together. But maybe they'd enjoy having me within driving distance. Surely, they'd still see me as successful even if I was no longer based in NYC.

Mom had just started retelling the part where she'd screamed and thrown her book when the screen door banged open, making us both jump.

But it was only Joan standing in the doorway. She looked like she'd just finished up her run. Her light gray tee shirt was dark in places with sweat, and the ball cap on her head was tugged low over her eyes. She had a tiny stub of a mostly gray ponytail sticking out of the back. And the scowl she wore had me swallowing uneasily.

I hadn't heard from my sister since the staff meeting, two weeks ago. She'd avoided me at work, and she hadn't joined us for dinner in the farmhouse once.

Joan had even evaded me at the Orchard Festival planning meeting two days ago. I'd found a seat by myself in the conference room at the Kirby Falls Public Library and taken diligent notes in my trusty notebook while the chairwoman of the committee had gone over festival procedures for vendors. Growing up, I'd always loved the Orchard Fest, and I was excited to work the event with my family this weekend.

It hurt to think my sister was so upset about my involvement with the farm that she was staying away as a result. That she'd basically rather have my input over her dead body.

"I'll go along with the Friday night food trucks and Candy's pumpkin-patch thing," Joan announced loudly and robotically, as if she'd practiced the words and hoped I'd be across a ravine when she delivered them.

I felt my eyes go wide in surprise, but I did my best to rein it in.

Joan continued, "We're already open through Halloween anyway. But there should be a budget, and Candy should call Will over at Grandpappy's to see if they have any excess produce they're interested in unloading. He'll give us a fair price."

Then she turned and exited just as abruptly as she arrived, the screen door snapping shut behind her.

Mom and I turned to glance at one another, our shock mutual, but my mother recovered quicker than I could.

She called out to my sister's slender retreating form, "You coming for dinner? I'm making spaghetti."

That was a low blow, I thought. Spaghetti was Joanie's favorite. Mom made the sauce and the meatballs from scratch, and Joan used to request it for every one of her birthday dinners as far as I could recall.

At my mother's invitation, Joan paused her long-legged stride.

Mom shot me a knowing look and a sly wink.

My sister muttered something under her breath that I was too far away to hear before calling over her shoulder, "Fine. I'll be there."

"Have a good day, honey," Mom hollered back, and I fought a smile.

Then I didn't bother fighting it because my sister was speaking to me again. Well, speaking in my general direction. Maybe I could get more out of her at dinner tonight. But the most surprising development was that Joan had agreed to the pumpkin patch. I was thrilled. And I was confident that moving forward with it would have a big impact on the orchard.

I couldn't wait to get to work. The budget would be upheld, and I'd call over to Grandpappy's like my sister wanted. They'd been on my potential vendor list anyway. I hadn't been to the big farm across the highway in nearly a decade, but I knew my parents were friendly with the Clarks, who ran the place.

"Thanks for the tea, Mom," I said happily, rising from my chair and heading toward the kitchen so I could put my mug in the dishwasher. "I better get started on the pumpkin patch."

My mother smiled back. "You have a good day, too, Candy."

I was in such a good mood that I didn't even mind it when the nickname slipped out.

I'd been loitering in the Apple House rather than my office, hoping to catch Mark, when he drove by. I had my laptop, cell phone, and my worn notebook laid out on the worktable.

When he spotted me beneath the covered awning, waving like a dork, he pivoted away from whatever task he'd been in the middle of and walked toward me. I watched as he glanced at the ground, but not before I caught the edge of a smile.

As I waited, my eyes drifted over Mark's body as he moved. His blue Judd's Orchard tee shirt was worn and threadbare, the sleeves straining around his defined biceps. He wore a five-panel hat that covered his dark blond hair, for the most part. The light-wash denim encasing his powerful thighs shifted as he bounded up the stairs of the Apple House's front porch.

"Hey," he said in greeting.

I dragged my horny eyes away because, oh my God, I'd totally been checking him out . . . for an embarrassingly long time. What was wrong with me?

Clearing the residual embarrassment from my throat, I finally managed an awkward, "Hey! Hi!" in return. *Good Lord.*

"What's up?" he asked, his blue-gray eyes sparkling, if I wasn't mistaken. "You looked like you had some news."

Oh, right.

"Yes! Joan came by this morning while Mom and I were having tea, and she agreed to the pumpkin patch. And Food Truck Friday. I'm getting started on everything."

"That's great," Mark said. "We talked a little about it. I'm going to work on getting the blackberries ready in the space behind the Apple House. They might not be ready next July for the u-pick operation though. New blackberries can be sour for a few seasons. But it'll be good to get them started—plan for the future. That space will work great, and it gets plenty of sun. I can bring clippings from some of the plants I have at home."

I frowned. "We'll compensate you for that." He was already shaking his head, but I persisted. "No, I don't want you to put yourself out. And I can help with the planting. You don't need to take this on if it's going to add to your workload."

"It's okay. We'll start small. They don't require a whole lot of maintenance once we get them set up. And you can help if you'd like."

Smiling, I said, "Thanks, I would." And then his prior words registered. "You have a garden at home?"

Mark nodded and put a hand in his jeans pocket before taking it back out again. "Yeah. Mostly vegetables, but I grow some fruit too."

"Let me guess. You dabble?"

He grinned at my teasing and then finally let out a chuckle.

I suddenly wondered how big and impressive this home garden really was. I'd bet my largemouth bass that Mark's backyard was a thing of beauty, a rural work of art. The more I learned about this man, the more I realized he was totally competent and proficient, and he excelled at whatever he put his mind to.

It was that surety that made it so hard to fathom Mark's situation with Hannah and their daughter. Whatever happened there must have been serious. I couldn't imagine steady and reliable Mark Mercer being anything but totally involved and utterly devoted to his child—no matter the distance or the circumstance.

Guilt had me glancing down at the worn worktable between us. "You don't get all your farming in at work?"

"I like to bring my work home with me," he said, pride evident in his tone.

It was nice to see him smile, to talk about something he obviously enjoyed.

I'd been worried after our last conversation on Saturday, at the farmers' market. I'd gone and asked about him being a dad and made things awkward. Mark's entire demeanor had changed, going stiff and becoming closed off. I couldn't say I blamed him. His personal life wasn't any of my business. We were co-workers, and, at times, it seemed like we were becoming friends. He had my back on my ideas for the orchard, and he was close with my whole family.

But I never should have assumed I had the right to ask about certain things. Parenthood was clearly a touchy subject for him. Despite what Bonnie had relayed during our lunch together, I had no idea what his actual situation was with Hannah and their daughter.

Gossip wasn't gospel, after all.

Without much thought beyond hoping to keep that tiny smile on Mark's face, I blurted, "I'm planning on taking a late lunch and going down to Apollo's to talk to Magdaline about booking their food truck for the first Food Truck Friday this month. Want to come with me?"

At my abrupt subject change and graceless invitation, Mark's expression dimmed. He clearly had some reservations about joining me. Maybe he was worried I'd corner him with more intrusive questions about his life.

"What time are you thinking? Apollo's will be packed for lunch," he said, shifting restlessly on his work-boot-clad feet.

"Oh, not until two or two thirty. I don't want to take up their time when they're so busy."

At my words, Mark's expression smoothed out and his shoulders lowered incrementally. "Okay," he finally replied. "That sounds good."

By the time two o'clock rolled around, I wasn't nervous about driving us downtown and spending my lunch break with Mark. I'd been too distracted and busy with work. Now that I had the green light from Joan, a few of my *maybes* and *wait and sees* were actually happening. I was doing further research, networking, and contacting potential vendors and local businesses to make these new undertakings a reality for Judd's Orchard.

When Mark and I walked into Apollo's, it was clear that the lunchtime rush had passed. There were three occupied tables and no employees in sight. We waited by the hostess stand while I breathed in the glorious scent of cheese and carbs.

"It's nice that some things haven't changed," I said quietly, eyes scanning the space of one of my family's longtime favorite restaurants. Growing up, we'd eaten here for Brady's birthday nearly every year. Mrs. Kouides would bring out a huge slice of chocolate cake with sparkling candles and lead the restaurant in a rousing rendition of "Happy Birthday to You." I had memories from special occasions and casual pizza-night dinners too.

My eyes lingered on the vacant booth in the back corner of the restaurant. The black vinyl was worn and there was a framed photo of the Aegean Sea on the adjacent wall. I'd brought Lo here the summer after our junior year. Her boyfriend, Joey, had cheated on her with Amber Wilson after prom. She'd found out, and I'd brought her to Apollo's to cheer her up . . . and to talk her out of keying Joey's Mustang. We'd eaten two slices of Mrs. Kouides's famous baklava cheesecake, and, in the end, she'd egged Joey's car while I'd been visiting my grandmother in Virginia.

"Well, some things have changed," Mark said, just as quietly. "They have that new sign out front, and Mr. Kouides took pastitsio off the menu after Gladys Oakley posted a copycat recipe in the Kirby Falls Facebook group."

I snorted. "God, that group is unhinged."

Mark's eyes crinkled at the corners in amusement as he slid me a glance. "It really is. And, you know, they started charging for parking on Main Street."

Gasping dramatically, I clutched the imaginary pearls at the base of my throat. "I bet the Facebook group had a lot to say about that."

Mark rolled his lips between his teeth while nodding. "Oh yeah. There was an organized boycott of downtown businesses and everything."

I sighed and shook my head. Then I considered what he'd actually said. "Wait. They charge for parking now?"

"Yeah. All street parking is paid."

"Shit," I murmured. "I need to go out and pay."

"It's an app, not a parking meter. I can show you. You just need your license plate number."

"I'll go grab that," I offered. We were in Mom's Passat, and I had no idea what the plate number was. "If Magdaline comes out, tell her I'll be right back to chat. I called ahead. She's expecting us."

Then I hurried out the front door before Mark could protest further or offer to take care of it himself.

Three minutes later, I'd successfully scanned the QR code on the parking sign I'd missed and navigated the app to avoid getting a ticket from local law enforcement.

I was walking the half block back to Apollo's on the sidewalk when someone stepped out of a nearby business, directly into my path. I pulled up short as did the woman who'd exited.

She was wearing all black, from her flowy tee shirt to her sneakered feet. The familiar head of curly blond hair whipped around at the abrupt sound that left my lips.

"Lo," I sort of squeaked.

A heavy beat of silence passed while we looked at each other.

"Candy, hey," my former best friend eventually said, and for the first time in our long and disjointed history, I couldn't read her expression. "I heard you were back."

I had the urge to lunge forward and wrap my arms around her. To tell her I'd missed her and it was so good to see her face.

I'd kept up with her on social media, but her posts were rare and impersonal—a random share for a local business or a funny meme. She hardly ever posted pictures of herself or her family.

It was also through social media that I learned Lo and Joey McClain had married two years after high school graduation. I hadn't been invited, but Lauren and Joey had been tagged in other people's photos. I remembered seeing those pictures on my way back from class and sitting down in the stairwell of my dorm, scrolling in disbelief.

Lo had worn a short white dress with spaghetti straps while Joey dressed in church attire—khakis and a white button-up with a striped tie. They'd looked like kids, and I couldn't believe she'd married someone without telling me. Her sisters had been her bridesmaids, and I could still recall the way that had stabbed at my heart. I hadn't been there. She hadn't asked me.

When we'd had our epic, last-blast road trip, we'd ended up in New York at the end of the summer, two weeks before the beginning of my first semester at Columbia. I'd been so excited for school to start, and maybe I hadn't hidden that well enough.

Lo was destined for the community college twenty minutes from Kirby Falls. She was planning on living at home and saving money. Education had never been high on her priority list. Our dreams had ultimately been very different.

The plan had been for Lo to stay with me and help me move into my dorm room. My parents were driving up with a boatload of stuff, but not for another week or so. I'd wanted that time to settle into my new life, but also to find a way to say goodbye to my old one—to say goodbye to Lo.

In the end, she'd saved me the trouble.

There hadn't been a fun move-in montage with trips to Target for bedding and posters. I never even got the chance to pretend Lo was my roommate until the real one showed up. As soon as we'd rolled into the city, my friend parked in front of my building and told me goodbye.

"We should just call it," she'd said. We'd had a great summer—a last hoorah. I was her best friend, but our lives were going in different directions. There was no sense in trying to keep in touch. Lo had called it *pointless*. Said we'd grow apart no matter what. School breaks wouldn't be enough, and it wouldn't be the same, so we should just stop while we were ahead.

Initially, I'd been too stunned to question it, but then I'd found my voice—gotten angry and started crying. Lauren had been stoic and sure in the driver's seat, her mind made up without any input from me.

She'd treated me like a high school boyfriend—someone not worth the time or energy of trying long distance with. But I hadn't been *just* some boy she was dating—those came and went. We'd had a decade and a half of friendship. You didn't throw that away—or at least, that was what I'd thought.

I still remembered standing on a cement sidewalk with a backpack on and a suitcase at my feet, watching my best friend in the world drive away. The soundtrack to my arrival on campus had been the sound of an engine and my own angry tears.

I'd heard later from my mom that Lo dropped out of college and got a job doing hair.

Belatedly, I realized the building my former friend had rushed out of was the Hairport, a beauty shop in downtown Kirby Falls. Of course. That made sense.

Instead of reaching for her, I crossed my arms over my chest. "It's good to see you. How have you been?"

"Good," Lo replied shortly.

I lifted my chin toward the building behind her. "You're at the Hairport?"

She nodded stiffly. "I do the best color in two counties."

I could feel my throat closing up at how painfully impersonal this was. Like I hadn't borrowed clothes from this person. Watched her smoke a cigarette when we were fifteen and then held her hair while she puked for half the night. As if she hadn't come to my house for dinner at least once a week our entire childhood. Like I was just some stranger asking intrusive questions that any resident in two counties already knew the answers to.

Forcing a smile, I managed, "Well, you were always really good at doing hair."

She'd braided and twisted my own into an elaborate style before the homecoming dance our senior year. Something she'd seen in a magazine and was able to recreate flawlessly.

Lauren's black sneakers shifted impatiently on the pavement.

In a rush of fear that she'd be gone again from my life just as suddenly as she had reappeared, I blurted out recklessly, with no thought of self-preservation, "Would you want to get coffee sometime and catch up? I—I—I can see that you're in a rush, on your way somewhere. But maybe when you have time, we could get together."

The silence stretched as Lo watched me struggle through the invitation. Whereas a moment before I couldn't read her expression, now her emotion was plain enough to see.

After a pitying sigh, Lauren said, "We're in really different places, Candy. I have a husband and two kids at home and not a lot of free time to grab drinks or coffee or brunch or whatever you usually do to catch up."

She said *catch up* like she thought I was hoping to convert her to Scientology or maybe get her in on the ground floor of my pyramid scheme. Instead of just hoping to try to know someone again—a person I used to know as well as I knew myself.

Although, maybe that wasn't right. Perhaps I hadn't known Lauren Walker at all because I never thought she would have been capable of leaving me alone in a new city and quitting our friendship cold turkey. Lo could be mercenary and painfully practical. She held grudges like a security blanket and didn't take shit from anyone. But in all our years of friendship, she'd never directed that part of herself at me. She'd defended me ruthlessly.

In the end, I'd felt like a cliché, and worse, an oblivious one. It was natural for friendships to fade away—especially following high school graduation. Long distance was hard to maintain for a romantic relationship, why wouldn't it be difficult for a friendship as well? Not that I'd ever gotten the chance to find out.

I'd been ignorant to think our lives wouldn't drift apart. I remembered feeling so stupid for being blindsided by what anyone could have probably seen coming, and then dumber still for being hurt by it.

The truth was, I'd never understood the reason for my quick excision from Lo's life.

And standing on a similar sidewalk—this time in my hometown—I couldn't comprehend the brush-off now. But instead of arguing or crying, I simply replied, "Sure. Okay."

"I need to run," Lo said.

"Right," I rasped. My throat was doing that closing-up thing and I was barely getting air, so I wasn't sure how that word managed to escape but it had, and I could feel my face flush as a result.

"Welcome home, Candy." And then Lo turned and left me behind just as easily as she'd done it the first time.

I didn't mean to stare after her like a dramatic teenager, but I honestly had a hard time remembering what I was doing out here.

Farther down the block, a figure stepped out onto the path—a strong, solid form. *Mark.*

Shit. Mark. We were supposed to be at Apollo's talking to Magdaline about the food truck. Seeing Lo had—

Lo passed by him just then, and I was close enough to see the way his eyes narrowed beneath the bill of his hat in recognition and then his gaze hurriedly searched the surrounding area until he found me, standing statue-still beneath an awning and incapable of putting one foot in front of the other.

Mark strode in my direction, his gait confident and sure but his expression hard.

God, I hoped he wasn't mad that I'd kept him waiting.

I told myself to get it together, and eventually, my feet got the message. Mark and I met in the middle and drifted toward the side of the path so that any foot traffic could easily maneuver around us.

"I'm so sorry," I practically yelled at the same time Mark said, "Are you okay?"

His softly uttered question was at odds with his intense stare and tight jaw. His words and genuine concern had all those messy feelings and throat-clenching tendencies of mine roaring back with a vengeance.

I wanted to be normal about this. Nothing had happened, not really. I ran into someone I used to know. I was being ridiculous by giving the exchange so much weight. It wasn't like losing Lo all those years ago.

Yet the truth was, I *wanted* to cry. Not just for the brush-off this afternoon, but for the girl I'd been seven years ago, for the friendship I'd mourned. How I'd called for months and hadn't gotten so much as a text in return. All those times I'd woken up crying in my sleep, sitting up afterward feeling embarrassed and disoriented in my dorm room. How those dreams filled with memories of Lo and home had gone on longer than I ever had anticipated. The way I'd tried to make new friends at a new school in a new city all while grieving a loss I didn't understand.

In my experience, losing a best friend was so much harder than losing a boyfriend. Maybe I'd never loved a boy that much, or maybe I'd known that finding your soulmate in the form of a friend was much rarer.

"Of course. I'm fine," I finally said, but *fine* came out with hardly any sound, just the shape of the word on my lips and tears pooling in my eyes.

Mark didn't do the panicked guy thing when presented with a woman's emotions. He just nodded, as reliable and assured as he did everything else. And then he stepped forward and wrapped me up in a hug.

I held on tight, my arms going around his waist, thankful and mortified and everything in between. I rested my chin on his shoulder and noted, gratefully, that I didn't see Lo's retreating form anywhere.

Mark was so warm and strong. I felt protected, inside and out. Like he wasn't just shielding my body but keeping my heart safe and secure as well. Mark was always careful and controlled; whereas, I was open and free with my affection. I patted arms and gave hugs and whacked shoulders and kissed cheeks.

I supposed I should have been embarrassed by Mark's pity hug and my display of emotions that had elicited it. But, somehow, I didn't think he was judging me.

He rubbed soothing circles on my upper back. I felt his calloused palms catch on the fabric of my tee shirt every so often, and I liked the contrast between his strength and how gentle he was capable of being.

"I'm being silly," I said, my voice steady once more.

"No, you're not." Mark's words were a quiet rumble against my chest. "Is that the first time you've run into her?"

I nodded. "It's just been a long time," I tried and failed to explain. He'd obviously recognized Lo. I didn't need to explain who she was to me. Apparently, he remembered. "It wasn't the reunion I guess I'd been hoping for."

The truth was, I hadn't even known I was holding out hope where Lo was concerned. Of course, I'd thought about what it would be like to see her again. That daydream had been on repeat often in the early days.

Maybe now that reality had passed, shattering every imagined scenario, I could stop wondering. I could finally close the door on my friendship with Lo and all those *what-ifs* and *what-might-have-beens*. I hadn't realized how much hope had sneaked through by leaving that door propped open.

Yet her sudden appearance and swift rejection had been a pretty effective one-two punch. It wasn't a knockout, but I was floundering on the ropes.

It was nice to have a steadying hand while I recovered.

"I'm sorry, Candace." And then a weighty pause. "It's hard to lose a friend, no matter how much time has passed. When you've been through a lot together, it takes a long time to tuck it all away. Forgetting is never really an option."

Oh, God. *Mark and Hannah.*

I blew out a long breath and squeezed him tight.

My loss had been nothing compared to Mark's. He'd lost a friend and a wife in Hannah Price. I didn't know what had happened in their divorce or what their relationship was like now. It wasn't my business. But it didn't sound like they were on good terms. With so much between them—a marriage and a child—I couldn't imagine returning to friendship or remaining amicable. Some situations were just too complicated and difficult.

Or maybe I was making assumptions all around. Maybe he wasn't even talking about Hannah.

But I thought he must be.

The truth of his loss wasn't owed to me. I was just grateful for his comfort, his friendship here and now.

Without offering any explanations, Mark pulled back. "We'll try Apollo's another day. Let's go somewhere else. Somewhere I think you'll like."

Confused and disoriented by the shift in conversation, I regarded him warily. "Okay."

Mark ducked inside the restaurant to let Magdaline know we'd reschedule our meeting. When he returned to my side, he held out his hand. "Keys?"

Fifteen quiet minutes later, we pulled into a small shopping center in Miller Creek. I eyed the building as Mark shifted the Passat into park.

"I think it was a burrito place back in high school."

"I think you're right," I murmured, squinting to see the sign over the door.

It wasn't a burrito place now.

At the realization, I turned my head to look at Mark. He was already waiting, bracing for my expression.

"You brought me to a pie shop?"

Mark's thumb tapped a beat on the steering wheel, and he looked a little unsure. "I thought you might like it. I don't know if they have Oreo mousse, but their apple pie is really good. And their sweet potato pie too. Well, everything I've tried here has been—"

"Thank you," I interrupted. My smile was on the wobbly side, but I was determined not to cry anymore today.

Mark had done such a nice thing for me. He'd remembered my favorite pie and brought me somewhere to make me feel better.

"This is perfect," I assured him.

Pied Piper's was bright and cheerful on the inside. I took in the picnic blanket–patterned tablecloths and the gallery wall jam-packed with mismatched frames of all sizes featuring illustrations of pastries and baked goods. It felt modern and fun, and I liked it immediately.

The employee behind the counter had pink hair and dark-rimmed glasses and welcomed us with a friendly smile and a bright hello.

Mark and I approached the dessert case, and I found an assortment of pies. My gaze lingered on the key lime and fruit pies, but then my attention found its way to a half-filled pie tin on the bottom row. The pale filling looked whipped and fluffy, but the glossy chocolate stripes on top were decadent and rich. I knew what I was ordering.

"I'll have a slice of the Peanut Butter Paradise Pie, please," I told the worker.

She grinned. "That's my favorite."

"Same for me," Mark said, and before I had a chance to react, he'd slipped some cash across the counter.

Instead of fighting him on it, I took the gift he'd given me—more than a slice of four-dollar pie on a Wednesday afternoon. A reprieve. A balm for my tender heart.

"Thank you," I said quietly, squeezing his arm gently in gratitude.

Mark's eyes were soft when he nodded, concern still lingering around the edges.

We took our slices, neatly arranged on vintage plates, and found a booth next to the window.

Mark waited while I took my first bite, as if to ensure he'd made the right decision bringing me here for carbs and comfort.

I closed my eyes as the cool sweetness flooded my mouth. The flavors blended perfectly as the slightly bitter chocolate swirled in among the creamy peanut butter filling. I may have moaned a little at the taste.

When I opened my eyes, Mark was still watching, his own pie untouched.

His gaze snapped up from my lips, and he quickly cleared his throat. "How is it?"

I smiled. "Amazing. Try it."

And he did.

We ate our pie at a small booth, where our knees brushed any time we moved. In between bites, Mark told me about finding this place and bringing pies to the holidays and celebrations he spent with my family. I asked him about the occasions I'd missed over the last few years, and he filled me in.

I felt a pang at hearing the moments Mark described. I'd been in a city far away, probably eating bites of takeout in between working or studying. And for what? So the family I loved could say they were proud of my work ethic and my commitment? After all this time—years gone by in sacrifice—I couldn't say if it was worth it. Actually, I knew the answer. I just didn't want to think it too loudly.

I pushed my doubts aside for the time being and listened as Mark recounted the time my dad burned a perfect circle in the backyard when he tried to deep-fry a turkey for Thanksgiving.

As we talked and laughed for the next twenty minutes, I couldn't help but think Mark had done what he set out to do. The encounter with Lo had settled into a fresh bruise, no longer the open wound it had been. I was feeling better, but it hadn't really been about the pie.

Mark's thoughtfulness in bringing me here made all the difference.

Now that I considered it, I was a little embarrassed by our conversation over the weekend when I'd said a pie restaurant was what I missed most about my time in New York. I hadn't been lying or anything, but what did that say about the life I'd left behind or how I'd been living it?

I didn't have close friends in the city anymore. My friends from college were scattered around the country. I had work colleagues and acquaintances, former professors, and references. There was definitely no one keeping in touch from Blakely Hammond Marketing on the Upper West Side.

Mark was sweet to remember that I had a soft spot for pie, and I appreciated the comfort he'd given me today when I'd needed it, along with the marked lack of judgment.

Of course, I wished things had gone differently with Lo. There was even a part of me that wished I'd just risked the parking ticket and stayed inside Apollo's with Mark in the first place.

But then another louder and more insistent part argued that I would have missed out on this—the unexpected detour, the conversation, Mark's sweetness that rivaled the pie, and knowing what it felt like to be in his arms.

MARK

The outdoor space at Firefly Cider was packed when I arrived.

A John Denver cover band played beneath the awning of the open-air stage. Bonfires burned around the perimeter of the space, the glow barely visible as the sun sat low in the evening sky. Nearly every table was full, as were the Adirondack chairs positioned throughout.

Nerves and learned behavior had me glancing at the folks seated and milling about, but I didn't recognize anyone. That alone made my jaw relax, but it didn't keep the anxiety at bay entirely.

Candace's event was starting in thirty minutes, and I caught sight of her at a long table on the back porch. She had several Firefly employees helping to arrange cider flights. The small three-ounce glasses were fitted inside holes in the wooden boards in groups of four, and I imagined there were different cider varieties in each glass.

Prepacked paper bags and bushels of apples were positioned on an adjacent table for sale alongside signage for Judd's Orchard and framed QR codes for payment.

Candace was busy and didn't see me approach, so I had a moment to watch her work as I maneuvered my way through the picnic tables and the sea of tourists. She wasn't wearing her fancy pantsuit tonight; instead, she had on jeans and a white Judd's Orchard tee shirt covered by an open flannel that looked soft and worn. Her dark hair was pulled back in a high ponytail, but it wasn't ruthlessly tamed and smoothed down like on her first day back in town. Today it was a bit looser, with a few strands framing her face and tiny wisps misbehaving along her hairline. She looked beautiful. She looked like she fit here, in this space, this town.

Candace moved quickly and confidently, smiling at her helpers and chatting as she went. She didn't appear flustered by the crowd or the folks wandering up to ask her questions before the event started. She looked completely in control and ready for the turnout, whatever that may be.

From what I'd seen on the social media posts from the orchard and Firefly, they'd sold advance tickets for the event as a way to gauge numbers and cover the cost of the cider. But they'd also intended to sell cider-and-apple-pairing event tickets at the door tonight.

As I ascended the steps to the covered porch, Candace glanced up and did a double take. "Hey! You came."

I nodded and tried not to focus on the way her smile lit up her entire face. I didn't want to read too much into her expression. Probably just surprise and relief at having an extra pair of hands.

"Great turnout," I said, dipping my head in the direction of all the customers milling about. "How can I help?"

Her gaze took in the matching Judd's Orchard shirt I wore before coming back to my face. "Thanks for coming out. I didn't think it would be this busy."

Candace waved me over behind the table and squeezed my arm in greeting when I reached her side. I could feel her sweetness and gratitude in the simple show of affection, and I resisted the urge to squeeze her back.

She showed me what she was doing—pairing up the apple varieties with the various ciders and positioning everything on the extra-wide flight boards. There were cups of McIntosh, Gala with peanut butter, Golden Delicious with a caramel drizzle, and slices of Cosmic Crisp.

The Firefly employees were set up to take the tickets, hand out the flight boards, and pass the customers a postcard-sized handout with a list of what they'd be drinking and eating.

Together, Candace and I worked for the next hour to prep the boards as they were steadily distributed. We got into a rhythm and barely looked up until Rhonda, one of the Firefly employees, nudged us and said, "We're through most of the preregistered tickets, do you have enough stock if we open it up and sell more?"

Candace glanced in the coolers beneath the table and did some quick mental math. "We have enough for fifty more flight boards."

Rhonda grinned. "These will go fast. People are digging it. We had to open up the field for more parking."

Candace thanked the woman who typically bartended but was pitching in tonight for the event.

Then Candace turned to me and smiled before letting out a huge sigh. "I'm so glad it's going well."

I eyed her and the visible relief that was plain to see on her face. I never would have guessed she had been nervous about the turnout or the success of the event she'd orchestrated and made a reality. She'd been so steady and sure all evening —cheerful with guests and workers, laughing and smiling the whole time.

"Were you worried?" I asked quietly as she passed me more cups of sliced apples.

She shrugged before crouching next to the coolers. "I mean, yeah. I hoped it would go well, but I didn't know for sure. I didn't want it to flop and let anyone down. Who knows? Maybe all these people are just here for the band."

I frowned. "They're not here for the band."

But Candace didn't respond. She busied herself, unloading the remaining contents of the cooler onto the table.

I crouched beside her.

"Candace," I said softly, stilling her hands with my own. She met my eyes warily. "You did the research. You talked to Jordan and Firefly about the logistics. You planned and you promoted. You did the work. Even if three people had shown up tonight, no one would be disappointed in you. This event isn't a reflection on you as an orchard employee or a Judd."

Candace listened as I spoke, but I could tell she wasn't entirely convinced. However, after a moment, she eventually nodded. "Thanks, Mark. And thanks for showing up tonight. It was nice to have backup."

"Anytime."

We worked to prep the extra boards and then we sold apples. An hour later, when all the stock was gone, I helped Candace pack up her things and take them to the parking lot. She was upbeat—no doubt riding the high from her success tonight.

After closing the lid of the Passat's trunk, she blurted, "Would you want to stay and have a drink with me?"

Her abrupt invitation surprised me, but it also had something warm and weighty flooding my veins. This was a drink. It was casual. Not a big deal, I reminded myself. Maybe she wasn't asking me to prom, but this *felt* just as important for the boy who still remembered what color her dress was senior year.

The corners of my lips turned up in anticipation, and I felt the *yes* gathering on my tongue. But then instinct took over. I eyed the crowds still milling about. The band had about a half hour left on their set, and while the outdoor seating area wasn't as busy as it had been earlier, there was still a good amount of people. Yet hardly any of them were locals. I could count on one hand how many folks I'd recognized tonight as Candace and I had worked side by side.

It was safe to assume that this wasn't the Kirby Falls Baptist crowd. It was mostly tourists, strangers—people who didn't know me. I'd take them any day over folks who assumed they did.

It was probably safe to stay and have a cider before heading out.

Plus, I wanted to. Despite my innate avoidance of my judgy neighbors and any places where they might show up, I'd come to Firefly because I wanted to help the orchard—and Candace. And, if I was being honest, I was eager to spend more time with her.

Yesterday at the pie shop had been nice. I hated that Candace was hurting over her encounter with her former friend, but it had felt good to do something to make her smile. Seeing her frozen on that sidewalk, left in the wake of Lauren's destruction, had me feeling helpless. The devastation written across her face made me want to protect her from getting hurt. The hug had been instinctual. Candace had needed comfort, and I'd been willing to give it. More than willing. I wanted to be the person she relied on. Her sounding board. A shoulder to cry on.

Maybe it was that same foolish desire to mean something to her that brought me here tonight. But I wanted to show my support. I needed her to know that she had someone in her corner.

In my hesitation, Candace rushed to fill the silence. "I know we have the Orchard Fest bright and early tomorrow, so if you need to turn in and head home, that's totally fine."

She was giving me an out. Smoothing over my indecision and shoring up her defenses—mitigating her expectations and tucking her disappointment carefully away behind a copy-and-paste smile.

I wanted this to be the last time I saw that careful imitation on her face.

"Let's grab a drink. That sounds good."

"You're sure?"

I smiled. "Yeah, I'm sure." I tilted my head back toward Firefly. "I saw some open chairs by a fire in the back. Why don't you go grab those before some leafer takes them? I'll go in and get the cider. What would you like?"

Candace followed the direction of my gaze. I could tell when she saw the unoccupied chairs surrounding one of the fire pits because her expression smoothed out, the doubt clearing from her face like fog burned away by the sunrise. I hoped she credited my hesitation to simply searching for a seat and not the real reason I'd been hesitant to stay. I didn't need another encounter like the one at the farmers' market. I wasn't eager for a repeat of the judgmental stares, ready gossip, and blatant ignorance. All with Candace as a witness.

She smiled and gave me her order, promising to save our seats by the bonfire.

When I returned with two seasonal Don't Fear the Reaper ciders in hand, I passed one to Candace where she was seated in a two-person wooden Adirondack chair. Each seat was connected by a small table in the middle.

"Thank you," she said and took a sip.

"You're welcome."

I placed my drink down between us and settled in beside her. The warmth from the orange flames was welcome as the night air grew chilly.

It was fully dark now, save for the firelight and the glowing bulbs highlighting the perimeter of the seating area. We were far enough away from the outdoor stage that we could speak easily to one another and be heard over the band's rendition of "Annie's Song." The remaining seats around our fire pit were empty.

"So how do you feel?" I asked. "Are you one of those introverted extroverts who needs time to recover after being around people?"

Candace smiled and met my gaze. "No, not really. I've always been fine around people. No recovery period required."

I nodded and picked up my cider. "That checks."

She laughed. "But not you though," she said confidently. "You'll probably need some quiet after all that peopling."

I snorted. "I'll need a week to make up for it."

Her amusement was contagious and soon we were just grinning at each other— sharing a moment of comradery after an evening spent in the trenches of working with the public, basking in the success of the night.

Candace looked relaxed and happy—her smile wasn't the watered-down version from earlier nor the overly bright one she wore for the leafers. It was like watching her come up for air.

The firelight painted her skin in warm golden hues. For a wild and reckless moment, I wished I had my camera so I could capture the contrast of light and shadow, the way the dancing flames lovingly highlighted the planes of her face —her high cheekbones, the straight line of her nose, the elegant column of her throat, the jut of collarbones just above the neckline of her shirt.

I forced myself to grip my glass and take another drink.

"I guess you prefer working in the fields, instead of with the people," she said a moment later.

The statement sounded like a question, so I answered, "I do. But I'm not opposed to helping out wherever I'm needed on the farm."

"Is that what you studied in college, agriculture?" Candace asked, almost tentatively as if she were skirting the edges of a particularly narrow balance beam.

I knew where her cautiousness came from. I hadn't reacted well when she'd brought up me being a dad. The instinct to shut down and protect myself had been unavoidable. It was obvious that Candace didn't want to get too close to the imaginary line I'd drawn, so she was proceeding carefully.

But it was easy enough to talk about this part of my life without thinking about Hannah or lying about our relationship. "Yeah, agronomy. Crop and soil sciences at NC State."

"That's a good school. Did you like living in Raleigh?"

I considered her question and then answered truthfully, "I did and I didn't. It was never going to be long-term for me. Raleigh is a decent-sized city, but you're surrounded by suburbs and pine trees and land, so it doesn't feel very urban. I liked it well enough, but it was never going to be home."

For better or worse, my home would always be Kirby Falls.

There were times I'd given serious thought to leaving. In the early months following my divorce, I'd considered packing up and going somewhere no one knew what I'd lost, what I'd been forced to give up. With my aunt's passing during college, I had no family to stick around for and no one to keep up with. Part of me had wanted to take the easy way out and leave, avoiding the gossip altogether by taking off and settling somewhere new—another farm in another state.

But I liked my life in Kirby Falls. I cared about the Judds and the orchard. I had a place here and people who meant something to me and a good job that gave me peace.

So, yeah. Maybe it would have been smarter to start over somewhere else, but the selfish, spiteful part of me that I managed to ignore most days, thought I'd already given up enough for Hannah Price. I didn't want to give up my home too.

"I used to feel that way about New York," Candace murmured as she watched the fire. "I thought I'd go to college and then come home."

"Why didn't you? Do that, I mean."

Her gaze stayed on the fire pit, but her lips curved in a wistful sort of smile that somehow made her face look sad instead of amused. "Not a lot of job opportunities in Kirby Falls for the field I chose. Once I got started on the path I was on, it felt too late to turn back or change course. Columbia, graduate school, internship. I needed to see it through."

I watched her for a long moment and wondered for the first time if there was more to Candace's return to North Carolina than she was letting on.

Her voice was soft when she said, "It's crazy to think we expect kids to know what they want to do with the rest of their lives when they're only seventeen or eighteen years old."

"I don't think it's ever really too late to alter your path. There aren't rules about starting over and trying again. Cages like that are ones you build yourself," I offered.

Candace swiveled her focus to me, her gaze searching.

I didn't know what was going on in her head or her heart, but I felt compelled to continue now that I had her attention. "You read stories about grandmothers going back to college or someone writing their first book at fifty. You're only twenty-five, Candace. You could do whatever you put your mind to."

Complicated emotions—ones I couldn't even begin to name in the shadow of our burgeoning friendship—swirled behind her eyes, but I was growing more and more certain that this little trip home wasn't just an extended vacation for Candace.

Suddenly, the folksy background music ended and a voice came over the microphone drawing our attention. "This will be our final song this evening. Thanks for listening tonight."

A smattering of applause over on the lawn gave way to softly plucked guitar strings.

When I turned back to face Candace, she was watching the stage, a smile playing on her lips.

"I used to love this song," she said. "I haven't heard it in years."

"I don't know this one," I admitted.

"It's called 'Matthew.' Mom used to play this John Denver album in the kitchen while she made dinner and I did my homework at the table."

We listened together.

I watched Candace as she mouthed the words and kept her eyes on the stage. We listened as the band sang about joy, love, and a windy Kansas wheat field. By the end, our pint glasses were empty, and I had the sense I'd seen a different side of Candace Judd. One that had only revealed itself in the firelight and would be gone again once the embers cooled.

I was glad I'd stayed for a drink, grateful for the chance to know her a little better. There hadn't been any demoralizing encounters with know-it-all neighbors. No one had accused me of being an absentee father. A crowd hadn't gathered with their pitchforks.

Maybe this could be okay. Going out, spending time in the community. Getting a drink with a woman I liked spending time with—a woman I liked, period.

Pulling her flannel tighter around her, Candace said, "Well, I guess we better get going."

"Busy day tomorrow," I agreed.

The Orchard Festival kicked off in the morning. It would be several days of what amounted to a farmers' market on steroids. The usual produce vendors would be joined by local artisans, craftspeople, and antique dealers. Booths would line Main Street for six blocks, along with a stage for performers and a tent for storytelling. There would be all manner of apple-related treats from hand pies to cider slushies to fritters and doughnuts. The celebration would conclude on Monday with a 5K road race and an afternoon parade.

Judd's would be one of the dozens of vendors. We'd be on hand, selling eight to ten different apple varieties to the tens of thousands of tourists who'd make their way through Kirby Falls for the festivities over the weekend. Our start time in the morning was around eight. Nick and Amy would be holding down the fort at the orchard with some part-time volunteers—mostly friends of theirs—while Candace, Brady, Joan, and I handled the festival, where the majority of the crowds would be.

"I'll walk you out," I told Candace.

Lightning bugs lit up in the distance as we made our way toward our vehicles. It was dark and cool, and the night was unbearably quiet. With feet crunching over the gravel of the parking lot, I felt very aware of the woman at my side.

Candace sneaked a glance in my direction and grinned before looking away. Sudden nerves buzzed beneath my skin, and a part of myself long-left ignored came roaring to life.

A normal person would notice her signals—the way she fiddled with her keys and delayed getting into her car. Any other man would see Candace nibbling on her bottom lip and think she was anticipating something.

She didn't know I wasn't a normal guy. That I didn't do this sort of thing. I didn't have drinks with women in my hometown or otherwise. I didn't go around waiting for signs and making moves. It had been a painfully long time since I'd kissed anyone.

Candace didn't know any of this because I hadn't told her. As far as she knew, I was two years off a divorce and a single dad who probably had some baggage. If she knew the truth, she'd know that my baggage had baggage, and nothing about my life was as it seemed.

That selfish, spiteful part of me reared its ugly head once more. Why shouldn't I get to act my age? I should have been able to lean in and kiss this woman. To still her nervous hands and slide my palm around her waist, tug her close, and breathe in her lavender scent. Feel the soft hairs at her temple as I pressed my lips there first.

Instead, I was thinking about how Candace didn't know the truth about me, and how if anyone saw us together, it would reflect poorly on her.

But I deserved to be happy.

And right now, nothing would make me happier than closing the distance between us and tasting the cider on Candace Judd's lips.

My heart pounded out a vicious beat—an internal alarm, warning me of the danger ahead. But I didn't care. I wanted this. I wanted her.

So I shifted forward a half step and whispered, "Candace."

She stopped messing with her keys and glanced up at me through her lashes. "Mark," she answered shyly. Then her full lips spread in a grin as I leaned close.

Candace's fingers gripped my nape as she rose up on tiptoes to meet me halfway. My nose brushed hers gently, and my hand did manage to find the dip in her waist as I worked to steady myself.

Then suddenly, a car door slammed somewhere nearby, followed by loud, abrasive laughter. Candace gasped in surprise, and we broke apart abruptly, like two teenagers caught in a backseat.

She met my gaze and then huffed out a little laugh.

"Sorry," I murmured and pulled my own keys out of my pocket.

"Why are you sorry?" she asked with a sassy twinkle in her eye. "They should be the ones apologizing."

I'd almost kissed Candace in a parking lot of a popular establishment where anyone could have seen. I knew how fast gossip traveled in this town.

What had I been thinking?

With nothing more than the promise of a kiss, I took an even bigger step back.

I could still feel her hand on my neck, her breath warm on my lips, the way she'd whispered my name—both a question and an answer.

Squeezing my fist around the key ring, I forced myself to look at her. To remember my place and what I had no business wanting. "I should get going."

Her embarrassed amusement gave way to confusion. "But—"

"Good night, Candace. I'll see you in the morning."

It took everything in me to turn and walk away. I didn't wait for my statement to land. I could hear the finality in my tone, and I knew she heard it too.

It was instinct to want to open her door and make sure she got on her way safely. But I didn't want to see the disappointment I'd caused. I didn't want to hear her questions or have to spell this out for her. I was a coward.

The night ended in something crueler than disappointment. It was a painful reminder. A wake-up call. I wasn't a normal guy, and I didn't deserve to be happy if I stole it from someone else. I would only mess things up for Candace.

The town pariah didn't kiss the hometown sweetheart.

And I needed to remember that.

When I got to Main Street the following morning, everything was already set up and ready to go. The volunteers must have been through at sunrise because neat rows of white tents lined either side of the street as vendors worked to unload their goods and set up their booths.

The Judd's Orchard tent was large and positioned directly beside the one for Grandpappy's. Will Clark was busy, unloading apples onto their tables.

As I approached, I noticed Joan and Candace were already present and accounted for as well as a big cardboard stand-up of a shiny red cartoon apple wearing a cowboy hat. I frowned, wondering what that was all about. It looked like one of those photo ops with a hole cut out for people to stick their faces through. Based on the size of the apple and the height of the face hole, I assumed this was for kids, and judging by the way Joan was eyeing it, I guessed the giant apple was Candace's idea.

Joan caught my gaze and rolled her eyes before turning back to where Candace lingered, clearly awaiting instructions. "I'll be back with the dolly. You two put the tablecloths on." And then she took off to where she'd parked the work truck.

Candace's wide hazel eyes darted to me. She looked wary, and I fucking hated that I'd put that expression on her face.

"Good morning," I said, making sure my smile was genuine and not as tight as my chest felt.

"Hey," she replied, and *her* smile was nonexistent.

I pointed to the cardboard apple. "What you got there?"

"Oh, it's for photos. I thought kids would like it. And it has all our social media handles on it for advertising. The parents can tag us, and I'll share the photos. Good for content."

"I like it," I told her sincerely. "It's a good idea."

"Thanks," she replied tentatively. Then Candace moved to the stacked gingham tablecloths that her sister had indicated.

I quickly stepped forward and grabbed the other end of the one she held, helping her spread the fabric across the surface of a long white table, desperate for some normalcy.

So, we'd almost kissed. It wasn't the end of the world. And it didn't even need to be the end of our friendship.

Things didn't need to get weird.

But the silence stretched like a rubber band pulled taut, just waiting to snap.

I could hear the shuffle of bodies and vendors chatting as they set up. Birds sang in the background and the cool morning breeze made the tablecloth rustle.

What you couldn't hear were the things I wanted to say. The way I felt twisted up with the need to explain myself. How I wanted to tell Candace I was sorry about last night—taking off that way—and that I'd had a really good time with her. I always had a good time when I was with her.

But I couldn't admit any of that. It would only lead to more questions and more lies. I couldn't be honest with her, and that wasn't fair.

Joan made her way back with the first load of apples, and Candace and I got to work organizing them on the tables to sell in pecks, half pecks, and quarter pecks. Joan was going back for a third load right around the time Brady strolled in with four coffees in a drink tray.

"Good morning," he called. "I brought caffeine."

"Thank you," Candace said. "And there's mini muffins in a bag beneath the table. A really friendly volunteer brought them by earlier."

Brady squatted to retrieve them. "Great. I'm starving."

A few moments of uninterrupted work later, Brady said conversationally, "Hey, Candy Cane. Why does your apple cutout have a cowboy hat?"

Candace turned to face her brother. "Because it's a small-town apple festival, that's why."

"Who do you know who wears a cowboy hat?" Brady challenged.

"Well, I don't know. People, I'm sure."

"This ain't Texas."

She huffed in annoyance. "Who cares? It looks cute with the hat on top. I like it, okay?"

"I like it too," I found myself saying suddenly. It worked to quiet the bickering siblings, but now I had both their attention. Candace didn't look convinced, and Brady looked delighted, which was never a good sign.

"Well, if you like it so much," Brady began, "I'll take your picture, and Candace can post it. You can be the first one to pose with the Cowboy Apple."

Attention and public scrutiny were the last things I wanted.

I glanced to Candace, who suddenly looked amused.

The threat of her cool reserve from earlier helped make up my mind.

"Fine." I nodded and crossed behind the Cowboy Apple. Crouching low and feeling like an idiot, I stuck my face through the cutout.

"Smile," Brady ordered cheerfully as he lined up the shot for far longer than was necessary. "Got it! They'll love this."

"Text me that," I heard Candace call out as I straightened. She wore a devious smirk.

Brady laughed and then moseyed around the side of the tent, face glued to his phone.

Heat was creeping up my cheeks, but Candace didn't look quite as standoffish as she had earlier in the morning. If I needed to embarrass myself on social media by posing with a giant apple to restore the peace, I guess that was fine.

Candace came to stand next to me. We worked in silence for a moment, packing apples into bags and lining them up on the table next to signs designating their variety.

"Thanks for being a good sport," she said, smiling.

"Of course," I murmured. "It was nothing."

"I won't really post it."

Her words loosened the anxiety building. Even if I thought I could handle the attention, I still didn't want it. Avoidance was second nature at this point in my life.

"Thanks," I finally replied.

We resumed our work, but I could tell it was there on the tip of her tongue. A question about last night. A desire to clear the air. The space between us vibrated with things unsaid.

I couldn't give her everything, but I could say something to ease the sudden tension that hadn't been there since that very first day when she hadn't remembered me.

I cleared my throat. "I had a good time last night . . . with you at Firefly." Candace's hand paused around a Golden Delicious apple. "I'm sorry I had to take off the way I did. But . . . but it's probably better that way."

Her hand finally gripped the apple, and she loaded it into a half-peck bag with the others. "I see."

I took a risk and bumped my elbow with hers. "If you have any more events on the calendar, let me know. I'll help out. I want to."

There was a brief pause before she tapped my elbow in return and replied, "Okay. If you're sure."

Keeping my eyes forward on the box of produce, I gave Candace another half-truth. "That's what friends are for."

Eventually, things got busy and I didn't have time to worry about what Candace was thinking. The four of us worked to stay stocked and to keep up with the lines of customers snaking down the side of our tent as the crush of bodies moved up and down Main Street.

With a positive attitude and a brilliant smile, Candace chipped in wherever she was needed. She took direction from Joan and worked tirelessly all day. She restocked apples and sold them to customers. Candace was friendly with the tourists and always stepped in to answer questions or talk up the orchard, undoubtedly knowing how much Joan hated upselling.

It was honestly a little hard to watch the way Candace so blatantly sought her older sister's approval. But Joan was truly oblivious, just going about her work and keeping her head down. Candace kept her spirits up, and I tried not to wince at every thoughtless, unintentional jab Joan made.

It wasn't until day one of the Orchard Festival was winding down that everything went to shit. The opening band had already taken the stage for tonight's concert. Even from three blocks away, we could hear the strum of the guitar and the beat of drums. Foot traffic had dwindled in the last half hour as people made their way to the end of Main Street that housed the stage and the food trucks. As a result, we were already packing up.

Eloise Carter, the formidable head of the Festival Planning Committee, stopped in front of our booth as the sun crept closer to the horizon, clipboard in hand and stern expression eating into the lines of her face. "Good afternoon. Where are Nick and Amy? I wanted to have a word."

Candace and Brady had taken the dolly and the first load of crates back to the truck, so it was just Joan and me left to speak with Ms. Carter.

"They're handling the farm this weekend while the rest of us see to the festival," Joan said, barely sparing the older woman a glance as she worked.

Eloise was no-nonsense and by the book. She was brutally honest and had no problem strong-arming people to get her way. She was probably after a permit for the Cowboy Apple or something else equally as tedious and ridiculous.

"I have some questions about their sponsorship."

Joan sighed and finally looked up. "Do you need their number, Ms. Carter? Pretty sure it's on your clipboard there." And then she gave one of the most powerful women in town her back and picked up another crate of apples.

It was times like this that I really appreciated Joan's general air of do-not-give-a-fuck. Eloise had a tendency to be an overbearing pain, but she'd met her match in the eldest Judd sibling.

The older woman eyed my co-worker for a moment, clearly displeased with the dismissal, before her laser focus zeroed in on me. "And you, Mr. Mercer. I suppose it's fortunate for the Judds that you aren't too busy with your familial obligations to tend to your work duties this weekend."

The implication landed as effectively as a slap across the face.

Familial obligations.

Right, the child she believed I was neglecting or not supporting or whatever bullshit gossip was circulating.

I was still frozen in shock at her blatant insult, but I registered the sound of a crate hitting the ground hard behind me.

Joan's voice was deceptively soft as she stepped up beside me, worn work boots even with my own. "Did you just—"

I halted her with a hand on her arm. Icy blue eyes met mine, and I shook my head. "It's okay. I got it."

After a bracing breath, I said flatly, "Ms. Carter, you'll need to reach out directly to Nick or Amy. We're packing up here and heading out, but we'll let them know you're looking to get in touch. Have a nice night, ma'am."

I waited until the woman made a note on her clipboard and then walked off to ruin someone else's day.

With a rough inhale, I turned to the rear of the booth, desperate to avoid any lingering festivalgoers. I needed a minute to steady myself, so I started breaking down empty boxes.

"Are you okay?" Joan asked as she approached. She took the box away from me. "You're not thinking straight. We need those for tomorrow's produce to bring back in the morning."

Shit. "You're right. I'm sorry." I took my shaky hands and stuffed them into the front pockets of my jeans to keep from balling them in angry fists. It was stupid to still let this shit get to me.

"I don't care about the boxes," Joan insisted as she did her best to catch my eye. "She had no right to say that to you. Damn busybody with nothing better to do than try to make herself feel important."

"It's fine."

"It's not fine," she argued. "She was running her mouth for no other reason than knowing it would get to you. Don't let her under your skin. She doesn't know you. She doesn't matter."

I huffed a humorless laugh. "Teach me how to not give a fuck, would you, Joanie?"

"It's a ten-week course," she replied deadpan. "I don't know if you could handle it."

That had my laugh from a moment ago turning genuine.

I finally met Joan's gaze and was disturbed to find it soft and concerned.

"I'm okay. Really," I tried to assure her.

Joan gave my arm a comforting squeeze—the most affectionate she ever really got. "Say the word and I'll steal my neighbor's goat and let it go to town on her award-winning roses."

Smiling, I nodded. "Let's keep workshopping it."

"I have a whole notebook full of revenge plots," she said seriously. "I'll add it to the list."

That reminded me of Candace and the worn notebook she carried with her everywhere, jotting down ideas as they struck. Maybe these two sisters weren't so different after all.

I peeked beyond Joan to see that Brady still hadn't returned. Candace had come back at some point and was busying herself boxing up the Judd's Orchard tee shirts we'd bring back to sell tomorrow.

"I'm gonna go help your sister."

"Okay," Joan said. "I'm going to go drag Brady away from the Grandpappy's tent by his ear."

I glanced over to see that she was right. Brady was parked in front of the Clarks' booth, leaning on the two-wheel dolly we needed to finish loading up for the night. He and Mac were locked in some sort of debate, but that was par for the course with those two. Mac had enough family members around her to prevent any real bloodshed. Actually, there was a cup full of straws on the table in front of her. She could probably do something lethal and inventive involving Brady's trachea that would, no doubt, finally shut him up.

"Yeah, better go rescue him, for his own good."

When I made my way over to Candace, she was nearly done with the merch.

"Thanks for packing that stuff up," I said.

Despite the awkwardness of this morning, Candace and I had worked pretty seamlessly throughout the day. She hadn't just been upbeat with the tourists. I'd been on the receiving end of her smiles as well.

"Oh," she squeaked, fumbling the shirt she'd been folding. "Of course. No problem at all."

She wouldn't meet my gaze, and I wondered if we were back to being weird with each other now that there weren't customers around. I didn't think she'd overheard my conversation with Joan from the back of the tent. Maybe she—

But then Brady and Joan were back, and there wasn't much time to get Candace alone to talk to her or gauge her reaction. We had to finish up so we could go home, then get up and do it all over again tomorrow.

As Candace kept her head down and avoided conversation for the rest of the afternoon, I tried not to let myself wonder about the alternative.

What if we'd kissed last night? Would we have flirted and teased today behind the scenes? Shared secret smiles and found ways to be in each other's space?

Catching sight of Eloise Carter in her bright green volunteer shirt down the street, I shook my head and forced those *what-might-have-been* thoughts away, grateful for the reminder.

I'd done the right thing taking a step back with Candace. It would keep her reputation and hometown sweetheart status intact. She didn't need gossipmongers like Eloise Carter catching wind of something brewing between us. She didn't need to be guilty by association.

Keeping her in the friend zone would keep her safe.

No matter how much I wished for more.

CANDACE

"So, you saw them what? Being affectionate? In a passionate embrace? Eye-fucking? Break it down for me, Candace."

I quickly swallowed the pizza roll I was eating and sucked in a cooling breath as the too-hot cheese threatened to blister my tongue. "Ow. Crap. No, I mean. Not really."

"How would you describe it, then?" Bonnie asked again.

It was Sunday night after another busy day at the Orchard Festival, and Bonnie had tomorrow off from teaching since it was Labor Day. The farm wasn't open to tourists on Mondays, and as exhausted as I was from working the festival all weekend, I was up for a late night with my new friend.

We currently had on moisturizing mud masks while we ate like frat boys on the living room floor of the garage apartment. The television was on in the background with a *Psych* rerun, but we weren't really paying attention. It didn't matter, I'd seen this episode like four times.

I'd confessed to Bonnie the scene I'd walked in on Saturday afternoon between Mark and my sister. I needed someone else's perspective. I needed to know if I was seeing something where nothing existed, or if I was simply freaking out because of the almost-kiss. Bonnie was playing the role of sounding board and reality wrangler while I let my imagination run away with me and scarfed down pizza rolls at an alarming rate.

"I don't know. I got a vibe," I tried to clarify. "Joan was squeezing his arm, and they were smiling together."

My sister was not an affectionate person, so voluntary touching was notable.

"They looked cozy," I added, sounding glum to my own ears.

"And you're jealous," Bonnie said without judgment before she popped her own pizza roll into her mouth.

I shifted uncomfortably, crossing my pink-pajama-clad legs. "I guess I thought we had a moment the other night. Mark's lips had been like a millimeter away from mine before we got interrupted. But then he practically set a new land-speed record getting away from me."

"Almost like he suddenly realized he had a girlfriend and probably shouldn't be Frenching her sister," Bonnie said.

"Exactly."

Although, I had a hard time imagining my grumpy sister actually getting laid and still being in such a terrible mood all the time. Annnd I should definitely not be thinking about Mark and assuming the sex would be good. Even though I knew it would be. He was good at everything. And so strong and capable, yet sensitive and attentive.

God, maybe that was why Joan had been so cold and angry since I'd returned to Kirby Falls. I'd been spending a lot of time with Mark—working the farmers' market and tackling the new projects for the orchard together. He'd even stood up for me at the staff meeting and backed me on my ideas. I bet Joan could tell I had a crush on him. I resisted the urge to hide my face in my hands.

The thought of being the *other woman* once again made me want to barf up my pizza rolls.

Bonnie paused with her wineglass halfway to her lips. "But why would they be hiding a relationship? They're both adults. Why keep it a secret?"

I considered that for a moment while I chewed another gooey, cheesy bite. "Maybe because they work together?"

"It's not like your family farm has an HR department," Bonnie countered.

"I don't know. Could be because of all the rumors about his divorce and his daughter. Or maybe he's just a really private person."

The truth was I didn't know for sure what was going on between Mark and my sister. But I did know that following our near-kiss at Firefly the other night, Mark had some very obvious buyer's remorse. If the runaway-bride act hadn't clued me in, the deliberate *nothing-to-see-here* vibes the following day had done it. Like a restaurant hostess, Mark had seated me firmly in the friend zone. I wasn't about to beg. If he had reservations—Joan-related or not—then I wasn't going to force it.

We worked together, and I had a life I needed to get back to. A career that was sure to take me out of sight and out of mind in a few short months. No need to make my time in Kirby Falls awkward.

Yet, to myself and maybe Lance Bass, I could admit that I had fun with Mark. Closing out that night at Firefly with a kiss would have been pretty fantastic. Yes, I was attracted to him. Who wouldn't be? He had that whole *gentle giant* thing going on. Kind, soft-spoken, competent, and able to bench-press the John Deere tractor out back. Plus, his rock-hard thighs didn't hurt either. I wanted him to wrap me up in his strong arms and kiss me on the forehead . . . and other places.

But if he wanted to be just friends, that was okay too. I could do that. And if he was secretly dating my sister, he needed to be a little more careful who he brushed noses with.

Bonnie's phone buzzed from the coffee table, halting the conversation, which was, honestly, probably a good thing. I should stop discussing Mark and rambling about Mark and thinking about Mark.

She snatched up her cell and read the screen. Her teeth chewed on her bottom lip as she typed out a careful response. Suddenly, I worried that my invitation to hang out tonight had started an argument with her husband.

I didn't want to be nosy, but the frown on her green-mud-mask-spackled face was pretty severe. "Everything okay? Do you need to go?"

Bonnie's brown eyes met mine and she forced a smile. "No. I'm staying here with you. We're having a girls' night." Then her phone buzzed once more and her gaze hardened. Her thumbs flew across the screen as she texted.

"There's nothing wrong with taking a little time for myself," she gritted out before turning the screen off and placing the device facedown on the table.

"Definitely," I agreed cautiously. I wondered what that was all about, but I didn't want to push if she didn't want to talk about it.

After the all-caps text message I'd accidentally seen back at the shaved ice shack, I'd gotten a vibe about Bonnie's husband. When she'd first arrived tonight, I'd asked after Danny, but Bonnie had given me a pretty vague "he's fine" in response. I kind of got the impression he took his sweet, thoughtful wife for granted. I didn't want to cause trouble for my new friend, but I also thought she deserved a night out, or night *in* as it were.

Instead of making things awkward, I checked the time and said, "We should probably wash this goop off our faces. Twenty minutes was up a while ago."

Bonnie prodded at the dried concoction covering her chin. "I'd be okay if it shrank my pores down to nothing. Most days I feel like they're visible from the International Space Station."

I laughed. "Come on. Let's rinse and then we can switch it over to your *Sons of Anarchy* show."

"Yes, please. You're going to love it." She let out a dreamy little sigh. "There is just something about a bad boy on a motorcycle."

I couldn't help but think of the photo of Bonnie's husband, Danny, on her lock screen. He was a thin white guy with a receding hairline and a new mustache he was trying out. He looked like the furthest thing from a leather-wearing MC member you could possibly get.

But maybe the fantasy was just something you squealed over with your girl-friends. Maybe the you who fantasized about bad-boy bikers was just as fictional as the fantasy itself. You didn't go home with the guy on the television screen. Daydreams looked different for everyone, and they seldom compared to reality.

My own whispered fantasy had taken the shape of someone so unexpected that teenage Candy wouldn't have known what to think. But here I was, twenty-five years old, back in my hometown, and crushing on a certifiable blast from the past. A man with quiet words, a deep voice, and a kind heart.

A man who was maybe involved with my sister.

Sometimes the fantasy was safer in your own head, like Bonnie's fixation on dangerous bikers.

I passed her a hand towel and said, "Amen to that."

The following weekend, I found myself in the foggy early morning setting up for a birthday party at the farm. Little Aiden Dorsey was turning five and, according to his grandmother, had a thing for tractors.

This was my third event since updating the Judd's Orchard website with details for party rentals. It was actually a pretty easy gig, and something I could manage for my folks on my own.

The parties took place during regular weekend business hours. I simply arrived early to mark the picnic tables reserved and set them up with party decorations, cups of fresh apple cider, and take-home baskets for each guest to pick up to three pounds of apples. All the party hosts needed to do was have their attendees show up. I welcomed everyone, stored any gifts, and slapped wristbands on the children planning to jump on the bounce pillow.

It was easy enough to accompany the party out to the fields and ensure they were going to the rows marked *Ripe for Picking*. The kids also liked it when I did a little demonstration on the best way to pick apples. Sometimes I hung around and snapped pictures for busy parents. It was fun, and I really enjoyed this part of my job. Making people happy and helping them make memories never got old.

We had at least one party on the schedule every weekend between now and our new closing date of January 1. Joan had agreed to stay open through December and set up the Christmas tree lot to see how things went. She wasn't ready to plant our own Fraser firs, but I'd found a tree farm north of Weaverville to supply us with trees to sell this year. I was feeling very hopeful.

Sales had been good since the farm opened for the season nearly a month ago. The two Friday Night Food Truck events had been well received, bringing in local families and out-of-towners alike. The cider-and-apple-pairing event at Firefly had been a huge success. We had two other local collaborations coming up in as many weeks, and it was my hope that we'd close out September with a nice net profit for the farm.

As I was straightening the confetti-patterned tablecloth on the first picnic table, I saw Mark approaching from the corner of my eye. It was chilly this mid-September morning, and he wore a dark green flannel over his Judd's Orchard tee shirt. He'd skipped the ball cap today, and I could see that his dark blond hair was freshly trimmed. Those blue-gray eyes zeroed in on me, and I forced myself to take a centering breath as I tugged the plastic tablecloth into place.

Mark and I hadn't spoken since the Orchard Festival's Sunday afternoon street fair last week. We'd both been busy with our respective duties this week. September was the most hectic time of year on an apple farm. Most of our varieties were ripe and ready for harvest. And there was the fact that I'd been avoiding him just a little bit.

But I couldn't really avoid him now.

"Hey," Mark said, voice rough with the memory of sleep. "I saw you had a party on the schedule. Thought I'd come help set up."

"Oh, thank you."

I didn't really know how to feel about that, but I did know I was tired of the strained conversation and my cowardly desire to hide out and avoid thinking about Mark and his lips and his lips in proximity to my sister. I needed to do something about this so we could move forward. He was clearly trying to put us back on solid *co-worker* ground. I needed to buck up and do the same.

"How many are coming?" he asked, eyeing the stack of baskets I had ready to go.

"Thirteen kids and their corresponding adults. Won't be too bad."

He started placing the balloon weights equidistant down the center of the long table. I used them to keep the tablecloths from flapping in the wind or flying away altogether. "Saw it was Ellie Dorsey's son's party."

I frowned. "The grandmother did all the communicating with me. I didn't realize."

Before I could comment further, Mark grinned. "I don't know if you remember, but she was in our grade. Star basketball player. Red hair. Ringing any bells?"

I whipped a paper plate at him like a Frisbee, and he laughed, catching it against his chest.

Grinning back, I asserted, "Yes, I remember Ellie." We'd been on the debate team together. I didn't realize she had a son though.

If Mark was back to giving me shit over forgetting high school classmates, then maybe this awkwardness over almost kissing wouldn't last forever. Perhaps we were on the other side of it.

"I can't believe Ellie has a five-year-old. That feels wild for someone our age." I froze, realizing what I'd said, unsure how Mark would take it. *He* had a child who was at least a few years old.

But he didn't react visibly or stiffen up the way I half expected. He just kept setting down cups decorated with apple-shaped polka dots at each place setting. "Yeah, I think her parents helped out a lot when her son was born."

"Back in New York, my friends would have thought it was crazy to have a baby before you were thirty-five. They used to joke that I practically wanted to be a child bride."

I didn't know why but heat was creeping up my neck at the admission and how callous it sounded. It didn't paint my friends—acquaintances and co-workers, really—in a very good light.

Mark looked up. "Were you engaged or something?"

It was one of the things that always made me feel out of place. People I'd interned with, or gone through graduate school alongside, could never understand why I wanted to start a family in the early stages of my career. After a while, I stopped telling people. It set me apart and made me feel like I didn't fit in. The country bumpkin with rural inclinations showing through her dressed-up city-girl costume. In reality, I was probably lonely and desperate for a semblance of family and the constancy of a committed, monogamous relationship.

But dating was hard in the city without putting your expectations out there from the get-go. I hadn't been in the market for a good time or something short-term.

That was part of the reason I'd been so disappointed by Emerson's deception. I'd thought there was good potential for a future with him. I'd assumed we were going somewhere. He was nearly thirty-six years old, after all. Turned out he was interested in having kids, just not particularly committed to keeping his marriage vows.

I pushed away the disgust I still felt at my horrible judgment.

"No," I said as I focused on my work and not on Mark watching me. "My friends just knew I wanted kids. There's a five-year plan in my notebook and everything. A family is on there."

When I risked a glance, Mark was frowning down at the stack of red napkins he held. I didn't know what I could have said that had him making that face, but I really wanted to stop talking about this and stop thinking about how far behind I was on that five-year plan.

"We have ten more parties booked for the season," I told Mark, moving over to decorate the final picnic table.

He moved with me, taking the other end of the tablecloth to spread it wide. "That's really great."

"It got me thinking about interest in educational tours and field trips for local schools. Depending on the grade level and group size, we could offer short, informative talks. You know, the life cycle of the apple, types of apples, bees and the importance of pollinators, that sort of thing. And then the kids could jump on the bounce pillow and pick apples to take home to their families."

Mark had paused partway through my speech. Now, he rushed to smooth the edge of the plastic tablecloth down. "That would be a good plan to implement in the future. I imagine it's too late to set something like that up this season, but maybe next year, if we find the right person interested in leading it."

I nodded, but his words caused something to twist uncomfortably in my belly. I didn't want someone else assuming the role of educator at the orchard. These strange proprietary feelings were unexpected. I was honestly jealous of this nameless, faceless person implementing my plan, which was just as irrational as it was ridiculous. I wouldn't be here next year. Of course, it couldn't be me. I was working the farm this season—*now*. It was selfish to want the role for myself when I knew I couldn't keep it.

My gaze strayed to Mark, where he was placing the apple baskets at each child's seat. His eyes found me watching him and he smiled, just one of his tiny, barely there grins that tilted the corners of his full lips.

Yeah, sometimes life wasn't fair and you didn't get what you wanted.

Feeling the need to get things back on the right track—the one to clearly labeled and boundary-inclusive Friendship Town—I cleared my throat. "Thanks for helping me set up for the party."

He made an amused sound, and I spotted his even white teeth as his smile widened. "It's sort of my job."

"Your job doesn't start for twenty more minutes," I argued.

A blush washed his face in sudden color, and Candace from last Friday would have given just about anything to know what thoughts heated those scruffy cheeks.

But then I caught sight of my sister in the distance. She was driving the tractor and hauling the giant apple crate out into the north fields. Fuji was on the schedule for picking this week. Mark would be out there with her.

Time to steer this ship into safer waters. "I appreciate your help," I said around a closed-mouth smile that doubled as a convenient shield. With my eyes carefully trained on his, I added, "You're a good friend, Mark."

At my words, he went utterly still. Mark watched me for a long moment before shoving his hands into the front pockets of his jeans. He nodded slowly. "Of course. Happy to help."

We finished setup fifteen minutes later. I thanked Mark again and watched him head off the way Joan had gone to start his own workday.

I'd done the right thing by establishing a boundary.

Even if I was wrong and Mark and Joan weren't together officially or openly or even at all, I didn't want my time here in Kirby Falls to be filled with drama and bad decisions. I didn't want the almost-kiss hanging over me like that—a fantasy, a daydream, a what-might-have-been.

Making it clear that we were back in friend territory was the safest way forward. He should know I was fine with that. There was no need to worry about me bringing it up. I wasn't going to jump him or something, no matter how attracted I was to him.

I had no desire to fuck things up even more with Joan. I wanted to prove myself to my sister. Show her I was a helpful member of the team, a good worker, someone she could rely on. So, maybe eventually, Joan might stop resenting me for being here.

I came home to get myself together and out of trouble.

Not cause more.

CANDACE

"What is that?"

I winced as Brady came to stand beside me on the dew-covered grass.

He took a step toward one of the pallets of two- to four-pound pumpkins. "Are these the ones for the pumpkin patch?"

A flush was climbing a rope ladder up my sternum, shaky and uneven.

I tried to clear the rising panic from my throat, but my brother spoke again before I could manage it. "Why are they so small?"

I stared at the bins that the delivery driver had unloaded behind the Apple House and willed them to be right. However, the roughly four hundred pie pumpkins didn't magically grow into jack-o'-lanterns perfect for a pumpkin patch. They stayed small and uncarvable. And if you listened closely, you could hear their little orange bodies saying, *Way to go, Candace*.

"I—"

"What the hell is this?" my sister's voice interrupted as she joined us in the early-morning sunshine.

I gave up and closed my eyes.

Ignoring the sound of approaching footsteps, I tried to figure out how to explain this monumental fuckup.

It was actually what I'd been doing before my brother had approached. That and frantically checking the invoice from Owensby Acres on my phone.

A light touch at my elbow had my eyes opening.

"Hey," Mark said quietly. "You okay?"

I hadn't realized he was also present and accounted for to witness my humiliation.

Things had been going so well too. In the past two weeks, Judd's Orchard had been booming with business. The birthday parties, Food Truck Fridays, and other events I'd been planning were doing so well. Regular posting and advertising on social media had brought tourists in by the droves. I'd even gotten a travel influencer on board to feature the farm this month on their channels.

And now that October was right around the corner, I'd been expecting this delivery from Owensby Acres so I could get the pumpkin patch set up and sorted this week.

Yet, the squash we were all staring at was another mistake for the Candace Judd Well-Meaning Hall of Fame.

"Candace," Mark tried again.

This time I was able to swallow around my embarrassment and nod. "I'm okay. Just surprised."

"Why would you order sugar pumpkins, Candy?" Joan had her hands on her hips as she walked between the pallets inspecting their contents. "They're good for making pie and not much else. How are we supposed to make a pumpkin patch out of these?"

"It was a misunderstanding. I'm so sorry."

"Did you buy tiny Christmas trees too?"

"Of course not," I replied automatically, but I made a mental note to check the order with Skytop Farm.

My mouth was dry, but I did my best to make my voice even when faced with my sister's obvious irritation and disappointment. "I'll fix this, Joanie. I'll call the vendor and see if they'll exchange them for carving pumpkins."

Her gaze narrowed in suspicion. "Did you order them from Grandpappy's like I told you to? I can't imagine Will would let you get hundreds of pie pumpkins without double-checking that's what you actually wanted."

"Well, no," I replied. "I mean, I tried. I called over to Grandpappy's, but all their surplus was spoken for this season. They were happy to put us down for next year though."

"Next year," Joan repeated flatly.

I couldn't know what she was actually thinking, but part of me wondered if she'd envisioned the pumpkin patch—and the rest of my ideas—as a passing fancy that she had to simply endure until I was gone again.

Ignoring the ache those thoughts produced, I admitted, "So I went with Owensby Acres off of Will Clark's recommendation. The price was nearly the same. I just didn't realize . . ." *That they were the wrong variety of pumpkin* went unsaid.

Mark hadn't moved from my side, and I was grateful for it because, from this angle, I didn't have to see the disappointment that was likely on his face.

Joan sighed and shook her head before walking off, and the sight made all my edges go brittle and weak.

A moment later, Brady's face entered my field of vision. He wore a *well, shit* expression. With a half-hearted punch to my shoulder, my brother said, "Tough luck, Candy Cane. You'll figure it out though. Let me know if you need help moving them." And then he, too, was gone.

Thankfully my parents hadn't wandered over to the farm yet. Then again, it might be best to get the humiliation over with in one fell swoop with all the orchard employees at once. It wasn't that my mom and dad would be angry. No, they'd be understanding and kind. And that was almost worse.

I couldn't believe I'd made such a stupid mistake.

When I could no longer take Mark's quiet, stalwart presence at my side, I finally looked over to find him watching me.

"I really messed this one up, huh?"

His blue-gray eyes were soft. "When I first started, I pressed a batch of apples that I thought Joan had set aside for that purpose. Turned out those were supposed to be bagged up and used as pre-picked for the store."

I winced. Typically, we pressed apples that had imperfections or were too small. The pretty apples, or the ones up to standard for selling, were sorted separately.

"Joan eventually got over it. Nick and Amy understood. Brady gave me shit about it for a couple of days. And I never made that particular mistake again." Mark tapped my elbow once more. "It doesn't feel like it right now, but it *will* be okay."

I nodded. He was right. In the grand scheme of things, this was a blip. But when you'd worked your whole life to be perfect, anything less than that was a personal affront. Not to mention how important it was to me to help my family and prove myself to my sister.

Rationally, I knew it was okay to make mistakes. People made them all the time. But there was a vicious little gremlin in my head that said it was okay for everyone else . . . but not for me. My brain fed and watered and tended that little gremlin like it was blue-ribbon livestock down at the county fair, and there wasn't a damn thing I could do about it.

I appreciated what Mark was trying to do though. He was kind to commiserate with me and share his own experience. And it was nice that he wasn't making me feel like an idiot.

"Thanks, Mark," I finally replied.

After heaving a sigh of epic proportions, I realized I'd need somewhere to put the three pallets of pumpkins. They were blocking the employee entrance to the Apple House where Mark and Joan brought in the apples for grading and wash-ing. Shit. What was I going to do?

And like he'd read my mind, Mark smiled and said, "Now then. You want to learn how to drive a forklift?"

Owensby Acres wouldn't take the pumpkins back.

But I came up with some solid plans to move the produce.

We would still be selling them in the Apple House throughout the month of October. I was currently working on setting up a mini pumpkin patch for kids. Complete with little wheelbarrows and tiny hay bales. Textbook adorable.

We were selling some of our squash at a discount to the local elementary school, thanks to Bonnie. She was going to do a pumpkin-painting project with all her students and had money in the budget to take over one hundred pumpkins off our hands. I'd kissed her on the forehead when she told me.

Mom and I were also taking orders for pumpkin pies for Thanksgiving. I was planning to help with those, and my mother was using it as an opportunity to turn me into a baker. Surprising the pumpkin spice right out of me, my brother volunteered to be on pie-making duty too. He said he was a natural and warned me not to get in his way in the kitchen. I fully planned on snapping him with a dish towel until he cried.

And, finally, now that the orchard had its liquor license, I was organizing a wine-and-pumpkin-decorating event for after hours in mid-October. That one was a small event for fifteen people, but it had already sold out. Honestly, I just really liked collaborating with Reggie and Aurora Holmes over at Lonely Mountain. They were wonderful people, and their wine was fantastic. We made a good team.

Despite the inauspicious beginnings of my pumpkin venture, I now felt confident that I could make this work. In the week following the delivery of the sugar pumpkins, I'd gotten the ball rolling on preparations for getting rid of them. All of them.

It was now Tuesday at the orchard—an off day from the public—and I was walking from the garage apartment over to my office in the Apple House. The early October morning was soft and gray, but I could tell it was going to be another stunning autumn day when the sun finally rose and burned away the low-lying cloud cover.

Following their harvest, the apple trees along the path were dotted with red and brown leaves, and the mountains in the distance were changing too. There was a patchwork of gold, orange, red, and maroon making a steady descent to lower elevations. It was a beauty to behold, and I couldn't believe I'd lived without this fall magic for so long. But it was more than the weather or the foliage. It was something special about my family and this farm. It was a sense of peace and comfort that had reignited in me when my plane had touched down and I'd breathed in my hometown for the first time in seven long years.

I didn't know if I could follow my six-step plan laid out in my trusty notebook and actually leave all this behind in three months. Maybe that was why I'd been dragging my feet on my job search. I hadn't even updated my résumé to include the work I'd been doing for the orchard—step two of six.

The truth was . . . I didn't want to leave. I didn't want to interview for a new position in a big city, be it New York or Atlanta or Nashville. I didn't want to pack my belongings and don my pantsuits and sit through budget meetings. I didn't want to work on a team where I was undervalued and taken advantage of and talked down to because of my age and my gender and my accent.

I wanted to read on the porch with my mother every morning. I wanted to work at the orchard with my siblings. I wanted to sit in that farmers' market booth until my butt went numb. I wanted to visit with my neighbors and get pizza at Apollo's. I wanted to get the pumpkin patch right next year. And I wanted to start field trips and lead educational tours on the farm.

None of it made a lick of sense, but there it was.

I also wanted to reminisce with my former teachers without getting a stomach ache and feeling like a walking failure. I didn't want to be one more high-performing child who failed to live up to their potential. Living and working in New York proved to my family and my town that I'd made something of myself.

Getting what I wanted, here in Kirby Falls, meant that all of the sacrifice and the schooling and the money and the quality education had been for nothing. That all my parents' hopes and dreams for me would be tossed aside so I could be something as inconsequential as . . . happy.

I shook my head, did my best to get rid of these pointless thoughts, and kept walking.

When I turned the corner on the dirt path, the Apple House came into view, and with it, three figures gathered around the side.

Mark, Brady, and Joan appeared to be staring at the exterior wall, the one that was on the other side of my office and faced the incoming gravel drive from the highway.

Curious, I approached. "What are y'all looking at?"

Brady scoffed. "I think it's obvious what it is."

"It is not shaped like the letter *M*, you asshat," Joan said in exasperation. It was the same tone she reserved for saying things she'd already damn well said. Ask me how I knew.

My eyes finally took in what I was seeing. The side of the Apple House was covered in little paint splatters. Vibrant reds, yellows, and blues stood out against the faded exterior of the whitewashed wood building.

I reached out to see if it was still wet, but Brady batted my hand away. "Don't do that. It's evidence. The sheriff's office is on their way. And then they'll likely make an arrest."

"Arrest who?" I said in surprise.

"It's obvious," my brother replied, crossing his arms in front of his flannel-covered chest. "The perpetrator behind this blatant and heinous act of vandalism was none other than MacKenzie Clark."

Mark groaned. "Come on, man. We've been over this."

Joan sighed loudly.

My gaze snapped to my brother. "What? Why would you think Mac would do such a thing?"

MacKenzie and my brother had been at each other's throats since birth. I didn't really know why, but they had a long history of pranks, torture, and general mayhem. However, I couldn't see the opinionated and sassy Clark cousin doing anything like this. Mischief and shenanigans were one thing—especially in the name of my brother's suffering—but this was something else. This was the destruction of property. This didn't impact just Brady. Paintballing our building affected Judd's Orchard and my family as a whole.

"Because she is a demon from hell. Plus, I've seen her shoot a paintball gun. This has her poor aim and indiscriminate attack pattern written all over it." He approached the splatters and gestured with his arms. "And if you look right here, it clearly forms an *M*."

I squinted and tilted my head. It did *not* clearly form an *M*.

"This is her calling card," Brady added. "She wanted me to know it was her."

My sister tipped her head up to the sky.

"Well, I don't see it," I said.

"Because it doesn't exist," Mark mumbled from where he'd covered his face with his hands.

"I don't have time for this," Joan said.

"That's right," Brady remarked decisively. "I'll handle it. You and Mark have Evercrisp and Cameos on the picking schedule this week. You go take care of that. And, Candy, you have the kids' pumpkin patch to finish up. I'll deal with the sheriff's department and give a statement. I'll get to the bottom of this. Don't you worry."

I winced. "Well, I wasn't really worried until you said that. But let me know when they're done. I have time this week. I can paint the exterior wall today and cover up the damage."

Brady ignored me at the sound of gravel crunching. Sure enough, it was an SUV from the sheriff's department. My brother took off in the direction of the vehicle, arms waving.

"Candy, do you think you can stick with him?" Joan asked. "I don't trust him not to be an idiot about this, and I don't want to worry Mom and Dad. They're taking the day off."

Shock flooded my system, but also a tiny little burning ember of hope. Joan asked me for help. Joan wanted me to handle something. She was still pretty standoffish in general since my return. After the tiny-pumpkin debacle, I was pretty sure she'd lost all faith in me.

"You—you want me to take care of it?" I stammered out.

She eyed me like she might be changing her mind already. "I have too much on my plate right now. Even you should be able to handle this."

I saw Mark flinch at my sister's statement, and admittedly, felt a pang of disappointment myself.

Even you.

That little flickering flame of hope felt a gust of wind, but it stayed lit.

Then Joan continued, "I figured you'd be able to help Boy Wonder over there deal with the sheriff's department. MacKenzie didn't do this. Probably some kids with nothing better to do, but I'd feel better if you kept an eye on Brady."

"I can do that," I readily agreed. "I'll head over now. You got it."

"Thanks," Joan said with a nod my way before she took off to start her day.

With a glance in Mark's direction, I saw he was watching me closely. "Good luck."

"Thanks," I said quietly.

Mark stuffed his hands into the front pocket of his jeans, a sympathetic smile lingering on his face. "I'll see you later."

Throwing a thumb over my shoulder, I said, "Yeah, I better get going too."

Rationally, I knew Joan only thought I was slightly more trustworthy and capable than our brother. But she'd still entrusted me with something. I was self-aware enough to know there was hope and sisterly devotion mixed up in there. Joan's attention was a spotlight burning a hole through my heart at center stage, and I didn't even care.

I would suffer through whatever stupidity Brady had locked and loaded and ready to go. I wouldn't let Joan down. She hadn't felt the need to handle it herself. She'd given me space in her life and the orchard, and I would take it— minimal as it was. Maybe it would lead to more. Conversations. Trust. A sisters-only group chat.

Okay, probably not that last one.

I just hoped I didn't crash and burn.

Three hours later I was feeling slightly less appreciative of the task I'd been given.

After I'd explained to the sheriff's deputies that, no, we did not have video surveillance on the property, they'd listened to my brother's long-winded explanation of events and then finally gone on their way with reassurances and promises to look into the matter.

Thankfully they'd agreed that it was likely bored teenagers and not our neighbor. Who, according to Brady, was a representative of our number one rival.

My brother had made it exactly forty-two minutes before he tried to get out of helping me paint over the vandalized wall by insisting on confronting Mac over at Grandpappy's. I'd told him he might hinder the investigation if he charged over there, accusations blazing. Then I'd rolled my eyes behind his back and grabbed the fresh paint can.

On the days when the orchard was closed to the public, we'd taken to eating lunch together at one of the picnic tables in front of the refreshment stand. Occasionally, Mom and Dad would join us, but mostly it was me, my siblings, and Mark in attendance.

Today, I was the last to arrive, and the only open seat was next to Mark.

With streaks of white paint dried on my worn jeans, I sat down at the table with last night's leftovers in my hand. I'd reheated a helping of Mom's baked penne in the microwave in my office.

It sounded like Brady and Joan were in the middle of a bickering match over my brother's vacation schedule. I ignored them and bumped Mark with my elbow, aiming for friendly and hitting the bullseye. "Hey, how are you?"

"Good," he replied quietly. "I'd ask how it went with the sheriff's department, but Brady already gave us the rundown while you were getting cleaned up."

I rolled my eyes and Mark chuckled, his shoulder brushing mine in the process.

"He is such an idiot," I muttered. And then I used the excuse of reaching for my water bottle to shift on the bench, putting a few more inches between our bodies. It felt safer that way. Friendlier.

The new distance didn't seem to matter because a moment later I felt Mark's thumb skim my temple and along the length of my jaw.

On a shuddering inhale, I pulled back in surprise to see Mark's waiting grin.

He lifted his hand to show me the paint on his thumb. "I think you missed a spot."

"Oh, geez." I released another unsteady breath. "I guess I did." I swallowed. "Thank you."

Mark held my gaze for a long moment before he nodded and went back to his lunch.

I could feel embarrassment flood my face. But I didn't really care about the white paint smudged across my skin. The reason for my sudden awkwardness was the way I'd reacted to Mark's simple touch.

Friends sat next to each other. They bumped legs and elbows and it was *fine*. Mark should have been able to casually wipe a drop of paint off my face without me making a big hairy deal out of it. Without my heart racing like a jackrabbit and my awareness dialing up to ten. I shouldn't have noticed the gentle way he'd touched me or how the rough pad of his thumb made my skin tingle. I needed to get myself together and remember my place.

Guiltily, I glanced at my siblings. At some point, the conversation had shifted to the opening of a new restaurant, but I caught up pretty quickly.

"It's in that little shopping center in Horse Shoe near the post office," Brady said after he'd finished chewing a bite of calzone.

"What's it called again?" I asked as I blew on a forkful of pasta and did my best to ignore the heat lingering in my cheeks.

"Flyers. It's Abby's new place. They serve wings and beer and the best rosemary fries you've ever had."

Abby was Cole Abernathy, my brother's best friend since kindergarten. They'd grown up going to school and playing soccer together. They'd even gone to the same college and roomed with one another in the dorms. Most friendships couldn't survive that, but nothing seemed to separate those two boneheads.

From what I'd gathered, Cole owned several successful restaurants in town and did everything from front-of-house management to cooking to bussing tables, whatever was needed. Flyers was just the newest one on his roster.

"Y'all are going, right?" Brady asked. "I told him we'd be there to support the grand opening."

"Sure. I'm in," I replied.

"I can't tomorrow," Joan said with no further explanation.

"What about you, Mercer? You coming?" Brady asked.

I eyed Mark discreetly. I could feel the side of his knee beneath the crowded picnic table, but I was ignoring it.

In the past few weeks, I'd been doing a lot of ignoring where Mark was concerned. We were firmly back in the friend zone, and that was safest for everyone. I was also ignoring the way that knowledge made me feel.

Maybe Mark was hesitating because he and Joan had plans—secret relationship plans—tonight. I shoved a bite of too-hot pasta in my mouth and then inhaled through the pain.

My eyes slid to Joan, who didn't seem to be giving Mark signals with her facial expression. She wasn't even looking at him. Her gaze was focused on her ham sandwich. I still wasn't sure what—or if—anything was going on there.

With another knee bump, Mark shifted uncomfortably and drew my attention again. "I don't know, man."

"Come on," my brother begged. "I'll buy you a beer. Abby's a friend. I want him to have a good turnout. Plus, I hear there's going to be a timed hot-wing-eating contest. I'll need moral support."

"Oh my God," I said with glee. "You should have led with that. I can't wait to see you suffer."

My idiot brother deserved it, too, after this morning with the whole MacKenzie-Clark-attacked-my-honor-and-my-home routine and the subsequent pouting. I couldn't wait to see him get his butt kicked in Scoville units.

Mark still looked unsure as he poked at his homemade rice bowl, but he eventually said, "Alright. I'll come."

Brady's grin was triumphant. He held his hand up for a high five, but Mark just gave him a look. Then my brother pivoted and held his palm out to me. I grinned and slapped it a little harder than was necessary.

"Damn," he whined, shaking out his hand. "Okay, this'll be great. Try to get there around six."

The following day, I had time to set up the hay bales for the pumpkin patch and put a second coat of paint on the side of the Apple House before I needed to shower and get ready for grand opening at Flyers.

The restaurant was packed with locals—plenty of residents I recognized. I loved that there were so many people here. Neighbors and families all present to support Cole. Even with the noise and the rowdy atmosphere, I had a smile on my face. There was something to be said for community and kinship.

After being away for the better part of a decade, I was surprised to find that I was comfortable in my hometown. I knew that sounded strange, but I'd never really experienced Kirby Falls as an adult, on my own terms. But here I was, waist-deep in my community and just as content here as I had been in Manhattan. I could drink a beer on a Saturday night or visit a food truck for dinner. Attend a restaurant opening where the staff wore matching tee shirts and people stood in line at a counter to order. It wasn't brunch in Brooklyn or a picnic in Central Park. But as much as I enjoyed my time up north, there was really no comparison.

I'd rather drink tea with my mother every morning than take my lunch break at the Met. While I was comfortable people-watching or reading on the subway, I'd rather walk through downtown Kirby Falls or drive along the highway with the mountains in the distance.

Both settings had a piece of my heart. Attending college in New York had helped me grow up, but Kirby Falls had raised me.

One was home, and the other was not. And my heart knew the difference.

Looking around now, I saw all these laughing, smiling residents, and I was flooded with the overwhelming sense of camaraderie and fellowship, neighborly love and devotion.

Smiling to myself, I took in the rest of the newly renovated space. The Flyers logo was front and center on the brick wall above the order counter, outlined in bright red LED lights. The menu was displayed on three screens overhead and showed all the various sauce options and heat levels.

I glanced around, looking for my brother, but I didn't see him. After a third person bumped into me and apologized, I made my way toward the back so I could get out of the main thoroughfare.

Mark was easy enough to spot in the crowded restaurant because he'd tucked himself in the corner at a booth for two and seemed to be the only point of stillness in the whole place.

"Mind if I join you?" I asked.

Mark looked up from his phone and straightened. "Of course not. Have a seat."

"Did you order yet?"

"No," Mark replied. "I saw them setting up for the contest and figured I'd wait until it died down a little."

My attention shifted, and, sure enough, there was a long table on the opposite wall being set up and covered with a vinyl tablecloth while people brought over chairs and placed them at intervals on one side. It looked like four brave souls were taking on the ghost pepper dry rub challenge.

"Apparently they have five minutes to finish five wings with no beverage. Anyone who completes the challenge gets a tee shirt and a free meal. But the person who does it the fastest gets their picture on the wall and a gift card."

I rubbed my hands together. "This is going to be good. Brady can't handle spicy food. I don't know what he's thinking entering this contest." Grinning, I added, "One time, when we were teenagers, someone dared him to eat a whole habanero. He barfed all night and wouldn't even touch a bell pepper for years afterward."

Mark laughed. "This should be interesting, then."

"Hey, Candy!" The unfamiliar voice caused me to startle in my seat.

When I turned, I found the grown-up version of a boy I hadn't thought about in years, standing beside our table.

Looking up, I smiled. "Hi, Jay. How are you?"

"I heard you were back in town," he said with a laugh, like he'd told a really funny joke.

Instinctively, my hackles rose. Was this going to be another awkward encounter where a former classmate wanted to reminisce or talk about my SAT scores?

"Yep," I replied. "I'm back in town."

"Remember that time you cut off all your hair in third grade? Everyone thought you looked like a boy. Man, I'd forgotten about that." Jay smiled dreamily.

My eyes widened because I had not been expecting that, and I wasn't sure if the embarrassing reminder was better or worse than rehashing my past accomplishments.

I finally settled on, "Yeah, wow. I'd forgotten too."

"You know—"

"I think we're going to grab some food," Mark interrupted with a hard look at the newcomer. "You have a good night now."

Jay stared at Mark like he hadn't even known he was there, and definitely didn't remember him from high school. But Jay must have had *some* social awareness because he eyed the muscles highlighting Mark's strength and presence, and wisely backed away. "Yeah, you too. See you around, Candy."

My finger drew a little squiggle on the varnished tabletop, and I laughed under my breath. "Thanks."

With a glance, I saw Mark watching me with a concerned expression. "I never liked that guy."

I smiled. "Well, it was a memorable haircut. Very unfortunate."

"Oh yeah?"

"Took two years to grow out," I admitted.

Mark's eyebrows drew together in sympathy.

"It even made the Humble Shelf."

"What's the Humble Shelf?"

My lips parted in surprise. "You haven't seen it?" He shook his head, still looking confused. "Well, it's this shelf in the living room of the farmhouse, on one of the built-in bookcases in the corner. Mom keeps childhood photos there— the really bad ones. Says it's to keep us humble. There's one of me with my unfortunate third-grade haircut. Another when Brady had braces and had to sleep in headgear." I laughed a little, remembering. "Oh and Joan at probably three or four during one of her birthday parties, surrounded by streamers and gifts and this Mickey Mouse cake, looking grumpy as hell, hating every minute of it."

"That's . . . wow. I can't say I ever saw Amy doing something like that."

"Well, it gets even better." I grinned. "It's basically her dream to show it to potential partners and embarrass me and my siblings. She wants to gauge how they might react and find them worthy or wanting. My mother, the romantic, thinks only someone who really loves you could love the unattractive, most awkward version of yourself. It obviously backfired anyway since we're all still single."

After my pronouncement, I watched Mark closely, curious if he'd have any sort of reaction. Surely someone who was in a secret relationship with my sister would make a face at hearing her called single. A secret smile, a narrowed gaze, *something*.

But, no. Mark just shook his head, his amusement plain at my mother's diabolical plans.

The sound of chairs scraping over linoleum had my attention going to the opposite end of the room.

"Looks like they're getting started," I said happily.

"Oh, no," Mark murmured.

"What is it?"

"Look who the last-minute entry is."

I followed Mark's gaze to where Cole Abernathy was squeezing in another chair. He stepped out of the way to reveal none other than MacKenzie Clark.

"Yikes."

Mac moved to take her seat next to—of course—my brother. They glared at each other in a way that probably wasn't good for their eye health.

But then Brady said something I was too far away to hear, and his angry features melted into a smirking grin. That seemed to make Mac even more irritated as she thumped down hard in her seat and made a valiant effort to ignore my brother.

The contest kicked off with a brief word from Cole. With a good-ol'-boy grin, he thanked everyone for attending and supporting the opening of the restaurant while a few cooks emerged and passed out red baskets containing the hot-peppered wings.

Cole introduced the contestants next. There was Baker Ramsey, a retired school teacher and avid *Jeopardy!* fan, followed by Beatrice Michaelson, a roofer from a women-owned-and-operated roofing business here in town. Next in the lineup was a teenage boy named Braiden Hixon, who I was ninety percent sure worked down at Bev's Sno-Kones. Then there was my idiot brother grinning and hamming it up for the crowd. And last, but not least, Cole introduced Mac Clark.

"It's like a train wreck," I said to Mark. "I know something horrible is going to happen, but I can't look away."

He chuckled.

"I've got five minutes on the clock," Cole called out as he held his watch aloft for the crowd. "Remember, y'all, you can use as much ranch dressing as you like, but you have to clean the bones and you only have five minutes. Then we'll get you a glass of milk, a bowl of ice cream, whatever you need to cool down. Although, I can tell you, it's not going to help. And you're really going to hurt later. Hope none of you have a big date tonight."

The customers laughed at the promise of impending gastrointestinal distress for those assembled.

But then Mac said, loudly enough to be heard, "Doubt Judd, here, has to worry about that."

More laughter from the crowd.

Brady's eyes narrowed, and he fired back, "Hope this doesn't cause problems with your IBS, Mac Attack. Did you consult your doctor beforehand?"

Mac shot him a look that could have singed his eyebrows off.

Cole clapped his hands. "Okay, let's get going before these two strangle each other. Remember, do not touch your eyes. Annnd, ready, set, here we *go!*"

In a flurry of movement, each of the five contestants lunged forward to grab their respective baskets. They tore into the first chicken wing, and the effects of the spice level were quickly apparent. Faces heated, deep red climbing across the cheeks of Baker and Beatrice. Sweat was visible on Brady's upper lip and where it beaded beneath his eyes. Mac's face was expressionless as she discarded the thoroughly cleaned bones from wing number one and then reached for the next.

The contestants were using the ranch dressing cup as a little swimming pool for their wings, all except the gangly teenager Braiden.

I nudged Mark with my knee. "Look at that kid go."

"He's a machine," Mark replied.

Baker tossed his unfinished third wing into the basket and scooted away from the table. "I'm out." His hands were shaking, and he looked like he was already experiencing some stomach upset. The staff rushed over with a bowl of ice cream, a glass of milk, and some wet wipes for Baker's spice-covered hands.

"One down!" Cole called. "And two minutes remaining."

MacKenzie and Brady were jockeying for space at the table, their elbows whacking into one another.

"Give me some space, you jackass," Mac growled around her chicken wing.

"Keep your bony elbows on your own side, you delinquent," Brady spat back. But he wasn't looking so good. My brother still had three wings to go, and time was dwindling. He was starting to sweat through his ball cap.

Mac's cheeks were the color of Red Hots, and she wasn't faring much better.

Moments later, the teenage underdog raised his hands in victory. "Done!"

Cole came over to inspect his basket, and the kid was declared the winner.

Beatrice the roofer dropped her final wing back into the basket and moaned, "Thank God," before the crowd erupted in applause.

Brady and Mac could be heard arguing throughout the aftermath of the ice-cream-and-wet-wipe delivery.

"You know, that kid's taste buds probably aren't even fully developed," Mac complained. "What is he, twelve?"

"Let it go, you sore loser," my brother said around a laugh.

"*You're* a loser," Mac snapped.

"I'm going to poke you in the eye with my wing finger," he said, reaching toward her face.

She grabbed him around the wrist as they struggled. "You mean, ring finger, you dumbass."

"You'd like to get your hands on my ring finger, wouldn't you," Brady said, still grinning.

MacKenzie growled something feral, and the squabbling intensified as she tried to poke him in the eyes with her spice-encrusted finger too.

Unable to hide my laughter, I asked Mark, "Should we intervene before they end up in the emergency room?"

He was already shaking his head. "Cole's got it."

And sure enough, Brady's best friend was wading in to separate them by tugging Brady up and out of his seat. "Come on, you two. Remember what happened at the opening of Carter Bistro downtown?"

Immediately Brady and Mac stopped trying to injure each other and actually looked a little sheepish.

"I can't feel my tongue," Brady mumbled as Cole helped him away from the table.

"That's probably a nice change of pace for you, bigmouth," Mac called sweetly. Then her eyes widened and she belched loudly.

"Ladylike, as always," Brady teased. But he was nearly to the front door and too far away for Mac to maim.

I turned to Mark. "Well, that was fun."

He smiled. "You know, it actually was. You want to stay for some food or are you heading out?"

Did I want to stay and have dinner with Mark Mercer?

We were co-workers. Besides, it was okay to have a beer and some chicken wings on a Tuesday night at the same table with someone you knew. This wasn't a date.

"Food sounds good," I replied. "I worked up an appetite watching my brother make a fool of himself."

Mark laughed. "Yeah, me too. I'll grab us some menus."

As he approached the counter to grab the laminated copies, I didn't let myself think about how nice it was to spend time with Mark outside of work. Or how comfortable I felt around him. Or the way his butt looked in his dark-wash denim.

Muttering a soft curse, I looked away.

This wasn't a big deal, I told myself sternly.

Mark and I were friends.

And I was determined to keep us that way.

MARK

It was around four thirty in the afternoon, and I was in the Apple House giving a batch of undersized apples a final wash and sort before loading them into the press when I heard Candace cursing behind me.

I turned to see her struggling to wheel the outdoor heaters over to the seating area in preparation for her event tonight.

After shutting off the water, I dried my hands and made my way to her. "Hey, want some help with that?"

Straightening, she blew a strand of wayward brown hair out of her face. "God, yes."

She had on a chunky mustard-colored cardigan over her navy-blue Judd's Orchard tee shirt and some light-wash jeans. The weather had been chilly for the last two days, which was typical for autumn in North Carolina. The season was a mixed bag. Some October days were similar to those in the summer months, just without all the humidity, or they could be rainy and cold with a wind so fierce it could rip the hat right off your head. About midway through the month, we were somewhere in between. Mild, sunny days with evenings that grew cold as the sun melted behind the hills.

Candace was preparing for her wine-and-pumpkin-decorating event taking place tonight. The temperature would dip down into the fifties before the end of it, so the attendees would appreciate the four freestanding outdoor heaters when the sun finally set.

"Sure thing," I said.

"I'm sorry if you were in the middle of something. I really appreciate the help."

"It's no trouble. I was just washing apples for the press."

There was a bit of an awkward shuffle as Candace still tried to help and I tried not to surround her body with mine. We were both trying to grip a tall silver cylinder that stretched over six feet tall and tilt it so the small wheels engaged on the uneven dirt and grass. When her ass bumped into my thigh for the fourth time, and she apologized—for the fourth time—I offered to maneuver the heater myself if she wanted to guide me and tell me where to put it.

Probably best to avoid touching her backside, even inadvertently. Things between us had smoothed out in the last month. The way we'd almost kissed at Firefly had faded into the background of the farm and being co-workers.

Candace was still friendly and easy to be around, so it was only my own stupidity that kept remembering how she'd felt under my hands that night, the way she'd whispered my name. The casual dinner we'd eaten together at Flyers had been a couple of weeks ago. While it had been fun to be with her like that, it was probably safer to keep our interactions limited to the farm. So I didn't forget that we were friends and co-workers. So I didn't start hoping for more.

I shook myself and righted the heater into position, ensuring it was level. Over the next half hour, we worked to get the remaining three heaters out of storage and positioned around the picnic tables. Despite the late hour, I figured I could stay and help bring the pumpkins over from the Apple House too.

Tablecloths were spread, and wine bottles and stemless glasses were acquired. Candace had brushes and paint palettes for all the attendees. She straightened the place settings with care, little tweaks here and there. So much of her time and attention went into these events, and I knew it carried over from Candace herself —the high-achiever, the go-getter, the dreamer with that notebook that went with her everywhere.

At three minutes to six, everything looked picture-perfect. But there weren't any guests.

The farm closed at five, and Nick and Amy and Joan had gone home for the day. Brady was on a dinner break and would be back any minute to help Candace with the event, and to make sure she wasn't alone. While the vandalism hadn't repeated itself, we still didn't have any closure on the situation. Brady had volunteered to work late tonight to help Candace close and lock up.

She was staring toward the road that entered the orchard—the still-empty road.

"This is great, Candace. You should take some photos for social media before y'all get started," I said, attempting to draw her attention.

She spun around. "You're right. That's a great idea."

"Still a couple of weeks until Halloween. You could probably schedule another one of these since the registration filled up so fast."

Candace was snapping photos of the table setup with her phone. "Yeah, well, if no one comes, it's probably a good indicator that I shouldn't try again."

I glanced at my watch. "There's still time."

She smiled at my optimism, but it wasn't the one she typically wore. This smile lacked the full force of her happiness, the joy she had for the farm. How she'd chat with tourists, work the refreshment stand with her mother, or coax a shy kid into an apple cider doughnut and a grin. Candace was usually so upbeat, it was disorienting to see her off-balance now. I felt helpless in the face of it.

"Do you think Brady accidentally latched the gate and they can't get . . ." Candace trailed off at the sound of vehicles coming down the drive. She brightened. "They're here."

I smiled. "Told you so."

Candace glanced back at me and grinned, visibly relieved. "Yeah, you did." Her attention snagged on the procession of vehicles as they drew closer to the parking lot. "That's Bonnie," she said around a laugh. "She didn't tell me she did this. Oh, and Mac and Laramie, too."

Her voice had gone soft and surprised. "I better go greet them," she murmured distractedly.

Candace took off toward the gravel lot, an excited little skip in her step, and I couldn't resist the smile that came over me as I watched. Her friend had shown up for her and made sure her event was successful following the pumpkin mix-up. After her awful encounter with Lauren Walker downtown, I was glad Candace had Bonnie, and Bonnie's friends and family by extension.

Part of me wondered if they'd keep in touch once Candace moved back to the city.

I figured her hurrying away from me now was as good a reminder as any. Candace didn't belong to me any more than she belonged to Kirby Falls. This was a temporary pit stop, a layover until she went back to her real life.

I realized, belatedly, that I hadn't been so innocent in my offer to help tonight. Yes, I'd heard her struggling with the heater and felt the need to be there for her, but I also recognized that work—on the farm—was the only safe way to spend time with Candace. Apparently, I was a glutton for punishment. It was important to keep out of situations where someone's lips could find their way to anyone else's, but I was still eager for her time and attention. Working late at the orchard was a safe enough way to do that.

Clearly, that lonely teenage kid with a crush still impacted my decision-making.

It was time for me to go and finish up my own work for the night. Yet, I stuffed my hands in my pockets and watched Candace walk away.

Candace

I barely let Bonnie get out of the car before I threw my arms around her. "I can't believe you did this!"

She laughed, her arms tight across my back. "Well, I knew how upset you were about mixing up the pumpkin order. So I thought I could help you and have a fun night out with my gals."

Bonnie was so sweet to support me this way. The registration for the sip-and-paint night had filled up inexplicably fast. Turned out, it was all my friend, and she'd brought reinforcements.

I leaned away to see her face better. "But this event was your idea. You told me I should set up something like this to bring in sales."

"Well, yeah." She grinned. "I'm a genius."

I laughed and squeezed her one more time because I was so grateful for her friendship. Finding Bonnie like I had—completely by chance and right when I needed her—had been one of the best things about coming back to Kirby Falls.

"Come meet everyone," she said.

Turned out Bonnie had brought a teacher friend from the elementary school along with her own mom, Patty, and her aunt, Maggie. I remembered Miss Maggie from the bakery over at Grandpappy's. She ran things over there and made beautiful cakes. I didn't realize she'd hired an assistant, but Chloe seemed really nice. She'd hugged me too, and I could smell the vanilla and sugar lingering on her skin. Chloe had introduced me to her friend Andie, who was pretty excited to be out for a kid-free evening.

Laramie Burke had graduated with me. I'd always liked her, and it was nice to see her now. I'd been meaning to try to catch up with her. She'd brought her best friend, Kayla, who I'd also shared some classes with. I welcomed them and pointed them in the direction of the picnic tables we'd be using tonight.

MacKenzie Clark was the next one to emerge from her vehicle. She hugged me and introduced me to the pretty blond woman climbing out of her passenger seat. Becca Kernsy was on vacation, but, apparently, it was an extended one, and the Clark family had absorbed her into their fold. I didn't have the whole story there, but she was as sweet as pie. She'd also been the friendly volunteer who'd assisted with setup during the Orchard Fest. It was a fun coincidence meeting her for real and having her at the orchard.

"Have you recovered from the hot-wing challenge," I asked Mac as we trailed the others.

She groaned. "Don't remind me. I had to cancel a date that night. Being doubled over with stomach pain isn't sexy."

I laughed, feeling so light and buoyed by gratitude that I thought I might float away.

"This looks great," Bonnie called to me when she reached the decorated picnic tables.

I took in the scene. It *did* look nice. With the sun setting in the distance, the sky was streaked with lavender and a pink so pale it should have been on a nursery wall. The hills were topped with gold and copper as autumn did its thing. And the farm only accentuated the natural beauty around us.

My guests were fawning over the setup and the pumpkins—the tiny palettes, paint sets, and water cups at each station. There were stencils for outlining and a cheese board to accompany the six bottles of wine I'd brought over from Lonely Mountain.

"You work magic, I swear," Bonnie added when Mac and I finally joined her.

"Thanks. Mark helped a lot actually," I finally replied.

All at once, I realized I'd walked off from him without a backward glance when the first car came into sight. My head swiveled, trying to find Mark among Bonnie's friends and family, but he wasn't there.

I'd been so relieved to see folks arriving, and then I'd been straight-up surprised to glimpse Bonnie's car as well as the others. I'd gone to welcome them, and in doing so, I'd left Mark behind. I needed to thank him for his help. Guilt hollowed my stomach at what I'd done.

My gaze strayed upward to where I felt warmth blanketing my skin. He'd turned on the propane and set all the heaters on low for us.

Instinctively, I took a step away to search for him in the Apple House, but Laramie called my name.

"Candace! I want to see Lance Bass. Bonnie told me about the fish in your office, and I almost died. I'm an NSYNC superfan. I need to see it."

But before I could answer her, Mac hoisted a bottle of Lonely Mountain pinot grigio and hollered, "You can have your picture made with Lance Bass later, Larry. Let's get these bottles open."

I glanced between the Apple House where Mark might be and all these women waiting on me to do my job. I felt pulled in too many directions.

I pasted on a smile and went to grab the corkscrew.

When I'd finished uncorking a bottle of Gandalf the Blanc, I passed the opener to MacKenzie who was waiting to open the second bottle. Just then, my brother came strolling across the grass from the direction of the parking lot.

He caught sight of Mac and stopped in his tracks. "Are you sure it's a good idea to arm her?"

I heard a low growl emanate from my side.

"And you're giving her wine?" he added helpfully. "Wow, sis. No self-preservation instinct in you at all. She's probably using her access tonight to case the joint."

"I've told you a hundred times, Brady Judd. I did not vandalize your property. It was probably someone else who finds you painfully annoying," Mac stated matter-of-factly.

"Oh yeah?" He smirked and crossed his arms over his flannel-covered chest.

"Yeah. We have a club and everything. We meet on Tuesdays down at the library. Only room big enough to hold us all."

My brother opened his mouth, but I cut in, "What are you doing here, Brady?"

He shot Mac one last glare before answering, "I'm working this event with you and closing tonight. I just got back from my dinner break."

What?

"I thought Mark was on the schedule," I argued. "He was out here helping me for over an hour."

My brother shook his head. "Nah. He was off at five. I'm your backup tonight. And good thing since you have a violent delinquent in your midst."

I ignored the bickering his comment sparked as my mind spun and my feet carried me across the grass.

Mark had stayed. He'd helped me move the freestanding propane heaters and then he'd hauled pumpkins and wine and paint supplies back and forth from my office. He'd positioned and decorated the tables while I'd arranged the cheese board.

And he was supposed to go home nearly two hours ago.

I mounted the steps to the Apple House and found him in the back near all the equipment, right where I'd interrupted him the first time. He said he'd been washing fruit for the apple press, and here he was, trying to finish the job after he'd helped me with mine.

I felt overwhelmed by want and gratitude and an ache in my heart that just wouldn't go away.

Mark was one of the best guys I'd ever met. He was so gentle and patient. Kind but unassuming. He took up only the space required when it was probably half of what he deserved. I'd never felt so safe with someone, so utterly cared for. Mark was reliable and comfortable, but only to the point that my heart started to race and my breath quickened.

I wanted to hold his hand. Sit around a bonfire. Read different parts of the same newspaper and let him make me breakfast. I wanted to run my fingers through his soft, short hair until he fell asleep with his head in my lap. Sit next to him at the dinner table at the farmhouse and keep my knee pressed right up against his.

I also wanted to run my hands over his body and experience his strength. Have him pick me up and put me on a counter, so I could get as close as I wanted—as close as I could get.

"Mark," I said, my voice too weak and confused and breathless to be heard over the sound of the water and the conveyor transporting the apples to the press.

So I stepped closer and pressed a hand to his warm back, gaining his attention.

When he turned and found me standing there, he smiled first, like his lips couldn't help themselves. I clung to that reaction, watching those blue-gray eyes crinkle at the corners and his mouth tip up in a subtle grin. But then he got a good look at me and the way I'd stepped into him—close, closer than I should have been, closer than I ever allowed myself.

His grin fell away, and his gaze moved over my face, looking for an answer I didn't have.

With a finger through Mark's belt loop, I tugged him to me, but a whisper of caution and uncertainty brought me up short.

"Are you with anyone?" I asked, desperate for the answer. After everything that had happened in my last relationship, I couldn't do this without knowing the truth. No matter how strained or distant our relationship, I could never knowingly hurt my sister.

Mark's confusion intensified, drawing his dark brows together beneath the bill of his cap. "What? No, I'm not seeing anyone."

Relief pulsed in time with my longing. I nodded. Then I rose on tiptoe and pressed my lips to his.

I thought Mark would freeze up or hesitate with the way I'd ambushed him, but he didn't. His lips parted on a sigh, and I traced the seam gently with my tongue. His hand found my waist in the sliver of space between my tee shirt and unbuttoned cardigan, and he gripped me with purpose. I loved it. It was a fraction of his strength, but it was something I longed for. I could feel the dampness from the water on his hands seep into the fabric, and it was proof that this was real. It was happening.

There hadn't been a pause or a jump scare to pull us apart at the last minute. No hesitation to slow us down. I kept my index finger wound through his belt loop, just in case. With my other hand, I cradled his scruffy jaw as we kissed.

His scent surrounded me. The bright shimmer of rainfall and garden soil and growing things. So much vibrant green that I could see it behind my closed eyelids. His touch was a balm, cooling relief from this painful crush I'd been hiding away and hauling around.

I let my hand drift to his nape, where I could run my fingers through his dark blond hair, the way I wanted, the way I'd imagined. Mark made a sound as my nails grazed his scalp. It was deep and wanting, a tug on a line that connected us and had me answering with a groan of my own.

I heard laughter come from out by the picnic tables, and I knew I should pull away. I'd simply walked off minutes ago, like someone in a trance, trying to make sense of Mark's actions. I had work to do and a group of women waiting for me.

And from the way I still held him by his jeans, I could feel the evidence of Mark's arousal on the backs of my fingers. This wasn't really the time or the place.

So I gentled the pressure everywhere we touched, slowing my movements to cool the need burning within.

The heels of my sneakers met the wooden planks of the Apple House floor, but Mark bent forward, following me down. I smiled against his mouth as I pressed one final kiss to his plush lower lip, which was just as soft as I thought it would be.

The hand on my waist loosened the fabric in its grip. Mark traced down the length of my arm until he found the point where we were connected, the belt loop I still held.

"I didn't want you to get away this time," I murmured shyly.

You only got one first kiss with someone, and the butterflies doing flips in my stomach were letting me know that this was one for the record books. If I'd been fifteen, the memory would have gone in a locked journal with some hearts and squiggles doodled in the margins.

Mark's smile was dreamy, a drowsy sort of affection that I wanted to snuggle up in.

I pressed my fingers to my lips as I regarded him affectionately. The soft skin felt tingly and swollen in the best way.

Mark's eyes tracked the movement and his expression grew thoughtful all at once.

"What is it?" I asked, suddenly worried.

"Before, why did you ask me if I was with anyone? Why would you assume that?"

My finger instinctively tightened around his belt loop. "Oh, that." I licked my lips nervously, tasting him there. "I thought you might—possibly—be my sister's secret boyfriend."

"What?" Mark's voice came out loud in the scant space between us, and my attention snapped to his in alarm. Lowering his voice, he spoke softly this time. "Secret boyfriend? Candace, what are you talking about?"

"I saw you and Joan at the Orchard Fest. I thought—I thought—"

Mark's frown deepened. "Saw us what?"

"Well, Joan was rubbing your arm. You two were close. It looked like she was comforting you or something. And then you were both smiling at each other."

Surprise gave way to thoughtful introspection as I spoke. "Candace, your sister and I are friends and co-workers. Yes, she was trying to make me feel better, but there has never been anything romantic between us. Not ever. I'm not—I'm not interested in her that way." He took my hand and squeezed. "Do you think I'd try to kiss *you* if I was?"

"Well, no," I admitted. "But you ran off that night and you wouldn't talk about it. You seemed to want to forget that our almost-kiss at Firefly ever happened."

With a shy smile, he admitted, "Because I like you, Candace. And I didn't want you to feel weird because we work together and have to see each other all the time . . . temporarily, at least."

I smiled too, ignoring the reminder of my looming deadline. "I don't feel weird. I like you too, Mark. So much."

With another tug of his belt loop, I had him wrapped up in a hug, my arms around his waist and his quiet laughter rumbling against my chest.

Feminine voices drifted in through the open-air space, and I could see now it was nearly dark outside. "I need to go wrangle this event, but more kissing later, yes?"

Mark chuckled again as I took a step back. "Yeah. More kissing later," he agreed with a grin. Blue-gray eyes lingered on my face, touching every part. It was as if he'd finally given himself permission to look and he didn't know where to start.

"And thank you for your help this afternoon. I meant to say that earlier, and just now before I attacked your mouth. Thank you for staying late and just generally always being there when I need you."

His expression was soft as he watched me. "Anytime."

Hurriedly, I pecked him on the lips and then took off toward the yard and the picnic tables beyond. Everything looked to be under control upon my approach. Someone must have taken the corkscrew away from Mac because I didn't see it embedded in my brother anywhere. The women were still chatting, and another two bottles of wine had been opened. The cheese board was mostly demolished, and when I came into view, all my guests cheered.

Grinning, I joined them. "Sorry about that. Are y'all ready to paint?"

A round of yesses met my ears, so I gestured to everyone to take a seat in front of a pumpkin. I showed them the stencils for anyone who wanted them and made sure everyone had the supplies they needed to get started.

With the pumpkin painting underway, I circulated and refilled drinks and paint as needed, chatting as I went and getting to know these women who were so important to my friend, Bonnie.

Mac shared a story about finding an entire naked family behind the storage shed over at Grandpappy's last week. Apparently, they'd been trying to take a weird photo op with a self-timer, their baby inside a pumpkin, and everyone else holding up squash from the farm's pumpkin patch to cover their private parts.

Everyone was laughing as she recounted the incident amid her shudders.

"I'm scarred for life, I tell you," Mac said as she put a final flourish on a black cat she'd been painting.

"I'm sure seeing a naked man for the first time was shocking for you." Brady laughed.

Thankfully Becca prevented well-deserved violence against my brother when she caught sight of something on the property.

She stood to get a better look and pointed at a furry body in the distance. "What is that?"

I squinted to see a groundhog standing on its back legs, ignoring us completely and eyeing the apple tree closest to it.

"It's a groundhog," I offered.

Becca took a few steps closer into the darkness, her long blond hair shining like a beacon. She pulled out her phone and started snapping pictures. "I've never seen a groundhog before." After another few shuffling paces in the animal's direction, she added, "It's so cute. I just want to tackle it."

At least six people all shouted, "No!" The groundhog took off into the field at a run.

Becca turned back to us and pouted. "Gosh, you guys. I wasn't really going to do it. Even I know better than that."

"No offense, babe," Laramie called. "But you're a city girl. We just had to make sure you weren't going to get yourself mauled and maimed."

I moved among Bonnie's friends and family for the next half hour, listening and laughing and just generally enjoying myself. This didn't feel like work. It was nice being surrounded by a group of women who were all kind and funny and included you in their conversations.

Seated beneath the warmth of the outdoor heaters, on the farm my family had built, I was happier than I could ever remember being. I liked these women, and I wanted them to be a part of my life—a life here in Kirby Falls.

As the voices and laughter swirled around me, I swallowed an awkward lump in my throat and wished for the hundredth time that I could stay. *I wanted to stay.*

But you couldn't always get what you wanted.

Movement up on the front steps of the Apple House caught my eye. In the bright glow from the floodlight on the corner of the building, I could see it was Mark. His hoodie was zipped up to ward off the chill and a small, secret smile was visible on his face.

I could feel an answering grin on my own.

He paused when his boots hit the grass and raised his hand in a wave.

My smile widened, and I waved back.

He gave me a long look with those pretty blue-gray eyes, and I felt it behind my sternum. There was something happening in the center of my chest. My heart was beating hard, but not so much in panic. More like a dance party with techno music and glow sticks and everything.

Finally, Mark gave me a nod and shoved his hands in the pockets of his hoodie before turning toward the parking lot and his waiting truck.

I could feel myself going soft and warm all over. I wanted to tuck him inside my heart and button him up behind my cardigan, keep him there forever. Mine to have and mine to hold.

An elbow nudged me in the side, and I jolted in surprise.

"Would you look at that," Bonnie said slyly next to me.

Oh, Lord. Had she seen me making googly eyes at Mark?

But when I glanced her way, her attention was focused on the next picnic table over.

I followed her gaze and felt my lips part in mutual surprise. "Holy crap."

Mac and Brady were sitting across from one another, and they were the only ones at the table. The other folks probably vacated due to their constant squabbling.

But they weren't fighting now.

Mac was still working on her pumpkin. However, she and Brady were clearly in conversation. He watched her while she made careful strokes along the surface of her pumpkin, and she glanced up at him frequently. They looked like they were having a completely normal discussion.

Suddenly, MacKenzie erupted into laughter, and Bonnie grabbed my arm. "What is happening?" she hissed. "Is the world ending?"

I noticed the other ladies at our table had quieted as well, drawn by the spectacle of Mac and Brady actually getting along.

"I'm afraid," Laramie said in a hushed tone.

"Is someone recording this?" I heard someone else whisper.

And then Becca murmured softly, "Classic enemies to lovers."

As we all sat silently and watched those two bozos behave themselves for once, I couldn't help but think that stranger things *had* happened. Maybe just because their relationship had always been one way, didn't mean it couldn't adapt. People could change. Futures shifted all the time and expectations along with them.

We weren't simply the sum of our past, I thought hopefully.

A breeze cut through the warmth from the heaters, causing me to shiver.

Just as suddenly, the tides shifted and Mac's voice rose in indignation as she pointed her loaded paintbrush in Brady's direction.

I heard a sigh from Chloe and a softly muttered, "Oh shoot," from Becca.

"Just shy of five minutes," Larry said in disappointment. "I owe you five bucks, Aunt Maggie."

Amid Mac's angry hollering, my idiot brother's laughter rang out, vindictive and delighted in equal measure.

Maybe change was too much to hope for in certain situations. I probably shouldn't let my imagination get away from me either.

twelve

MARK

Nerves made my grip on the small Tupperware container unsteady, and I nearly fumbled it when I took the front stairs two at a time.

I needed to calm down.

It hadn't taken long for the warm afterglow of my kiss with Candace to get snuffed out. Last night, on the drive home, reality had come crashing down with no room for subtlety or the tender, hopeful feelings I'd been entertaining.

Dread sunk like a weight, cold and heavy in my chest. We'd kissed and it had been perfect, but what the hell was I supposed to do now?

There were things about me that Candace didn't know, and, even worse, things I couldn't tell her. At best, she just thought I was private about my life. But more likely, she thought I had a daughter out there who I never saw or acknowledged.

In a delirious daze from her lips and her scent and her taste, I'd agreed to more kissing, but what did that even mean? We'd need to keep this—whatever it was —between us. If her family and the town found out, any sort of association with me would have a negative impact on her. They'd whisper about Candace behind her back. I couldn't stand the thought of my reputation ruining hers.

But here I was, twelve hours later, heart in my hands along with some pumpkin scones.

Tightening my hold on the plastic container, I poked my head into Candace's office. She wasn't there, but she must have just stepped out. The overhead light was on and so was her electric heater. It was early, but she was an early riser. I'd wanted to stop by and talk this morning, try to figure out where we went from here.

As I stepped more fully into the room, I caught the scent of lavender that always seemed to cling to her hair and her skin. It was soft and delicate, but it had arousal flooding my system along with memories of her fingers firm around my belt loop and her nails on my scalp. All I could do was shake my head at myself. Shifting uncomfortably, I moved to place the scones on her desk.

I'd pack up my heart, but leave the scones.

It was a good thing she wasn't here to accept the breakfast and my barely coherent thoughts. I'd probably just stand there staring at her like a lovesick idiot. I was fifteen with a crush all over again. Except now I knew her—the real her—not the half-formed idea I had in my head. She was kind and funny and beautiful in a way I couldn't have known when I was simply an infatuated teenager.

Distantly, my brain warned that I was a little more than infatuated this time around.

I probably needed to get my shit together before we had this conversation anyway. If I was smart, I'd just put things to rest, tell her there was no point in moving forward and we should go back to being friends. I knew we had an expiration date with her plans to leave in the new year. But it was that same threat of her impending departure that made me think we could do this—keep this secret for a few short months.

It would be easier to keep a relationship under wraps if it had an end date. I wasn't selfish enough to try to date her for all the world to see. I didn't want to hurt her. She could leave Kirby Falls once more as one of its best and brightest— a hometown darling untainted by my past and my decisions.

Maybe Candace could be mine for a little while, and it wouldn't hurt so bad when she left.

Intent on heading out, I stepped closer and placed the Tupperware on the desk. In doing so, I caught sight of her laptop, off-center on the scarred wooden surface and open to a webpage. My attention snagged on the job listings. *Market research manager. Sales and marketing position. Product marketing. Brand manager and client relations.*

I'd known Candace was leaving from the start. When her parents had mentioned the return of their youngest daughter, they'd said she was taking some time away from the city and was coming home. I didn't know what might drive someone away from their city and current position, but maybe Candace was exploring her options, seeing what else was out there.

Either way, none of those job postings were in Kirby Falls.

It was a stark reminder—a disappointment I didn't have any business feeling.

I glanced away from the computer screen to the mounted fish on the wall. Its large orange eye stared knowingly.

Shoving my hands in the pockets of my jeans, I started for the door only to be stopped when Candace walked in, breathless and already grinning.

"Hi. Good morning. I saw your truck."

She was wrapped in a green sweater that made her hazel eyes glow warm and golden. Candace looked so damn excited to see me that I nearly confessed to what I'd seen on her laptop.

I could feel the judgmental weight of Lance Bass's lifeless, frozen gaze at my back.

Everything I'd planned to say this morning left my head in a rush. I cleared my throat. "Hey. I brought you some pumpkin scones," I told her, pointing to the plastic container like a jerky marionette.

"Thank you," she replied happily, already moving to retrieve them. "These look great."

While she broke off a piece of crumbly breakfast pastry and popped it into her mouth, I tried to make the words come. But seeing her scrambled every option on the table.

Before I could decide on the best path forward, Candace finished chewing. "This is delicious. Thank you for making those for me."

I was ready to admit that Wenn had actually made them, and we'd been out shooting again last night at Craggy Peak, but then she said, "Would you like to go out to dinner tonight? Or grab a drink after work?"

She looked so fucking hopeful that my throat closed up. My frantic heartbeat was the only thing getting through, and I knew if I tried to speak, my voice would shake with the force of it.

Candace Judd was asking me out on a date. Like that was the next logical step after making out in the Apple House. And maybe, for a normal person, that was.

I didn't have the luxury though. For a moment, I tried imagining what it would be like to be a regular guy on a date with someone like her. But as the town pariah, I was so far removed from that option, the daydream just wouldn't stick. Hell, it wouldn't even materialize.

Instead, I thought fast. How could I fix this? I didn't go out in Kirby Falls. I avoided restaurants. I didn't attend trivia nights or play rec-league softball. There was no frequenting of bars or breweries. That outing to Flyers's grand opening had been an exception, not the rule.

Trying to extrovert myself now, with Candace on my arm, was a path to disaster. I'd make her look bad. People would judge her, gossip about her. Paint her with the same tainted brushstrokes they smeared across me.

The thought of what she'd be subjected to had my voice emerging too sharp, the edges jagged and forceful. "I can't go out with you." Regret was instantaneous. My hands balled into fists inside my pockets.

Candace's bright, hopeful expression died a thousand deaths.

"I just mean," I blurted inelegantly, "I'm more of a homebody. Why don't you come over? I'll make you dinner."

"Really?" she asked tentatively, the light creeping cautiously back into her expression.

"Yeah. I'd like to have you over."

Her grin turned sly. "Can I see your garden?"

I laughed—probably sounding unhinged—as relief flooded my system. We could do this. If she came to my house, I wasn't putting her reputation at risk. "Sure.

You can see my garden. You can even harvest some sweet potatoes and beets to take home."

"I can't wait."

When I realized we'd just been standing there staring at each other for a full thirty seconds, I straightened. "I'll text you some menu options today. Then I'll pick up groceries after work. Is six thirty okay?"

She nodded. "Sounds good."

I swallowed uncomfortably but knew I needed to get this next part out. "I know this is new, and I know you're leaving. I don't have any expectations, Candace. I like you and want to spend time with you. But do you think we could keep this thing"—I motioned between us—"private for the time being? I don't want to make things weird at work or with your family. Can it just be you and me?"

Candace's face stayed mostly the same, but I saw her swallow, the tendons in her neck going tight. Her warm smile became less defined, like a handout that had been photocopied one too many times. I hadn't seen Candace's copy-and-paste smile for weeks. Those initial brittle encounters had tapered off to genuine happiness during her time in Kirby Falls.

The fact that I'd put it on her face now made a hole open up in me.

But then her expression cleared like a summer day, and she said, chipper as a Girl Scout, "Of course. That makes sense. My mom would probably start planning our wedding if she knew." She laughed at that, and it sounded so true and real that I started to doubt the disappointment and tension I'd witnessed just moments ago.

"Well, I'll let you get to it," Candace said.

I scrutinized her face, but she looked at ease. "I'll text you in a bit. Think about what you want tonight. I'll make it for you."

She nodded.

Then I stepped close to her because I couldn't not. My hand cupped her cheek, fingers threading into soft sable hair.

"Is it later?" she asked around a mischievous little grin that I ached to taste.

"Yeah," I breathed, and gave in.

I felt her smile change, transform into something welcoming and wanting as her lips parted. She tasted like the tea I knew she favored in the mornings, honey-sweet.

Her hand found its way to my chest, resting on the soft flannel I wore. I wondered if she could feel my racing heart. It hadn't calmed since she'd stepped through the door, eager and breathless, happy to see me in her space.

The kiss stayed slow and intent. I wasn't about to let things get out of hand when her dad or her brother could walk by at any moment. I wanted her, but I respected her too.

Finally, when my hands shook from the effort to keep myself in check, to stop myself from moving down her body, I placed a tiny bite on her bottom lip and pulled back, resting my forehead against hers and breathing the same air.

"More kisses later?" she asked.

My eyes were closed, but I knew she was smiling.

"More kisses later," I confirmed.

Then I made myself leave before later came too soon.

Eleven hours later, I opened my front door and forgot what I was doing.

Candace stood there, outlined by the setting sun, and I wondered how I'd ever get through dinner. She looked so beautiful. I felt like I'd been hit with a tranquilizer dart, right in the chest, and it was trying its best to take me down.

She'd done something with her hair. It hung in long loose waves that were somehow both elegant and casual.

The jeans she wore had a rip at the knee, and I felt like a damn Victorian viscount getting a glimpse of forbidden ankle.

Clearing the addlebrained desire from my throat, I finally managed, "Come in."

Candace beamed, her curious gaze bouncing all around.

Instead of stopping to let her snoop, I took her coat while she toed off her shoes, and then I led her into the kitchen. "Can I grab you something to drink? I have a red ale from Trailview, the cranberry seasonal from Firefly, and a bottle of pinot noir. Or water or sweet tea."

"You don't have to stipulate that the tea is sweet," Candace said with a grin. "We're in North Carolina. That's a given."

"It actually took me a while to warm up to it. I drank unsweet until after college."

She gasped dramatically, teasing me before finally answering, "I'll have that cider, please."

I grabbed the bottle from the fridge and popped the top before pouring it into a glass. I could feel her amused gaze on me the whole time, and I only barely managed not to spill anything.

"Thank you," she said, accepting her drink. Her pleased smile hadn't gone anywhere.

"What?" I asked.

"I could have drunk from the bottle, Mark. You didn't need to put it in a glass."

Warmth crept into my cheeks. "It gave me something to do with my hands."

She laughed. "Stop being nervous. It's just me."

Just her. God, if she only knew. There was no *just* about it.

She'd made me a nervous wreck at seventeen. And now, the sight of her in socks, standing in my kitchen, was a daydream so casual and devastating that I wasn't sure I'd recover.

I busied myself checking the doneness of the potatoes I had on the stove.

Candace gave me some space and sat down at the table, sipping her cider. "So what did you make me?"

She'd only mentioned a cashew allergy when we'd texted earlier, and she insisted that she liked every kind of food except for celery because "that shit tastes like chewing on wet hair." Since I hadn't had much to go on for menu options, I made something relatively easy that I usually put together for myself a couple of times a month. I knew it had a high success rate.

"Oven-roasted pork loin, steamed red potatoes, and a basic table salad with red wine vinaigrette."

"Wow," Candace breathed.

I chuckled. "It's pretty simple."

"Not for the uneducated," she argued. "Let me guess. Did you grow those red potatoes yourself?"

I kept my back to her as I pulled said potatoes off the stove. "Uh, yeah."

"And did you make that red wine vinaigrette from scratch?"

I drained the water into the sink. It was mostly the steam from the potatoes that made my face flush, but I eventually admitted, "Maybe."

Candace cackled happily. "I knew it."

I tossed the quartered root vegetables in a bowl with fresh herbs and a bit of olive oil, then covered it with aluminum foil to keep warm.

Before Candace could tease me any further, a sound came from the back deck, just beyond the screen door. It was a strange but familiar combination of rusty car door and crying baby.

I couldn't believe I'd been so distracted I'd forgotten to put his food out.

"What was that?" Candace asked.

I wiped my hands on a kitchen towel and grabbed the cat's bowl from beneath the sink. Busy with opening the can and dumping the contents, I didn't notice Candace going for the back door.

"Wait," I said, but it was too late.

She slid the door open, and the cat darted right in. "Ohhh. A kitty. I didn't know you had a cat."

"I don't. Don't touch him," I cautioned. "The cat's feral."

She looked down at the gray beast who sat placidly in the middle of the kitchen and then back at me.

I rolled my eyes and set the bowl down for him before backing away slowly. Holding up my left hand, I pointed to a white slash beneath the knuckle on my middle finger. "See this? He did it two years ago. I was feeding him inside because it was rainy out, and the wind blew the door closed. Ornery thing thought he was trapped and went wild. He jumped up and knocked over everything on the counter, and then clawed the devil out of me when I tried to help him down."

Candace watched the big cat as it crouched over the bowl, chewing politely. The traitor.

"Maybe he's experienced personal growth," she said thoughtfully. "Perhaps this cat is ready for a second chance to be rehabilitated."

I let out a disbelieving sound that made her laugh. Then she wandered over to the open doorway and peeked out on the deck. "So, what's his name?"

My brows lowered in confusion. "Who?"

"The cat."

"It's not my cat."

She glanced back to me, eyes alight. "You feed it?"

"Yeah."

"Every day?"

I shifted on my feet. "Most days, yes. He doesn't always stop by for a visit."

Candace's glossy pink lips suppressed a smile. "I'm assuming you built that multi-level cat mansion out there on the back porch."

I hesitated and her grin erupted. "Well, yeah. But it's only for bad weather, and I read you should never put out soft pet beds for feral cats in winter. So there's hay instead to keep him warm."

"Riiiiiight. No name. Not your cat. Got it."

I ignored her teasing and tried to distract her. "Want to see the garden before it gets dark?"

"Yes," she replied enthusiastically.

I had a couple pairs of shoes lined up on the entryway rug for when I went outside. Candace slipped her feet into a pair of my oversized clogs without asking, and another little dart whistled straight into my chest.

The damn cat followed her out and meandered over to its water bowl.

Candace's borrowed shoes thumped across the wooden decking until she reached the top step. Then I waited as she stopped and stared.

My throat was tight with anticipation, and I couldn't say why—couldn't put a name to it—but I felt helpless and raw. She was seeing the most important parts of me, I realized. The things I kept private, kept for myself, in my home—my sanctuary.

I stepped up beside her and tried to see my garden through new eyes. The planter boxes now held autumn vegetables: leafy collards, beets, vibrant butternut squash, pumpkins, and more. Some were ready for harvesting, while others, like the bok choy and cabbage, would need another few weeks.

Candace's head turned toward the back corner of the yard where the greenhouse stood. I'd built it two summers ago. It wasn't very big, but it suited my purposes. I had some small projects in there, but mostly it was where I started everything from seed, giving plants a safe place to take root.

Then her head swiveled to the other corner, where the rope hammock hung between two sturdy tree trunks and the stone circle of my fire pit sat. I had a couple of chairs over there as well, and wood stacked against the fence line for burning. It might be chilly later, but we could have a fire after dinner if Candace wanted. I envisioned her socked feet propped up in my lap while she sipped another cider. The amber flames glowing across her skin. My jacket draped across her shoulders.

Yeah, maybe a fire was a good idea.

Eventually, Candace turned and met my gaze. I saw a mixture of wonder and quiet disbelief on her pretty face. "This is amazing, Mark."

Pride burned warm in my chest.

I liked my home. I'd made it mine after Hannah left. But I hadn't shown it to anyone else in a long time. I loved it, but I didn't expect that others would too. However, it suddenly seemed important that Candace liked my house and my garden and my space. I wanted her here . . . for as long as I could have her.

"Will you show me your plants? What you have growing?"

"Sure." I placed my beer bottle on the deck railing and reached for her hand, intending only to help her down the porch stairs in my unfamiliar and ill-fitting shoes, but when we reached solid ground, she kept her hand in mine.

I led her along and pointed out the vegetables in the various beds, explaining how I cycled them out and what would be there in the spring and summer months. I showed her where I had different berry bushes and a small patch of asparagus near the porch lattice.

Then I led her over to the greenhouse, so she could see the lettuce seedlings and the herbs I grew in there year-round for cooking.

"Were those herbs for the steamed potatoes from in there?" Candace asked after she'd exited the small structure. There wasn't enough room in there for the both of us to move around, and I'd wanted to give her space to explore.

I nodded. "Yeah. Italian parsley, basil, and oregano."

"What do you do with all your produce?" she asked, her hand sweeping wide to encompass the backyard.

"I have a neighbor I share some with. In the summer months, I usually bring some to your family. Your mom makes pickles with the cucumbers. I have a friend who likes to bake, so he gets some of the zucchini and pumpkin harvest. Then I can a lot and donate to the food bank downtown what I can't eat myself."

Her hazel eyes brightened, and she took a step closer to me. "I would love to learn how to can."

"I can show you," I offered. "I make jams and jellies too."

Candace shook her head in amusement and moved right into my space, her slender arms wrapping around my waist. "Jams and jellies. Mark Mercer, you are the perfect male specimen, I fear."

I barely had time to wonder what to do with my hands before she pressed her lips against the underside of my jaw and then stepped away. Holding out her fingers, Candace said, "We better get inside. Don't want that home-cooked dinner to get cold."

I followed her across the yard, up the porch stairs, and back into the house. The cat was nowhere to be seen, but that wasn't unusual for this time of day.

Side by side, we toed off our shoes on the entryway rug. Candace insisted on setting the table, so I pointed out the necessary cabinets and drawers. I couldn't help but wonder if she'd remember her way around the next time.

It was definitely too soon to start thinking that way, but I didn't seem capable of casual at this point. Despite all my internal warnings and self-assurances, temporary was going to have to be enough where Candace was concerned. And if I found myself heartbroken come January, I only had myself to blame.

She asked me more about the house and the garden during dinner. We talked and ate, and Candace complimented everything I made. It was nice making a meal for two instead of meal-prepping for one and freezing leftovers.

I liked having her in my space and seeing her comfortable enough to ask for seconds and offer to help wash dishes. I didn't let her, but I liked that she asked.

While I loaded the dishwasher, I told her to go snoop around the living room. "I know you're dying to."

Her cheeks went pink, but she laughed and made a beeline for my bookshelves.

I kept one eye on her as I rinsed our plates and cutlery. Her attention was focused on some of the framed photographs I had positioned around the room. They were mostly landscapes that I'd taken, several from Craggy Peak, others from Juniper Point and Lake Archer.

As I was closing the dishwasher door, I noticed Candace take a step back and survey the room, a frown drawing her dark brows together. It was almost like she was looking for something or doing a final once-over for an item she'd missed.

The paranoid part of me thought she was probably confused, checking for photos of a daughter I didn't have. She probably assumed that here, in the privacy of my own home, there'd be some evidence of the little girl I never mentioned or discussed, even if I didn't feel comfortable sharing her with the world.

I realized, all at once, that this wasn't going to work. If Candace and I were going to have something—even temporarily—I couldn't keep lying to her about my past. I didn't think I could stomach it.

It was one thing to have strangers and neighbors gossiping about me behind my back, or to my face, in some cases. I didn't really care what those people thought because they weren't important. They could have the lies and chew on them for as long as they liked. It was unsettling to think Candace might believe those same rumors. And expecting her to swallow the lies made the thought of being with her impossible.

As I watched her turn in a slow circle to better take in the room, I knew I needed to make a choice.

I could put a stop to whatever was happening between us. Keep my secrets and my lies.

Or I could tell her the truth—something Candace deserved if we were going to move forward.

After drying my hands on a kitchen towel, I took a deep breath and walked into the living room.

"Can we sit down?" I asked. "I need to tell you something."

thirteen

MARK

"What's up?" Candace asked slowly, eyes shadowed with worry.

She was sitting next to me on the couch, but I'd never mistake this for a relaxing movie night. There was distance between us, with the weight of the upcoming conversation, and I'd been the one to put it there.

I swallowed thickly, then licked my lips. "Listen, Candace. I don't really date."

"Ohhh," she murmured as if a lightbulb had gone off. "You prefer hookups."

"What? No. I don't—I don't do that either."

"Because you don't like women?" she wondered.

A startled laugh jumped up and over the truth trapped in my throat. "No, Candace. I like women. Well, I like you."

She smiled a little at that. "But you don't date."

"Not really. No."

Candace looked thoughtful. "Because you have a daughter?"

I watched her for a long moment, unsure how to begin. It wasn't a story I'd ever told. I knew Candace was leaving. I knew this thing between us—new and tentative—was temporary at best, destined for failure at worst.

None of this was really my secret to tell, but I knew I could trust her.

"Remember last month, at the farmers' market, you asked me about being a dad?"

"Yeah," she replied sheepishly.

"Well, I wasn't truthful with you, and, for that, I'm sorry. Hannah and I got married in college, but it's not what you think."

The words felt like a tangled mess. Where to start? How much to say?

"You have to understand how important Hannah was to me at the time. Her family—the Prices—basically took me under their wings. You probably heard the rumors back in school, but my mother died when I was young and I never knew my father." I swallowed that old, familiar hurt and made myself say the rest. "My aunt moved us to Kirby Falls when I was in middle school, and she didn't—she wasn't capable of giving me a homelife like kids should have. The Prices lived next door, and they welcomed me. Hannah was my first real friend."

Hesitating, I wondered what to say next.

Candace's hand slipped into mine. When she squeezed gently, I realized I'd been silent too long.

Tilting my head, I met her gaze—patient, kind, and completely open. "But in college, we grew apart. By junior year, I hardly saw her. She came to me then because she needed help. She—she got pregnant, and the father of the baby didn't want her to keep it. Hannah knew how her parents would react to a child born out of wedlock, so she asked me to help her."

Candace's lips parted in surprise.

"So I married her," I admitted. "We got special married housing on campus, and I stayed with the baby so Hannah could finish up her final semester and gradu-ate. Then we moved back to Kirby Falls. I bought this house with the money I'd saved for school. She got a job teaching at the elementary school. Things worked for a while."

That might have been an exaggeration, but, at the time, it had felt true enough. I didn't love Hannah romantically, but she was my friend. And we had Lyndsey.

"I always meant to go back and finish my degree, but I got my job at the orchard. I was happy there."

While that was accurate, it wasn't the whole reason. Truthfully, I got caught up in my fake marriage and my fake life. And then later, after it all went wrong, I was all alone, missing a kid that wasn't even mine.

Those early days back in Kirby Falls had been about performing, showing off our young family. There had been constant dinners with Reverend and Mrs. Price. Church picnics where everyone wanted to see Lyndsey and hold her.

It was like college had never happened. Everything revolved around the Prices. My entire world was back to the limited view I'd had as an adolescent, but instead of Hannah being my young savior, I'd been hers. I played the role of a loving husband; there was no part of being Lyndsey's father, though, that I had to fake.

Another squeeze of my hand brought me back to myself. I looked down to where Candace's fingers wrapped around mine and told her the rest.

"Lyndsey was just over a year old when Hannah told me she wanted a divorce. She'd been dating someone she met online, and she was leaving to be with him. They're married now. Live in Tennessee, outside of Nashville."

"She just . . . took the baby?" she asked, disbelief coloring her tone.

"Yeah. Hannah thought a clean break would be best. Lyndsey was too small to remember me." Saying those words were just as terrible as thinking them. Knowing they were true was a different kind of wound.

Candace was quiet for long moments while I wrestled with my emotions.

We just sat there, the truth heavy between us, her hand firmly holding mine. Finally, she said, "I don't understand. What was the plan long-term? You were just going to stay married to Hannah? Sacrifice your own future and happiness? Or did you—did you love her?"

I shook my head and met her gaze. "No. We didn't ever really get that far. We weren't married long, and so much of that time was spent surviving with a newborn. Maybe, eventually, we would have discussed the future . . ." As my voice trailed off, I thought about the reason why we'd probably never gotten to that point. "Right after Lyndsey was born, Hannah tried to kiss me. I was gentle with her but told her no. She was my best friend, but I didn't love her like that. She played it off like it was fine, just hormones. But looking back, I don't know."

Part of me thought that was the beginning of the end. Once Hannah realized we'd never be a family in truth, she'd gone out and looked for a better option. I guess she'd found it.

Candace made a sympathetic sound. "Then not long after, she said she was seeing someone else?"

"I couldn't give her what she was looking for," I admitted, feeling that old familiar shame rise up. Maybe if I'd just tried, kissed her back, it would have made our marriage real. Maybe someday I could have loved her. Maybe I'd still have Lyndsey if—

"You gave up your whole life, Mark," Candace said, her voice sharp enough that it pulled me out of my regrets. "You shouldn't have had to give her your heart, too."

I didn't know what to say to that.

Candace added, "I'm sorry for what you lost. And I'm sorry you were ever put into that position in the first place. It wasn't fair and it wasn't right."

I felt my brows furrow. "It wasn't like that, Candace. I don't—I'm not mad—"

"You should be," she argued. "Hannah took advantage of your friendship. She used you, cheated on you, and then cast you aside when you were no longer convenient. Let me guess, you never once cheated on her. I bet you honored your marriage vows even though they were fake."

My heart rate had picked up steadily as she spoke. Now it felt like I was halfway through a ten-mile run. Why was Candace saying these things? I didn't tell her the truth to bash Hannah or to gain sympathy for myself.

Of course, I'd kept my vows. Even when Hannah had blindsided me with a divorce, I didn't go out looking for a way to get back at her. Maybe we hadn't married for the right reasons, but I never saw it as a free-for-all. Marriage wasn't about keeping score or keeping things even. It wasn't every man for himself. At least, not for me.

"It wasn't like that, Candace. Besides, it's over now anyway."

"It's not over. You're still in this town, and everyone thinks it's your choice to not be in your daughter's life. When the truth is that Hannah took her away from you."

I was already shaking my head, frustration forcing the words through gritted teeth. "She's not my daughter. I have no claim on that little girl. No rights."

But Candace ignored me, eyes blazing with anger on my behalf. "Does her new husband think you're some deadbeat dad? Please tell me her parents know the truth. That she's not perpetuating this lie from three hundred miles away?"

Her words had my throat going tight, and I couldn't answer. But by the way her face fell, I knew she'd figured it out.

Anger and shame swirled together in an irrational vortex. I dropped her hand. My voice was gruffer than I intended when I demanded, "I don't want to do this. I didn't tell you the truth so you could throw it in my face. I told you because I couldn't stand the thought of lying to you. Of being with you and you not knowing me."

After a few moments, Candace took a deep breath and pressed her knee gently against mine. "I'm sorry. I shouldn't have reacted that way. You're right. You were telling me something sensitive and private, and I made it about me. I'm so sorry, Mark." I heard her swallow. "We can drop it. Talk about something else. Or I can go, if that would be better."

Now that my own breathing had evened out, I could think again. Did I want Candace to go? Was this how I wanted our first date—or whatever it was— to end?

I tapped her knee with mine and met her worried gaze. "You don't need to go. I was thinking about having a fire outside. Maybe we can sit out there and talk?"

A tentative smile touched the corners of her full lips. "I'd like that. And if you want to tell me more about Lyndsey, I'd love to hear about her."

A welcome ache flared to life in the center of my chest. I hardly let myself *think* about the little girl I'd lost. I definitely never talked about her. There wasn't anyone I *could* talk to. Hannah had cut off contact over two years ago, following our divorce. And to her parents, I was public enemy number one. The Prices had stopped being my family when I let their daughter leave the state and marry someone else. As if I had a choice. I wasn't going to stop Hannah from living her life. Our friendship had grown twisted and tainted by then, but I still wanted her to be happy. I wanted that for her daughter as well.

The offer to open up and talk about Lyndsey felt like a gift.

"Yeah," I finally replied. "That would be nice."

***

Candace

My first date with Mark Mercer was *not* going how I'd expected.

I never could have anticipated sitting around the fire pit in his gorgeous backyard while the quiet man told me about his marriage of convenience to his childhood best friend. I didn't even think those were real outside of historical romance novels. But here the modern example sat, clearly suffering from the trauma of the experience, from the unbelievable selfishness of his ex-wife and former best friend.

I'd listened to Mark reveal the truth of his marriage with shaking hands and so much unspent rage that I could hardly think straight. If I'd been thinking, I probably wouldn't have blurted out all that stuff about Hannah, but it had been hard to resist.

But seriously, fuck Hannah Price. I couldn't believe she'd put Mark through so much. He'd given up his education and his future to save her from her terrible family. He'd assumed the care of a newborn and obviously fallen in love with that baby, because hearing him talk about Lyndsey now was heartbreaking. Hannah had asked all of this of Mark, and then left him holding the bag when a better option came along.

She clearly only worried about her own relationship with her parents while she ignored the fact they were Mark's only family too. It was unforgivable that Hannah left for Tennessee, content to let everyone think that Mark didn't love or care for his child. I'd seen the gossip firsthand, what the Prices had let perpetuate in their daughter's absence. It was cruel and unfair after all Mark had done to protect Hannah.

But from Mark's reaction earlier, acknowledging Hannah's terrible behavior wasn't welcome. He was too loyal for his own good. Mark was still protecting the shy girl he'd befriended in middle school even though she was a grown-ass woman who needed to own up to what she'd done.

Beneath my simmering anger, however, was the realization that Mark Mercer was, probably, the best man I'd ever met. He'd kept Hannah's secret to his own detriment. He had sacrificed his own happiness for that of a friend. His loyalty and integrity were unmatched.

I'd known he was a good person from the beginning. His quiet, gentle nature had immediately put me at ease. And now, in knowing the truth about his relationship with Hannah, I'd learned just how selfless and big-hearted he was. As a result, my own heart ached at all that Mark had endured.

"Was she a good baby?" I asked gently.

Mark took a sip from his beer and tucked the plaid fleece blanket more tightly around my feet.

Following his tense confession in the living room, Mark had led me back outside. He'd built a roaring fire, scooted my chair close, draped the cozy fabric across my legs, and pulled my feet into his lap. The night air was chilly, but there wasn't any chance I'd get cold. Mark would never allow that.

He smiled as he gazed at the flames, distant, as if calling up a memory he'd hidden away, uncovering the cobwebs and bringing it out into the light. "No, not at all." His quiet laugh pierced a hole in my heart, and I felt my nose sting all of a sudden. "She spit up all the time. Like a little geyser. Hannah had trouble breastfeeding, so we gave Lyndsey formula. For a while, we tried different ones, in case she had sensitivities, and then different types of bottles. But she never seemed to have stomach pain or anything like that, she just spit up a lot. There was one day where I had no clean tee shirts left, and then she threw up on my bare chest and I just gave up trying to smell like anything other than spoiled milk."

I smiled as I watched the firelight dance across his face.

The thought of big, strong, baby-wearing Mark did ridiculous things to my ovaries. This was not the time.

"And then," he murmured followed by another aching, memory-laced laugh, "she didn't sleep, and if she did, you had to be holding her. There was this two-month stretch where she cried in the evenings. Every night at seven. Like clock-work. But I figured out, if I wore her in the front carrier and danced around our tiny apartment, she'd settle. And if I played Ed Sheeran, she'd be content. Basically, Ed Sheeran saved my life."

He'd given me a list of reasons why Lyndsey hadn't been a good baby, but he was still smiling, looking so utterly fond that I had to pinch the outside of my thigh to keep from crying.

I cleared the emotion from my throat and said seriously, "You should send him a fruit basket."

Mark caught my eye and laughed. He looked almost grateful. As relieved as someone could be while discussing something painful.

I wondered if Mark had ever gotten to discuss Lyndsey since Hannah had ripped her from his life. Who could he confide in? I assumed no one else knew the truth. He carried these memories and never got to share them. Maybe Mark needed this. Maybe it was a good thing.

I wouldn't make him regret telling me the truth. Even if I hated Hannah Price and thought she deserved a scarlet A and a come-to-Jesus moment with her family. He'd trusted me with this secret—one that he guarded fiercely. Being the person Mark opened up to was humbling.

"You know," Mark said eventually, after his laughter subsided, "I knew she wasn't mine. But she felt like she was. All those nights when she wouldn't sleep unless I was the one holding her, they meant something. When she was about eight months old, she refused to take a bottle from anyone but me. Even Hannah couldn't soothe her. I knew it wasn't right, but I liked being her favorite. I might not have been her real dad, but she picked me. This little baby who didn't share my blood, never had my eye or hair color. She didn't know any better, but she was still mine for as long as I got to keep her."

My eyes burned as the pressure behind them built, but I didn't want Mark to stop talking.

A sad smile crossed his lips as he stared at the fire. "After they moved away, I got hung up on the most unexpected things. Like how I'd never get to coach Lyndsey's sports team or go to a dance recital or watch whatever it was she was interested in as she grew. Because that would be the fun of it. To see her get big and change and figure out all the things she loved most. To see the person she'd become. Maybe she'd play the piano or learn to sing. Or maybe she'd love animals. Or maybe she'd need her dad to coach her soccer team someday."

My quiet sniffle drew his attention.

"Hey, don't cry," he said, rubbing comforting circles over the tops of my feet. "I shouldn't have told you all that."

I wiped away a tear from my lower lashes. "No, Mark. I'm glad you did."

"Crying on the first date isn't a great start." Then he froze as if realizing what he'd just said. "Not that this is a date. I just—"

"It is," I interjected with a reassuring smile. As far as I was concerned, this was the beginning of something. My heart was soft for Mark Mercer and getting gooier by the second. I could feel myself slipping further and faster into something dangerous. "It's a date. I'm glad you told me those stories. I like hearing about Lyndsey. Thank you for trusting me with the truth."

"I just didn't want to lie to you. I didn't want you thinking what everyone else thinks about me."

The urge to blame Hannah for Mark's reputation was admittedly strong, but I knew he wouldn't appreciate or welcome it right now. "I understand," I said instead.

"That's why I asked you if we could keep this"—he gestured broadly between us —"under wraps. I don't want all the rumors and gossip to touch you. I don't want people to bad-mouth you if you're seen out with me."

"I understand," I repeated.

And I did . . . for the most part. It didn't make it easier to swallow though. I knew Mark was doing what he thought was best. He was trying to protect me from small-minded busybodies. But hiding our relationship brought up past insecurities.

Emerson had made me feel like a dirty little secret, and those feelings really impacted my self-worth after I found out he was married and a no-good cheater.

The idea of being someone else's secret didn't sit right, but I told myself it wasn't the same. Mark was a good person. He might be misguided in his attempt to protect me, but he didn't intend to hurt me. He didn't know about Emerson and the affair. He didn't know I'd been fired. He didn't know about any of that because I hadn't told him. However, now wasn't really the time to bring all that up or to demand a public relationship.

I didn't care what gossipy church ladies thought about me or how dating Mark might impact my reputation in Kirby Falls. I wanted to be with him, but it wasn't just my decision to make.

A nasty little voice in my head whispered that if I did demand he date me openly, when I left and things ended, I'd be just as bad as Hannah Price, leaving him with a mess to clean up. I could envision the whispers and the horrible posts in the Kirby Falls Facebook group. How Mark had broken my heart, or worse, run me out of town—just like his ex-wife.

People didn't want the truth when a lie suited their needs just fine.

I wouldn't be careless with Mark's heart or his life in our small town. I refused to be another selfish person using and abusing him.

I reached for Mark's beer bottle and took a sip before passing it back. He smiled, pleased.

Then for the next little bit, we sat back and enjoyed the night and the fire and having someone to share it with.

My eyes scanned Mark's amazing backyard. The time and care he put into his garden oasis was obvious. From the beautifully tended plants and crops to the greenhouse to the patio, it was clear that Mark's home was important to him.

Seeing it tonight, with the stars bright and clear overhead and the smell of wood smoke thick in the air, I knew I'd been given a gift—a welcome I'd do my best to deserve.

Being in Mark's garden felt sacred. I'd known he was an intensely private person —for reasons all the more clear now. Between the gossip about his divorce and how little time he spent out and about in Kirby Falls, I'd sort of assumed his home was his safe space, the place he felt most comfortable. Where he didn't need to worry about whispered words and hurtful rumors.

Yes, this place was, indeed, magical. Like a hidden treasure that didn't exist on any map. A secret I felt compelled to keep.

I was intensely grateful he'd shared it with me.

Yet, for as much as this place was his sanctuary, it was also his prison.

MARK

More than a week went by with Candace knowing the truth, and nothing fell apart. The world didn't end.

But I still had moments of panic when I considered what I'd done, what I'd revealed.

Life at the orchard continued as usual. It was nearly Halloween, and the pumpkins were almost gone. We still had a couple of varieties of apples available for the tourists to pick, and weekends continued to be packed at Judd's.

For the next couple of weeks, Joan and I would be busy getting whatever was ripe off the trees to sell pre-picked in the Apple House before the first freeze hit and all the fruit dropped. We'd been lucky so far with a mild autumn. The plan was to also use what we picked at the end of the season for the first cider pressing next year.

Then we'd be navigating the extended open season with Candace's Christmas tree setup. Joan and I would be chipping in along with everyone else to get the tree lot arranged on the property and figure out the ins and outs of that operation. Candace had a meeting on the calendar to go over those aspects.

It seemed like Candace had a plan for nearly everything. Her advertising, social media posts, events, and collaborations with local businesses had definitely impacted the bottom line this season. We'd seen an increase in the number of tourists through the gates, making our busiest months even busier.

Even Joan couldn't deny her sister's hard work and dedication to the farm. She was still a little standoffish with Candace, but she didn't openly object to the changes Candace was implementing. I thought she might be coming around even if there still wasn't any sisterly bonding happening. At this point, Candace spent more time with Bonnie and Mac than she did with Joan.

I knew it bothered Candace. We'd talked a little about it the last time she'd come over for dinner, two nights ago. I'd told her to be patient. That she was doing all the right things, and Joan would come around. But part of me realized there was a clock counting down until Candace left, and, eventually, Joan would be too late.

I tried not to think about the deadline looming over Candace's time in Kirby Falls. Two months didn't feel like nearly enough time to see where things went with us. We'd taken it slow so far. Candace had agreed to keep our relationship private, and she'd been to my house three times for dinner. We'd had another night out by the fire, and then two nights ago, we'd watched a movie, snuggled together on the couch in my living room.

I didn't want to rush her into anything she wasn't ready for, but with her body draped across mine, I'd been hyper-aware of every breath she took and every time she shifted in her seat. It was hard enough to be close to her at work and not kiss her in her office every morning. To sit next to her at the picnic table while we ate lunch together and not hold her hand. But I could wait as long as she wanted. Despite the stopwatch on her time here, what was happening between us wasn't a race.

It was Friday, and we had a long day ahead. The orchard was open to tourists, and then Food Truck Friday would close things out around eight o'clock. I thought there might even be a band on the schedule for the night.

"Hey," I said as I poked my head into Candace's office twenty minutes before the gates opened.

She glanced up, a bright smile ready and waiting on her pretty face. "Hey, you. What do you have on the agenda for the day?"

Unable to stop myself, I drifted closer to her desk. "Picking Gold Rush in the east field."

Her fingers played with the edge of her notebook, the one she brought everywhere. "I know it'll be late when I get off tonight with the band and the food truck being here, but I thought I might bring some dessert over afterward. Would that be okay?"

"Sure."

Candace worried her bottom lip. "And if I wanted to stay the night? Would that be okay too?"

I took in her nervous fidgeting and the abuse she was inflicting on her plush lower lip. Then I thought about what she was really asking. Smiling, I replied, "Yeah. That would be more than okay."

"Yeah?"

When I couldn't take her tentative worry anymore, I closed the distance between us and leaned over her desk. Cupping her cheek, I pressed a quick kiss to her lips, trying to alleviate her hesitancy and her nervousness. Doing my best to address the part of her brain that told her she had to question herself with me.

I wanted her at my house and in my space. I wanted her all day, every night . . . for as long as she'd let me have her.

Eventually, I pulled back, brushing my nose gently against hers before confirming quietly against the soft skin of her lips, "Yes. Stay."

Reluctantly, I straightened and released her.

Candace beamed up at me. "Okay."

"Okay," I repeated, like an idiot. I needed to get out of this lavender-scented office before I did something embarrassing, like ask her to marry me. "I'll see you later."

"Bye, Mark."

"Bye, Candace." Then with a glance over her head, I added, "Bye, Lance Bass."

Her happy laughter stayed with me, keeping me warm on the chilly October morning.

I offered to help Candace and Brady close, but Candace told me to go ahead and she'd see me in a few hours. I used the time to pick up around my already clean house, change the sheets, shower, and trim my beard.

Candace still had another hour at the farm, and I was pacing around my house feeling absurdly nervous. I'd had to go out and get condoms from a convenience store in Miller Creek because I didn't have any in the house. I hadn't needed them. Despite being divorced for two and a half years, I hadn't dated or hooked up with anyone. And with the circumstances surrounding my marriage, I hadn't been with anyone since college—since before Hannah and I had gotten married.

I kept one eye on the clock and tried to rein in my worries.

Truthfully, I hadn't really let myself think about this, the reality of being with Candace. What it would be like, how she'd taste, the sounds she'd make. Fantasies were supposed to be filthy, but the kinds of things I thought about regarding Candace Judd were embarrassingly innocent, yet no less vulnerable.

Swinging in the hammock together on a spring afternoon, her slender body cocooned in my arms while light filtered through the trees overhead, highlighting the gold strands in her hair. Taking her up to Craggy Peak for a night shoot while she sat in the bed of my truck, starlight glittering in her eyes. Working side by side in the Apple House on a busy Saturday, sharing smiles and secret touches. A bottle of lavender-scented shampoo sitting in the shower on a shelf right next to mine.

My fantasies were forbidden in a different way. The most obvious reason was that they could never happen, not for any length of time anyway.

Candace was leaving. She was my co-worker. She was a Judd. I couldn't screw any part of that up. And I couldn't change the truth of it either.

But there was also the secret part of me that *did* wonder what it would be like— all of it. The sound of her moan vibrating against my lips, the softness of her inner thigh, *and* that damn shampoo bottle.

That reckless, curious part was living out another fantasy when I opened the door to Candace's quiet knock.

She'd showered and changed. Her long hair was slightly damp and bound in a thick braid that draped over one shoulder. I liked thinking that she'd rushed a little, eager to get here, impatient to see me. I didn't have wet hair to show for it, but I did have an anxious path I'd worn on the carpet and my heart racing at the sight of her.

She held a bakery box in her hands and a large tote bag slung over one shoulder.

"Hi," I said, opening the door wide and relieving her of her burdens.

Candace removed her shoes and socks and left them by the front door.

"Hey," she finally replied, a little too loud considering how close we were.

I fought my smile and led her into the kitchen. "How'd it go tonight?"

"Oh, uh, it was good. The empanada food truck always draws a crowd, and the band was nice. Just instrumental acoustic covers. It was a good vibe. Is it hot in here?"

I placed the white box on the counter and turned to see Candace fanning her face with one hand and awkwardly attempting to shrug out of her denim jacket with the other.

Oddly, seeing her sudden bout of nerves helped to calm me. It was nice to know I wasn't the only one affected by the possibility of tonight.

With sure steps, I closed the distance between us and helped ease her jacket the rest of the way off, tracing her arm beneath the fabric. "I can turn down the heat if you like."

"No, that's okay," she said, following this with a deep, centering breath.

"Candace," I murmured quietly. Her wide hazel eyes snapped to mine, a little more green than gold in this light. "We don't have to do anything you're not ready to do. We can eat the dessert you brought and watch another movie. There's no pressure here, okay? No expectations."

She nodded along as I spoke, but then as soon as I stopped, she pushed up onto her toes and kissed me. It wasn't tentative or cautious. Candace kissed me like she couldn't help herself. And then just as quickly, she pulled back, keeping her eyes closed a moment longer.

"I know you'd never put any pressure on me, Mark. But I—I want this. I want you. It's hard to be around you at work. I want to touch you and kiss you." Her hands splayed across my chest as she spoke, smoothing the fabric of my tee shirt. "I'm just nervous all of a sudden. I care about you, and I want to be good for you. I—"

Leaning forward, I cut her off with my lips. Then as I pressed featherlight kisses to the corners of her mouth and her cheeks and her eyelids, I admitted, "You don't have to worry about that, I promise. Just you being here, that's all I want." Another duet of soft kisses along her jaw. "That's all I need."

Her fingers curled in the waistband of my jeans as I moved my lips gently along the column of her throat. The backs of her fingers were cool against my abdomen, but she didn't need to worry about keeping me close. I wasn't going anywhere.

Candace made a sound, low in her throat as my tongue dipped into the hollow beside her collarbone, so I did it again.

My fingers flirted with the bottom edge of her sweatshirt, before drifting beneath. Charting a path from her waist to her ribs, I let my rough palms skim her skin. A trail of gooseflesh erupted in my wake.

"Mark," she breathed, as she shifted on her feet, impatient and eager. I knew because I felt it too. We were wearing too much clothing, and while I wanted to take my time, I felt the edge of urgency pushing me forward.

Reaching down, I loosened her grip on my pants before threading her fingers through mine and leading her down the hallway to my bedroom. It wasn't the master suite, but it was the room that had been mine since I first bought the house. I'd never seen a reason to move to the bigger space after Hannah moved out.

Candace didn't bother to stop and look around. She lifted my shirt and brought it up and over my head, content to explore my body rather than the room we occupied. Her hands traced reverent lines across my chest and over the rounded tops of my shoulders. Nails scored lightly down the length of my arms. I sucked in a breath as her curious touch found its way along the muscles of my abdomen to the ridges of my hips.

"Can I take these off?" Candace asked politely, her grip once again on the button of my jeans.

At my nod, she added, a little less politely, "I'm kind of obsessed with your thighs."

Surprised laughter shot out of me, and she grinned in response. "I'm probably going to bite them."

I laughed again. The sound cut off abruptly as she followed the fabric of my jeans to the floor, dropping to her knees as she tugged the worn denim. She was fully clothed, and I was standing in my gray boxer briefs while she knelt at my feet. "Candace," I managed hoarsely.

But she ignored me and leaned in to press a rough, wet kiss to the top of my left thigh. Her nails dragged up my calves, over the thin skin behind my knee, and I made an involuntary sound at the sensation.

She looked up at me then, her smile a touch wicked and infinitely more confident than it had been in my kitchen minutes ago.

My brain short-circuited, and I placed a steadying hand on the mattress to my right. "Maybe you should come back up here."

"What if I want to stay down here?" she challenged, her grin widening as she deliberately brushed her nose against the skin of my inner thigh.

I swallowed. "Then this will all be over very quickly."

"That's okay. We can do other things."

It was the image of all those other things flashing through my mind that had me hurriedly pulling her to her feet. "You're wearing too many clothes."

"Should we match?" she teased.

"Yes," I agreed and gripped the hem of her sweatshirt. Then I met her gaze and asked with intent, "Can I undress you, Candace?"

She nodded.

I lifted the soft blue fabric over her head, feeling a rush of heat as I uncovered miles of gorgeous skin. She wore a delicate white lace bra with flowers embroidered all over it. My hands felt big and clumsy at the sight. I realized I'd paused a moment too long when Candace reached for the button fly of her jeans herself. She shrugged the denim over her hips and revealed underwear that matched.

I got it together just enough to steady her as she stepped out of her pants and tossed them to the floor.

Then she walked right to me, arms winding around my waist as she pressed all that warm skin against mine.

It was a relief to have her this close, to pull her tight and feel her heartbeat just as ragged and impatient as my own. In the circle of my arms, she let go of my waist and reached back to undo the clasp of her bra. The fabric was trapped between us until Candace shimmied a little and it fell away. Next she tucked her thumbs into the waistband of her underwear and slid those down her legs. I felt the drag of the delicate lace all the way to the floor.

Then Candace stepped back and I got a good look at her.

I was sure characters in a movie or a book would say their heart stopped at the sight of such beauty, but mine was beating too hard and too fast for that to ever be the truth. Blood rushed in my ears, accompanying the frantic pounding in my chest. She was all gorgeous long lines—hair, legs, torso—and rosy brown nipples. A full bottom lip captured between her teeth. Toes curled into the gray carpet beneath her feet, and a steady golden-brown gaze as I did nothing but look.

"You," I started, but then had to clear the overwhelming want from my throat. "You're beautiful, Candace."

She released her tortured lip and smiled before pressing her bare body to mine once more. Now, only my boxers were in the way.

Her thumbs dipped an inch inside my underwear, and she repeated against the shell of my ear, "Should we match?"

"Yes," I breathed in answer.

And she lowered my boxer briefs to the ground. My erection was hot and hard between us, and as I felt Candace's hand wrap around my length, my eyes closed.

"You're beautiful, too," she whispered.

A gruff chuckle escaped my lips. I was too rough around the edges to be beautiful.

My laughter died as quickly as it started. It had been so long, and I was getting too close too soon, so I willed myself to pull her off me.

Guiding Candace backward, I had her sit on the edge of the bed and lean back.

Then it was my turn to get on my knees.

She was soft against my mouth, everywhere I touched. Her legs shook as my lips dragged along her knee, the inside of her thigh, the very heart of her. I slid my tongue along her seam and felt restless hands search for purchase in my short hair.

Candace squirmed when I sucked on her smooth skin, so I did it again and again. I moved closer as her hands tugged helplessly at my scalp, wedging my big body deeper between her spread legs, helping her drape her thighs over my shoulders.

Those fantasies, the ones that had made me wonder about her sounds and her taste, were being rewritten with every pass of my tongue. The truth emerged more vibrant and intoxicating than any daydream.

When I finally pressed one thick finger inside her wet heat, I felt the desperate rhythm of her release and heard the sharp gasp she made as a result.

Candace fought to pull me closer as I kissed my way up her body. I relished her seeking touch, her panting breaths warm against my neck. And when I grabbed the condom from my bedside table, I was so damn grateful she'd found her release because I wasn't going to last. She felt too good, too soft, too perfect under my hands.

Nails scraped down my back when we were finally joined. I had to stop and just breathe, my head bowed against her shoulder as her legs lifted to wrap around my back.

"Is it later yet?" she whispered.

I smiled into her smooth skin before I brought my lips to hers. The reminder and her kiss helped to ground me, to soothe the impatient edge that begged *more* and *now* and *faster*.

We kissed for long minutes as I set a steady rhythm and she matched me with every roll of her hips. Her thighs held me as I rocked into her. My hands found her breasts, her hips, the delicate curve of her cheek.

Then I let my fingers drift to the place where we were joined. Candace jolted as I touched her, her rhythm faltering momentarily as I worked her sensitive flesh in circles over and over. I wanted to get her there—with me. I wanted to hit that quickly rising peak together.

As her breath sped and her muscles tightened, I kept my pace and my patience. I was rewarded by a gasping moan and Candace's delicate inner muscles pulsing around me.

When I couldn't hold back any longer, I closed my eyes and let myself go. Pleasure forced a groan from between my lips as my movements became jerky and inelegant.

I flipped us so that I didn't crush Candace, and the warm weight of her across my body had contentment settling somewhere deep within.

As I returned to myself, soft lips grazed my temple. I could feel her fingers tracing the planes of my face.

Then she settled too, her head coming to rest on my chest as I worked to even out my breathing.

Those old fantasies didn't hold a candle to the woman in my arms. I couldn't have known before, how the reality of her would compare to the utter inadequacy of my imagination. But now I did. And I wasn't sure I'd ever recover.

When I emerged from the bathroom a few minutes later, Candace was standing in the kitchen in her pajamas.

She'd told me to meet her there for dessert after I cleaned up. I'd kissed her forehead and tried to remember how to walk.

She'd just put a slice of cake onto a plate when she turned and caught sight of me. Her gaze lingered over my bare chest before dipping down to the cotton lounge pants I wore.

It was silly to feel my cheeks heat at her appreciative stare, especially after what we'd just done, but I liked having her eyes on me. And I liked having the freedom to look back even more.

"What you got there?" I finally asked.

"Caramel cake from the Orchard Bake Shop." She set the knife down and licked a bit of frosting off her thumb.

I swallowed and Candace grinned.

She set two plates on the kitchen table and took a seat. I grabbed two forks and joined her.

Before any awkwardness could settle in the vacant chairs beside us, my phone buzzed from where I'd left it charging on the counter.

I went to check it, just in case there was an emergency at the orchard or Nick or Amy needed something, but it was a text from Wenn. I'd seen my friend a few weeks ago. We'd gone up to Craggy Peak to get some sunset shots. He'd fed me pumpkin scones, and I'd brought him a lager he liked from Trailview Brewing.

Wenn: Reports of aurora visibility as far south as Mount Mitchell. I can't make it out tonight, but if you aren't busy, you should see what you can get.

Seeing the northern lights this far south was extremely rare. I didn't bother setting up any forecast alerts for it, but folks from the photography group we were in checked aurora activity religiously, on the off chance we got lucky here in North Carolina.

I glanced up as Candace took a bite of dessert. Her lips wrapped around the fork, and she made a grateful little sound as the sugar hit her tongue.

It would be after ten by the time we got up there, but it would make for an experience to remember if we could see any of the pinks or greens twisting their way across the sky. And with a long exposure, I'd be able to pick up even more than what was visible to the naked eye.

"What?" Candace asked when I'd been staring too long at my phone.

"How much of that cake do you have?"

"I should have worn all black," Candace said as she slumped low in the passenger seat of my truck. Her eyes darted out the window, but her voice was laced with unbridled excitement.

"We're not robbing a bank," I argued.

"But we *are* breaking the rules."

I rolled my eyes but smiled before shifting the truck into park. "You are such a goody-goody," I teased as I opened my door to put the chain back across the path.

"Well, yeah," she called, scooting into the driver's seat to shout after me. "That's kind of my brand."

I chuckled and clipped the barrier back into place.

After we'd shuffled vehicles, putting Candace's car in my garage where it wouldn't be noticed by nosy neighbors, we'd made good time on the drive up to Craggy Peak. We'd caught Wenn's pal at the visitor center just before closing and had given him a large slice of caramel cake to look the other way while we accessed the official-use-only trail for park and emergency service vehicles.

After a quick glance at the aurora projection for the night, it looked like our best odds of catching the phenomenon was between 11:00 p.m. and 2:00 a.m., so our chances were pretty good. It wouldn't take me long to get set up. There wasn't anything discernible in the sky as of yet, but we had plenty of time.

Candace had been more than happy to tag along. Now, sitting in the passenger seat in plaid pajama bottoms with my NC State hoodie swallowing her, she was practically bouncing from excitement.

We reached the overlook, and I passed Candace a headlamp. "It's really dark up here without ambient city light. I don't want you to trip over anything. I'll set up some blankets in the truck bed if you want to hang out back there while I unpack my equipment."

"Okay," she squeaked. "I can help."

With our headlamps on, Candace and I unrolled a mattress pad I used for camping and covered it with a couple of flannel-lined sleeping bags. It was in the low fifties currently, so not too cold, but if we stayed out here for any length of time, I didn't want Candace to get uncomfortable.

I positioned my tripod and showed her my camera while I clicked through the manual settings.

"So, what's different about trying to capture the northern lights?" she asked, her gaze focused on the screen.

"Well, with a longer exposure, the camera lens is capable of capturing more light than the human eye ever could. It'll make the colors more impressive as well as the light from the stars. Everything will be brighter than what you see with the naked eye."

I searched the sky, and to the west, I could see faint pink hovering over the layers of dark mountains. Pointing, I showed Candace what we were looking for. "I'll set up here with my wide-angle lens, turn off my autofocus, dial the aperture way low—maybe 1.4—and raise the ISO for light sensitivity, since it's so dark tonight. Then I'll use my remote and try some different times. Maybe five-, ten-, twenty-, and twenty-five-second exposures. And then we'll see where we land and adjust from there."

"This is so cool," she said eagerly.

We worked together over the next half hour, taking test shot after test shot. Candace asked me questions, and I explained what I was doing. It was nice having her with me. Usually, Wenn and I worked side by side in comfortable silence. We'd talk a bit, share our settings if something was working particularly well, but despite there being two of us, it wasn't really a group activity.

I liked sharing this part of myself with Candace. Like with the garden at home, she was interested in the things that interested me. Usually, I was a quiet guy, but talking to Candace about my hobbies made me feel good.

Later, when we were stretched out in the bed of my truck, sleeping bags spread open to keep us warm, we watched the way the pink in the sky steadily intensified. There was even a sliver of green visible. You couldn't see the colors shifting or the auroras dancing like in the Arctic Circle, but it was still a sight to behold—not something I ever thought I'd see in the mountains of North Carolina.

I had my arm around Candace, and she was tucked up against my side, her body warm and welcome. I thought this might be the most perfect night of my life.

"When did you get into photography?" she asked.

Her voice was quiet in the night, the only human sound among the insects and the rustling leaves. No doors slamming or engine noise from the highway. There was peace in knowing we were the only people for miles and miles.

"I took a class in college and really enjoyed it. Then I got back into it when I moved back to Kirby Falls. There are so many beautiful places to shoot around here. I joined a photography meetup group in Asheville a few years back. That's where I met Wenn."

"Ah, the mysterious aurora borealis insider."

I smiled into her hair, the lavender scent competing with the crisp autumn breeze and winning by a mile. "That's him. He's also the mysterious baker who utilizes my zucchini."

Grinning, she moved until her top half was draped across my chest, then she looked down at me with a scandalized expression. "Utilizes your zucchini, does he? I thought that was my job."

I laughed out loud, and Candace appeared so damn pleased with herself that I swatted her on the backside. She gasped dramatically, and I leaned up to capture the sound with my lips.

Eventually, we shifted so that she was fully on top of me as we kissed. Her hips shifted restlessly, seeking friction, and with the thin layers separating us, it wasn't a hardship. She felt good on top of me.

As my hand found its way beneath the cotton of her pajama pants to palm her ass, Candace pressed something into my other hand.

I broke the kiss and gave a surprised laugh. "Now, where did this come from?"

She grinned, unrepentant. "I stole it from the box at your house."

"Wow. Did you have *plans*, Candace Judd?"

She bit her lip and shifted her hips a fraction. I stifled a groan as her hot center pressed more fully against my painfully hard erection.

"I like being prepared," she finally replied with another sexy little thrust.

"I didn't think a goody-goody would have sex in public."

"Semi-public sex," she argued with another roll of her hips.

I clutched the globes of her ass to still her. "Outdoor sex," I countered.

She laughed and I felt the sound everywhere. "You got me there."

Then Candace started moving again, grinding atop me, and I didn't have it in me to continue the debate.

The night was gorgeous, we were completely alone, and I'd make sure to keep her warm.

CANDACE

"Candy!"

I froze at the sound of my mom's voice.

I hadn't thought she'd be on the back porch this morning. It was cold. Steal-the-breath-from-your-lungs cold. I knew because I was the one dressed in thin sleep shorts and Mark's stolen college hoodie, running across the yard in my sneakers with no socks on, trying to get into my warm apartment.

I'd backed out of Mark's garage fifteen minutes ago while he'd watched from the doorway in nothing but a pair of jeans until I was out of sight.

Late November wasn't messing around. Frost coated the grass in all directions, a glistening layer that crunched underfoot. I could see my breath puff out white and impatient as I turned to face my mother with goose bumps coating my skin.

I'd been successfully doing the walk of shame and sneaking back into the garage apartment behind the farmhouse several mornings a week for the last month.

Well, maybe not so successfully if my mother's huge knowing grin told me anything.

With a sigh, I detoured to my parents' back porch and closed the screen door as quietly as I could, hoping like hell that my dad was still asleep, or just literally anywhere else while I had this conversation with my mom.

She patted the cushion beside her, and after I took a tentative seat, she shared her blanket, throwing it over my legs.

"You want some tea?" she asked before a sip of her own.

"No, thank you," I replied primly, grateful for the blanket but dreading when I inevitably had to get back up again.

I needed a hot shower. My hair was a tangled mess, twisted and tugged on from Mark's hands the night before. I'd thrown it up in a messy bun this morning with the intention of cleaning up as soon as I got home.

But here I was, sharing a love seat with my mother while I still smelled like Mark's sheets. And I was pretty sure I was sporting beard burn on my neck.

Casually I reached up and removed the elastic band, attempting to smooth the strands down to cover my throat.

"You know you don't need to be embarrassed, honey."

Oh, I begged to differ. No one wanted their parent catching them after sneaking in from spending the night with their boyfriend. Especially a secret boyfriend I couldn't even admit to seeing. And it wasn't like Mark could spend time with me in the garage apartment, not unless we wanted to hide his truck in the fields and try smuggling him in without setting off the new motion-sensor floodlights on the property.

I sighed.

Yes, things with Mark were going great. We'd had a solid month together so far. Homemade dinners at his place. Takeout pizza and movie nights on his couch. Bonfires in the garden. Taking photographs up at Craggy Peak and Juniper Point. And nights in Mark's bed.

He brought me flowers from his greenhouse for my office. We worked together in the Apple House, and then he'd helped me get the space ready for the tree lot that had kicked off last weekend, following Thanksgiving.

Mark had joined my family for the holiday too. While it had been nice to sit beside him at the dinner table, I couldn't do more than press my knee against his. I wanted to hold his hand or tease him about the pie we'd baked together and burned the night before because we'd gotten distracted. But secrecy was still paramount, and I had to be careful with my glances.

We still parked my mother's car in his garage whenever I came over. When I spent the night, I always woke up to a blaring alarm on my phone, signaling it was time to hide what we were to each other, reminding me to get home before someone noticed me missing.

I knew Mark was only doing it for me—for my reputation, and to prevent any awkwardness at work. However, some days it was harder than others to remember the reasons why.

When I was dressing in the dark and pressing sleepy kisses to Mark's mouth, I felt like I was, once again, someone's dirty little secret. Guilt hovered just beneath the surface even though I wasn't doing anything wrong. I was only being with someone I cared about, someone who cared about me in return. There was no secret wife and child this time, no adultery or workplace misconduct. But sometimes my heart had a hard time separating the past from the present.

"You're an adult," Mom continued, drawing me out of my worries. "And you don't need to hide. You can be honest with us. We've only ever wanted you to be happy, whatever that may be."

Her tone changed at the end. I glanced over to read her expression, but she didn't appear anything beyond open and reassuring.

Briefly, I wondered if my mother could see the secrets I was keeping. Not just my month-long relationship with Mark, my parents' favorite employee, but the other things I was hiding beneath the surface. The truth about my return to Kirby Falls. My reluctance to leave. How I hadn't done more than update my résumé and glance at job listings. The way I couldn't bring myself to apply for a single position anywhere.

For a moment I considered coming clean, admitting that I didn't want to find another job or move back to the city—any city. I wanted to stay right here and work on the farm with my family, live in my hometown, and be . . . happy.

But then my mother smiled and patted my knee. "We're just so happy to have you here, Candy. Even if it's just for a little bit until you need to get back to your life. Your father and I want you to feel comfortable while you're home, and if that includes having a . . . *playdate*, shall we say—"

"Oh, God," I groaned in mortification.

"—then that is fine with your father and me."

"No, it's not!" my dad yelled from just inside the doorway to the kitchen.

I covered my face with my hands as my mother laughed.

"He's kidding," she said happily while attempting to pry my fingers away from my heated cheeks. "He knows you're a grown woman. And sometimes women have needs—"

"Nope," I said and stood abruptly, casting the blanket off my legs in the process. I'd rather get hypothermia than have this conversation. "I am not mature enough to discuss this." Without making eye contact, I hurried toward the screen door. "Thank you for understanding, Mom. Let's never speak of this again. I will see you later."

"Bye, sweetie!" she called. Her amusement followed me across the lawn.

I picked up my pace as the wind nipped at my bare legs.

<hr>

Maybe it was the run-in with my mother and all the feelings it brought up, but afterward, I'd texted Mark to see if I could stay over the following Sunday night.

Monday was his day off next week, and I figured I could just go in late in the hope that we could wake up together, or at the very least, without an alarm getting me up and out of bed before daybreak.

Sunday rolled around, and I parked my car in the garage as usual. Mark made cabbage roll soup for dinner. Apparently, I'd gone twenty-five years without realizing I liked cabbage, or maybe I just liked it the way Mark made it, in a creamy tomato base with rice and ground beef. Either way, dinner had been cozy and comforting, much like the man himself. With it being December, I'd been in the mood to watch something festive, so we streamed *Die Hard* and argued over whether it was a holiday movie or not.

Later, when we were in bed, I felt like I should give Mark a heads-up about Mom. I didn't think she'd made the connection between us—I doubted she'd be able to hide her excitement if she'd accurately pieced together who I was having a *playdate* with.

Good Lord.

My parents loved Mark. He was their star employee and an honorary Judd son. If my mother thought we were seeing each other, she'd go ahead and book the venue for our wedding reception and put together a list of names for her future grandbabies.

I felt an ache at that. Mark would make a great husband and father.

Deliberately pushing those sorts of wistful thoughts away, I turned off the light on the bedside table and snuggled closer to his side. "So, Mom caught me sneaking in the other morning."

Mark stiffened, his warm body going rigid at my words.

I hurried to add, "She doesn't know about us."

"You didn't tell her?" His voice was cautious, quiet, as if he'd expected me to fold beneath my mother's early-morning inquisition. Maybe I was reading more into his tone simply because the room was dark and I couldn't see his facial expressions. Maybe I was hearing accusations where none existed. Maybe I was being too sensitive about all this secrecy because of my past. Chances were high it was all three.

"No, Mark," I replied evenly. "I know you're not ready for that. She only wanted to assure me that she didn't care if I was . . . seeing someone. She knows I'm a grown woman, and she didn't want me to feel like I needed to sneak in and out of my own apartment like a rebellious teenager."

"I see." His body relaxed on a long, slow exhale.

"So I thought I'd skip the alarm in the morning, go in a little late."

He pressed a kiss to my temple. "It would be nice to wake up together."

I breathed a little sigh of relief. Mark *did* want me here. "Yeah."

"And not have to shake your comatose body awake, because you could sleep through a tornado."

I squawked in mock outrage and pinched his side. The skin was easily accessible since Mark was wearing boxer briefs and nothing else. "It's not my fault I'm a heavy sleeper!"

He yelped out a laugh and twisted away from my grabby hands. "Honey, there's being a heavy sleeper, and then there's you. I check your breathing at least once a night."

Seeking retribution, I pressed my ice-cold feet against his side.

"Holy shit." He jerked, reaching for my toes to still me and then sandwiching his warm hands on either side of my bare feet. "Are you cold? Why didn't you tell me? I can turn the heat up."

His sweetness had me pushing my grinning lips against his shoulder. "I'm fine. My feet just stay cold."

Mark rubbed my skin as if trying to transfer his body heat to me. "You're sure?"

"Yep."

Then he turned on his side to face me, taking my feet and tucking them securely between his muscular calves. Strong arms came around me next, calloused fingers drawing shapes I couldn't identify on the skin of my back. I nuzzled my face against Mark's chest, and the last thing I remembered was stubble on my forehead and soft lips telling me he'd keep me warm.

I woke up suddenly the following morning. The kind of disoriented emerging that happens when you lie down for an afternoon catnap and wake up four hours later. I could have been in another country for all I knew. But when my abrupt consciousness started to make sense, I took note of the fact that bright sunlight streamed through the curtains, filling every corner of Mark's bedroom.

The man himself was seated beside me, fully dressed and freshly showered. He appeared to be holding back laughter, but I forgave him because he also held two cups of steaming coffee. The scent filled my lungs as I groggily pushed up onto one elbow.

Alas, our dreamy wake-up montage complete with slow, sleepy lovemaking in dim early-morning light had not come to pass.

"What time is it?"

"Almost ten," Mark replied, passing me a mug and making sure I held it securely before releasing his grip on the handle.

"Shit," I murmured.

He smiled. "I didn't want you to sleep too late. I didn't know what you had going on at work today."

The first sip of caffeine had parts of my brain coming slowly online. "Why didn't you get me up sooner, when you got up?"

Mark's grin widened.

I groaned. "You tried and I didn't budge?"

He nodded. "You looked really cute all curled up and dead to the world."

I groaned again. "Mom used to have to get a spray bottle to wake me up for school."

Mark chuckled and took another sip of coffee.

"It would be nice to be a normal sleeper . . . She said I used to talk, too."

Mark smirked but said nothing.

I sat up straighter. "Wait. What did I say?"

He hid his growing smile behind his Kirby Falls Farmers' Market mug.

"Marcus Mercer, you better tell me right this minute."

Then he did laugh outright. "Marcus is not my first name."

"I know. But I don't know your middle name, so I had to make up for it."

Reaching forward, he swept a strand of hair off my forehead. I could only imagine what a mess it was. "It's Jeffrey."

Before I could further demand he recount my sleepy nighttime mumblings, he stood and made for the doorway, calling as he went, "I'll make you some breakfast. Don't go back to sleep."

"Okay," I agreed, struck with a sudden wave of affection that had my voice emerging quiet and choked.

That sense of warmth and fondness went absolutely nowhere when I eventually unwound myself from the blankets and stood. Because there, on my feet, were a pair of oversized men's wool socks.

I looked down at the thick fabric that definitely hadn't been there the night before. Flexing my toes, I thought about Mark's sweetness. He was always considerate and gentle with me, always made sure I had what I needed—that I was safe and comfortable and content. He was steadfast and loyal, the first person to help out in any situation. Mark volunteered his time and his generosity and he took care of the people he cared about.

He was in the kitchen right now, making me breakfast despite the late hour, because he knew it was my favorite meal.

I made my way to the bathroom across the hall and grabbed my toothbrush from right next to Mark's in the holder. Then I retrieved an elastic from the countertop and did my best to tame my wild brown hair into a high ponytail. After I finished up, I took off everything but the socks and went to the kitchen.

Mark was at the stove, with his back to me, but he must have heard me approach because he said, "What do you want in your omelet? I have those mushrooms you like and a few cherry tomatoes from the greenhouse. I'm out of bacon though."

When I stayed quiet, he glanced at me over his shoulder and promptly dropped the spatula he'd been holding.

Grinning, I approached slowly. Then I reached around his body to twist the dial closest to me and turn off the heating stovetop.

"What are you—"

His words cut off abruptly as I lowered my naked self to my knees before him and undid the button of his jeans.

Mark's eyes went dark and watchful as I tugged his zipper down and shifted his pants and underwear just far enough to free his hardening cock from the confines of his clothes.

"You don't have to—" he tried to say, but he was again interrupted when my tongue dragged up the underside of his erection.

I watched him swallow thickly as I reached the head, swirling my tongue and collecting the drop of liquid at the tip. Then I brought my eyes to his as I took him deep inside my mouth.

Mark made a rough sound and reached back to steady himself on the countertop.

He looked at me with so much patience and gentle restraint that some trouble-making hellion inside me—one that had never seen the light of day—wanted to make him lose every ounce of that careful control.

And that was what I set out to do. With hands and lips and tongue and teeth, I fought to drive Mark wild. I relished every strangled moan, each whispered *fuck*. The way his eyes absorbed my movements and how well I took him.

There was power in giving pleasure, and with the way Mark was looking at me, I felt consumed with it.

His thighs shook beneath my fingertips, and I knew he was getting close. He tugged hard on the line of his restraint and balled his hands into fists. So I smoothed my palms up his legs and used one to grip his length and the other to cup his balls, and I redoubled my efforts.

When Mark finally grasped my ponytail and wound it around his fist, the seductress buried deep inside this consummate good girl gave a victorious shout and a devastating smirk. I bobbed my head in time with his urging, and soon enough, Mark's movements stilled as he found his release, his panting breaths the only sound in the room.

When he'd recovered, Mark helped me to my feet and opened his mouth, the very obvious offer to reciprocate poised on the tip of his tongue. So I kissed him instead. What I'd done had been for me too.

When I finally pulled away, Mark's hands were cupping my ass. Grinning, I said, "I'm going to get dressed and then head to work. Bonnie's meeting me after school, and we're finishing up the float."

Judd's Orchard was part of the annual Kirby Falls Holiday Jamboree, and the parade was happening this week. Normally my family drove a tractor or a truck and threw out candy, but this year, I'd designed a float. It was still rural-parade appropriate, on a trailer hauled behind a pickup truck. But it looked amazing, and I was so excited for the event.

"Do you and Bonnie need any help tonight?"

I got an intense amount of pleasure out of Mark's loose, still-dazed expression. I smiled and shook my head. "We're almost done. I'm taking her out to dinner as a thank-you."

"You'll come over after?" His sneaky hands had returned to my backside and he gave a squeeze.

"Yeah." I laughed, attempting once again to extricate myself. "And I'll take those mushrooms and Swiss cheese in my omelet if you're still offering."

Reluctant fingers trailed along my hips as I pulled away and he replied, "Anything you want."

CANDACE

The Kirby Falls Holiday Jamboree was kicking off tonight with the annual parade on Main Street. This had always been one of my favorite local events growing up.

Our town had other parades celebrating the Fourth of July as well as the Orchard Festival, but the holiday parade was the only one that took place at night, when everything was bright with twinkle lights and utterly magical.

I remembered the wonder and excitement of staying up late, drinking hot cocoa from vendors, and catching handfuls of candy as they were thrown from passing vehicles and floats. And then later, riding in the back of a pickup truck, representing Judd's Orchard, my legs swinging off the tailgate while my siblings and I waved to friends and neighbors and visitors.

There was something enchanting about the celebration, and Christmas had always been my favorite holiday.

Being able to participate in the parade tonight was something I'd been looking forward to.

This weekend was probably the second biggest draw for tourists behind the Orchard Festival in September. The Thursday night parade started festivities. Holiday markets would happen Friday through Sunday on the same stretch of Main Street that saw farmers' market vendors and Orchard Festival attendees.

However, the wares would be less fresh produce and more along the lines of handmade gifts. Local artisans would occupy booths and encourage folks to take home hand-thrown pottery, Christmas ornaments, original artwork, and much, much more. Food trucks would be on site as well as vendors selling hot chocolate, kettle corn, candy apples, and peppermint bark.

December weather was unpredictable for an outdoor event in the mountains, but snow this early would be a rare occurrence. Most people would need to bundle up though, especially for the parade tonight.

Currently, we were lined up a mile away from the parade route, over on Elliott Avenue. Streets had been blocked off, and all participants had been directed to follow a twisting, turning map and jamboree volunteers to a very specific location to ensure the procession went as planned in exactly one hour and fourteen minutes.

Mark would be driving the Judd's Orchard work truck at a crawl while pulling the trailer supporting our float. I was already in my costume and straightening and adjusting the decorations before the rest of my family arrived.

The theme was Santa's Apple North Pole Wonderland. With Bonnie's help, I'd constructed a giant sleigh down the center of the trailer. There was quite a bit of glitter involved as well as battery-powered twinkle lights. In the rear of the sled was a raised platform for my parents, who would be assuming the roles of Santa and Mrs. Claus. Twinkle-light reins led from the front of the sleigh to another platform that would hold my sister, Joan, our apple-loving Rudolph.

The sleigh was set in and among Christmas trees from our lot, all decorated with red and green apples and strands of popcorn—courtesy of Bonnie's Kirby Falls Elementary School art students.

Brady and I planned to walk behind the trailer as apple-worker elves. Our costumes included apple-picking bags that were filled with treats, and our job was to pass out candy to kids, hand orchard coupons to adults, and just generally ham it up for the crowd.

The float behind ours was Miss Sally's Tiny Dancer Academy. I'd gotten their playlist and routine schedule from my former ballet instructor, so I knew what to expect and didn't need to play music from our own float. Brady and I had even worked out a short dance routine that I was pretty excited about.

I tapped one bell-topped pointy boot and slipped off my white gloves before reaching into my skirt pocket. With a quick flip to the front-facing camera, I grinned and took a selfie. My eyes were bright with shimmery silver makeup and looked more green than brown in the late-afternoon light. The curved tip of my elf hat dipped down low over my forehead. And you could just barely see the tops of my red-and-white suspenders peeking out from beneath my recently curled brown hair. I looked festive and happy. Santa's little helper.

But hopefully, this text would put me on the naughty list.

I fired off the image along with a short message just as Mark climbed out of the driver's seat. He'd been scooting us into position, something we'd had to adjust regularly during the parade setup to ensure everyone was where they were supposed to be. Eloise Carter, the head of festival planning in Kirby Falls, was probably somewhere with a clipboard, devil horns, and a whip—not the sexy kind.

From my position at the end of the twenty-four-foot-long trailer, I watched Mark straighten and pull his phone from his jeans pocket. As soon as his eyes locked on the screen, he smiled—the small, secret tilt of his lips that I loved so much. He hadn't even had a chance to read the text yet, his thumb just now tapping to unlock it.

That immediate smile in reaction to my name popping up on his screen had me swooning. My heart was room temperature butter, left out on the counter to soften. Destined for something miraculous like a bowl of chocolate chip cookie dough or this man's love.

Like a sneaky little elf, I observed the change that came over Mark as he read my text. Unaware of my spying, his eyes widened at what he saw on his phone and then he laughed. I was too far away to hear it, but I knew exactly what it sounded like. I could feel the phantom exhale against my neck, the rumble of amusement from his broad chest, like the best sort of memory.

That low sound of happiness was something I'd grown familiar with over the last few months. In the bed of his truck with a camera in his hand, in the firelight glow, in the darkness of his bedroom, his eyes on me.

Mark's pretty blue-gray gaze found me now, the laughter in his eyes so recent that I could still see the wisp of it before it softened into something aching and fond.

Mark kept his affectionate stare trained on me as he closed the door to the truck and walked my way.

I wondered at the sight and felt certain that anyone who saw him looking at me like that would know in an instant where we spent our nights and how we filled our hearts. It could never be interpreted as anything other than what it was. And I imagined the look I gave him in return answered pretty definitively.

Our expressions fairly shouted our intent, not to mention our body language. It said, these two idiots were stumbling their way into love and hiding it from the world, as if that could stop it. An unobtrusive, weightless fall, despite things like time and place and small-town politics.

When Mark reached my side, I kept my hands—and my lips—to myself when all I wanted was to step into him and make sure all the people lingering in the setup line knew this man belonged to me. And still, we were close to touching, the reckless possibility of it. The way my torso leaned in, like he was a star and the gravitational pull was unavoidable. How his shoulders relaxed and his fingers twitched at his sides, reaching for me reflexively before his brain could catch up and bring him to heel.

Mark's voice was low and amused when it emerged. "To answer your question, yes, I am very into that costume. Feel free to wear it when you come over tonight."

I grinned. "That, sir, is the correct answer."

His smile was a little wicked, and I wondered what he was thinking about doing to me later, but before any truly naughty ideas could materialize, Mark's gaze snagged on something over my shoulder. He took a big step back and shoved his hands in the front pockets of his jeans. His warmth and his vibrant green scent abandoned me abruptly.

I didn't have to look to know someone was approaching. A moment later, my brother's voice, accompanied by jingling bells, identified the reason for Mark's sudden retreat.

"You know, I didn't think I was a fan of suspenders, but I look good," Brady proclaimed with a snap of the red-and-white elastic that matched my own.

I gave him an annoyed look, mostly frustrated that he'd interrupted. "They're candy-cane patterned. It's not like you'll have an occasion to wear them again."

"I just meant, now I know I can pull off suspenders. I'll get a normal pair and wear them to the next wedding or fancy event I have to go to." My dopey brother frowned at Mark's clothes. "Sorry you're stuck driving the truck and don't get a costume, Mercer."

"That is fine by me," Mark said gamely.

Mom and Dad were the next to join us. My mother looked pretty cute in her red velvet dress with white faux fur accents. She even wore a short white wig and had gold-rimmed round glasses perched on her nose. Dad was grinning in his Santa suit, complete with beard, hat, and furry boots.

I showed them where they'd be positioned on the float. I'd tucked a few water bottles out of sight for them and added some cushions for the wooden bench seat to make sure they were comfortable on the platform.

"Honey, this is amazing. Everything turned out beautifully," my mother gushed as she took in the sparkling display.

"Yeah, Candy Cane," my dad said, "you did a wonderful job. We'll be the hit of the parade."

I smiled. "Thanks, y'all."

Funny how my family's nickname wasn't such a painful reminder anymore. It just felt like a connection to my past, one that I was happy I got to experience again, being home this fall.

Nervously, I checked the time on my phone. Joan wasn't here yet, and we were twenty-two—no, twenty-one—minutes out from the start of the procession.

Mark gave me a knowing look. "She'll be here. She knows how important this is to you."

That was what had me worried. I'd been home for three and a half months, and I didn't really feel like I'd made any type of progress with Joan. Yes, she tolerated me better at the orchard. I supposed she was less hostile. She didn't openly question my motives anymore, but she still looked at me like a squatter on *her* family's land.

We didn't have conversations that didn't involve the farm. She never asked how I was doing or if I wanted to grab dinner. Joan made me feel like an outsider and, at times, even unwelcome and unwanted.

It was eight minutes to five and the sun was setting fast when Joan finally approached, winding her way through the little girls in sequined costumes gathered at the float behind us.

I straightened from where I'd been repositioning some garland along the outside of Santa's sleigh. Disbelief had my mouth dropping open.

"Where's your costume?" I asked before I could think better of it.

Joan seemed taken aback by the float, her surprised blue eyes scanning the lights and decorations until she found me right smack-dab in the middle, several feet above her. Her eyes narrowed. "I'm not dressing like a reindeer, Candy."

"Why not? It's your part on the float. You're Rudolph."

She looked at me like I was insane. "Why in the world do I need to wear a fuzzy brown suit and antlers on my head to sell apples?"

I forced myself to take a deep breath. My sister was a practical person, rarely frivolous or given over to fun or whimsy. "It's a theme. See"—I pointed to everyone else in turn—"Dad and Mom are Santa and Mrs. Claus. Brady and I are elves. The float is decorated for the theme, Joan."

"How the hell was I supposed to know that?"

It felt like there was steam gathering behind my ears, and some pent-up, rage-filled, resentful part of me possessed my mouth. "Well, let's see. There were like twelve family meetings about the parade and float decorating that you conveniently missed. You would have known about the costume if you'd bothered attending."

Joan sighed like I was the biggest idiot on the planet. "I'm a grown-up, Candy. With grown-up responsibilities."

"So am I!" I finally snapped. "I haven't been your bratty little sister in a long time, Joan. If you'd bothered to notice, I'm twenty-five. I have a great credit score and a fucking investment portfolio. I'm not a kid. Stop treating me like one."

Silence rang in the wake of my pronouncement. I might have been shouting. I didn't know. All I could hear were my angry heaving breaths and the deafening sound of blood rushing in my ears.

Vaguely I noticed Mark coming over, concern etched between his dark brows, but I couldn't pay him any mind because I was so mad that I could hardly see straight.

This confrontation with my sister had my heart going a million miles an hour. *My sister*. Someone I'd loved and respected and admired all my life.

She was staring at me in stunned shock, but then her eyes defaulted to narrowed slits.

I realized suddenly that Joan was not perfect. Far from it. Maybe she was a great daughter and a devoted orchard employee, farmer of the fucking year. But I'd made allowances for her for far too long. I'd taken every single snide remark in stride—all the bitter negativity she'd wielded so subtly.

Since I'd been back in town, my sister hadn't even given me a chance. It went beyond a pumpkin patch or a parade float. It was the eye-rolls and the constant mistrust. She treated me like an incapable child hell-bent on stealing her inheritance. All these painful realizations were swirling around inside me. I didn't have room for anything rational.

Joan was selfish and single-minded and astonishingly bad at communicating. She expected everyone to be just like her—just as dedicated, just as hardworking, just as fanatical about the farm as she was.

And I'd committed the cardinal sin. I'd left. I'd devoted my life to something that wasn't Judd's Orchard.

But I was done paying for it.

"Maybe we should take a minute," my father said at the same time my mother cautioned, "Girls, you both—"

"You know what—" Joan began, but stopped abruptly when she placed her hand on the side of the float to brace herself. It must have been at a crucial, weight-bearing point because the hanging garland dislodged and landed in a sad little serpentine coil at her feet before systematically popping off at the remaining intervals until the entire length of the trailer was garland-less and unadorned.

My mouth dropped open in horror as my hard work was once again dismissed and discarded by my sister.

I heard Brady mutter a low, "Oh shit," from somewhere.

Logically, I knew that Joan's harmless touch probably dislodged an already loose staple and the resulting chain reaction had been bad luck.

But whether you were two or twelve or twenty-five, there was nothing logical about fighting with your sibling.

"How could you!" I yelled.

"That was an accident." Joan held her hands up in the universal sign for hold on a minute, but I would *not* be holding on for any length of time.

In a fit of blind rage, I grabbed the closest thing I could find—a shiny red Rome apple decorating the Fraser fir to my right—and chucked it at my sister. It missed her by a mile but practically exploded on impact. Bits of apple flesh and juicy innards splintered off the asphalt as my sister jumped to the side.

"Hey!" she shouted.

But I didn't care. I grabbed another—a Granny Smith this time—and threw it at her head.

"What the hell?" she shouted when it caught her in the shoulder instead. "Great way to prove you're an adult, Candy. Jesus Christ."

But I was on a roll. "It's Candace!" I screeched.

I grabbed apple after apple along with strings of popcorn and plastic snowflakes and threw them all in my sister's direction. She ducked and shouted and picked up pieces of apple and popcorn from the ground and threw them right back.

I had sticky juice splattered across my face and my costume, popcorn stuck in my hair, and I was pretty sure I'd lost a fake eyelash.

My parents were hollering, trying to intervene, and, at one point, I heard Brady shout, "You have to eat those apples. You know the rules!"

The next piece of fruit was aimed at him. "I will strangle you with those suspenders, Brady. Shut. Up!"

I'd just turned back with my arm cocked and loaded when I caught sight of Mark stepping in front of Joan. He plucked half a McIntosh apple out of her hand and then turned to face me.

"You two are going to stop this right now." Mark didn't raise his voice, but he did sound like he meant business, like a teacher at the head of the classroom, disappointed in his troublemaking pupils. "You're going to ride on this float and act like adults." He glanced between me and my sister. "And then you're going to sit down and have a conversation like rational human beings."

Surprisingly enough, we did stop.

Giving me a death glare and a wide berth, Joan hopped up and took her position at the front of the sleigh without her costume and covered in the remnants of our apple battle.

Brady ran over to Burke Hardware and borrowed a staple gun to fix the garland bunting on the side of the float.

My parents climbed aboard and produced Oscar-worthy North Pole smiles and waves.

Mark plucked the missing eyelash from my hair, handed me a handkerchief for my face, and squeezed my arm. Then he got behind the wheel and shifted into drive.

In the end, we only delayed the parade by six minutes.

However, the event had lost some of its luster. My excitement waned to practically nonexistent due to the fight with my sister. I felt embarrassed by my actions, but underneath the shame and guilt was still a fresh dose of hurt that we'd gotten to that murderous, apple-slinging point in the first place.

I still smiled and waved and tossed candy to children and neighbors. Marveled a bit over the lights and music and the sense of community. But I felt dim around the edges, fuzzy and indistinct—like a chandelier that'd blown half of its bulbs.

When the parade was all over and we'd hauled the trailer back to the farm, my father ushered Joan and me onto the screened porch of the farmhouse and left us there. Side by side, we sat in cold, awkward silence on the wicker love seat. It was dark save for the light coming from the kitchen inside. My mother tossed two blankets at us and told us we couldn't leave for at least twenty minutes.

I didn't know what kept my sister from just getting up and going. Maybe it was the fear of disappointing our parents. It was one of the few things that proved we were actually related. Or perhaps Joan was feeling a little bit of the guilt-shame combo that was currently hunching my shoulders and restraining my tongue.

When it was clear she was going to be as pigheaded about this conversation as she was about everything else, I decided to start with honesty.

"I got fired from my job in New York. That's why I came home."

In my periphery, I saw Joan turn to look at me. I could feel her gaze, heavy and questioning, on the side of my face.

I swallowed. "Well, I didn't technically get fired. I was forced out. I got involved with my boss who stole my ideas and passed them off as his own. Then I found out he had a wife and a baby I didn't know about, and it just fell apart from there."

Joan was quiet for a moment before saying very matter-of-factly, "That guy sounds like a dick."

A surprised laugh shot out of me.

The silence stretched between us again, not quite as tense this time. Less like a tightrope between two skyscrapers and more like a game of tug-of-war.

With her eyes fixed forward again, Joan said, "I always wanted to work on the farm, not in the passive way that Brady is involved, like he has nothing better to do. But like I felt it in my bones. I loved the land and working with my hands, being a part of something—a cycle, nature, a legacy. I always knew that this was where I belonged."

Somehow I could tell she wasn't done talking, just ordering her thoughts. So I stayed quiet.

Finally, she glanced at me. "I loved it here and you never did. You couldn't wait to get out of this town, away from the farm. It felt like you needed to be rid of all of us, too."

Heat flooded my cheeks and shame slithered in my belly. Every argument I could have made died on my tongue. All of what Joan said was true. I *had* been eager to escape. At the time, making something of myself meant something bigger and better than Kirby Falls. Ivy League, big city, sophistication, career-driven professional. All the things I thought equaled success. A dream that felt juvenile now in the face of Joan's hard work and dedication.

"You swooped in here this summer with your pantsuits and your big ideas, acting like you belonged here when, for the longest time, you thought this place was the worst place someone could be."

I considered my determination and my forced positivity over the past few months. I'd been the physical embodiment of fake it till you make it. Joan had seen through all that. Of course, she had.

"But I realize now," my sister said, "that you were young and . . . so different than me. It's hard not to remember the girl you were. Maybe it's the age difference, but I have a difficult time seeing you as anything but my baby sister."

I nodded because I got that. "I have a hard time seeing you as anything but my perfect big sister."

Joan scoffed. "Perfection is just an idea. Something people kill themselves trying to achieve. It's not any more attainable than world peace or being universally beloved—unless you're Dolly Parton."

I smiled. "I guess I thought Mom and Dad already had the best daughter for the farm. I felt like I needed to chart my own path to stand out."

"I'm sorry that I made you feel like you needed to run away to do that."

"And I'm sorry," I said, "that coming home disordered your life and put a strain on things around the farm. I was just trying to help."

"I know that," Joan admitted. "And it's not like I really gave you a chance to discuss stuff with me. I should have told you that some of your ideas made more work for the rest of us instead of being bitter and angry about it."

I nodded because that was true too. And then because it should be said, I added, "I'm sorry I threw all that shit at you this afternoon."

Surprising me once more, Joan laughed, the sound a little foreign to my ears. "Actually, I was pretty impressed. You finally stepped up and defended yourself. Stopped acting like a kicked puppy while making me out to be the champion of the kickball league."

I smiled and looked down. I *had* let Joan walk all over me.

Now that the adrenaline and anxiety from this conversation had worn off, I was getting cold. I tucked the fleece blanket more securely around my thighs.

"Your accent is back," Joan said.

"I know." I chuckled. "I blame being around Mom. When I was in the city and we'd talk on the phone, I'd be dropping *g*'s off the ends of words for days after."

My sister laughed again, still rusty but getting looser.

In the silence that followed, so many memories flashed through my mind. Joan in braces learning to drive the old pickup truck with single-minded focus. Sitting with my parents at Brady's high school soccer games and hearing my mother gasp every time an opposing player challenged him for the ball. Helping my dad string Christmas lights on the front porch. Listening to my mother hum and roll out cookie dough.

Maybe Joan was remembering things, too, because after a moment she said, "I was hard on you, and I'm sorry for that. Despite what you may have once believed, I'm not perfect. But I sure am prideful. I'll do better, I promise."

It meant something that my sister was apologizing. Too often in families, folks just put the past behind them like it never happened. They ignored the hard parts and never talked them out. Never managed to say their sorries. They took for granted their bonds by blood and birth and assumed that connection wouldn't weather away over time.

I didn't want to wake up in twenty years resenting my sister because she couldn't own up to her mistakes. And I didn't want her to do the same with me.

"How about I'll stop thinking of you as perfect, and you'll stop thinking of me as that single-minded teenager who lit out of town on graduation day for greener pastures? It may have taken me some time, but I love my home, Joanie." I took a deep breath for courage and added, "In fact, I want to stay."

"Is this the first time you've said that out loud?"

"Yeah," I admitted.

"I could tell." She grinned. "You look like you're going to barf."

I laughed into the cold December night. "Yeah, well, admitting you'd rather go back to where you started feels like a waste of time and money and heartache. Mom and Dad sacrificed so much for my education. At first, I couldn't believe I'd even gotten in to an Ivy League school. It had felt prestigious, like I wasn't just some backwoods redneck from the middle of nowhere, not if the admissions folks at Columbia University thought I was good enough. How lucky was I?"

Despite the distance from home, it seemed like looking a gift horse in the mouth if I'd turned down Columbia and went to a nearby state school. It was an opportunity. More importantly, it was in my plan.

"Luck didn't have a single thing to do with it," Joan argued. "You worked your ass off in school. You earned that admissions letter. And you went to college and learned and grew as a person. If you'd have turned down Columbia, stayed close and given it up, you would have always wondered. Now you know, right? You know what else is out there. And sometimes that's what growing up is all about."

My sister was right. I *would* have always wondered.

"If you want to stay. Stay," Joan said simply.

I twisted my fingers nervously beneath the blanket, wishing it were that easy. "You wouldn't hate having me here?"

"I would not hate having you here. And you know Mom and Dad would be thrilled. You have to remember, your idea of success is unique to you, and it's even different now than it was when you were eighteen. Why would two small-town farmers who love their community and their family and their life ever think that a career in New York City is the only path to success? They wanted it *for* you because they love you, and that was always your dream. They'd probably even be proud of you if you were something horrible like a congressman. You could run a pyramid scheme, and they'd say, 'Look at our baby girl.'"

I'd started laughing at *congressman* and kept right on going, whacking my sister on the arm.

Joan was smiling too. "Their love is not tied to a college loan payment, Candy— Candace," she corrected softly. "You're minimizing a lifetime of love and pride."

So many emotions battled for dominance: shame, guilt, love, affection, regret, heartache, disappointment. Coming home was complicated, and I'd known it all along, but staying . . . that might be the simplest thing of all.

My sister was right. I needed to give my parents more credit. And it was okay to change and adapt, remake myself over again. Who the hell knew what they were doing at eighteen, anyway? Holding on to something just for the sake of holding on wouldn't do anything but give you calluses. I didn't want to hang on so tight to this one thing that I let everything else go.

I wanted to be in Kirby Falls with my family and my friends . . . and with Mark.

It was as if Joan had reached into my brain and pulled out the knowledge. "And staying would definitely make your dating life easier." She gave me a knowing little smirk. "Now that you've found a good guy and all."

"I—I don't know what you mean," I managed to stammer out as shock and panic flooded my system. I was one more epiphany away from a hard reset.

My sister rolled her eyes, but she was amused. "Any idiot could see the way Mercer looks at you. Come on now."

Her words made me feel warm, filled me up.

It seemed to go okay the first time, so I gave her another truth. "I love him. A lot. I'm *in* love with him."

"Good," Joan replied, nudging me with her elbow. "I'd hate to have to kill you for breaking his fragile heart and running off our second-best employee."

I snorted. "And the best employee is?"

"Me, obviously," Joan said with zero humility. "Did you think it was Brady?"

I laughed hard at that and she joined in.

This was maybe the longest and best conversation I'd ever had with my big sister. "I was hoping it would be me."

The sharp edges of Joan's wicked humor softened, and the smile she gave me was warm and welcome on this cold night. "The ranking system is just for permanent employees. I guess you'll just have to stay if you want to be a contender."

Then she bumped me with her elbow again. "You think it's been twenty minutes yet. It's like the North Pole out here."

I cut her a glance, but she was already watching me. "Too soon, Joanie."

Then we both burst out laughing.

I felt lighter than I had in years.

seventeen

MARK

I was waiting for her when she knocked.

I'd gotten home from the parade more than an hour ago, tense and worried over the conversation I knew needed to happen between Candace and her sister. I just hoped whatever was said didn't do more harm to their relationship than good.

Opening the door, I was surprised to find Candace just how I'd left her.

"I'm realizing now that I probably should have showered or at least gotten all the popcorn out of my hair before coming over."

My laughter was soft as I reached for her hand and led her inside. "How about a bath? I'll wash your hair and you can tell me what happened."

Candace's hazel eyes brightened. She nodded and then followed me to the bathroom I never used.

I'd remodeled the primary bedroom and attached the en suite right after Hannah and I had moved in. It was wide and spacious with a white claw-foot tub and subway-tiled walk-in shower. The room was painted a soft robin's-egg blue and the fixtures were all antique bronze. But there was no toothbrush resting on the counter or towel next to the sink.

Candace took in the space with wide eyes. I turned on the water to warm, and after adjusting the knobs of the faucet, I straightened and said, "I'll go grab a couple of towels and some soap."

When I returned with my supplies, Candace was already undressed and sitting in the bathtub with her knees to her chest. She'd wrapped her arms around the tops of her long legs and her dark hair streamed down her smooth back. She looked relaxed and beautiful. I thought I'd been pretty stupid not to use this bathroom until now.

There was a stool next to the still-filling bathtub. It was mostly decorative, a place to set a watch or a pair of earrings, but it suited my needs. I shifted it beside the white porcelain and sat.

Candace pivoted, placing her hand on the edge of the tub and resting her chin atop it.

I smiled down at her and reached for the pieces of popcorn trapped in her long strands.

"Thank you," she said. "This is really nice."

Eventually, I leaned over and turned off the water. The sudden quiet seemed to echo with a hundred things I couldn't bring myself to say.

Tilting her face back, I took a wet washcloth and began gently wiping away her glittery elf makeup. "So how did it go with Joan?"

She hummed as the fabric passed over her closed eyelids. "Pretty well. We talked. She apologized and I apologized. We're both going to try to do better."

"That's good," I said, relieved. Joan could be stubborn, and I knew how badly Candace wanted to connect with her sister. If they'd made peace, that was a very good thing.

Her eyes were still closed when she admitted quietly, "I feel pretty dumb for the whole fight before the parade."

As I considered what to say, I nudged Candace toward the center of the tub and tilted her head back. With the mason jar I'd brought from the kitchen, I wet her hair over and over until it was shiny and saturated.

Eventually, I replied, "I think it needed to happen. I don't know if you and Joan would have talked it out otherwise."

"Still embarrassing," she said with a self-deprecating laugh.

"Let's go with 'a period of personal growth.'"

Her smile brightened.

I watched her for a moment. With her eyes closed and her head tilted back, she was so trusting, so open—gorgeous beyond belief. I wanted to lean forward and taste her wet skin, trail my hand along the surface of the water, reach beneath.

My eyes shifted to the bottle of lavender-scented shampoo I held in my hand, and I had to take a steadying breath.

Our deadline was fast approaching—less than a month—and Candace hadn't shared her plans for the future or her exit strategy.

She was rooted in every aspect of my life—my work, my home, my damn heart. I didn't know how I was going to let all this go when the time came. How I'd scrub this house of memories all over again.

She spoke a bit more about the conversation with Joan, how they'd been mistakenly viewing each other for years.

I was quiet as I listened and washed her thick hair, soaping up the strands and massaging her scalp. My fingers brushed away droplets along her hairline and trailed them down the elegant line of her throat.

Candace was all graceful compliance, tilting her neck this way and that as she spoke. She made these appreciative little groans that had me shifting on my stool.

After I'd rinsed out the last of the conditioner, she opened her brilliant green-gold eyes and murmured, "You're really good at this, you know?"

"Thanks. It was always my dream to work in a salon."

She laughed, causing ripples to fan out around her in the soapy water. When the water had settled but happiness still lingered on her face, she clarified, "I meant, you're really good at taking care of people."

I took a towel and dried her ears, not knowing what to say. Taking care of someone was what you did when you loved them. To me, it was as simple as that. I'd known I loved her for a while now. It wasn't news to me, but it might not be what she wanted to hear.

"You're always taking care of me," she explained as she twisted her wet hair on top of her head and used a clip to hold it all in place. "Making sure I'm comfortable and content."

I thought of my past life, with a wife I couldn't make happy. I considered this empty room and the attached bedroom that hadn't been used in over two years. Maybe I was only now learning how to take care of someone. Maybe Hannah had been right to go out and find a partner who could look after her in all the ways she deserved.

I picked up a washcloth and massaged some of Candace's shower gel into it. Then I gently unwrapped her arm from where it rested around her knees. I worked the wet, sudsy fabric up the length of her forearm and asked, "Are you comfortable now?"

She smiled over at me. "I don't think I've ever been this relaxed in my whole life, Mark."

Her words made me warm with pride, or maybe it was the steam from the bath or the way she looked so damn beautiful beneath my hands.

I dragged the cloth up and over her shoulder blades, around to her other arm. She lifted it wordlessly for my ministrations. Then Candace stretched out her long legs until her red-painted toes touched the end of the bathtub, exposing her breasts above the waterline. Her skin was shiny with moisture, a bit flushed from the heat of the water, and her perfect nipples were tight in the cool air.

Gooseflesh pebbled in the wake of the washcloth as it passed over her skin.

With a voice so deep I hardly recognized it as my own, I asked again, "And now? Are you still relaxed?"

I didn't know whether she recognized the direction my thoughts had taken, but she regarded me with dark eyes. Then slowly, she leaned back, using her hands for support, and opened herself even further to my gaze.

"Can you keep washing me?"

In answer, I brought the fabric to her neck, gently brushing back and forth along her collarbones. The corner of the washcloth dipped low, dragging over one pert nipple. Candace's breathing picked up, and I could feel my heart pounding in my chest, so fucking eager to do this for her—to take care of her, to make her feel good.

My hand dropped down, caressing her breasts through the cloth I held. I watched her lips part on a soft moan, and her eyelids closed once more.

I started to lower the cloth below the water, across her taut stomach, when her voice stopped me. "You should probably take that shirt off. Wouldn't want to get your sleeves wet."

The request seemed innocent enough, but when I'd drawn the fabric over my head and tossed it onto the bath mat with Candace's clothes, I found her eyes taking me in.

"The pants, too," she said with a mischievous smile. "I'm a splasher."

My grin was amused, but I slipped off my jeans as she requested, happy to play this game with her.

When I sat back down on the stool in nothing but my boxer briefs, she propped one long leg up on the side of the tub. I fished the cloth out of the water and resumed washing. The fabric slid easily over her smooth calves. I took a few slow passes behind her knee that had her squirming before dragging the terry cloth up her thigh.

Candace placed her foot back into the water but left her bent leg spread wide. As my hand dipped below the surface to pay particular attention to her hip and side, the washcloth slipped from my hand. She didn't seem to mind as my touch drifted over her stomach. A fast exhale came between parted lips, and Candace tilted her hips ever so subtly.

I took the direction and dipped my hand low, the pads of my fingers finding her center, smooth and warm, even in the bathwater.

Her head was still tipped back, eyes closed and features relaxed, as I took three fingers and circled her clit slowly.

I'd been half-hard the moment I'd started washing her, but, now, my arousal was straining the fabric of my underwear. Suddenly, I was grateful she'd asked me to remove the constricting denim.

She made a low whimper when my middle finger drifted down to her entrance and pushed slowly inside before I returned to the apex of her thighs, focusing my energy there. I watched her full lips and her panted breaths, the way her breasts moved above the water. Candace was straining toward release and getting close, but then her eyes opened and she looked at me.

She straightened and stilled my hand, and I worried I'd done something wrong, misread a signal. Maybe she couldn't get there like this—with just my fingers, in the water.

But then she smiled and reached over the side of the tub for a towel. Candace stood quickly and stepped out onto the rug. I steadied her hips as she ran the fabric quickly over her skin. She was still damp a moment later when she surprised me and climbed into my lap.

Jesus.

She was a welcome weight in my arms. Her center pressed down on my erection as she straddled me on the stool. I wrapped my arms around her tight when she leaned in to whisper, "I didn't want to come yet. I wanted you to be inside me."

I pressed my lips to the skin of her shoulder, still damp and unbelievably warm. "Whatever you want."

I felt her reach between us and pull the front of my boxer briefs down.

I groaned as she gave me a few firm pumps before inching her hips forward and positioning me at her entrance.

"Candace," I breathed out roughly. Her delicate, soft skin—the heat of her—enveloping just the tip made me lightheaded with want.

"Can I?" she asked. "I wanted to feel you. Just you."

We'd used condoms in the weeks we'd been together. Always careful. Always controlled.

My confusion must have registered in my stillness and hesitation because she pulled back to look at me and clarified, "I have an IUD and I've been tested."

I wanted it—the possibility of feeling her like this, with nothing between us. The intimacy of it. The trust.

It wasn't like I needed to admit I'd been celibate for five years before she came along—she knew the truth of my marriage and the vows I'd kept. So, I simply nodded and replied, "If you're sure?"

In answer, she kept her soft gaze locked on mine as she lowered herself down. The heat and the pressure and the stunning pleasure of her bare skin had my eyes slipping closed as a groan escaped my lips.

My forehead dropped and rested against her collarbone as she rolled her hips and then found her rhythm—legs spread wide, raising herself up onto tiptoe, and then falling on my length. I let my hands skim her shoulder blades, her back, and then lower, cupping her backside as she ground against me.

A thousand images flashed behind my closed eyelids as we moved together—things I had no business wanting, desperate wishes for tomorrow and next year and forever—until they all evaporated in a brilliant blinding light. Candace's inner muscles contracted around me and her arms clutched my shoulders in a desperate grip, so I held her tight in case she was feeling what I felt—like I might come undone when this was all over, as insubstantial as a memory, faded and lost.

Her release triggered my own, and the sensation was nothing I'd ever felt before. I couldn't stop touching her skin. I couldn't get close enough. My lips lingered everywhere I could reach.

When our breathing finally evened, and Candace's skin pebbled from cold, we cleaned up and climbed into bed, still touching, always touching.

I woke when it was dark but still early. We were in the same positions we'd gone to sleep in. I was flat on my back with Candace tucked into my side, her head resting on my shoulder and her cold feet nestled beneath my legs.

A moment later I realized what had woken me. I'd heard Candace mumble in her sleep a few times before. Mostly it was indecipherable, but occasionally there were a few words I could pick out. One time she'd said, "Bubble gum snow cone," and I'd been quietly amused, smiling into the dark of my bedroom before drifting off again beside her.

But I wasn't smiling now.

Candace repeated her quiet admission three more times before she released a deep breath and rolled over.

Love you. Love you. Love you.

As I watched the steady rise and fall of her back—clad in one of my tee shirts—I couldn't help but want to hear her say it again when she was awake. But then the reminder of a slim silver laptop stole into mind. The job listings. Her intent to leave Kirby Falls . . . and me behind in just a few short weeks.

I couldn't ignore the fact that whatever she was dreaming right now didn't match what she wanted in the light of day.

Eventually, I climbed out of bed, too restless to settle.

It was a few hours later when I heard her alarm go off. I'd already set my mug down on the kitchen table, prepared to go back in there and shake her awake, maybe bring her a cup of coffee too. Let the sharp scent do what the blaring alarm couldn't, but before I could rise, the sound switched off.

A few minutes later, I heard the door to the bathroom close, and I figured she was up and not passed back out again.

Enough time went by that most of my coffee was gone and I'd gotten lost in my own thoughts when I noticed Candace enter the room from the hallway.

My mug hit the table with a graceless thunk, and my mouth dropped open in shock.

This time, Candace wasn't standing naked in my kitchen, in only my wool socks. She *was* wearing my clothes though. Candace stood at the threshold in a black hoodie I hadn't seen in over seven years.

"Why— How?" I stammered. "I didn't think you even remembered."

She slowly approached, a secret little smile turning up the corners of her kiss-swollen lips. "I remembered, once I placed you as Mark and not Mercer. I found an old yearbook the day after we were reintroduced. It all came flooding back when I could put your face with your name."

"And you kept it?"

Candace took the seat next to me, her bare knee pressed to mine. "I did. I brought it to school every day leading up to graduation, with the intention of returning it and thanking you. You were so sweet to help me the way you did. Not many teenage boys could handle talking to a girl about her period, but you kept me from embarrassing myself. I was grateful, Mark."

I remembered that day. Of course, I did. I'd been a nervous wreck trying to get the words out, to speak loud enough for the object of my very one-sided crush to hear.

"When I didn't see you before I left town that summer, the hoodie came with me. Made the move from dorm room to dorm room, and eventually apartment to apartment. It was comfortable and cozy and it reminded me of home."

Shaking my head in disbelief, I muttered, "Teenage Mark can die happy."

Candace laughed. "Would you like it back?"

The question, so innocent and teasing, had me going quiet suddenly. Did I want this piece of me back? One that was more hers now than it had ever been mine.

Part of me wanted to smile and shake my head. *You already stole my fucking heart, what's an old hoodie?*

But the bigger part—the one who'd replaced a crush with the real thing—couldn't manage it. I couldn't do this anymore. I couldn't love her and watch her leave. I didn't know how to protect myself because the damage was already done. She'd just dealt the final blow with a black hoodie.

As I remained quiet, I watched concern crease her dark brows.

My hands shook, so I clasped them together on the wooden tabletop. "I don't think I can do this anymore, Candace. Be casual or temporary or whatever the fuck we are."

I didn't say, *I can't sleep from wanting you. I can't lie beside you one more second knowing you can't be mine. I'm in too deep. It's not the same as having your body. I want your heart too.*

I'd been cowardly these last few weeks. She hadn't mentioned applying for jobs or interviewing, and I didn't want to push. Afraid that the reminder of how temporary everything was might put an end to us sooner.

It had been a mistake to let myself fall deeper into the fantasy. I could see that now.

"Mark," she said, drawing my attention from the regret swirling among my thoughts.

"Do you know what I do every time you leave?" I asked suddenly. I didn't give her the chance to answer. "I make myself watch. I force myself to look. When I wait in the garage while you drive away. When you go inside the farmhouse or the Apple House or your office. When you climb in your car in the afternoon after work. I watch and I wait, and I try to get used to the idea. I try to get used to watching you go. It's inevitable. You're not meant for here. Kirby Falls is just a stopover until you find your way back to where you really belong. And I think" —I swallowed the roughness from my throat—"I think I didn't prepare myself nearly well enough."

CANDACE

I try to get used to watching you go.

At his words, a film reel of Mark Mercer flashed through my mind. Patient, loyal, solemn-faced Mark waiting in a parking lot with his hands shoved in his pockets. Watchful blue-gray eyes making sure I got inside safely, no matter where I was. A steady, stalwart form standing guard just for me, in work boots and a five-panel hat.

All those gentlemanly gestures, all those thoughtful images, turn into something heartbreaking in an instant.

"Mark," I tried again, reaching for his clasped hands. But he wouldn't look at me. "I don't want to be temporary or casual either. I should have been upfront with you. I'm so sorry. I should have told you weeks ago that I wanted to stay."

It was like that final word was a key turning in a rusty lock. Mark's head snapped up, confusion wrinkling his brow as disbelief warred with the hope I felt mirrored in my own chest.

I threaded my fingers through his. "There's no job for me back in New York. I— I don't want to go back. I want to stay in Kirby Falls. For months, I thought Joan didn't want me here—until last night. But the bigger part was having my self-worth tied to some corporate job, an image, an idea of success that no longer fit with my happiness."

"What does that mean?" Mark asked, his fingers gripping me back so, so tightly.

"It means I'm staying. As of twelve hours ago." I smiled. "I'm sorry I didn't tell you right away. I should have." I glanced around the kitchen, looking for the words, the ones that had eluded me last night in the bathtub. "Honestly, I was a little scared."

"Scared?" he wondered softly, drawing my attention back to him.

"You didn't really sign up for a girlfriend. This has all been"—I paused, then swallowed uncomfortably—"secret. I didn't know how my staying would affect that. If you'd still want me."

"Of course, I want you," Mark replied immediately. "Of course, I want you to stay . . . if that's what will make you happy."

"I think I haven't let myself get used to the idea yet. It's so new, and I have a lot to take care of. My apartment in New York, the rest of my things, buying a car. My parents were so sweet and excited when I spoke to them last night—when I asked if I could stay. But part of me is probably always going to worry about disappointing them or letting them down or making them regret sending me to such an expensive school."

Mark shifted in his seat, sliding his bent leg between mine and slotting us together like puzzle pieces. "You have to know how happy they are to have you here, Candace. They'd rather have you home than a thousand miles away using a degree they paid for. They'd rather you use it right here."

It was a truth that would take some time to get used to. For so long I'd told myself that my parents loved what I did, that they were proud of my career and the person I'd become *because* I'd gone away. Even hearing their reassurances yesterday hadn't done enough to dispel those long-held beliefs that told me I needed to earn their love and affection with a high-paying salary, an office, and a big fancy life.

When I'd spoken with my parents the previous night, I'd seen the shine in my mother's eyes and the joy on my father's face. But believing it would take some time.

You couldn't rewrite history without penciling in a little regret.

I nodded and confessed, "I know they love me. And I love them. Spending time here and working together these last four months have been amazing—just what I needed after leaving the city. My parents have always been supportive of me, and now I get to support them and the farm. Do you remember that day I told you about wanting to organize group tours at the orchard? And set up field trips and educational talks?"

He watched me carefully. "Yeah, I remember. The day you told me you wanted a family."

I felt heat bloom in my cheeks, suddenly very aware of the things I'd revealed about my five-year plan to the man I was now currently in a relationship with. Ignoring my shy discomfort, I nodded. "I got so irrationally irritated at some hypothetical future employee who could potentially implement my plan some-day. At the time, I didn't think it could be me, but I wanted it. Badly. That wasn't the first time I thought about staying in Kirby Falls, but it was when I realized I was lying to myself in thinking New York was going to be able to make me happy anymore."

With a sheepish smile, I admitted, "I want to man the Christmas tree lot, and I want to be here in the spring and plant a field of lavender. I want to see the blackberries grow in the summer. And I want to do it all with my family . . . and you."

"Good," Mark murmured. "I want that too." Then he cupped my still-heated cheeks and kissed me. His touch was reverent. It felt like gratitude and relief. Like he'd been up early trying to figure out how to break things off and now he didn't have to.

He pulled back but didn't stop touching me. His thumb stroked my cheek tenderly.

It was probably renewed happiness along with that same lingering relief that had me saying with little forethought, "I know it was different before, when we thought this was short-term, but what do you think about telling people now? About dating for real?"

Mark had been so worried about what people thought and how they might judge me as a result of us spending time together out in the open. And while I didn't have those same fears, I hadn't felt right forcing his hand when he was the one who'd be left with more gossip when I left town. Now that I was staying, though,

I wanted to reassure him. We could face the whispers together. Despite what people thought about him, I knew what had really happened with Hannah and Lyndsey. And I wanted to be with him, openly, where my family and friends and everyone could see.

But I realized my enthusiasm may have been somewhat premature.

Mark hesitated, blue-gray eyes searching my face, before he leaned back in his seat. I tried not to see the distance he'd put between us as deliberate and meaningful.

Finally, he replied, "Yeah. Sure, we can do that. You mean tell your family?"

I hoped my smile was encouraging. "Yeah, I'd like to tell my family. They adore you. They'll be so happy. And I'd like to stop hiding and sneaking around. Go out on a date or hold your hand, if I feel like it. I know you're worried about how people will react, but I don't care about that. I know you, Mark. I know the truth. Those other people—the small-minded gossips—they don't matter."

He nodded slowly in response, but I could see the worry in his eyes. And maybe that was part of why I hadn't told Mark about my last relationship. I didn't want him to think I was manipulating him, and I didn't want him to agree to date me openly only because he knew about my hang-ups surrounding the secrecy. I'd tell Mark about Emerson and the affair when things weren't so messy, when we were more settled.

I squeezed his hand. "It'll be okay. You're already planning on coming to dinner at the farmhouse on Sunday, right?"

"I told your mother I would."

"That's great. Joan and Brady will be there too. We can tell them then."

"Okay," Mark agreed.

And as he nodded and squeezed my hand in return, I told myself that everything would be alright.

***

Following my early-morning conversation with Mark, I'd driven back to the orchard to get ready for the day. With the Holiday Jamboree crowd in town, it was set to be a busy one on the farm.

The Christmas tree lot was doing well. Joan and Mark were helping out with that. Today, my brother had the day off, and I was on the schedule to work with Mom in the refreshment stand. We had hot chocolate with homemade marshmallows, warm apple cider, and a variety of cookies and treats for sale. The bounce pillow was still open for kids to play on, and despite the December chill, we had Food Truck Friday happening tonight. It was the final one of the season, and now that I was staying, I could get the calendar ready for next May when those Friday festivities would resume.

I smiled at the thought.

Mark and I texted throughout the day, but when I invited him over to the garage apartment that night for pizza and a sleepover, he said he'd already picked up groceries and wanted to cook for me at his house.

I didn't start to worry until the following day. I remembered the way Mark had hesitated when I asked if we could tell my parents and bring our relationship out into the open. Now that we were closing in on family dinner tomorrow, I was growing concerned that Mark had changed his mind—or maybe he hadn't been ready in the first place.

I scrutinized every expression, every touch. The way he'd declined coming to the garage apartment and offered to make dinner instead. How he had me park my car in his garage, just like always.

Maybe he needed more time to get used to the idea. I thought a dry run might help before we gathered at the farmhouse tomorrow and told my family the news.

Mark and I were both off at five today, so I invited him to go with me downtown to check out the rest of the Jamboree festivities.

On my way to refill the hot cider urn, I pulled out my phone.

Me: Want to hit the Holiday Market after work? We can bundle up and check out the booths. Maybe grab dinner downtown.

Almost immediately, dots appeared on the screen as Mark typed out a response. I bit my lip and kept my gaze glued to my phone as the dots stopped and started twice more before disappearing altogether. Disappointment had my eyes closing and a weary sigh escaping.

I didn't wait any longer. I shoved the phone in my pocket and went back to work. I knew I'd taken the chicken way out. I could have run down to the tree lot on my break and asked him face-to-face, but texting Mark felt safer when I had unease brewing in the pit of my stomach.

Thirty minutes later, I had three unread messages waiting for me.

One from Bonnie: *How do you feel about a Christmas party at Grandpappy's next weekend, after closing? Mom and Aunt Maggie are hosting and said to invite the whole Judd bunch. Can we bring these two farms together without bloodshed? LOL*

The next was a message from Joan—an image with a short text: *This would be a good one for the Instagram account.*

I smiled as my eyes scanned the picture. Mark was standing just outside the string lights marking the perimeter of the tree lot. He had a Fraser fir—wrapped in netting and ready for transport—hoisted over one strong shoulder while two little girls in puffy jackets stood before him. The girls looked like twins, around three or four years of age. They wore matching pink coats and white leggings beneath tiny tulle skirts. In the image, they were frozen mid-leap, excited over their Christmas tree purchase. Two men who were clearly their parents stood behind them looking just as joyful. And there was Mark, grinning down at the children, a look so soft on his face that my heart ached at the sight of it.

The third and final unread text was from Mark, sent five minutes after my original invitation: *Sure, that sounds good. I'll meet you in your office after work.*

I stared at the screen and wondered if I was pushing too hard. Was I being unreasonable? Or was I reading too much into a twelve-word text message. I didn't know. I was too in my own head to be rational right now. Too concerned about Mark's perceived hesitation, and overanalyzing everything as a result.

If Mark wasn't ready to be with me for real, could I be okay with that?

We'd been seeing each other for over two months. I didn't want to be anybody's secret, but I knew Mark meant well. He wasn't hiding me away because he was cheating on his wife. I told myself this wasn't the same as what had happened with Emerson.

Mark wasn't using me, and he'd never do anything to intentionally hurt me.

So why did it feel like I was setting myself up for heartbreak?

Mark

It was nearly dark when we arrived downtown. The streetlights were burning, and the holiday decorations were lit. Twinkle lights wreathed all the trees lining Main Street, and giant ornaments dangled from the lampposts. Store windows were decorated with hand-drawn winter scenes and smiling snowmen. Carolers walked along the road, stopping to perform on every other corner. And in front of the courthouse, there was a giant Christmas tree lit with multicolored lights. A big sleigh was positioned for folks to pose in for photographs. It was a bright and festive wonderland. It just needed some mountain snow, and the image of a picture-perfect small town would be complete.

The vendor booths and food stations would be open until 8:00 p.m.

It would be a miracle if I made it an hour.

When Candace had texted and asked me to walk the Holiday Market with her, I'd had a moment of wild panic. Her invitation felt intentional. It had seemed like a test. I knew she wanted to bring our relationship out into the open, and I wanted that too, but I'd been living a very private life to protect myself. This felt like borrowing trouble, opening myself up for more gossip and more attention. Not only me, but Candace too.

This wasn't working the farmers' market together or hanging out at the orchard with her siblings. Tonight was a declaration of intent—the beginning of our relationship for all of Kirby Falls to see.

I didn't want her to, but part of me worried that she'd take one lap with me downtown and regret her decision to stay. I worried that whispers would follow in our wake. That curious eyes would monitor our movements, our glances, and our very public path together.

I'd resigned myself to being a hermit. It seemed safer to avoid people than to engage with them. I didn't make waves in Kirby Falls. I kept my head down and my business my own.

Giving in to Candace's idea for a night out went against all the safeguards I had in place. It would take some time to get used to being deliberately in the public eye.

I sincerely hoped there would come a day when I wasn't aware of the neighbors and residents sitting behind in their booths, watching us wander. When I wouldn't read into every glance or raised eyebrow, but that day was not today.

"It's not as awesome as our sleigh," Candace said.

Distracted, I glanced up and frowned. "What?"

Clad in a winter toboggan with a pom-pom on top, Candace thumped the side of the painted plywood. "The sleigh. Don't tell Eloise Carter, but I think our Judd's parade float sleigh is much more authentic."

I swallowed and tried to focus on Candace's bright, teasing grin instead of Vera Sterling and Sheila Jessup walking behind her with their heads bent together and their gazes locked on us. The women were retired, but they kept busy enough with the goings-on in town.

Shoving my hands in my pockets, I agreed, "Yeah, it's definitely nicer."

"Right?" She hopped in and shifted on the wooden bench seat. "This has no padding. Very uncomfortable. Santa would definitely get a splinter. Plus, someone drew a penis on the dashboard."

I didn't respond, all too aware of the feminine voices and raised eyebrows from over Candace's shoulder. She patted the seat next to her. "You okay?"

"Yeah, I'm fine." I ducked my head and joined her on the hard bench as Vera and Sheila shuffled away.

Ms. Sterling ran a bed-and-breakfast a few streets over and was a Sunday morning regular at Reverend Price's church. Sheila Jessup hosted a local podcast and was the administrator of the Kirby Falls Facebook group. My breath quickened at the thought of the damage they could do.

"Let's take a selfie," Candace said, positioning her phone in front of our faces. "The tree looks nice behind us."

She leaned into me, pressing her cheek against mine and smiling wide. I couldn't seem to relax my jaw, but I managed an approximation of a grin.

As Candace led me back out onto Main Street, I briefly looked in the other direction but didn't see the older women.

We kept walking, stopping so Candace could say hi to the Clarks manning the tent for the Orchard Bake Shop. They weren't selling apples, since the harvest was done for the year, but the bakery at Grandpappy's stayed open year-round and did good business for breakfast. They also provided local desserts and wedding and event cakes. It made sense that the Clarks would have a Holiday Market booth to promote the Bake Shop.

Maggie Clark was the head baker over at Grandpappy's. She was a kind person. She'd always been friendly with me, but the knowing look she cast between me and Candace still made me shift on my feet uncomfortably. While Maggie and Candace exchanged pleasantries, Laramie Burke shot me a huge grin. Without saying a word, she simply handed me a container of peppermint bark I hadn't ordered, then gave me a sly wink.

I stepped away from the table a few paces, needing some distance and room to breathe. The chill in the December air did very little to cool my heated skin. I could feel nervous sweat causing my undershirt to cling to my shoulder blades.

Candace glanced back at me and her smile died abruptly at what she saw in my expression. She excused herself from Maggie and whatever they'd been talking about—a Christmas party or something. I couldn't focus on the specifics I'd overheard.

When Candace reached my side, she slipped her arm through mine and asked, "Are you feeling okay?"

I nodded, very aware of her nearness, my heartbeat, and the way I still couldn't seem to catch my breath. "Yeah, probably just hungry."

Candace brightened, no doubt thinking that this was an easy fix. We'd just walk down the street, arm in arm, and into a restaurant where we knew the staff and they knew us. She didn't know this paranoia went deep.

But I was grateful she'd shaken off her concerns. I couldn't stand to see the worry on her face—worry over me. She wanted to be here, and I needed her to have a good time. It was important that this outing be what she wanted.

I just wasn't sure how to ignore the way my body was reacting. The constant awareness, the tension radiating out of every pore. I felt like I was on alert for danger, flooded with adrenaline as if this were a hostage situation and not simply a downtown street fair.

It wasn't even rational. I knew most of the folks weaving in and out of booths and shopping along Main Street were tourists. But rational didn't matter in the face of my fear.

Yes, I was used to avoiding the whispers and the stares and the attention from the people I *did* recognize. I typically just pushed it all down. But with Candace, it was different. When the rumors and gossip only affected me, I could ignore them. But now . . . I had her to think about. I was conscious of every lingering look and worried about all of it.

"How about Apollo's? I could go for some pizza," she offered. Her hand slipped down the length of my arm and she laced her fingers through mine.

I nodded, the motion jerky. "Sure."

We only had to walk two blocks to get to the Greek restaurant. I steered Candace gently away from the booths on the street—too many recognizable faces.

When we stepped inside Apollo's, I couldn't even appreciate the scent of bread and garlic. The restaurant was packed with people and, in the center, was a large party. It looked like four tables had all been pushed together to make room for the group of women laughing and talking. There sat Vera Sterling and Sheila Jessup with ten or twelve other women from the church.

My hand slipped from Candace's grasp.

The hostess was busy seating the folks in front of us.

Candace frowned at the group of women. "Isn't that—"

"I need to go," I blurted as self-preservation—along with a healthy dose of cowardice—kicked in.

She spun to face me, concern etched into every line of her face. "What's wrong?"

"Nothing. I just—I just don't want to eat here."

Her hazel eyes searched my face, then dropped to my chest where my breaths were coming fast. Hell, maybe she could see the way my heart pounded in my chest too.

After a quick moment that felt like a lifetime, Candace nodded.

When we reached the sidewalk, I sucked in the cool mountain air, trying desperately to clear my head. My feet carried me on autopilot toward the parking garage. Candace and I walked to my truck, not touching, not speaking. No taking a meandering path to peek in booths or to look at ornaments or hand-carved bowls.

Candace stayed silent on the drive to my house, and I wasn't capable of talking. My hands stayed white-knuckled on the steering wheel as my breathing gradually slowed and the panic receded.

By the time I turned onto my dead-end road, my muscles had relaxed, but the silence inside the cab felt thick and weighty. Candace wasn't looking at me, her stare focused on the closed garage door as we idled in my driveway.

I knew I needed to say something—to explain myself—but it still took a few minutes for the words to come. "I'm sorry. I know—I know I handled that badly."

"Can you explain it to me, Mark? I don't know what I did wrong."

My gaze snapped to her, but she was still facing forward, worrying her bottom lip. "You didn't do anything wrong, Candace. It's just . . . me. My fears and my hang-ups. I've been avoiding people and places like that for so long. I think it's just going to take me time to get used to it."

"Time to get used to being with me, where people can see us?"

"It was one thing when it was just me I had to think about. But now there's you, and I feel like I'm"—I paused, searching for the right words—"like I'm sullying your good name. Like Sheila Jessup is going to share a picture of us holding hands in the Kirby Falls Facebook group and people are going to wonder what the hell you're doing with the town pariah."

"Mark," she sighed. Candace reached for my hand, but my fists were clenched again. She simply laid her palm on top of my knuckles, giving me warmth and comfort even when I didn't know how to accept it.

"You're not the town pariah," she argued. "You were forced into an impossible situation and now nosy gossips want to judge you without knowing the truth. If you can ignore them, I can too. I know who you really are. Their whispers and stares and stupid Facebook group aren't going to scare me off."

My hand had loosened as she spoke and now her fingers were wrapped protectively around mine.

"I'm sorry about tonight," I said quietly. "I wanted you to have fun."

She shook her head. "I shouldn't have pushed. It's okay to need time. To adjust."

I was grateful for her patience and her understanding, but after tonight's failure, I felt broken beyond repair. How long would she be willing to wait on me to go to a movie together, to hold her hand on Main Street, to walk her down the damn aisle? It wasn't fair. My weakness shouldn't affect Candace and the life she hoped to lead—one that any normal person in a relationship would want.

"I just don't want you to feel like you need to defend my honor, Mark. The people who would gossip about you—about us—do not matter. There's freedom in not giving a fuck." She laughed quietly, and I did too.

But then she sobered and squeezed my palm. "I really am sorry I forced the issue today."

I made myself meet her eyes. "No. Don't apologize. You didn't ask for anything unreasonable."

Candace nodded. "I think"—she sucked in a bracing breath and stared down at our joined hands—"I think I'm extra sensitive about being secretive because of my last relationship."

I'd asked her before if she'd been engaged, but, beyond that, she hadn't talked about her romantic past.

"I was dumb," she said with a pained smile. "I got involved with my boss at my last job. He was older and sophisticated and seemed to value my ideas and my work. But because we worked together and I was his direct report, he wanted to keep things quiet."

Unease twisted my stomach.

"I agreed because I understood where he was coming from," she went on, attention still locked on our hands in her lap. "I wanted to be taken seriously in my position at the firm, and sleeping with your boss didn't look good from any angle. But I kept being a secret. He stole my work and passed it off as his own, and I didn't call him on it because I thought I was being a supportive partner. And then one day his wife came into the office. I didn't know he was married," she rushed to add. "I never would have done something like that. He didn't keep pictures on his desk. He never mentioned her. But we never went out. He would only meet me at hotels. I think I got caught up in hiding the truth, in sneaking around, the subterfuge of it all. I ignored the very obvious signs. And then I just felt like someone's dirty little secret."

I closed my eyes as anger tightened all my muscles. Fury that she'd been manipulated by a very obvious power imbalance, and regret that I'd brought her back to a place where she had to hide her relationship.

No wonder she'd wanted reassurances. Of course, it was important to her to be with someone now who was proud of her—who wanted to show her off.

Her thumb stroked mine gently as she admitted, "Once I knew the truth and confronted him, I was forced out so I wouldn't make trouble for the company. I came home to get myself together and to lick my wounds. I thought you should know the truth. I'm sorry I didn't tell you sooner. I was . . . I was embarrassed."

Swallowing down the guilt lodged in my throat, I said, "I am so fucking sorry I put you in another situation where you had to hide any part of yourself." Finally, unable to stand the defeated slope of her shoulders, I pulled her into my chest and held her. "I wish I could go back and change things. I wish I'd known. I'm sorry, Candace."

A different kind of fear gripped me. One that whispered more than gossip. It painted the very real picture of what would happen if I didn't get my shit together. I would lose Candace. I would drive her away with my baggage and anxiety.

"It's okay," she said, voice muffled against my fleece jacket. "I understood your reasons. I just wanted you to know where I was coming from. Why I rushed things tonight."

"You know, I could never—not in a million years—be ashamed to be seen with you. I'm so sorry that someone made you feel like a secret instead of the treasure you are."

I couldn't expect her to stay hidden away, not when she was staying in Kirby Falls now. I was so grateful she'd made that decision. I'd never felt relief like that, but today, amid my panic and worry, I'd forgotten how lucky I was to have her here, for good. I didn't have to say goodbye or tuck my love away. All those futures that used to keep me up at night—the innocent fantasies and the hopeful daydreams—were now at my fingertips, just within reach . . . if I could manage to hold on to them.

"I'm fine being patient with you, Mark. Your fears and your feelings are valid. You can't change overnight. You've been keeping yourself safe by staying away. It's not right for me to try to drag you out into the open. It's going to take time, and that's okay."

With the soft pom-pom of her hat brushing my cheek, I nodded because she was right. Years of learned behavior couldn't be undone overnight. I didn't want to keep disappointing her by going too fast and failing or having a panic attack on a street corner.

But I would keep trying, keep working to get comfortable among my neighbors. And we would tell her family the truth tomorrow. They deserved to know. Candace shouldn't have to hide part of herself from her siblings and her parents. They meant too much, to both of us.

I wasn't going to let my fears interfere with my relationship with Candace. I loved her and wanted to be with her. Tonight, with the past peeking around corners and triggering all my anxieties, I'd lost sight of that fact. But moving forward, I'd remember who I was fighting my demons for, because Candace was worth it. Our future was worth it. I refused to let my past mistakes keep ruining my life.

Amy Judd knew more than she was letting on, and she was letting on a lot.

Candace and I were the first to arrive for Sunday dinner. Nick had dragged Candace into the kitchen to help set the table and pour drinks for everyone. He said it was because neither one of them could cook worth a lick, so they better find some other ways to be useful.

Candace's mother—who'd prepared the beef stew currently simmering away on the stove—had asked me to get down a box of holiday decorations from the closet in the living room. The Judds had their Christmas tree positioned in the front window, but it didn't have any ornaments on it yet.

"I'll get it ready this week," Amy said as I placed the box on the worn carpet next to the six-and-a-half-foot-tall white pre-lit artificial tree. "When there aren't kids at home to beg you to decorate, it's easy to get lazy about it."

"You finally got Brady out of the house," I teased. "You almost sound like you want him back."

Amy laughed. "I wouldn't mind. He's a good cook and he cleans like you wouldn't believe. But he hogged the bathroom more than both my girls put together."

I grinned and watched in amusement as Amy casually drifted over to the built-in bookshelves in the corner of the room and said, "See how meticulously his hair was styled?"

I followed to get a better look.

By the time my eyes found the photo she'd indicated, I realized where my steps had taken me. *The Humble Shelf.*

I'd wandered into the trap before I fully realized it was set.

I eyed Candace's mother, but she was still pointing at a preteen Brady with dyed-blond tips and an unfortunate puka-shell necklace.

"I imagine it would take time and plenty of hair gel to get it into position," I replied cautiously.

Amy laughed.

But then my eyes wandered, searching for Candace's youthful face. There she was with the third-grade super-short cut she'd told me about. It hadn't been *that* bad. She was smiling so hard in the picture that I felt my lips twist before I gave them permission. She had on a purple baby-doll dress over black leggings as she posed in the school photo.

Next to it was another framed picture, an image of Candace in her early teens. She had a mouthful of braces and was holding up an award on eighth-grade graduation night. I recognized this version of her—the hardworking overachiever, the girl in the accelerated classes, the one who gave reports to the class without a tremor in her voice. My thumb stroked the smooth corner of the wooden frame before I replaced it on the ledge.

My gaze scanned to the next picture of Candace on the shelf below. She was maybe five or six years old and stuffed in the narrow backseat of a Judd's Orchard work truck with a slightly older Brady. It looked like they were mid-battle. The lines of their bodies were indistinct and blurred with motion so quick, the camera couldn't keep up. His arm was locked around her head while she dug an elbow into the top of his thigh.

Again, my grin came unbidden. I didn't have siblings, so I lacked the lived experience of loving someone while also looking for any way to irritate them. Brady and Candace had struck a good balance as adults. They called each other names and stole each other's food, but they'd be the first ones to step up if their sibling needed help with a flat tire, or a ride to the airport, or a prank on a shared enemy.

Despite the inherent violence, it was endearing to see this photo of them in a moment of diabolical sibling rivalry.

"I didn't know children could fight so much until Candace came along," Amy said, startling me. I'd been lost in the framed photographs and had forgotten she was there.

She ignored my obvious surprise and watched me carefully. "Joan was different, unconcerned with things like bickering and fighting. It was probably the age difference as much as her personality. But Brady and Candace were close enough, with only three years between them, that they fought like cats and dogs. Oh, they had fun too, but I'll never forget the day she tied him to the rolling desk chair and put makeup on every inch of his face. He got her back by putting eighteen slugs in her bed."

I choked on my laughter and Amy grinned, enjoying my reaction.

My eyes drifted back to the girl with braces, the one who'd become my teenage crush in just a few short years. The classmate I never had the nerve to talk to. The homecoming queen who lived in my hazy memories.

And now, the daydream laughing with her dad in the next room.

When I turned back to Amy, I found her watching me, a soft smile on her face and hazel eyes so much like her daughter's. She didn't have to say anything, I already knew what she was thinking. So I simply smiled back.

"Are y'all coming to eat or what?" Candace called suddenly from the kitchen.

Just then, the front door banged open, bringing with it Brady and Joan and a burst of cold December air.

The six of us squeezed around the kitchen table and ate hearty beef stew ladled over creamy whipped potatoes. The Judds teased and laughed, and I mostly watched and listened while Candace's leg pressed against mine beneath the poinsettia-printed tablecloth.

And when Candace grinned and broke the news, the only two people who were surprised were Nick and Brady. Joan simply grabbed another roll from the basket and told Brady she wasn't surprised he hadn't solved the mystery of the Apple House vandal with detective skills like that.

Amy gave us that same soft, knowing smile I'd seen in the living room, but this time, her hazel eyes were filled with unshed tears as she hugged us both.

nineteen

MARK

"And you're sure you're okay with going to the Christmas party?" Candace asked from the passenger seat of my truck a week later. She was worrying her bottom lip again, and I hated that I'd made her so fretful.

I offered up a reassuring smile as I turned onto the long drive that would lead us to Grandpappy's. "Yeah. I think it'll be fun."

The Clarks were good people. I knew nearly everyone who'd be attending simply due to sharing a town and being neighbors in the same line of work. I wasn't particularly worried about them judging Candace for dating me. She'd become good friends with Bonnie and Mac and Laramie in the months since she'd returned to Kirby Falls.

Plus, the gathering at the farm across the highway had the added benefit of taking place after hours. Or it would be. Candace and I were headed over a little early to help Bonnie set up. There were a few cars and stragglers in the parking lot, but the farm closed at five on Sundays, so the Clarks had decided that would be the best time for their holiday party.

When we got out of the truck, Candace still looked a little nervous, so I reached over and threaded her fingers through mine.

I didn't know that I'd ever been over to Grandpappy's during the holiday season, but their decorations were very festive. Our steps slowed as we entered the main gate from the parking area. The freestanding ticket booth was closed at the late hour, but it had been turned into a tiny elf house complete with a red-and-white signpost announcing the North Pole.

"Whoa," Candace breathed as she took in the General Store. It had large-bulb multicolored lights strung all over and the log cabin–like structure had been decorated to look like a gingerbread house.

Garland and white lights were draped along every fence line. We followed the main path past the field they typically used for a pumpkin patch. Now it held a vast collection of evergreens, in all shapes and sizes. The Grandpappy's Christmas tree lot was twice the size of the one at Judd's. We continued walking until we ran into MacKenzie.

"Hey, y'all," she greeted. "I'm just going out to round up the rest of the tourists. We have a few folks who can't read the closing time on the sign out front."

"We came a little early to help Bonnie," Candace said.

Mac pointed with her radio in one hand. "She and Danny are down by the gazebo. They were bringing some tables over."

"Thank you," Candace replied. "We'll go find her and see you in a little bit."

"Good luck with the stragglers," I told Mac.

She grinned, her red lips taking on a maniacal glee. "Oh, they'll need the luck. I can't wait to boot them out."

Candace and I laughed as Mac took off in the opposite direction, her long dark ponytail swinging happily as she went to ruin someone's day.

"Does she know Brady's coming?" I murmured quietly, in case she could hear me.

"I warned her," Candace replied just as softly. "Maybe that's why she's wearing red. So the blood won't show."

Chuckling, I wrapped my arm around her shoulders and directed us down the path to the gazebo and the pond.

Without the apple cannon going this late in the year, the Clarks had installed a fountain in the center of the water. It had a light feature shining on the spray that was just visible in the waning afternoon light. The alternating red and green would be fun when the sun finally set in the next half hour or so.

A raised voice drew our attention away from the pond, and our steps slowed at the same time. I followed the sound of two figures squaring off in the middle of the gazebo. Bonnie and her husband, Danny, were too far away for us to hear the details of the argument, but it looked pretty heated.

Candace and I came to a complete stop, and I could see the worry on Candace's face for her friend.

A moment later, Danny uttered something low and harsh and then stalked off through the trees.

Bonnie finally turned to face us as we approached.

"Are you okay?" Candace asked.

Bonnie forced an exaggerated smile and said, "Of course! Thanks for coming to help set up."

A beat of silence passed where I realized Bonnie was content to ignore what we'd witnessed. She wasn't going to get into it. Maybe because I was here.

But one thing was for sure, I'd be keeping my eye on Danny Jensen for the rest of the night.

"Sure," Candace replied brightly, her smile straining at the edges. "Put us to work."

"Mom and Aunt Maggie outdid themselves on the treats. There are, like, twelve different kinds of cookies." Bonnie grinned and it was more genuine this time. "They already decorated the food tables. Maybe you can help me unwrap all the dishes and fill some drinks? Becca and Larry are already up there. They'll help too."

Candace nodded and, seemingly unable to help herself, reached forward and squeezed Bonnie's arm. "Yeah. I can do that."

Bonnie squinted in the distance, and I turned too, worried that Danny was coming back. But it was just Brady, walking down the path to join us.

"Mercer," Bonnie said, "maybe you and Brady could bring up one of these round tables. Just in case we need more seating than the picnic tables that are already in front of the Bake Shop."

There were a few white tables and chairs set up around the large gazebo. I nodded. "Happy to."

We greeted Brady when he arrived, and he agreed to stay and help me cart the table up the hill. Bonnie and Candace took off a moment later to prep the food.

"Mercer, we haven't really gotten a chance to talk about you dating my sister."

I eyed Brady skeptically. While he'd been surprised at dinner last week, he hadn't indicated he was upset. I didn't think he had a problem with my relationship with Candace, but the guy was a wild card. You could never tell what he was going to do.

"Okay. Let's hear it."

With a commiserating look, he went on, "I know she can be a real pill. She is annoyingly extroverted. And don't tell her I said this, but she's good at nearly everything. It's disgusting. Oh, and she talks in her sleep."

"I know."

Brady made a face. "Gross, man. Keep that shit to yourself. She's my sister."

I sighed and kept my gaze flat.

He continued unaffected, "She's super competitive. Don't ever expect to win a game of Monopoly or anything without her being a brat about it. Oh, and her morning breath is rank. Don't let it scare you off."

"What are you doing, Brady? Aren't you supposed to be warning me away? Threatening bodily harm? Holding a grudge that I'm dating your sister and we hid it from you?"

He looked thoughtful for a moment. "Well, I don't love that you went behind our backs, but I figure you had your reasons. Plus, Candace is an adult. I don't need to come over here and threaten to break your kneecaps or slash your tires. You're the best fucking guy I know, Mercer. You're not going to break my baby sister's heart."

I shook my head, feeling a smile tip up the corners of my lips. Brady was often ridiculous, and rarely serious, but his endorsement meant a lot. "Thanks, Brady. I won't—hurt her, you know."

He nodded solemnly and then straightened, his gaze darting over my shoulder.

I turned to see Candace jogging toward us, a frantic sort of energy radiating from her.

Brady's posture and demeanor changed. He crossed his arms and said loudly, "You better be good to my sister!" Then he winked at me. "Or you'll have to answer to me!" He gave me a subtle thumbs-up just as Candace reached us, and I rolled my eyes.

"What are you doing, doofus?" she asked, eyeing him warily and clearly noticing that the table we were supposed to be transporting had been abandoned on its side, legs half folded in.

"As your protective older brother, I'm making sure Mercer here knows the score."

"Oh, Lord," Candace groaned.

My mind drifted to the tense standoff from earlier and Danny Jensen's angry features. I placed a hand on her elbow and drew her attention, suddenly worried about what brought her back to the gazebo. "Is everything okay up at the Bake Shop?"

"Yep," she practically squeaked, and my eyes narrowed. Her gaze darted toward the path and then back to me. "I came to help Brady with the table because I need you to run back to the truck and grab my toboggan for me. I'm freezing."

My eyes searched her face. Something was going on. Candace looked off-balance, and it was at least fifty-five degrees today. We weren't even wearing our big winter coats. Why would she want a hat all of a sudden?

If it had been my birthday, I would have said she was trying to lure me somewhere for a surprise party. But since it wasn't, I just looked at her a moment longer while she practically squirmed under my scrutiny. Finally, I nodded. "Okay, I'll run back to the truck."

A breath gusted out of her and she smiled widely. "Thank you!" Then she kissed me on the lips, and Brady made a gagging sound in the background.

They bickered about PDA while folding in the remaining table legs as I walked off in the direction of the parking lot.

Halfway there I remembered that Candace hadn't even brought her toboggan. The knitted pink hat with the pom-pom on top was, at this very moment, hanging on my coatrack by the back door. She'd worn it last night when she went out to see the cat. Her daily attempt to try and sweet-talk him into letting her pet him.

With a shake of my head, I spun around by the entrance to the General Store and pivoted back toward the Orchard Bake Shop, where the festivities were taking place tonight. I figured I was too late to intercept them and carry the table the rest of the way. Candace and Brady were likely already there.

A few minutes later, the long narrow building that housed the farm's year-round bakery came into view. It had a covered front porch with plenty of picnic tables for tourists to enjoy their treats, or for a weekend Christmas party for Grandpappy's employees and their friends. There were a lot more people milling about now. I spotted a handful of Clarks sitting and drinking and carrying dishes out the half door of the Bake Shop.

The rest of the Judds had arrived too. Joan was chatting with Will and his girlfriend, Becca. And Nick and Amy were talking to Will's father, William.

I caught sight of Brady and Candace positioning the table they'd carried while Maggie Clark directed them.

Chloe—the other Bake Shop employee—was at the order window while a man I didn't recognize and a little girl with blond hair waited.

Mac was nearby with the stragglers she'd rounded up, and she tapped her foot impatiently, clearly waiting on the man and the child.

Stepping onto the wooden decking of the covered porch, I muttered a polite "excuse me" to a pregnant woman whose back was turned, blocking the way to where I was headed.

"Oh sorry," she said as she pivoted out of the way, and I stopped dead in my tracks as the voice and the face registered.

"Hannah," I said in surprise.

She looked the same as the last time I'd seen her, over two and a half years ago. Well, except for the very obvious pregnancy. But then again, I'd seen her pregnant too. She was wearing jeans and stylish boots with heels, so maybe her ankles weren't quite as swollen this time around. Her hair was longer than it had been, but she was still the spitting image of my ex-wife, and for the life of me, I could not understand what she was doing here.

"Mark," she breathed.

Before I could recover, Hannah's parents stepped up beside her. Reverend Price had aged in the last few years. I hadn't heard from him at all since the divorce was finalized. His once salt-and-pepper hair had gone completely gray. He still wore wire-framed glasses that gave him a wise and studious air. He and his wife stared at me with twin expressions of contempt so acute they must have practiced them in the mirror every morning.

It took me a minute, but I realized that Candace had known. I bet she'd sent me to the car to keep me away. It was especially obvious once I glanced over and saw the horrified look on her face as she witnessed this painful reunion go down. The Prices must have been part of the group Mac was so looking forward to escorting out. But she probably couldn't give a proper boot to the local Baptist preacher and his family.

All of a sudden, awareness stole through me. If Hannah was here, then that meant—

My gaze scanned the area for a stroller or a baby in someone's arms. But Lyndsey would be three years old now—four next month. She wasn't the chubby-cheeked, happy infant from my memories.

Once my brain caught up, I remembered. Slowly, I turned my head to the order window, twenty feet away. The man and the little girl were still there, only now he was holding her. She laughed while Chloe grinned and handed her a cookie.

My breath came out like I'd taken a punch. Greedily, I cataloged all the changes. The hair that was long and slightly curled at the ends. The way her body had grown. But her face—with those striking green eyes that belonged to neither me nor her mother—was so familiar that my chest felt tight.

"Mark, I—" Hannah cut herself off, but I still didn't look away. I couldn't. Lyndsey was right here, and it had been so long.

The little girl leaned forward, hand outstretched, and I had a moment of panic as she lunged out of the man's arms. But he caught her smoothly as she and Chloe shared a grinning high five.

"That's what it looks like when a real man takes care of his family."

The words were unemotional and matter-of-fact, in a voice from my past. The same one that had given me patient instructions on how to drive a stick shift and how to replant a tomato seedling. The same man who'd prayed over every dinner I'd shared at his table since I was twelve years old.

Candace must have reached my side at some point because her gasp was what finally turned my attention away from the scene at the order window. It took a lot to drag my gaze away. I wanted to linger over all the changes in Lyndsey that I hadn't noticed right away. I ached to step closer, to hear her little voice.

Abruptly I realized that the Prices must have decided on Grandpappy's for their family outing because they'd been sure they'd never run into me here. Hannah didn't come back to Kirby Falls. I hadn't seen her since she moved to Tennessee, a month before the divorce was final. But she was here now, practically begging me with her gaze not to cause a scene, not to make waves, not to reveal the truth.

"Daddy, let's just go," was what actually came out of her mouth.

But no one moved. Hannah's father kept his gaze trained on me.

I felt Candace's hand slip into mine.

"Reverend," I said in greeting. "Mrs. Price." And finally, "Hannah, how have you been?"

My former best friend bit her lip, looking miserable.

"You don't get to ask that, young man," the reverend asserted. "You gave up your family, and you don't get to worry about how they are now."

I didn't reply. There was nothing I could say. No defense I could mount or argument I could pursue without revealing too much.

Awkward silence descended once more.

It wasn't my voice that emerged into the charged atmosphere next. "How can you stand there?" Candace snapped angrily. She'd dropped my hand and stepped slightly in front of me. But her words weren't directed at Reverend Price, she was staring directly at Hannah.

"How can you just let him take the fall for you over and over? You can't even say hi? Be friendly? Ask how he's been since you upended his life?"

I placed a staying hand on Candace's arm. She was practically vibrating, and I realized this was about to go very badly.

"Candace," I murmured quietly in her ear, but her attention was wholly on Hannah.

Briefly, Hannah looked surprised by Candace's presence, how this former classmate had elbowed her way into this situation, the way she was positioned protectively between us. Hannah's eyes moved back and forth between us until they narrowed to slits in realization. Then she raised her chin and said, "You don't know what you're talking about. This is none of your business."

"I know more than you think," Candace gritted out. "And a hell of a lot more than your own family. You're a selfish brat who's content to throw a good man under the bus. Do you like playing the victim? Is that what it is?"

"Candace," I hissed as my pulse thundered and panic slithered up my spine.

But she didn't hear me. "Did you know that he gets accosted on the street by your father's church ladies? They bad-mouth him and spread lies about him all in your honor. You're a lying, narcissistic user."

Hannah's mouth opened and closed but no sound came out.

The next voice I heard was the reverend's. "What is this all about, Hannah Marie?"

"Candace, stop," I hissed, trying to maneuver around her.

But she was determined. "After everything Mark did for you," Candace continued, flinging her arms wide and dislodging my hold. "He protected you. He married you. Saved you from being pregnant and disowned. He kept your secrets and went along with your lies. And you never even once thought about coming clean, helping him in return."

Before she could say more, Lyndsey barreled into Hannah's side, grinning happily and wrapping herself around her mother's legs. Hannah managed to look away from her accuser and reach for her daughter, mustering up a pained smile. "Hi, baby. Did you get your cookie?"

All I wanted was to watch—to look at Lyndsey up close. Instead, I forced myself to use the disruption to grab Candace's hand and tug her away from the scene she'd made infinitely worse.

The man who'd been with Lyndsey at the counter was staring at the tense standoff in confusion. Candace was still red-faced and angry, but she let me lead her away.

Hannah listened as her daughter kept up a steady stream of chatter, but she looked brittle, like one strong breeze would shatter her.

It was the final glimpse of the group, though, that had me even more desperate to escape. Reverend Price and his wife were staring at me. And they weren't wearing their rehearsed expressions of disapproval. They looked utterly shell-shocked.

I ignored the questions in their gaze, the sudden awareness, the disbelief.

As I led Candace away from the Bake Shop, I noticed everyone's eyes were trained on us. Neighbors and friends and Candace's family too. But I couldn't focus on that. Something tragic and terrible settled like a weight around my neck.

I couldn't believe Candace had been so reckless and rash. She'd taken it upon herself to cast doubt and suspicion on my marriage to Hannah. She'd practically revealed the truth right there for everyone to hear.

My breaths were coming fast, sawing in and out, as my steps quickened and my heart pounded. I dropped Candace's hand, desperate to get away from the mess she'd made. Her footsteps trailed me, but escape was my only concern at present.

Vaguely I heard Mac announce that it was time for all farm visitors to go due to a private event.

My feet carried me farther onto the farm, off the worn dirt path and over grass, until I reached the gazebo, right where we'd started. With my hands on my hips, I paced to the railing to stare out at the water. But I didn't see the ripples on the surface or the fountain in the center. The red and green lights didn't register over the blood rushing in my ears.

When I could manage a full breath, I turned to face Candace. She stood in the middle of the gazebo, her arms crossed, her face flushed, and her gaze focused on the wooden planks beneath her boots.

"That wasn't your place, Candace."

She nodded slowly but still wouldn't look at me. "That's probably true, but I couldn't just stand there and let them treat you like that."

"Do you understand the damage you just caused?"

Finally, her eyes rose to meet mine and anger flared anew. "I was protecting you. You deserve to have someone stand up for you."

I was already shaking my head. "Not like that. Not at someone else's expense." Candace opened her mouth, the argument ready and waiting on her tongue, but I shook my head again. "No, you don't get to decide that. It's not your job to breeze back into town and upend everyone's lives. You don't have the right to mete out justice as you see fit. I planned to honor my word to Hannah."

Candace released a frustrated breath. "I am so fucking tired of you defending that girl. She's a monster. And what has all that honor gotten you, Mark? While Hannah plays the victim with her family and her friends and everyone in this town, you stay home. You don't go out. You hide away to keep the peace. You're the villain of *her* story when you should have been the hero. People gossip and hold something against you that isn't even true. You don't correct them. You don't defend yourself. You live this small existence. It's not fair!"

Her shouted words echoed across the landscape, and I felt them vibrate painfully through my bones.

Of course, I lived with the decisions I'd made. And yeah, at times, I resented Hannah. After all, she got to lead the life I'd agreed to . . . without me in it. There was a three-year-old holding her hand right now who didn't even remember me. It wasn't just my reputation I'd lost. It was bigger than that, and Candace didn't have the right to question the way I lived now as a result.

As I struggled to steady myself, Candace took a step closer and lowered her voice. "Aren't you tired of living a lie that's not even yours? Aren't you tired of being held hostage in your own home?"

"My life is quiet," I argued. "It's small, and I'm okay with that." I'd lost the only family I'd ever known, and Candace wanted to focus on trivialities, like how I stayed home on Friday nights.

She pressed her hands together in a pleading gesture. "It's small because you've accepted it as your due. You don't think you deserve more, so you're settling for less. You let Hannah whittle you down and for what? So *she* can save face because she's too cowardly to admit the truth? She's not a kid anymore. You don't need to keep making excuses for her. She used you and then cast you aside when it no longer suited her. And she's not sorry. She's not even here. She ran away so she wouldn't have to see you and face what she'd done. Kirby Falls isn't her home anymore. It's yours, but you're a prisoner here, Mark. Can't you see that?"

Her words were salt in an open wound, one I'd ignored and left untreated for a very long time. Pain and anger had me lashing out to protect myself from the new threat—Candace and her accusations, a dozen things I didn't want to think about all while an image of a little girl I barely recognized flashed behind my eyes.

"You were the one who saw Kirby Falls as a prison," I countered spitefully. "You were the one who needed to run away to make something of yourself. Maybe everything and everyone here is just too small for you, Candace. This is my life, and I like it just fine."

"You're happy?" she challenged.

"I'm fine," I insisted.

She drew in a slow breath and watched me for a long moment. "I'm sorry for what I said back there. And how I said it. You're right. It wasn't my place, but I couldn't stand there—"

"You should have let me handle it," I interrupted.

Hazel eyes flashed incredulously. "Handle it? You were paralyzed by the sight of that little girl. The one Hannah ripped out of your life."

"Don't," I warned, that old hurt now fully reopened, pulling angrily at the stitches helpless to keep it closed.

"I couldn't let them say that stuff to you," she insisted as her frustration mounted, "knowing you'd just stand there and take it."

"Stop."

"You'd take the abuse like you'd earned it."

"Candace, please," I begged.

"No!" she shouted. "I love you and I'm not going to stop!"

I stared at her in disbelief, but she didn't look sorry, just determined.

I imagined hearing her declaration any other time. Around a bonfire. Riding shotgun. In the bed of my truck, staring at an ocean of stars.

Not wielded like a weapon in the heat of battle. Not used as an excuse or a defensive maneuver. An explanation and a justification.

Suddenly Candace released a shuddering breath and a sad little laugh, as if she'd just realized she'd admitted she loved me by slinging it at me with a clenched fist. "You might not care about defending yourself, but I'm always going to be on your side, whether you want me there or not. You're the best person I know. I don't want that to be a secret—how good you are."

With a quiet sniff, she brought her thumb up to her cheek and flicked away an errant tear. "I'm sorry." Her voice broke at the end and her face crumpled. She spun quickly before I could say anything—what, I didn't fucking know. And then she darted up the path and away from me.

I stayed frozen. It felt like someone took a hammer to a gong inside my chest. Past and present were colliding in a clang of emotions all while my heart pounded out a rhythm of dread.

Amid all the thoughts swirling in my head, one emerged shakily to the surface. I realized that I'd lied to Brady earlier. God, not even an hour ago. I'd been so sure I'd never do anything to hurt his sister, but here we were.

She'd done what she thought was right. Maybe she'd been rash and emotional, reacting badly on my behalf. But I *had* hurt her.

And she'd hurt me too.

Maybe that was what love was—giving someone the ability to wound you. A finely honed weapon with the means to leave a permanent mark. A blade, quick and sharp between the ribs. Because that's what it felt like as I struggled with the pain coursing through me.

And like nothing at all had changed, I stood there and watched her walk away.

286

twenty

MARK

Monday happened to be my day off, and I was grateful for it.

After Candace marched away from me yesterday, I'd avoided everyone, skipped the Christmas party, and made the slow trek to the parking lot alone.

Twenty-four hours later, and I still wasn't ready to talk to Candace or face well-meaning sympathy from the Judds.

Sleep hadn't come easy last night. I missed Candace in bed beside me—her soft warmth, her lavender scent that lingered faintly on the pillow, even her sleepy mumblings—but I was still twisted up over what had happened. I didn't know how to handle missing someone, loving them, and being angry at them all at the same time.

Rather than sleep, I'd replayed the events of the day over and over in my mind. Each time, my memories snagged on something new and painful. The way Hannah had gone from miserable to inconvenienced at Candace's appearance. How suspicion had slowly entered the reverend's features. The little shoes with sparkly butterflies Lyndsey had on her tiny feet. How defeated Candace had looked when she'd wiped her angry tears away.

Now, the afternoon sun was shining, and I was sitting out on the steps of my back deck drinking a beer in the cold. My gaze found the raised beds near the fence line. I had a polytunnel protecting my baby lettuces. They were nearly ready for harvesting after a long growing season sheltered by the plastic sheeting over half hoops.

A few minutes and several sips later, the cat wandered across the grass and toward the porch.

"You're early for dinner," I said.

His winter coat was in. The gray fur looked full and thick on his large frame. Yellow eyes scanned me briefly as he mounted the stairs.

With a sigh, I set my beer bottle down beside me, preparing to stand and get the beast his dinner. But before I could rise, the cat walked up to me, as casual as could be, and climbed into my lap. He placed one tentative paw on the thigh closest to him and then gracefully crossed to the other leg before sitting down like we did this all the time.

Alarmed, I left my arms and hands out to the side and froze, pretty sure I was going to get mauled any minute, but the cat simply looked out over the yard, sitting happy and content.

"What is happening right now?" I said quietly.

A moment later, a sound reached my ears. I tilted my head as I registered the steady thrumming coming from the vicinity of my lap. The damn thing was purring. I'd been feeding him for over two years. He'd barely wandered into the house, and I had a scar on my hand that had been his panicked handiwork. And now, the little shit was purring.

Swallowing, I cautiously moved my right hand. Slowly, I brought it close to his head. After a delicate sniff, the cat shocked the hell out of me by rubbing his face beneath my palm. I held my fingers gingerly as the cat worked to basically pet himself using my hand. Eventually, I extended a finger and crooked it beneath his chin. The purring rumbled louder in the quiet afternoon, and I felt a hesitant smile turn the corners of my lips. I didn't dare speak again lest the sound disrupt whatever tentative peace we'd brokered.

I couldn't wait to tell Candace. She'd been desperate to tame this furry beast, always talking to him while he ate his supper and bringing over cat toys to tempt him inside. She'd been convinced I needed a pet to take care of. A sudden ache had the smile slipping off my face.

I sighed and the cat looked up. His rusty meow wobbled from the vibrations of his purr. Maybe Candace had been right. Maybe this cat was rehabilitated and ready to try again.

After another few minutes of cautious petting, he stepped off my lap and went over to the water bowl I refilled daily. I rose and opened the back sliding door, leaving it open while I went in to prepare his dinner.

The cat followed, and when I placed the now-full dish of cat food on the kitchen floor, he walked over casually and started eating. I watched for long minutes as he consumed the offerings and then swiped a rough pink tongue over the side of his paw to clean his face. When he was finished, he wandered into the living room, like it was totally normal, and curled up on the couch.

I stood dumbfounded on the threshold as he closed his eyes and appeared to go to sleep.

"What brought all this on, huh?" He blinked sleepy yellow eyes my way and then ignored me, repositioning and curling more fully on his side. "What made you decide you could trust me all of a sudden?"

The cat didn't answer.

I didn't have much time to mull it over. A knock sounded at my front door, and I wondered, irrationally, if it was Candace.

Suddenly, the distance I'd craved last night and all day today abandoned me. I wanted it to be her. I wanted to hold her and apologize for the way things had gone down yesterday. I wanted to tell her I loved her too. I didn't want to go another minute without setting things right.

With time and a bit of distance, I could see where Candace was coming from. The righteous indignation on my behalf. The anger and worry she'd been unable to contain. If the tables had been turned, I would have hated watching anyone hurt or demean her the same way. Hadn't I inserted myself a time or two already? With her family, her sister, at the damn farmers' market when someone called her Candy instead of the name she preferred?

I couldn't imagine standing by while someone took advantage of her or tore her down, broke her heart, upended her life, and made her out to be the villain. So, yeah, maybe Candace hadn't gone about it the right way, but I could see that she'd stood up for me because she cared. And that meant something.

But it wasn't Candace at my door. It was a vision from my past and the least likely person I could imagine darkening my doorstep.

"Reverend," I greeted, and then stood back. "How can I help you?"

"Can I come in for a moment? Have a word?"

I pulled the door open wider in answer. Some ingrained part of me who'd always sought his approval felt the same urge now. I'd been the grateful child, the helpful neighbor, the charity case, and the respectful son-in-law, so there were lots of people-pleasing parts to choose from. Nerves and nostalgia battled for dominance, but mostly I just felt sad that I'd devoted so much of my life to someone who'd cast me aside without a backward glance.

Reverend Price didn't bother removing his jacket. Instead, he surveyed the living room briefly, noting the cat on the sofa, before sitting in one of the club chairs by the window. I wondered if, in that momentary glance, he remembered helping me refinish the floorboards after Hannah and I first moved in, or the time he watched Lyndsey take her first steps beside the coffee table in the center of the room.

I wiped my palms down the front of my jeans and sat in the chair opposite.

"Mark, I want to apologize." He leaned forward and rested his elbows on his thighs—a departure from his typically ruthless posture. This was his counseling pose, the bearing of an everyday man connecting with sinners. "Hannah relayed the truth of what happened—back in college. Her mother and I are grateful for what you did for our daughter and our grandchild. Decker, also, was unaware that you weren't Lyndsey's biological father. He shares our gratitude."

At my blank look, Reverend Price clarified, "Hannah's husband. He's a good person and a wonderful father to Lyndsey. He loves her very much."

I nodded. I'd only registered the unknown man at the farm the previous day in his proximity to Lyndsey, and then I hadn't thought of him again. But I was glad Hannah had someone decent in her life. I was even more grateful that Lyndsey had a solid, loving presence—a father she deserved. From the look of things, their family was growing, and I didn't begrudge them that either. I wanted Lyndsey to have a wonderful life with parents who adored her.

"It was wrong of Hannah to lie, but she made a mistake and has asked us and the Lord for forgiveness."

I noticed the reverend didn't say that Hannah had been wrong in assuming they'd disown her for showing up pregnant out of wedlock at twenty years old. I guessed if my love was conditional and hypocritical, I wouldn't advertise it either.

He also failed to indicate whether Hannah would be asking *me* for forgiveness. He was here in his daughter's place, after all.

I resisted the urge to shake my head, realizing suddenly how much anger and resentment I still carried. The same emotions I'd forced down for years. Mark the reliable. Mark the safety net. Mark the pushover, the scapegoat, the doormat, the fall guy.

Candace had been right. Hannah was selfish and self-serving. Even now, she was playing the victim. Her father was here apologizing. Sure as hell wasn't her.

The reverend clasped his hands loosely together. I had to give him credit, he held my gaze, unflinching and direct as always. "I can't imagine how difficult that must have been for you, when Hannah left and took Lyndsey with her. You were always such a devoted husband and father in the short time you were married. I think we were all surprised and confused by the news of your separation. We were disappointed, of course."

The steady cadence of his voice—instructional and unwavering, never raised—brought me back to our conversations as an adolescent. The same man who'd known me since I was a shy, withdrawn twelve-year-old . . . and had never once invited me to call him by his given name.

"If you'd like me to speak to Hannah and Decker about granting you time to see Lyndsey, I would be willing to do so."

My gaze sharpened at the offer. It was a carrot dangling at the end of a string, a cruel suggestion in an attempt to assuage his own guilt.

But at what cost? Upheaval for Lyndsey? Trauma for me? Hannah was undoubtedly selfish, but she was also right. That little girl didn't remember me, and having a weird uncle show up at her birthday parties would only confuse her. It would keep the pieces of my broken heart jagged. Lyndsey was never mine, and she never would be. I was grateful for the time I got to spend with her, a very short year of my life.

It wasn't *all* Hannah's fault. When she left, I should have been braver and fought harder for the part of my family I did love. But I'd been too busy being a martyr and taking the fall.

I hadn't spoken since we'd sat down. I realized I didn't owe the reverend anything. I didn't need to reassure him, alleviate his guilt, or accept whatever too-little, too-late apology he was peddling. The Prices had no problem disregarding me over the years.

But that wasn't the sort of person I wanted to be. Revenge and vindication weren't the standards I lived by.

"I appreciate the offer," I finally replied. "But I don't want to confuse Lyndsey or try to make a place for myself in her life when it would only serve my own purpose. She has a father now, and that"—I cleared the emotion from my voice—"was all I ever wanted for her in the first place."

"You're a good man, Mark."

That's what it looks like when a real man takes care of his family.

I didn't point out that it was that standard for masculinity that he'd thrown in my face yesterday, back when he thought I was a deadbeat.

When I remained quiet, Reverend Price stood. He didn't hold out a hand to shake or offer any more platitudes, but he did hold my gaze and assert, "There won't be any further problems from my flock. I'll see to that."

Problems. What a way to describe harassment and cruelty. *Flock*, too, seemed too tame for the kinds of people he guided from the pulpit.

I rose and nodded before making my way to the door.

The man left as quietly as he came. He'd never been the type for dramatics, just quiet resolve and unyielding expectation. And he wasn't a part of my life anymore.

Perhaps there had been a time when the Prices were my family. But their love and affection always had a price tag.

I thought of Amy Judd and her kind face and knowing smile. Nick on the back of a tractor, a supportive slap on the back. A seat at their table and a welcome at the farmhouse whenever I wanted it. Holidays, birthdays, and Tupperware slipped into my hand at the end of the night. No questions or judgment about my failed marriage. Joan gripping my shoulder and threatening revenge on judgy neighbors. Brady and a trivia night text message for as long as I could remember.

For years I'd had a prime example of how acceptance worked in a loving family. No qualifiers, no hoops to jump through. The Judds worked together and loved together and supported one another every step of the way, whether it be a home-cooked meal, or tough love and a blanket on the back porch. It was support that spanned time and space. It was a welcome home and a surprise pickup from the airport after seven years away. Their kind of love was limitless and unconditional.

I just hadn't realized I'd been included in it all along.

As I stood in the center of my living room and contemplated the family I'd been blessed with, I felt cool air blow in from the back door. I'd left it cracked for the cat in case he had buyer's remorse and panicked, thinking he'd been trapped inside.

My gaze cut to the couch, sure the long-haired beast would be long gone, but there he was, still curled up on the soft cushion, as if he'd always been there—like that particular spot was already his.

A moment later, I felt my phone vibrate in my pocket. I smiled down at the text message on the screen before casting another glance over to the sleeping feline.

With the device clutched in my hand, I thought it might be time for me to be brave too. It wasn't too late to change your plans, to live a new sort of life, one that was bigger and louder than what the voice in your head told you that you deserved.

So I typed out three letters and hit send before I could change my mind.

Trailview Brewing was packed that night.

People crowded around wooden picnic tables, locals and leafers alike. Tourists might not be in Kirby Falls for the autumn leaves, but they were content to travel, seeking the small-town holiday experience just as readily. With Christmas only two weeks away and plenty of events planned between now and then, the leafers wouldn't let up until after the new year.

I slipped through the crowd on my way to the bar as old, lingering anxiety made itself known. I caught myself scanning faces and bracing for impact. Then I told myself to fight my fears and fight for the life I wanted—one that was open and free and whatever I wanted it to be.

I forced a slow inhale and kept walking to place my order.

With the cold weather, the brewery had lowered the sides of the clear canopy enclosure and cranked the heaters up. I wouldn't need the heavyweight winter jacket I wore once I got settled.

With a glass of Trailview's brown ale in one hand, I skirted the edge of the trivia host's table and looked for Brady among the masses.

He found me first, standing on the bench like a drama queen and spreading his arms wide. "Mark Mercer, as I live and breathe."

I rolled my eyes and headed toward him.

He'd climbed down by the time I reached his table, but he was still grinning as I took a seat across from him.

"How the hell are you?" he asked. Then I watched the immature-frat-boy persona fall away and read real concern in his eyes. He'd witnessed everything that had gone down at Grandpappy's yesterday too.

"I'm okay," I replied honestly. But hopefully soon there'd be the potential for more than that.

I clinked my glass to his and took a sip before greeting the two other men at the table. Cole Abernathy was on my left and Jase Wilcox sat across from him. They'd both been friends with Brady since elementary school, and I'd been around them plenty in the years I'd been working for the Judds.

"Good to see you," the man nearly everyone called Abby said. "And thanks for coming out to Flyers's opening a couple of months back. You took off before we got a chance to talk."

"No problem. It was great. I hope business is good."

While Abby gave me an update on his newest venture, I thought back to that October evening with Candace, legs folded beneath a too-small table, our knees pressed together. The way I'd wanted her—her time and attention and love—but I'd forced all those complicated feelings aside, held myself back, and tried my best to be her friend instead. I'd been scared to wish for more, too afraid of losing her before I even had her.

Maybe love and loss would always be tethered together in my mind. Two sides of the same coin. I hadn't experienced one without the other. But I didn't want my relationship with Candace to come down to a coin toss.

"You ready, Mercer?" Brady asked, pulling me out of my thoughts and holding out his pint.

As the intro music for Trivia Night began, I let myself sink into the experience—one I'd avoided for so long. The simplicity of it. The novelty. The community.

"Yeah," I replied. Then I clinked my glass to his again and gave myself permission to have fun.

There was room for more in my life. I'd made it small on purpose. And I'd kept it that way to ensure my safety. But I could take up space. I could grow, and I didn't have to do it alone.

I had a life I loved—or the potential for one. It was time I started living it.

CANDACE

My office was freezing Tuesday morning when I got in. The fact that it was December and five thirteen in the morning probably had something to do with it.

I turned my electric heater to the highest setting and wrapped myself in a blanket I kept on the back of my desk chair. Then I pulled out my trusty notebook and flipped to the page I'd been scribbling on all day yesterday. **Things to say to Mark** was in bold at the top of the lined sheet. Making a list had helped to order my thoughts after I'd calmed down.

When we'd had our fight on Sunday, I'd been too emotional and reactive to really express myself. It was hard to make a good point when you were shrill and unsteady on the inside and just as shrill and unsteady on the outside. I'd walked away because I knew I wasn't getting anywhere while the shame I felt just made me more and more defensive. My adrenaline had needed to dissipate and my good sense to return. And I'd needed to stop shouting I loved him mid-rant.

I face-palmed and groaned as I remembered the utter shock on his face at my angry love confession.

A soft knock on the doorframe had my head snapping up.

"I saw the light beneath the door. Thought I'd check on you," Joan said by way of greeting. She was decked out in her winter running gear. Dark leggings hugged her slim, muscular legs while a quarter-zip pullover covered her top half. She wore a headband over her ears, and her cheeks were already a little pink from the cold.

"Oh, you know," I hedged.

Joan looked amused. "Just torturing yourself and being miserable?"

"Yep. That's the one."

She came in, closed the door behind her, and took the narrow uncomfortable seat in front of the desk. "He'll come around. He knows you didn't mean to hurt anyone."

My eyes drifted toward my notebook, but I didn't see the myriad of apologies written there in my hasty scrawl. I only remembered the panic on his face, the total devastation while he'd dragged me away from the Prices. The way his anxiety had increased tenfold when he realized that all eyes were on us and the scene I'd caused.

"I don't know, Joanie. He has every right not to forgive me."

"Bullshit," she said without heat. "That Price girl deserved everything you said and more. I've had to watch people give him a hard time for years. Bitten my tongue while people like Eloise Carter made him feel less than, treated him like some deadbeat who doesn't pay child support instead of the damn saint he is."

My eyes lifted at the realization. "That day at the Orchard Festival?"

My sister nodded. "She was running her mouth, and Mercer did what he always does. Turned the other cheek. That hypocrite preacher must have instilled more than Mercer ever realized."

My heart ached at the memory. Mark had told me there was nothing romantic between him and Joan when I'd accidentally spied their tender moment in the tent. Now I was grateful for the comfort she'd offered him in the face of needless cruelty.

I tugged the blanket tighter around my shoulders. "Yeah, but that's just Mark. And I did the exact opposite."

I'd attacked Hannah. Not that she was innocent, but the only thing she'd done to provoke my ire was breathe in my vicinity.

But I'd had months of knowing the truth. I'd kept my feelings to myself. Mark didn't want to discuss his decisions, and he didn't want to hear my opinion on Hannah and her childish manipulation. It became harder and harder to watch him hide himself away, and me along with him, as a result.

"I shouldn't have inserted myself into his business," I added. "A confrontation is the last thing Mark ever wanted."

But something bitter and vindictive had claimed me that day. When I'd seen Hannah standing there, looking so inconvenienced by Mark's very existence, I'd wanted payback. And then her father had swooped in with his self-righteous crap. I'd just snapped.

I'd imagined that scene a dozen times in my head. A phantom battle that played out in my imagination. So it hadn't been difficult to call up the words, the accusations, the truth. But in the process of calling Hannah out on her shitty behavior, I'd put aside Mark's feelings, and I'd broken his word by breaking mine. He'd told me the truth about his marriage in confidence. Not as ammunition to be used against him.

"Maybe so," Joan admitted. "But you *are* his business, Candace. His life affects yours. You're in a relationship now. You're teammates. And I know what it's like to watch people hurt themselves at the expense of others. He would have taken Hannah's secret to his grave and suffered every day for it. Honor and devotion are admirable traits when the people you're sacrificing for deserve it. I know you were just trying to protect him, and, deep down, Mercer knows it too."

"I hope so," I said, my voice watery.

"You want to go on my run with me? Might help clear your head? At the very least you wouldn't be stuck in this freezing office with that creepy-as-hell fish on the wall."

I frowned. "Don't talk about Lance Bass that way."

She shook her head, but she was smiling.

"I think I'll skip the run today," I finally answered. "But maybe tomorrow?" I figured I'd be up anyway. It wasn't like I was sleeping well with all that was weighing on my mind.

My sister nodded and stood. "Okay. I'll text you."

I smiled, grateful for the effort Joan was making. "Sounds good."

"And don't beat yourself up too much, Candy Cane. Mercer will come around."

I sure hoped so.

For the next hour, I busied myself by researching the lavender field I wanted to grow in the rear acreage on the farm. It was almost seven when there came another knock at my office door.

A moment later, Mark stuck his head in.

"Hi," I said quickly, hopping to my feet on instinct as my temperamental desk chair squeaked in protest. My blanket fell away from my shoulders and landed somewhere behind me, but I was too focused on the man before me to care.

"Hey," he said softly, closing the door behind him.

He stood there, just inside the threshold, watching me for a moment. And I used the time to drink him in in return. He wore a tan work jacket open over a cozy-looking flannel. Mark looked solemn, as always, but there was something cautious in his gaze. He was being careful with me, and I hated it.

It had only been a day and a half since our fight, but the distance between us felt bigger than that. It was like I'd dug a trench with what I'd done. Mark on one side and me on the other.

I could only imagine what he saw, looking at me like that. Messy bun on top of my head and dark circles beneath my eyes. Worry consuming me as I nibbled nervously on my bottom lip.

Finally, when I couldn't take the silence anymore, I blurted, "I'm sorry. I'm so sorry, Mark. You were right. It wasn't my secret to tell and I broke your trust. It was wrong of me to think I knew best when it was your life I was talking about. I understand if you can't forgive me, but I wanted you to know that I'm sorry for hurting you." I'd started crying about halfway through my apology, and by the end, I could hardly get the words out.

Mark closed the distance between us and cupped my cheeks in his hands. Using his thumbs, he attempted to wipe away the tears that were falling. Finally, he pulled me against his chest and rubbed my back. "Shhh, Candace. It's okay."

"It's not," I mumbled into the soft fabric of his hunter-green flannel.

I felt him inhale and exhale a huge breath before resting his chin atop my head. "I've never had someone stand up for me like that before. Yes, your family has always been good to me. Treated me like one of their own despite all the rumors and gossip. But I've never had someone who was all mine. A person who'd stand between me and the rest of the damn world. Someone who'd put me first, no questions asked. I didn't know what to do with that kind of love, Candace. I didn't know how to deserve it."

It broke my heart to hear how alone Mark felt all his life. Raised by an aunt who didn't appreciate the gift she'd been given. One who, instead, acted like she'd been saddled with her sister's kid. And to be taken in by a family who manipulated and took advantage of him, followed by years of self-imposed isolation.

I was lucky to have a loving family. Parents and siblings who would drop whatever they were doing to help me. But my family didn't just love me in the big ways. They loved me in the quiet ways too. The ones that made late-night grocery store runs when I was on my period, and sewed buttons back onto my sweaters before school the next day. The money found and freely given for school trips and college applications and anything I needed to help me succeed.

I'd had a lifetime of love, and Mark had missed out on all of it.

I felt my chin wobble, but I made myself pull back to see his face. "You do deserve it. You deserve every good thing."

His hands slid down to my waist, his thumbs passing over the fabric of my shirt the same way they'd collected tears on my cheeks.

Mark's lips tilted up in a soft smile—the one I loved so much—and he said matter-of-factly, "Well, if that's true, then the only thing I want to deserve is you. I want your sweetness and light. I want to work beside you on the farm. I want your cold feet in my bed and your shampoo in my shower. I want a home and a family with you someday. I want to love you for the rest of my life, Candace. I'm sorry for Sunday when I couldn't say it back. I couldn't hear it over my own fears."

I shook my head as happiness at Mark's words fought with the shame I felt over my earlier admission. "I never should have told you like that. But it was true then, and it's true now. I love you. So, so much."

He pressed a gentle kiss to my lips that spoke of forgiveness and understanding. Then he whispered against my skin, "I don't want to hide anymore."

I returned his kiss with one of gratitude and joy. "I can't wait."

We sold the last Christmas tree off the lot at Judd's on December 23. Well, the last one to a customer. I didn't count the seven-foot tree that was currently in the back of Mark's pickup truck.

We were closing down the orchard for the season and then setting up the tree in Mark's living room to decorate that night while *Die Hard* played in the background.

We'd been ornament shopping earlier in the week, and I'd picked out the tree skirt while Mark selected the multicolored lights.

I wanted to make some new memories with Mark for the holidays, come up with traditions of our own.

Tomorrow would be the second annual Christmas Eve celebration over at Lonely Mountain Winery. Reggie and Aurora had invited friends, neighbors, and local business owners for an evening of wine and appetizers, potluck style. Mark and I were bringing his favorite nacho cheese dip. I couldn't wait to see the decorations at the vineyard. It would be a chance to dress up a little and eat my weight in cocktail shrimp. I'd also heard there would be a string quartet and dancing on the heated patio. Swaying in Mark's arms to instrumental covers of Taylor Swift's songs sounded like the perfect night.

Next on the list of holiday festivities was brunch at the farmhouse on Christmas Day. Mark had joined my family for the last two Christmases, but it would be my first holiday brunch on the farm in a long time.

"Do you want your present early?" Mark asked.

Running my fingers through his soft, dark blond hair, I glanced away from the blinking lights of the Christmas tree and down to Mark, his head resting in my lap. "That would be cheating. Christmas isn't for two more days."

He suppressed a smile. "But no one would have to know. You could just open it early."

I bent down and pressed a quick peck to his waiting lips. "No, thank you. I'll wait until Christmas Day."

He groaned, "Such a good girl."

"That's right," I teased, liking the way that sounded a little too much.

Then Mark tugged me down again. The kiss was longer this time. He threaded his fingers through my hair and cupped the back of my neck. I shivered at his touch.

Eventually, he flipped our positions. I was lying on my back while he hovered over me. I squirmed as his strong thighs bracketed my hips, relishing every point of contact and how very secure I felt.

Our mugs of hot chocolate were long forgotten on the coffee table as we touched and tasted. The television screen was black, and the bright lights from the Christmas tree cast the room in a magical, twinkling glow.

"Do you want me to give you your present early?" I gasped out as Mark's lips traced a line from my sternum to my belly button.

"Yes," he murmured, the word slurred against my skin. "Always."

I arched my back, eager for his touch. "So impatient," I teased.

"I'll show you impatient."

Then he placed a gentle bite against my ribs that had me grinning.

I spent the next hour wishing I hadn't been so determined to wait.

When we were once again snuggled beneath the lights of the Christmas tree, wrapped up in nothing but a blanket and each other, I couldn't help but think I was right where I belonged. A perfect alignment of past and present while the fates looked on in amusement.

I had my family and the farm. A place I loved and a community I called home. And I had a man to share it all with. Someone who'd stand between me and the world, and lend me his sweatshirt if I needed it.

I smiled at the thought and placed a kiss on his shoulder, tasting his salt and his heat and his strength. And feeling beyond grateful for second chances and small towns.

There had been a time when coming back to Kirby Falls had seemed impossible —worse than impossible, it had seemed like failure. I'd held on to a dream with both fists without ever noticing that it had changed shape in my clutching hands.

But somehow I knew that Mark and I would keep growing and encouraging one another. We'd keep loving and forgiving, all the while being grateful for the chance to do it all together. Our dreams would take shape, and we'd give them room to grow. I didn't know what the future held, but as I squeezed Mark's hand and snuggled closer to his side, I knew I wouldn't have to face it alone.

The following week, we decided to spend New Year's Eve at Firefly with our friends.

It was cold, but the night was clear and bright. The fire pits were lit, and the outdoor heaters were cranked up to high on the back porch. A band played and folks congregated at picnic tables and children ran through the winter grass.

It was still pretty early though. Three hours until midnight.

As I made my way toward our group around the fire pit, I carefully balanced the two ciders I held in my hands.

I could see Mark standing among the others, arms crossed, navy-blue toboggan covering his short hair. The orange flames from the fire highlighted him like my own personal bearded beacon. Suddenly he laughed at whatever Brady said, and I was grateful for my idiot brother putting Mark at ease.

We didn't hide anymore. Our relationship was out in the open, but we still liked our quiet moments at home—one we shared. I knew Mark had some things to work through. It took time to change years of learned behavior. He'd talked about speaking to a therapist, and I supported him wholeheartedly. I thought there was a lot of trauma surrounding Hannah and Lyndsey that he needed to acknowledge, and seeking a professional would probably be the best way to go about that.

My eyes scanned the rest of our group. Joan was sitting down, having a quiet conversation with Laramie. Will Clark and his girlfriend, Becca, were snuggled up on an Adirondack chair while Becca chatted with Chloe. Her boyfriend,

Jordan, went back and forth between us and his staff to make sure everything was running smoothly at Firefly tonight.

Bonnie and her husband were listening in on whatever story Brady told, but their body language was a little stiff. A familiar tension took hold when I thought about my friend. I didn't know what was going on in her marriage, but I knew she didn't want to talk about it. Whenever I brought up her husband or things at home, she blew me off—pretended that everything was just fine. So I did my best to make myself available—a safe space for whatever she needed, whenever she was ready for it.

Before I could stare a hole through Danny Jensen's head, a little boy darted in front of me, causing me to pull up short. Hard cider sloshed over the rim of one of the glasses I held, but I grinned down at the little rascal. He beamed back with two front teeth missing, like he knew he was cute.

"Tommy, apologize," came a stern voice from beyond the boy.

I swallowed and looked toward the table where the voice originated, knowing who I'd find when I looked up.

"Sorry," he said sweetly and then went to join his mother at a huge picnic table filled with adults and children.

I met Lauren Walker's steady gaze as she said, "Sorry, he's a handful."

"No worries," I told Lo. Then I gave my former best friend a nod and went on my way.

I didn't let the shock of seeing her ruin my night. I thought I'd finally made my peace. Saying goodbye the summer after graduation might not have been on my own terms, but it was now. I was staying in Kirby Falls. I had to be okay with seeing visions from my past. That didn't mean I had to relive them.

Run-ins with Lo would be inevitable, but I'd survive. I refused to let all my good memories of our friendship be tainted by the abrupt end of it. Lo could forget me all she wanted. I would remember, and then I'd move on . . . the way Mark was moving on.

He'd told me about the visit he'd received from Reverend Price. How it hadn't been enough, but it had given Mark the closure he needed.

Our pasts were like that sometimes. It was easier to close a door and lock it without having to wonder if it would ever open again. Keeping it cracked left plenty of room for disappointment.

When I reached my friends, Mark accepted his drink and slid a hand around my waist. A warm whisper against the shell of my ear asked, "You okay?"

Because of course, he'd noticed.

Staying close, I nodded. The scruff of his beard tickled my cheek. "I'm good."

We spent the next few hours drinking and laughing as the groups with kids slowly trickled out.

Eventually, Mark and I ended up in the grassy area in front of the stage while the band belted out a pretty solid rendition of "Faithfully" by Journey. The song ended and the singer announced a time check. One minute until midnight.

Even though we'd stopped dancing, I still had my arms around Mark's neck while he held me close.

"Sooooo," I said.

His lips curled. "What?"

I did my best to look coy. "Since we're here at Firefly, I wondered, are you going to kiss me when the clock strikes midnight? Or were you thinking about dodging my lips and running away again?"

Mark gave me an amused glare. "Cute."

I grinned.

Before I had the chance to tease him further about our parking lot miss from a few months ago, he leaned in deliberately and captured my lips with his.

I had planned on telling him I thought it turned out just fine, but then I stopped thinking altogether. Vaguely I heard the sounds of the countdown all around us. But, for once, I didn't care about breaking the rules.

This was right where I belonged.

———

Our first book club meeting was happening over at Chloe and Jordan's house. It was technically Becca's book club, but she lived on the side of a mountain, and with the slight chance of snow in the January forecast, none of us wanted to risk it.

I'd just grabbed a plate of snacks and joined everyone in the living room when Chloe welcomed a late arrival.

I breathed a sigh of relief when my sister slipped her shoes off and passed Chloe her puffy black jacket to hang up.

With all the people, the chatting, and the extroverting, I knew this wasn't really Joan's thing. But one afternoon a few weeks back, she'd stopped by my office and seen a book on my desk. It turned out Joan was a big reader. I couldn't ever remember her toting around worn paperbacks on the farm or at the dinner table, but we'd talked for half an hour about my book club's latest selection. Then I'd invited her to join us.

And until right this minute, I hadn't been sure she'd show up.

But she murmured quiet hellos to all the ladies present and then took the seat beside me on the sofa.

"Hey," I said and held out my plate.

"Hey," she replied and snagged a party meatball on a toothpick.

The discussion was a good one. I'd been in book clubs before where people didn't read the book or they were too uppity to select romance titles for their monthly picks. But this event was nothing like others I'd attended in the past.

Becca came prepared with discussion questions, and everyone joined in and shared their opinions. Mac and Laramie got into it a little bit over the hero's domineering tendencies. But the rest of us sided with Larry in thinking Rhys Winterborne was elite-level book boyfriend material.

My sister mostly listened from where she sat at my side, but I heard her quiet laugh a time or two and felt buoyed by it. I was grateful that she was making the effort. Ever since the Parade Float Fight of 2023—as Brady referred to it—we'd been much more honest with one another. I still had moments of big-sister hero worship and she still made fun of my wall-mounted bass, but our relationship was real in a way it never had been.

My life was totally different now than it was six months ago. My five-year plan was blown completely out of the water. But I liked the way it looked from this side. The pieces sparkled like floating confetti—like strings of twinkle lights on a North Carolina night or a blanket of stars in the black velvet sky.

I had more than I ever thought I deserved and a farmer waiting for me at home.

MARK

One year and eight months later

I could hear the enthusiastic pitch of Candace's voice long before I reached the front steps of the Apple House. It was followed by a chorus of second graders' cheers and shouts.

I bit down on my smile as I took the stairs two at a time, eager to see her. In the nearly two years we'd been together—a year of that married—I hadn't been able to curb that desire to be close to her. And now, especially, the protective urge was strong.

A moment later, Candace came into view. She was in front of the information board in the back of the Apple House. She'd cleared off the space and put up materials about pollinators and the life cycle of the apple tree shortly after setting up her curriculum.

Her parents and Joan had fully supported Candace's idea to start group tours and field trip visits, complete with educational talks followed by a tour of the fields. Kids got to ask questions and then pick their apples to take home.

"Make sure you lift, twist, and pull," Candace said brightly.

Everything about her glowed. Not just because she enjoyed this part of her job on the farm most of all, but because once the second trimester had hit, she'd stopped feeling nauseous and miserable all the time.

I crossed my arms and leaned against a pillar behind the group while she finished up her instructions for the students, who were seated with their teachers hovering on the periphery.

Candace wore denim overalls with her Judd's tee shirt underneath. The blue fabric was pulled slightly taut across her small belly. The bottoms of her jeans were rolled up above bright yellow rain boots. We'd had a stretch of rain, so things were a little soggy lately, but she must have slipped those on when she got to her office. She hadn't been wearing them when we left the house together this morning.

Something about the combination of overalls and rain boots had me shifting restlessly on my feet. Maybe Candace had unlocked a new kink, because she looked so damn adorable. I wanted to pick her up and fuck her with the boots still on.

Just then, she caught my eye and winked. "Now, kids. Look for your teachers and follow them outside so you can get your apple baskets."

Then she skirted the group of children rising from their seats and motioned me toward her office.

After stepping inside, I closed and locked the door, cutting off the noise of excited chatter as everyone filed out of the Apple House.

I met Candace in front of her desk and slipped my hands around her waist. "Hey. How are you feeling?"

She grinned and snagged my belt loop like I might get away. "Oh, I'm good."

"Not too tired?" I confirmed. I didn't want her to wear herself out.

"Nope."

"I can take the kids out into the field. You can stay here and put your feet up."

Candace shook her head. "No. Joan is actually coming up right now to get them. I only had to do the educational talk and intro. She has Georgie with her today, and you know he loves leading everyone through the fields."

I nodded, relieved that Joan and George were handling things.

Then my hands shifted, as they often did, across the swell of her stomach. "How's our little guy?"

Blissful happiness stole over her features, and I felt my own emotions answering in return. "He's doing great. Just baking away."

Candace's pregnancy hadn't been a surprise. We'd been trying since we got married, both of us more than ready to start our family. But it was a consistently exhilarating experience to see her like this.

"Good," I replied and leaned down to press a kiss to her soft lips.

While my mouth moved over hers, my fingers drifted up to the straps of her overalls. I gave a little tug and murmured against her mouth, "I like these."

I felt her smile. "Oh yeah?"

"Mm-hmm."

Then I picked up her laptop and moved it to the chair behind me before lifting Candace and settling her on the surface of her desk. We'd finally replaced the battered desk and squeaky chair that she'd inherited when she moved into the space.

"I like these too," I repeated and tapped the side of her rain boot with my hand before moving to graze the sensitive spot behind her knee.

She gave my bottom lip a quick bite and grinned. "I knew you would."

I unclasped first one overall strap and then the other. "And how did you know that?"

"You're so practical. I knew you would appreciate them."

I pulled back and frowned a little. "That doesn't sound like a compliment."

"It really is," she argued. "Plus I knew you'd want me to leave them on while you bent me over the desk."

"Candace," I groaned and dropped my head to the top of her shoulder.

She giggled, likely knowing how tempted her words made me. The image alone had me fully hard behind my zipper.

Slowly she slipped off the desk and stood. Her overalls dipped low in the front as her straps fell away.

"You've got to stop treating me like a delicate flower," she insisted.

But I *did* worry. And I wanted to be gentle with her, especially when she was carrying our son.

Reaching up, Candace cupped my cheeks and gave me a slow, deep kiss. "I promise you're not going to hurt the baby and you're not going to hurt me."

My hands tightened on her hips as she fished out the hem of her orchard tee shirt and peeled it up and over her head. Her bra was black and lacy, and I liked it on just as much as off.

As if she could see my resolve crumbling, she smiled.

I sighed and demanded, "If you get uncomfortable, you'll tell me to stop."

She nodded earnestly but ruined it a second later by smirking. "I don't anticipate being uncomfortable at all." Then she shimmied the remaining denim fabric over her hips and took her underwear with it.

That devilish smirk stayed firmly in place as she pivoted and leaned over her desk, elbows braced beneath her shoulders.

Instinctively, my hands rose to skim over her backside, my rough palms leaving gooseflesh in their wake.

Subtly I reached around her, feeling for the edge of the desk.

"I'm fine, Mark," Candace said, exasperation and amusement fighting for dominance in her tone.

Then she wiggled back against me and I slipped my hand lower, eliciting a soft moan as she tried to spread her boot-clad legs wider, making room for my touch.

My gaze snagged on the fish mounted over her desk, but I didn't stop my ministrations. "You know I hate that fish watching us. Are you ever going to get rid of it?"

In the last year, she'd updated nearly her entire office. I'd helped install bookshelves along the back wall. We'd stripped off the wood paneling and painted the room a cheerful pale yellow. There was new furniture. And Candace had picked out some art prints for the wall from some artist out in Colorado. We'd even cut out a window so she had some natural light. Thankfully, the shades were drawn now.

Candace gasped dramatically. "Get rid of Lance Bass? Never."

Then I dipped my middle finger low and pushed inside her. She gasped again for an entirely different reason.

I smiled at the sound and bent, pressing a lingering kiss to her shoulder blade. As my finger stayed busy along with the heel of my palm, I knew I'd never get enough of moments like this—secret and stolen with my achingly beautiful wife.

But as much as I liked hiding ourselves away and fooling around in her office, I craved the life we were building together even more. One that was embroiled in the community and supportive of one another. We were part of a family, a legacy, and a team. The Judds had already been mine, but now it was official. I was grateful for the parents I had in Nick and Amy, and for the brother and sister I'd gained in the process.

Candace had made me her world, but, truthfully, I was just happy to have a place in it. One with the love of a woman I deserved.

I'd spend the rest of my life showing her just how much.

The fun in Kirby Falls continues with MacKenzie and Brady's enemies to lovers romance in Leaf and Let Die, *coming May 27, 2025 to Kindle Unlimited. I can't wait for this one, y'all.*

Want more of Mark and Candace? Check out a bonus epilogue for Leaf It to Me *when you sign up for Laney's newsletter HERE!*
If you have trouble with the link above, scan the QR code:

acknowledgments

I wanted to give a huge shout out to **Sky Top Orchard** in Flat Rock, North Carolina. Margaret and the team were so kind to help me with research and answer my farm-related questions. It was fun to get a tour of one of my favorite orchards in the area, and the apple cider doughnuts didn't hurt either. Thank you, Sky Top!

also by laney hatcher

Kirby Falls Series

Take It or Leaf It: A Grumpy Sunshine Slow Burn Romance

Leaf It To Me: A Small-Town Slow Burn Romance

Leaf and Let Die: An Enemies to Lovers Small-Town Romance

Cozy Creek Collection

Fall Me Maybe

Bartholomew Series

First to Fall: A Friends to Lovers Historical Romance

Second Chance Dance: An Enemies to Lovers Historical Romance

Third Degree Yearn: A Second Chance Historical Romance

Last on the List: A Surprise Pregnancy Historical Romance

Smartypants Romance

London Ladies Embroidery Series

Neanderthal Seeks Duchess

Well Acquainted

Love Matched

Find bonus content, reading order, and other news at my website:

https://laneyhatcher.com/

about the author

Laney Hatcher is a firm believer that there is a spreadsheet for every occasion and pie is always the answer. She is an author of stories both old and new where the HEAs are always guaranteed. Often too practical for her own good, Laney enjoys her life in the southern United States with her husband, children, and incredibly entitled cat.

Find Laney Hatcher online:
Facebook: https://bit.ly/3s6KnuY
Newsletter: https://bit.ly/3SbXg2v
Amazon: https://amzn.to/3IaOwU7
Instagram: https://bit.ly/3s4IRcS
Website: https://laneyhatcher.com/
Goodreads: https://bit.ly/3BD0Gme
TikTok: https://www.tiktok.com/@laneyhatcherauthor
Threads: https://www.threads.net/@laney.hatcher

Newsletter sign up